SOFIE
&
CECILIA

SOFIE

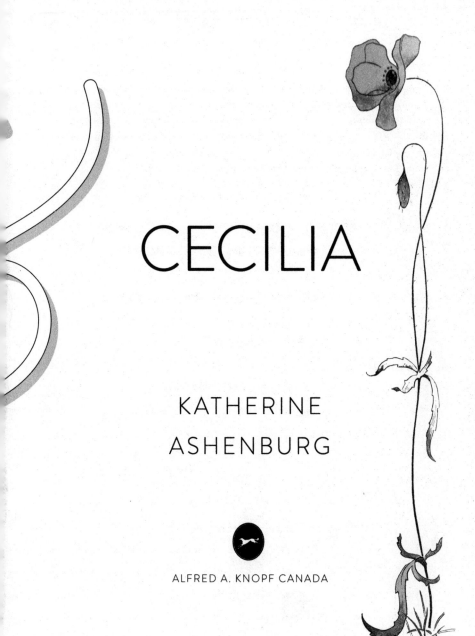

CECILIA

KATHERINE ASHENBURG

ALFRED A. KNOPF CANADA

Library and Archives Canada Cataloguing in Publication

Ashenburg, Katherine, author
Sofie & Cecilia / Katherine Ashenburg.

Issued in print and electronic formats.
ISBN 978-0-7352-7268-2
eBook ISBN 978-0-7352-7269-9

I. Title. II. Title: Sofie and Cecilia.

PS8601.S435S64 2018   C813'.6   C2017-905119-9

Book design by Kelly Hill

Cover images: (lady with flower) © Lyn Randle / Trevillion Images; (brush
strokes) © Lara Cold / Shutterstock.com
Interior images: © Dover Publications, Inc.

Printed and bound in the United States of America

2 4 6 8 9 7 5 3 1

Penguin
Random House
KNOPF CANADA

To J., who gave back my gift,
and to M. and S., wise counsellors.

CONTENTS

PART ONE

Prelude

IT WAS DURING that first visit to the Vogts' house that Sofie Olsson
and Cecilia Vogt began to know each other. Their husbands were
friends, but the two women had only met in passing at gallery open-
ings and exhibitions. Lars Vogt had been trying to arrange a visit
for months.

"You must bring your wife and all your children," he wrote to
Nils, "and any cats and dogs if you have them."

Sofie refused to bring Oskar, who was a baby. The four older
children, three girls and a boy, would be quite enough. The Vogts
were collectors, and she hoped the children would remember not to
touch their things.

Nils had fixed some old sleigh bells on the carriage, and they
made such a clamour that the farm horses the Olssons passed along
the way neighed in alarm. He told the children the horses imagined
that the king must be coming. That made the older ones laugh, but
Birgitta, who was four, was round-eyed and silent at the idea of
horses expecting the king.

Leggy stands of birch and pine edged the road, their boughs
high above the ground. Every so often they passed a cluster of

dark-red houses outlined with white corner boards, like a child's drawing of a village. Early in the morning, when they left home, belts of fog held the trees close, but by the time they reached Siljevik, Lake Siljan glittered in the morning sun.

The Vogts' yellow house sat behind its long garden, just at the edge of the village churchyard. Lars waited on the porch like a handsome tortoise slowly opening his eyes in the brightness. He smoked slowly and deliberately, as if he did not want to wake himself up too abruptly. He embraced Nils with special warmth, and shook hands with the others, even Birgitta.

"Later," he told them, "we'll visit my mother next door. She has to know everything that goes on here. But first the grown-ups need some coffee and the children some cinnamon rolls. Then we'll have a tour."

The front door opened, and Cecilia Vogt appeared.

"Welcome," she smiled at Sofie, over the milling children. The husbands called each other by their last names, as male friends did, but friendship was still in the future for their wives. If indeed it happened, they would move from Mrs. Vogt and Mrs. Olsson to first names. Small, with eyes the colour of forget-me-nots, Cecilia was a few years younger than Sofie. Almost everything about her was chic, beginning with her narrow, childlike feet in shoes that looked like gloves, the leather was so fine and the fit so close. She moved quickly, spoke quickly, probably thought quickly. Only her big, clattering laugh was neither elegant nor brisk.

Sofie was not especially tall, but Cecilia was so petite she almost felt that her height was a mistake. She had chosen a long, full, red jacket for the visit, one she had made herself, with black velvet scrolls appliqued on the yoke and pockets. She knew Lars Vogt loved red too—he often painted Cecilia dressed in scarlet. But it was Cecilia who admired the contrast between the jacket's mossy velvet scrolls and the hairy, loosely woven wool.

A maid brought a tray with coffee and rolls out to the table on the porch. Now that he was fully awake, Lars's long, purposeful fingers moved constantly, rolling a cigarette, rearranging the cream and sugar, drawing a picture for six-year-old Sonja of her doll drinking coffee. Sofie had brought her knitting, a pair of black stockings for Nils. She left the porch to see about milk for Birgitta, leaving the stocking on her chair, and by the time she returned, Lars had taken up her needles and turned the heel as deftly as any woman.

While the men congratulated themselves on finally getting together in Siljevik and laughed their way through shorthand remarks about other painters, their wives smiled at each other across the table, unsure where to begin. Spring had been late that year, they agreed. Sofie thought, Why do we always say that? Spring is guaranteed not to arrive in Sweden until the middle of May. She said something flattering about the formal beds of flowers in the Vogts' garden. "But you are a gardener too," Cecilia replied. "I can see that from your husband's pictures."

Sofie's garden, if you could call the space between their house and the river a garden, was wilder, the bulbs and perennials multiplying, travelling and dying according to their own, unknowable schedule. Indoors, at the big windows facing the river in the workroom, she grew the Christmas cactuses, geraniums, lilies and paperwhites that appeared in Nils's pictures. He often painted her, secateurs in hand, head cocked to one side as she studied a plant, coddling and disciplining it into shapes he could use.

"It's odd, isn't it," Cecilia continued, "feeling familiar with someone before you know them, even familiar with their house, from paintings you have seen of them? Seeing you here, I think of your husband's portrait of you holding your first child."

When Sofie looked at that painting, which she rarely did now, she wondered if the fugitive curls from her topknot had ever echoed the shape of her soft, thick eyebrows so perfectly. Behind the determined look of the young woman's round chin and straight mouth, there was a glint of something still undecided.

"I'm glad you know that picture," Nils said to Cecilia. "Sofie says I do not paint her face any more, just her big French sun bonnets."

Sofie knew he expected her to laugh along with everyone else, so she did. Nils painted her in sun bonnets over and over, the broad brim hiding her face as she bent over her mending in the garden or strung beans on the back steps. Floppy brims and loose dresses. She could not complain that he tented her in fabric, because she designed the dresses herself. These days, often all that showed of her in his paintings was a pair of hands, cutting, pruning, knitting, shelling, kneading.

Nils, as he often did when he and Sofie were in company, was playing the comic, exaggerating his devotion, calling her his idol and pulling out chairs for her with great flourishes. She looked amused, as if this were happening for the first time.

Nils turned to Lars. "Sofie has brought you a gift."

It was Lars's birthday, and she had sewed him a cushion, modelled on the long, thin coach cushions the women made in the south of Sweden. Hers was black felt, appliqued with hearts and clouds, and embroidered in red with Lars's initials and birth date in the corners.

Lars and Cecilia held it up together, and Cecilia ran her hands over the thick felt, appraising it. Sofie felt a prick of uncertainty. She thought it was good, but it would be easy enough to find it a childish effort for a trained painter. She had, after all, studied with August Malmstrom at the Academy of Fine Arts, but perhaps the Vogts did not know that. Lars gave the cushion one of his thorough examinations and thanked her.

"How cleverly you put it together," he said, "taking all the old traditional things—hearts, initials, the colour scheme—and paring them down and rearranging them to make something that is modern. And then, the one thing that is completely modern, the stylized clouds."

So, it was all right then. Still, she wondered what Cecilia thought. He is the artist, she told herself, why should his wife's reaction concern you? But it did. Something about Cecilia's confidence made Sofie want her approval.

Cecilia led the way as Lars explained about the house. He had grown up in the village, but Cecilia was from Stockholm, from a Jewish family of textile manufacturers. Although she and Lars had been in the house less than a year, they had started a library and a folk school, where adults could learn to read and write, and where people who still practiced the old crafts passed on their knowledge. Cecilia did all the administration. And now she spoke the Siljevik dialect with the servants and in the village.

Markus, who was eight, was impressed by the house's modern inventions, the central steam heating that included hot water, the toilet inside the house, and especially the telephone, hanging self-importantly on the wall in a room off the kitchen. Although it had been Siljevik's first telephone, the numbers had recently been reassigned, and the Vogts' number was four. The pharmacy was given number one, and the children thought that was most unfair.

Cecilia mentioned that she was thinking of putting in a second telephone, for long-distance calls. She used the telephone every day, arranging Lars's commissions and exhibitions and negotiating with his clients, but she did not want this clumsy machine in her green-and-gold study. Here was a kind of artist's wife Sophie had not seen before. All the planning and efficiency was impressive, but Sofie did not think she envied it. Yes, with a wife like Cecilia, a man would have more hours to paint, but would Nils want such a wife?

Sofie need not have worried about the children touching the Vogts' pottery or weavings. The Dalarna furniture the Vogts collected did not interest them either, but the Hall, with its Viking look and high, sloping timber ceiling, did. While the children chased each other around the billiard table, Lars pointed out the old textiles hanging on the walls and the shelves of folk pottery. The Vogts' pieces were as fine as people had said, but the thing she had not expected was the books—the Swedish first editions behind glass, from the seventeenth and eighteenth centuries, and the shelves of English novels ranged above the sofas.

Lars had already turned to leave the Hall, when she said, "But the books."

"Oh yes," he said off-handedly, "those are Cecilia's."

Sofie held up her hand to keep Cecilia beside her while she scanned the novels. Many were old friends, and others she had never heard of. As a girl, she had read all of Victoria Benedictsson and the other Swedish writers, but once she could read English, she preferred British novels—more brightly coloured, peopled with more outrageous eccentrics, thicker, richer, wilder.

"I see you have most of Dickens's books. Which do you like best?" And then, without waiting for an answer, because she noticed something else, "So you like Mrs. Gaskell too. I have not read her, but I mean to, perhaps this winter."

"Please, borrow any you like," Cecilia urged her. "*Cranford* is very popular, but I would suggest starting with *North and South*."

Sofie said, "I would like to borrow *Cranford*, please." Seeing surprise bloom and fade on Cecilia's face, she added, "And *North and South* too, if that is not too much."

The men were not interested in Mrs. Gaskell and had gone ahead to the bedrooms. Eventually their wives followed, still quizzing each other about their favourite novels. The furniture in Cecilia's bedroom was Louis XVI, ivory and gold, with spindly-legged chairs and tables that looked as if they were standing on tiptoe, awaiting their mistress's orders. Thinking of the heap of unanswered correspondence on Nils's desk, some of it probably six months old, and her own makeshift bedroom in a corner of the little girls' room, and the constant struggle to tidy the toys, Sofie said to Cecilia, "I don't know which I admire more, the beauty of your things, or the perfect order in which you live."

Cecilia said, "But it is your house that is famous throughout Sweden."

"And we still don't know what to make of that," Sofie said, and she and Nils laughed. This time, it was genuine.

Lars's bedroom, a few rooms away from Cecilia's, was painted bright red, his bed under a silky red canopy like a general's on campaign. Although the house was full of paintings, Lars had only one in his bedroom, a watercolour he had commissioned from Nils called *In the Studio*. One of Nils's favourite models, Margit, brunette and slim except for the gentle swell of her belly, posed nude in front of a full-length mirror. Nils was reflected in the mirror, a paintbrush raised at his easel, scrutinizing Margit with eyes half-shut. She stood with her arms akimbo, thumbs at her waist and fingers meeting at her back. It was a position that raised the breasts. Hers were small, and young.

Sofie watched the men looking at the picture. She had heard the innuendos about the Vogts' marriage, but an artist's life always attracted rumours. Sofie tried not to pay attention to rumours.

"Lovely thing," Lars said happily.

Whether he meant Margit or the painting was unclear.

In the afternoon, while the men looked at Lars's engravings in the studio and the Vogts' maid watched the children running around under the trees, Cecilia took Sofie into the village church. In the midday sun, the light inside was cruel. High white walls, clear glass windows, a white ceiling sectioned like a honeycomb. Everything was exposed, unlike the churches in Spain or Italy, where the darkness was filled with clutter—relics, votive candles, stained glass, holy water fonts.

And yet, Sofie thought, even here, in the Protestant north, even in all this whiteness and light, much is hidden.

"It is beautiful," she said finally, turning from one austere corner to another, "but rather bleak. There is nowhere to hide." She had to smile at the silliness of wanting to hide in a church, but there was a tremble at the edge of her smile. When Cecilia turned toward her with an answering smile, her guest's eyes were brimming with tears.

"Mrs. Olsson, what is it?" she said, taking a step toward Sofie. "Do you want to sit down?"

The wooden pews, fenced in behind doors that shut tight, promised as little comfort as the rest of the church. Sofie wiped her eyes hard on her red sleeve.

"No, it's nothing, please don't even think of it. I'm sorry, I'm being so foolish."

Cecilia waited.

To fill the growing silence, Sofie said, "It's just that I am weaning the baby, and I find I am ridiculously tearful at these times."

She thought, How stupid this must sound to a woman who has no children. And how indelicate to mention it to a stranger.

"If you are sure you are well enough, then . . ."

"Yes, perfectly well, thank you."

Still a little hesitant, Cecilia turned back to the church, pointing halfway up one of the columns. "The only bit of colour is the preacher's golden perch," she said. "No wonder my husband prefers the churches in the south."

Sofie nodded, rubbing her moist sleeve against her jacket to dry it.

Markus had brought his fiddle, and after an early dinner he played for them in the Hall. When the songs had words, the two older girls sang them, holding hands. Sonja was shy, Marianne not. They performed an Irish song that was new to the Vogts.

> *When I was single I wore a plaid shawl*
> *Now that I'm married I've nothing at all.*
> *Ah but still I love him I'll forgive him*
> *I'll go with him wherever he goes.*
> *He bought me a handkerchief red, white and blue*
> *But before I could wear it he tore it in two.*

Sofie noted, not for the first time, that the lyrics and music went in different directions. The words suggested a plaintive melody, but it was brisk and matter-of-fact. She could feel Cecilia watching her, and she took care to show that she was quite herself again.

Askebo, 9 June 1901
Dear Mrs. Vogt,

Thank you for all your bounteous hospitality, right down to the very welcome provisions for the journey home. I hope Markus's fiddling did not bore you too much, but I could see how eager he was to play under that wonderful high roof. I spent some time this morning working at the Dalarna braiding. Yours is precise but airy, and mine is not! But all goes well enough, in my slapdash way, until the end of the row, when things fall apart. When we see each other again, if I still haven't worked it out, I will ask for your help.

I found myself in the strangest reverie during the ride home. Do you ever look back on your wedding day and feel surprised at how your life turned out? I was so young, and so sure that Nils and I were making a new kind of marriage, something that my parents, for all their care for each other, hadn't known. But perhaps they too thought they were at the start of a new thing. Maybe everyone who gets married thinks that.

I wonder, what is giving me these curious thoughts? Nothing, I suppose, but seeing your beautiful house and watching spring advance, hour by hour.

With thanks again for letting those noisy children and their grateful parents invade your sanctum,

With best wishes,
Sofie Olsson

Cecilia sent a prompt answer. Probably she does everything promptly, Sofie thought as she extracted the letter from the mailbox. The baby was fussy, so she had taken him out for some fresh air while she walked up the road to the box. The wind blew in his face, which made him laugh, while she read Cecilia's letter.

Siljevik, 17 June 1901
Dear Mrs. Olsson,
    How delightful it was to have you and your family here, although the day sped by too fast. You are a lucky woman to have so many healthy, spirited children.
    Yes, I agree, we knew very little of life—although we thought we did—when we embarked on the vast sea of matrimony. I could never have dreamed of the satisfaction I have had sharing my life with Lars, watching him receive acclaim here and abroad and, of course, taking up our projects at home.
    Please come again soon. Next time, I'll teach you another braiding pattern, one I like called "Moon and Stars."
    Cordially yours,
    Cecilia Vogt

Sofie folded the thick, smart letter paper back into the envelope, away from the baby's sticky grasp. She's telling me to keep my distance, she thought. No doubt I was stepping too close to delicate ground.

SOFIE

Chapter One

1882–1887

WHEN SOFIE FALKNER entered the Academy of Fine Arts in 1882, it was fewer than twenty years since women had first been admitted to the school. That fact did not interest her particularly. She couldn't have said what *did* interest her—probably colour and line and trying to get the right amount of shade and light in a drawing. No doubt her parents, so harmonious, so laissez-faire as to what she and her two younger sisters did, encouraged her dreamy side. There was nothing she needed to fight against or for, she had everything she wanted. So she drifted across life, content, silent for long periods, absorbed in her own fancies, like one of those insects who skim just above the surface of the lake.

Hallsberg, where the Falkners lived, was a little town with an enormous train station. Mr. Falkner went further, describing it as a railroad junction with a town loosely tacked on. Trains came late to Sweden, but by 1862 the western line between Stockholm and Gothenburg, a journey of fourteen hours, was finished. Hallsberg was midway between the two cities, and people began to say that you had to go to Hallsberg to get anywhere. The Falkner girls played and learned their lessons and ate and slept to the hollow, regretful sound of train whistles. Sofie always heard an apology in their hooting, "I'm-sorry-but-I-must-do-this, I'm-sorry-but-I-must-do-this."

The Falkners enjoyed their own company, so they spent most of their time in their house on Vastra Storgatan. The house was dim and full of hiding places. Everything in it aspired to the sculptural, from the pressed-wood chairs with their bas-relief arabesques to the repoussé brass plant pots to the massive carved breakfronts and credenzas that supported columns, pilasters, rosebuds and birds perpetually in flight. Nothing was content with a flat surface, everything was three-dimensional. The chairs were upholstered with cut velvet, and even the walls were covered with embossed leather.

Since their parents made very few rules, the daughters invented their own. Strict, arbitrary laws determined when the pocket doors between the main reception rooms could be opened and closed, what borders and diamonds in the parquet floors could never be stepped upon or calamity would follow, who could lift the purple brocade cushion off the window seat in the parlour and open the secret compartment underneath it, and under what circumstances the tiny, unlit room off the kitchen that held the brawny black safe could be entered. Later, people talked about those old-fashioned houses as glum and forbidding, but the Falkner girls colonized every cranny and dark corner.

They took piano lessons, singing lessons and, for one year when a dancing master lived in Hallsberg, dancing. But Sofie's favourite time was Wednesday afternoon, when Mr. Lindstrom came to the house to teach drawing and watercolour painting. He was a large, loosely knit man who was always perspiring. Sometimes he absentmindedly picked up a painting rag, rather than his handkerchief, to blot his forehead and spent the rest of the lesson with a blue or green gash across his face. The girls kept their composure by not looking at each other when that happened.

Mr. Lindstrom would arrange apples, pears and a jug on a table in the old nursery, or a broken chunk of bread, a triangle of cheese and a glass, and the girls would set to work. On a spring day, Sofie would look out at the garden and wonder how the hydrangea climbing the stone wall could be translated onto paper, but they never worked out of doors or painted anything live. When Mr. Lindstrom inspected their work, he would stand in silence and after a while he would say, "I see. I *see*. I see." It was as if they were painting a secret, and his job was to discover it.

Her father wished, mildly, that Sofie would apply herself more to the piano.

"That's something you can do all your life," he told her. "You can have all your children around the piano, singing while you accompany them. Or you can play duets."

But when Sofie was meant to be practicing, she kept a little pad of paper on the piano bench. The pad filled up with sketches of Miss Ivarsson, the piano teacher, her sisters and her cat, Mus. Of the three girls, Margareta played well, but Miss Ivarsson sighed over the other two. Martina was a tomboy and sat down at the piano with scraped forearms and knuckles and blackened fingernails.

"Wrong notes, or dirty nails. Not both," Miss Ivarsson ordered in vain.

Sofie's nails were clean, and she concentrated on Czerny's exercises or Schubert's songs to a certain extent, but her pad of paper called to her in a way the piano never did.

Life in Hallsberg was pleasant. No one spoke in anger and the house was full of the smells of comfort—gaslights, wood burning in porcelain stoves, cloves, almonds and cardamom, the damp earth that gave minimal life to the rustly, odourless ferns in their jardinières, furniture polish. In truth, there was too much furniture polish, because they had one maid too many. Mamma was too soft-hearted to let poor Mina go, so Mina, who was a little slow, endlessly dusted and then polished the columns and festoons and cherubs that weighed down the furniture.

When Sofie graduated from the local high school, to everyone's surprise she wanted something that could not be had in Hallsberg. She wanted to study at the Academy of Fine Arts in Stockholm. It was the only time that anyone remembered her taking a stand.

Her father was baffled.

"Sofie, your pictures are charming," he said. "Mr. Lindstrom tells me you have a gift, especially in your flower paintings. And all that will make your home, your married home I mean, attractive. But tell me why"—gently pleating his brow—"you would want to go to Stockholm to study art. I've never heard of a woman painter. I mean, a professional painter, not one who paints on china or does watercolours."

"Yes, you have, Pappa. Amalia Lindegren."

"Amalia Lindegren." He thought for a minute. "Is she the one who paints those sad children? Peasant cottages?"

"Yes. And Mr. Lindstrom told me she is a member of the Royal Swedish Academy of Arts. But that's not the point. I don't know if I want to *be* a painter, in the way that you are a businessman. I just know I want to learn how to paint. It's all I want to do."

Her father looked at Sofie as if to say: From one of your sisters, I might have expected something like this. But from you, no. She returned his look, levelly.

"But where would you live in Stockholm? How would you get there?"

So. If he was worrying about practicalities, it was going to be all right. Mr. Lindstrom had murmured something about "life classes" perhaps being a problem for her father. She was unclear what life classes were, and perhaps her father was too. Apparently he was not going to raise the issue.

"Pappa, you're always telling us we live at the crossroads of Sweden. I would take the train, of course. And there are families near the school who rent out rooms to female students."

———

When Sofie arrived at the Academy in September, she was directed past the studios and lecture halls on the main floor, up to the third floor and then to the back of the building. Making her way up the stairs at the same time was a wiry young woman who seemed to know where she was going. Out of breath from the climb, she introduced herself as Hanna Hirsch. Interpreting Sofie's tentative smile as a question about their destination, she explained, in short bursts, that the women had been given their own enclave in the school to placate the instructors and male students who had protested their admission in the 1860s. Their presence would lower standards, they had claimed, water down the curriculum and make the school a byword for amateurism. To guard against those dangers and preserve the virtue of the women, they were isolated as much as possible.

The segregation was so complete that Nils always claimed he never knew the female department's exact location in the Academy's crumbling old buildings. "I only gathered its general direction," he told Sofie later, "from the constant aroma of coffee. The word was that you poor women studied as diligently as we men were diligently lazy and absent."

Perhaps it was true that Nils hadn't known where the women worked. Or perhaps that was his way of saying that they were nothing to him, since he, too, disapproved of women studying art.

The coffee that fuelled the women's work may have been strong, but their course of studies had a hole at its centre. The missing part was the "life class" that had embarrassed Sofie's teacher, Mr. Lindstrom. Since the goal of every serious painter was large historical subjects, mastering human anatomy through nude models was essential. The male students started by copying engravings, then drawing arrangements of wooden blocks, then copying plaster casts of statues from Greece and Rome and ending up in the Life School, where they drew nude models, often in classical poses. Even for the men, an ease with studying nudes was relatively recent at the Academy. A plump, pear-shaped janitor still working there in Nils's day had served as a "female" nude when the students had only been allowed male models and back views. By the time Nils was a student, female models and front views were common, but the students still occasionally tormented Emil, the janitor, by pretending that the model of the day was ill, and that he must leave his mop and hurry to the life class.

For the female students, life classes were out of the question.

To the end of his life, Nils remained angry about the shoddy teaching, atrocious conditions and outmoded standards at the Academy. Although as a student she understood less about the old-fashioned standards, Sofie also realized that in its vastly more self-satisfied way the Academy was almost as limited as Mr. Lindstrom's teaching. But for her it was enough to spend her days with paints, easels and colleagues who were happy to discuss how the sun could light one particular shrub, apparently deliberately, while everything around it remained in the shade. Then—the more interesting question—how to paint that convincingly.

After classes the students went out to supper at one of the cheap restaurants around the Academy. Over pea soup and pancakes, they argued about the eighteenth-century engravers, their own Tessin versus his more famous French contemporaries, the new French vogue for painting out of doors (unheard of at the Academy) and the relative merits of their teachers. Sofie lived in Ostermalm, which was a longish tram ride away from the Academy, at the house of her mother's cousin, whom she called Aunt Eugenia. Her parents had made that a condition of her going to Stockholm, but Sofie returned to Ostermalm only after supper.

People who wore their hearts on their sleeves interested Sofie, as well as people who knew, quickly and sharply, how they felt. Opinionated and keenly critical of herself as well as others, Hanna Hirsch, who had climbed the stairs with her on the first day of classes, became a friend. In her final year, Hanna's teachers encouraged her to enter the historical competition. The competition subject that year was "Luther burns the papal bull at the Wittenberg square"—a typical challenge involving antique buildings, crowds, a few important personages ("showing as much leg or at least as much stocking as possible," Hanna said darkly) and the triumph of Protestantism. She had hardly begun when she realized, as she told Sofie, that she could not go on with "such rubbish." Hanna did win another, less important award for her own choice of subject, a lamp-lit study of her mother and sister, but the faculty considered her a malcontent.

Sofie managed to evade the big historical subjects, and Professor Malmstrom did not press her. He was kindly but took no particular interest in her work. That did not surprise her, nor even particularly disappoint her. She kept on, like Hanna, painting small, domestic scenes—her sisters chasing each other in the garden, her father winding the curvaceous Dalarna clock that stood in the front hall, poor Mina dusting the clothes press in the master bedroom, her arms extending across its great breadth in a clumsy, one-sided embrace. When the Impressionists' liking for such subjects reached Sweden, Sofie and Hanna joked that they had been in the vanguard. And yet, even when she chose her own subjects, Sofie was not quite satisfied. There was some other way she wanted to paint, or some other subject, but she did not know what it was.

Sofie's parents wanted her to come home after she graduated, but she was not ready to return to Hallsberg. She compromised by continuing to live at Aunt Eugenia's, while she shared a drafty studio above a bakery with Helena Jolin. She and Helena had studied together at the Academy, and it was through Helena that she met Nils Olsson.

The Jolins were giving a dance at their house on Kungsgatan, and Sofie stood in the drawing room at the beginning of the evening with Helena's father. The room was crowded like an obstacle course with ottomans, plant stands and tiny side tables. A ginger-haired man made his way easily through these hindrances, as if he were a habitué of such places, and shook hands with Mr. Jolin.

"Sofie, my dear, this is Mr. Olsson. Olsson, Miss Falkner."

She knew Nils Olsson by reputation as a successful illustrator for periodicals and books who had lived in France. The Jolins probably thought him a presentable example of their daughter's artistic leanings. He looked merry, even slightly mocking, but Sofie could see he missed nothing. Only a very slight rigidity of the neck gave him away, if you were watching closely.

She and Mr. Olsson sat together between two dances. Her dress was the colour of a blush, if a blush could be worried into endless ruches and bypasses and gathers and then gift-wrapped strategically in black velvet ribbons. She thought it was beautiful. Her arms, which were good, were bare from her wrist-length gloves to the short puffed sleeves. She sat very erect, holding a nosegay of camellias. Between her tightly laced corset and her padded and poufed bustle, there was no allowance for relaxing. Mr. Olsson asked her, without a great deal of interest, "Were you at school with Miss Jolin?"

"No," she said, "that is, yes. We were not at high school together, but at the Academy."

He winced, as if he had a sore tooth and she had touched it. "Horrible, wasn't it?"

She was used to critical art students, but his rancour, especially some years after he had graduated, seemed extreme.

"I loved it," she said, telling the simple truth.

Either he didn't have the energy to set her straight or he didn't think it would be worth his while. As if he were obliged to follow a worn-out formula, he asked, "And what are you doing now?"

She explained about the studio she shared with Helena over the bakery. She added, "Helena and I worry that we will never be able to paint again without the combined smell of yeast, warm rolls and turpentine." Mr. Olsson gave no indication that he found that amusing.

It seemed quite normal to Sofie that she had little to say to an accomplished man seven years her senior but, afterwards, Nils would never tell the story to the children without mentioning that he'd had to suppress his yawns until they got up to dance, each with another partner. He usually added, "Not a single fibre in me was vibrating."

Helena's mother disagreed with Nils's impression. "That Sofie Falkner is not like everybody else," she said to him later, at supper. "There may be weeks when she doesn't say one word, but then she'll suddenly open her beak and she always says something that is sound, right, witty or even funny."

Nils would make that part of the story too, but Sofie thought Mrs. Jolin's opinion was an exaggeration, in both directions. She was neither so silent, nor so witty.

They met again, a few weeks later, in Jakobsbergsgatan. Sofie had been riding in the Djurgarden, and was just leaving Andersson's Livery, dressed in her riding habit.

She said, "Good afternoon." Nils did not recognize her, so she told him her name, and he remembered. He seemed to be in a better mood. They exchanged a few pleasantries, and parted, but he had already changed his mind about Sofie. She was more interesting, he would say, wearing her tall hat and holding a whip than in her pink ball dress.

"Especially holding the whip," she would add.

Chapter Two

1887–1889

AFTER SOFIE HAD shared the studio with Helena for a winter, her parents agreed that she could spend a year painting in France. She settled in the village of Grez-sur-Loing, a place she found rather sad, although it was popular with British, American and Scandinavian artists. The Loing was a sluggish tributary of the Seine, southeast of Paris. Grez had two inns willing to lodge artists and a romantic, many-arched bridge. Other than that, there was nothing picturesque about it, which suited the painting style of the day.

Even in Grez, the women did not study painting with the men. Sofie and two other Scandinavian women, Emma Dahlberg from Bergen and Dorotea Jonasen from Copenhagen, worked with Monsieur Lavartin. When Dorotea lost her way in a painting, she pressed the small of her back, as if it ached. "It's not my back," she would say, "it's my so-called talent." Dorotea was engaged to be married, and Monsieur Lavartin gave her a set of dishes as a wedding present. His note suggested that before she left Grez for the wedding in Copenhagen she should take her brushes and paintbox down to the river, and launch them out on the water.

Because, he wrote, as a married woman she would no longer wish to be an artist, but a housewife. He had praised her draftsmanship; he had seemed genuinely impressed by her work. But a married woman, he repeated, as if no one would dispute this, would not wish to be an artist.

The Scandinavian artists in Grez were a raucous group, famous for their epic toasts and parties that went on all night. Nils Olsson had returned to Paris, about an hour away by train, where people said he lived with a French woman, one of his models. But he spent most of the spring and summer in Grez, where he was the feverish centre of the Scandinavians, full of practical jokes and comic projects. He was always sketching their dinners, their trips to the river to bathe, their painting excursions. When they had a spur-of-the-moment fancy dress ball, he drew Sofie costumed as a Moroccan woman on her way to the well. She had draped herself in a bedsheet, with one shoulder bare, found a pair of hoop earrings in the market and begged a jug from her landlady, which she put on her head. With her dark hair and eyebrows, it was almost convincing—her striped stockings and court shoes were the only false notes.

Sofie suspected that underneath the high spirits, there was another Nils Olsson. He supported himself as an illustrator, but his career as a serious artist had stalled. He had never been awarded a travelling scholarship from the Academy, the most important mark of its approval. Nor had any of his paintings, other than a workaday portrait of a friend, been chosen for the Paris Salon. The studio-based oil painting he had learned at the Academy was passé in France, where the critics were championing realistic water-colours of contemporary scenes, painted out of doors. At first, Nils had resisted. What serious painter would throw over the classical subjects? How could watercolours compete with oils? But eventually, like everybody at Grez, he attempted the new style.

Grez, 20 May 1888

Dear Mamma and Pappa,

Thank you so much for the jam and the coffee. How sweet it is to taste the good old Swedish lingonberries again, although I have to confess that I have become devoted to the French marmalade we eat at the pension. Mme Desmoulins makes it herself and I would ask her for the recipe, except that I doubt we could get Seville oranges in Hallsberg. Watching Madame's face when I present her with the coffee beans will be a picture, as the French pride themselves on their excellent, very strong coffee!

You will remember the Stockholm illustrator Nils Olsson, whose sketch I sent you, of me running upstairs in the pension in my sheet after a bathe in the river. The other night, some of the painters had an informal exhibition of their latest work, in which he showed the most wonderful picture. It is everything we were not taught at the Academy. No hero from history dressed and posed in a studio, but a peasant boy, homely, resting in a field in his crumpled grey jacket. He sits, under a moody sky, next to a ragged thistle bush bigger than he is. He has tilted his face so that only one huge ear shows, and the sun shines through it, turning it red. The only other dash of colour is a clump of poppies in the far distance.

Some of the others compared it to a painter we all admire, Jules Bastien-Lepage. Bastien-Lepage painted a peasant girl in a similar setting and called it *Poor Fauvette*. And yes, it is very fine, but the title tells it all: it has a degree of sentimentality that is completely absent from Olsson's picture. Bastien-Lepage's girl is very pretty. Wrapped in a rough piece of cloth, she wears cast-off shoes that are far too big for her. Olsson's boy on the other hand is so natural, he is not pretty and his jacket is filthy, but you can feel the truth with which it is painted. I could not stop looking at it. Finally, so as not to hurt the feelings of the other painters, I forced myself to move away and look at their work.

As for me, I keep on with the same small subjects, a girl dressed for her first communion, a mother knitting while she watches her baby son. But now, like Nils Olsson but without half his talent, both painter and subjects have gone outdoors. I work, as the French say, *en plein air*!

Thank you, Mamma, but there is no need to send the faille suit or the dinner dress. I have my blue serge suit and the brocade dinner dress with me, and that is more than a hard-working art student will have occasion to wear. What I do need is another painting smock, but I will get that here in Grez.

Much love to all of you, and don't forget Mus in that, your Sofie

The artists in the little colony included a young man from Glasgow named John Lavery. He painted Sofie in a hammock overlooking the patchy river. She was half-turned out of it, leaning to pick up a cup of tea from a little rush-seated stool, so that half her face was hidden by the hammock.

"There," he said, pulling the gold bangle on her wrist slightly downward. "I'd like that to show a little more."

Born in Ireland, Lavery was dark and not terribly tall, with a chiselled face and an attractive ease. He stared at his canvas, then at her. Her big brown skirt filled the entire width of the hammock; one hand held the hammock's web for support while the other reached for the blue-and-white cup. He made a minute adjustment of the cup on the stool.

"That's very good, there, the way you are holding the hammock. How is your own work going?"

"Oh fine, I suppose."

He looked inquiring, so she had to say more.

"For years I wanted to work out of doors, and now I see the difficulties—the changing skies, the weather that doesn't follow our schedule, the work of finishing the rough sketch later in the studio. But I am much happier with the change, and Monsieur Lavartin is a great help with getting the right buildup of colour."

"Have you finished the picture of the little goose-girl?"

"Not quite. It's strange, but no matter how artless or unselfconscious you think a person is, the act of posing can make them look so unnatural. That's what is happening with my goose-girl."

Lavery said nothing, but she knew he was listening while he added some black to her brown skirt. She wished she could think of something else to say to him. Out of the corner of her eye, she saw the muddy, grey-brown river. She felt the twist of her back, such a cruel pose to hold, and an unfamiliar stirring in her body. Was it the pressure of the hammock around her hips and buttocks, or Lavery's intent, unblinking attention? To cover her confusion, she gave a small laugh and continued.

"The goose-girl reminds me of what my mother said, when I was trying to explain this new kind of painting to her. She said, 'That's interesting, dear, but I still don't see why it's so much better to paint peasants harvesting turnips than the trial of Socrates.'"

They smiled at the naivete of parents.

Still darkening her skirt, he asked, "And what is it like for a woman artist in Sweden these days?"

A woman artist in Sweden. She had never thought about that, which was embarrassing. If he had asked Hanna Hirsch, she would have had a great deal to say about women artists in Sweden.

"I . . . I don't really know how it is for them. I suppose I'll find out when I return."

Lavery called the picture *Tea by the River*. Once it was finished, Nils Olsson began to claim the seat next to her when they sketched out of doors, and she did not pose for Lavery again.

One day, she and Nils painted a peasant woman in a vegetable patch, carrying a large basket. Nils drew her in profile, her head wrapped in a white cloth, standing near some pumpkins. Sofie drew her from the back, wearing the same cropped jacket, gathered skirt and clogs. Nils refined his in the studio, the orange pumpkins the only bright note in the blue-green-grey palette. She never got around to finishing hers, so it stayed sketchy and impressionistic. There were trees in the distance, under a moody sky, and no pumpkins. It was overcast and gloomy, like Grez in general. But her painting was good. Even she could see that it was good.

She fell in love with Nils Olsson's paintings before she fell in love with him. After the boy by the thistle bush, he painted a stooped old man leaning on his stick, and sisters picking pears in an orchard. Compared with the slow tedium of oils, the speed that watercolours demanded suited him and his paintings had a warmth that was never maudlin.

About the painter, Sofie took more time. She watched his manic enthusiasms and his occasional absences when melancholy overtook him. The other Scandinavians told her that he had grown up in one of Stockholm's slums, carrying water and chopping firewood as a small boy to add to the family's pitiful income. His father was an angry, unpredictable labourer who disappeared periodically. His mother took in laundry to support the family.

It was flattering to be singled out as the one he teased most and the one he sat next to when a group went out sketching or painting. Without ever seeming to put down his brush or pencil, he kept up a joking commentary about her work, her dirty smock and her snub nose. He filled the margins of his paper with cartoons of her, big-eyed, "potato-nosed" as he called it, with ears and curls sticking out. The other women told her,

"Nils Olsson likes you," and she pretended to disagree. But she liked hearing it.

She saw there was some need under his bravado that she might or might not want to meet, but she never knew whether she gave in to him in spite of that or because of that. Years later, she thought, I was right to resist. And probably right to surrender.

Her father saved the letter in which Nils asked for her hand, and gave it to her.

> Grez, 30 September 1888
> Dear Mr. and Mrs. Falkner,
>   I am a man and I love your daughter. That is the important part. I am also an artist, and will work all my life to support Sofie. Our dearest wish is for your blessing.
>   Yours,
>   Nils Olsson

Her father responded by saying that was all he needed to know. He added that Sofie had known what was best for herself since she was a little girl.

For her part, Sofie felt sure that her father had made some discreet inquiries about Nils, and was more or less satisfied. Probably he was pretending to be more easygoing than he actually was.

Although they agreed to the engagement, her parents wanted her to continue with her plan of studying for a second year in France, this time in Paris. The art "academies" in Paris sounded impressive, but by now Sofie realized that often they were nothing more than a retired model who would rent a big room, hire a younger model and put a label on the door, the Academy So-and-So. Anyone could pay a fee and come and draw the model. Once a week, a teacher would appear and criticize the work. The Scandinavian students agreed that the Colarossi studio was the best. Sofie and another Swedish woman, Julia Nyman, moved in together in a room on the Rue Vavin, and painted at the Colarossi studio.

When Sofie was learning English at school, she had read Mary Wollstonecraft's *Letters Written During a Short Residence in Sweden, Norway and Denmark.* Writing at the end of the eighteenth century, Miss Wollstonecraft had been struck by the liberty given to engaged couples in Sweden. Women passed from the reign of their fathers to the reign of their husbands, she wrote, with that one important intermission. Engaged women had a freedom they would never know again, and their parents were deliberately blind to the intimacies of the couple.

Miss Wollstonecraft's account was still controversial in Sweden, where middle-class parents defended the reputations of their daughters. But now, almost a century after she wrote them, Miss Wollstonecraft's ideas had a new currency. Sofie and her friends debated them while they painted.

One Saturday, as the spring sun tried fitfully to break through Paris's grey skies, a few of them took a local train to the nearby countryside. They set up their easels overlooking an apple orchard.

"Objecting to intimacies before marriage for women is irrational," Emma Dahlberg insisted while she frowned in concentration at the colours on her palette. "Men have always been permitted sexual freedom, so why not women?"

That was bold, but Emma often was bold, at least in words. Still, Sofie doubted, privately, that Emma put her theory into practice.

"Logically, I don't disagree," Dorotea Jonasen said. She was trying to get a man who was pruning one of the apple trees into her painting, but he moved too quickly as he cut dead and low-hanging branches. She could not think and chase the man on paper at the same time, so she put down her brush. "But it doesn't feel right. I will not avail myself of liberties until I am married."

Sofie and Emma exchanged glances; they suspected otherwise.

Privately, Sofie was more concerned about Nils's attitude. Apparently he had not read Mary Wollstonecraft. He kissed Sofie's hand, her cheek and—but not for long—her mouth. She wondered why he did not make love to her. Perhaps he wanted her to be more innocent and inaccessible than she was to make her seem as different as possible from his mistress. Sofie had never discussed the mistress's existence with him, but Nils's living arrangements in Paris had been common knowledge in Grez. Of course, that was over now.

There came a Sunday in May when the weather was like summer. Sofie had invited Nils to lunch without mentioning that Julia was going away for the day with a sketching group, to the forest at Fontainebleau. When he arrived, the table in their little sitting room was set for two. *Sole véronique*, she told him. She had bought a cookbook at one of the bookstalls along the Seine. The grapes, as it turned out, were a bit sodden and the fish drier than she had hoped. But he was full of praise, and took a second helping. After the cheese, he stood to stretch his legs. She stood too, and kissed him.

"All that Chablis has made me sleepy. Let's just lie down for a while and close our eyes. Julia won't be home until the evening."

Nils looked startled, but she took his hand and led him to her bed, behind a tablecloth she had pinned to a clothesline. The Chablis helped. Her heart was beating like a church bell, in a way that would have been alarming except that everything seemed to be happening at a distance from where they stood. Almost casually, she loosened her blouse. Unfastening her stays, as always, took some doing and, laughing, she asked for his help. She pinched in her sides while he freed the hooks and eyes. His hands trembled.

Afterwards, she lay on her back, watching the afternoon sun light up the jacquard pattern on the tablecloth. Nils lay curled around her with his face in her shoulder. The wine had worn off and she hurt, which she hoped was temporary. She was aware of two smells. One that came from her underarms was like celery salt, an essential ingredient when Alma, the cook at home, made meatballs. It was sweat, she realized, after some initial uncertainty—she had not had much occasion in her life to produce sweat. The other smell combined something yeasty with a tinge of bleach. It was a clean smell, that seemed to be coming from the sheets. Nils cupped his hand on her side and said, "My angelic girl, you are so kind. So, so kind."

Kind. It was not the word she would have chosen, but she judged that the afternoon had been a success.

When he told her, it did not seem outrageous. Or even particularly momentous. She didn't actually take much notice, perhaps because, like almost everything he said in those days, it was so loving. His look, as he said it, of being delighted with her—that was the main thing. She heard him saying, "Your paintings are very fine, Sofie. Quite . . . accomplished. But, of course, with our marriage, that chapter closes." Really, she couldn't remember the exact way he put it. She understood his meaning, that she would not be painting once they were married. But all the talk was a kind of interruption, a noise that threatened to distract her from what she thought of as the real story. How they were going to marry, going to have their own place, do things as they liked, be together forever, be enchanted with each other. That was what mattered. She didn't put it to herself that, after all, it wouldn't be impossible to live without painting. Because even to think that way made it sound more important than it was.

When her teacher had told Dorotea that a married woman would not continue painting, Sofie, along with the other Scandinavian women, had enjoyed a bit of indignant huffing. But it was easier to discount a middle-aged teacher than your fiance, especially when Nils's attitude seemed somehow flattering. He wanted Sofie to concentrate on him and the family that was to be, and that was romantic.

Still, she could not follow him in all his opinions about women artists. At dinner one night in the Hotel Laurent, the artists' talk turned to Rosa Bonheur, the French artist most famous for her large paintings of cows and horses. Nils laughed so hard he almost choked when he talked about Mlle Bonheur applying to the police for the necessary permission to wear trousers while sketching at the stock-yards. His friend Holger slapped him on the back. They had gone through this story a dozen times, but it never failed to convulse Nils and at least a few of the other men.

"And with her hair cut as short as a man's," Holger added, get-ting into the well-worn spirit of the exercise. "When you saw her in her black trousers and coat, you didn't know it was a woman!"

"Well, *some* sort of a woman . . ."

There were appreciative snickers all round, some a little mechanical by now. Most of the women looked as amused as the men. Sofie kept her face blank. If Nils thought Rosa Bonheur was ridiculous, perhaps she was, in some way that escaped Sofie. But she did not find Rosa Bonheur's paintings funny, and she would not pretend that she did. She concentrated on remembering one of them, a wonderful crowd of horses at a livestock auction.

Hanna Hirsch was having none of it. "She painted animals because the French Academy refused to let her study human anat-omy," Hanna said, more forcefully than necessary because everyone knew that but was choosing to ignore it. "Refused her out of prudish-ness. At the stockyards, which could turn the stomachs of many men, some perhaps around this very table, she could study all the anatomy she needed. And who in her right mind would drip her skirts in the blood and offal that litters the floor there? You could skate on the blood. Of course she wore heavy boots and old trousers."

Georg Pauli, another of the Swedish painters, said, "If she did not choose her subject, you would never know it from the painting called *Ploughing in the Nivernais*. It is superb what she does with four bulky cows and a farmer driving them through great reddish-brown clods of earth."

Quite suddenly, Sofie loved Georg Pauli. Not in the way she loved Nils, a love that consumed her with desires to touch him, to put her hand in his pocket so she could feel where *his* hand had been, to feel their knees meeting under the table. She loved Georg in a way that meant, "You are a fine person, and I salute that."

But Rosa Bonheur had had to give up too much—love, children. Sofie saw no reason to make those sacrifices.

Nils ignored Georg Pauli's praise of Rosa Bonheur. He turned the conversation to two male painters in the new, realistic school they all admired.

"That is the kind of work we should be concentrating on," he said scoldingly, as though he had not led the group in mocking Bonheur.

Chapter Three

1891–1893

M ARIANNE WAS BORN in the second year of Sofie's marriage. She and Nils had returned to Grez, and they gave the baby a French name. When she was six months old, they left France for Sweden. At first they lived in Sodermalm, a working-class neighbourhood in Stockholm, while Nils and his colleagues formed a group they called the Opponents. The Opponents worked feverishly on an exhibition designed to show the conservative Swedish art world what it could learn from the new French painting. The exhibition included seven paintings by Nils and was a tremendous success.

Two years later, in 1893, they moved to Gothenburg and a boy, Markus, was born. Nils taught at the Valand School of Art, denouncing the ideals of classical beauty that had warped his own education and introducing his students to the fresh air of modern art. They had a small flat close to the school, with a distracted maid named Berta. In between school terms Nils was often away, studying monumental art in Paris and frescoes in Italy, or travelling in Holland.

Sofie's parents came to meet their grandson, and her mother spent hours with Marianne and the baby. Her father preferred talking with Nils about art. Would France retain its supremacy? What did he think would be the ideal education for an artist? What about these new fellows, French mostly, who apparently took off their spectacles before they began painting? Sofie had no idea that her father was so knowledgeable about art. Then again, if Nils owned a shoe factory, her father would have made it his business to be equally well informed about the shoe market.

No one needed to be informed about *her* work, she thought. It was obvious that she was nursing Markus, trying to teach Marianne her colours and numbers, and working with Berta to tidy, clean and put meals on the table. No wonder she fell into bed at night exhausted and yet feeling that she had let the day slip through her fingers.

When Nils was not travelling and not overwhelmed with his own work, some of their happiest hours were spent sitting up late at the newspaper-covered dining table, painting their china. They had ordered plain porcelain dinner plates from Rorstrand, fired at a low temperature or "biscuited." Each plate was to be decorated with a different flower, and sent back to Rorstrand for a second, higher firing. It felt to Sofie like old times, when Nils had sat next to her painting out of doors in Grez, trading suggestions, compliments and mock insults. The decoration had to be painted with a rapid, unfaltering hand. Nils went like lightning, instinctively knowing how stems and flowers would wind around the plate. She, who pored over flowers in Gothenburg's Botanical Gardens, needed a little time to map their route before she plunged in, because there was no going back. They needed blooms that insinuated themselves around the rim, in a look reminiscent of Nils's beloved eighteenth century. They ruled out gladioli and irises—too stiff. Both claimed the nasturtium, with its tendrils clambering irrepressibly over everything, its little outbreaks of buds and its leaves as round as saucers. In the end, Sofie surrendered the nasturtium to Nils, and contented herself with the moss rose. It too was pliable, even with its thorns.

One thing she had kept from her painting days was the shape of her clothes. When she was pregnant, her dresses were waistless and loose, like a painting smock. She found she liked that, whether or not she was pregnant. (To which Nils said, encircling her waist, "But you are always pregnant." It did seem that she had no sooner weaned the new baby than she was pregnant with the next one.) In England, she read, this style was called Aesthetic Dress, and had been taken up by the disciples of William Morris. So-called New Women, who supported female suffrage and were in revolt against corsets and the other constraints forced on women, also favoured it. Sofie wasn't in revolt against anything, but it was pleasant not to have a waist, or stays, or a weighted skirt, just a loose body of unpressed pleats that hung from the yoke like a child's tunic. She designed a few dresses of her own: the trick was to have some eye-catching decoration, usually applique or embroidery, at the yoke and sleeves.

When Marianne was born, all Sofie had wanted to do was nurse her, watching the baby work to keep up with the first milk that came in quickly and then relax into more measured swallows. She ran her knuckles along the curve of Marianne's cheek and watched her laugh well up. Nils thought she doted too much on the baby.

With Markus, she was strangely sad and always tired. He was more demanding than Marianne, but by no means a difficult baby. But Sofie did not particularly want to live. That sounded so dramatic, but it felt the opposite of dramatic. Everything was heavy, so awkward she didn't know how to pick it up. She still loved Marianne, she supposed because it was a kind of habit. Loving Nils seemed less of a habit, but she carried on with him. And he was so absorbed in his work that he did not notice much that was happening at home.

It was for the baby that she felt painfully, guiltily little. She wondered how it would end, and whether she would have to spend her life pretending to care for him. Loving Marianne was like eating warm bread and freshly made butter, it felt so natural and wholesome. Loving Markus seemed impossible, like swallowing nettles.

"He is so homely," she had complained to her mother when her parents visited Gothenburg.

"He is not," her mother said. "He is perfectly handsome."

But she knew her mother was lying, to save her feelings. Or to save Markus? She knew Marianne was the most exquisite baby ever born, and Markus one of the least attractive. Years later, when she looked at photographs or Nils's paintings, she saw that Marianne was not as beautiful as she had thought and Markus nowhere near as homely.

It was early summer and Markus was ten months old when the idea came to her. She had gone into the nursery to make sure he had settled. In his sleep, he breathed a double breath, with a catch between the first, shorter breath and the longer, second one. As she watched in the dark she thought, I need to draw him. At least, to draw him. Maybe not paint him, but at least to fix on paper those cheeks, the slope of his eyes that was like Nils, the mildly pointed chin. She felt quite calm and not particularly disloyal to Nils, because she knew she would not need to do this again. And that it was important.

Nils had gone sketching with friends to one of the nearby islands. There would be no problem finding the necessary privacy. She took the baby to the Botanical Gardens, while Berta watched Marianne at home. There was plenty of room for paper and drawing pencils at the foot of the carriage. In a bosky little cul-de-sac where the sun slanted down on a border of mayflowers and lady's mantle, Markus played with a ball of yarn. The velvety, cupped leaves of the lady's mantle, each one holding a single drop of dew, tempted him, but his crawling was still too unskilled to take him from his blanket to the border. Sofie spent the morning drawing him. Then she took him home and drew him some more while he surrendered to sleep, on his back, his arms and legs splayed. Only one thing was missing in her sketches, and that was his strawberry-blond colouring. After the children were in bed for the night, she made some rapid watercolours by lamplight. Nils was meticulous about his paints, but she left them in perfect order.

By the end of the day, Markus was hers. She loved him, loved his haunches that were like small hams, the way he rocked back and forth trying to crawl and then thought better of it, the way he hoisted himself up on a chair, mostly with his right arm, and crowed triumphantly once his chin was level with the seat, the way he moved his blocks around, searching methodically for some magic block-formula that eluded him.

Her "day off," as she thought of it, had worked, where Markus was concerned. But it left her feeling rather flat, at times even short-tempered. The next time Nils went away, a week later, she took the children on a picnic to the park that surrounded Skansen Kronan, the octagonal fortress that guarded the city. Marianne cried and then pouted because she wanted to climb up to the lookout at the top—even for her fat, determined legs, the steps were too steep. Markus fussed more than usual. The day was a very long one.

Sofie kept the sketches and watercolours for a while in her recipe folder, between the instructions for Mamma's apple cake and Mrs. Hedlund's gingerbread. But she did not need them. And when Markus was five and they moved permanently to Askebo, she burned them with the other rubbish.

Chapter Four

1897–1898

WHEN SOFIE WAS a girl, the Falkners spent their summer holidays in Askebo, a village in Dalarna where two of her aunts lived in an old cottage on a river. In 1897, after Aunt Karolina died and Aunt Emmy moved to a nearby town, Sofie's father, who owned the cottage, gave it to Sofie and Nils. Askebo was like hundreds of villages—a sprinkling of houses, farms and an old church along the winding river. Falun was the closest town, with a mine whose copper produced the dark red paint that covered most of Sweden's cottages. The Olssons' cottage was painted Falun red and, depending on her mood, Sofie found that charming (it was so Swedish) or boring (it was so Swedish).

Since there was nothing distinguished about the cottage, they added and renovated in bits and pieces, when they had the time and money. They stayed in Gothenburg for one more school term, and moved to Askebo in 1898. Nils was selling enough that he no longer needed a teacher's salary. By then, there were four children, Birgitta and Sonja having followed Markus. Little by little, they added a verandah, opened up the ceiling in the nursery and robbed the dining room of its view of the river by building the first studio in front of it. Nils did small, fanciful things, sculpting a gargoyle of himself for a roof truss, for example, and topping a chimney with a weathervane in the shape of a palette signed with his initials.

Askebo, 25 June 1898
Dear Mamma,

Thank you for the embroidery patterns, which arrived yesterday. That kind of handcraft always reminds me of Mrs. Greger from down the street, and those huge green apples she was eternally embroidering on orangey-red wool. I don't remember ever seeing anything she finished, just those giant fruits multiplying on her wool.

No one will ever like the Askebo house as much as we do, we are doing such odd things that suit us alone. Aunt Emmy came to visit, before we are ready to have visitors, but when will we ever be ready for that? She was most dismayed by the second-floor room where the little girls and I will sleep. We have taken away the ceiling, to make it more spacious, and we look right up to the roof. And we have taken down the aunts' curtains and put shutters on the inside, no curtains. A bare wooden floor so the girls can push their doll carriages and build with their blocks. My bed lies behind a simple curtain strung up on a pole. Aunt Emmy said it looked like a dungeon. Oh dear, you see what I mean.

Marianne loves playing little mother with the baby, and she and Sonja quarrel, each claiming "Birgitta's my baby!" "No, she's my baby!" It quickly becomes tiresome. Nils has painted a picture of me nursing the baby, but actually she is weaned, sooner than the others. My milk dried up, who knows why, and for the last few sittings I had to pose with a doll, which was strange.

I feel a bit listless, perhaps because the house is still so unsettled. It does not seem to bother Nils: he works all the time on his mural for the girls' grammar school in Gothenburg.

*Once we had assigned the rooms on the second floor for
bedrooms, a reading room and a guest room, there was no
place for my desk. Nils's bright idea was to put it in the hall,
so that is where I write to you. The good side of this decision
is that I am easy to find when Nils or the children or the
maid need me; the bad side is the same! What is the opposite
of a hideaway? That is what I have.*

*Love to you and Pappa
from six of us,
Sofie*

Reading it, she thought, No, this is not a good letter. She tried
again.

Askebo, 25 June 1898
Dear Mamma,

Thank you for the embroidery patterns, which
arrived yesterday. You are right, I should stir myself and
stop moping, and get interested in some handcraft. I will
look more closely at the patterns and, once I get the hang
of them, perhaps I will design my own.

While Nils was in Stockholm I had the panelling
installed in the dining room. I could see that the workers
were surprised that we would line the heart of a Swedish
house with cheap tongued-and-grooved wood, the kind
you see in an ordinary cafe or a railway waiting room.
But it would be silly to waste expensive wood on walls we
are going to paint forest green and obscure with pictures
and shelves for some of our favourite pieces. I did not dare
go ahead with the green until Nils returned. Reluctantly,
because he had wanted something more formal, he
agreed—he says my colour sense is better than his.

But he has come up with all kinds of ingenious

solutions and pretty touches. He cut a window in the
wall in his bedroom that looks down onto the studio,
so he can see the progress of his painting from that angle.
Then he painted a garland of oak leaves all around the
opening. For the lovely old clock we bought in Paris, he
made a bracket for the dining room wall, and then he cut
a square in the bracket and in the shelf beneath it for the
clock's weight. So simple and space-saving!

Marianne and Sonja love playing little mother with
the baby, and Markus would happily spend all day at his
workbench. Thank you again for such a fine birthday
present. Nils is terribly busy with his mural for the
Gothenburg Girls Grammar School. I confess I feel a bit
listless, but no doubt everything will be better once the
house is more settled.

Love to you and Pappa,
from six of us,
Sofie

She dreamed that all Sweden was tented in the thick wool on which
women embroidered. Piano covers, curtains, lap rugs, bed coverings
were all pressed into service, and no one in Sweden could see the sky
for these dark pieces of wool. Plums, grapes, irises and pears embroidered in loud colours grew on the wool, a good thing because there
was no sun where the real things could grow. Underneath, where
people walked, the threads stretched, taut and criss-crossed, a web
that could never be disentangled.

Later, when people talked about their Askebo house and their
family as a model, Sofie found it all rather exaggerated. Letting in
as much light as possible and choosing bright colours rather than the
sleepy darkness that filled so many houses was unconventional,
she supposed that was obvious. And the idea that children should

not be consigned to the nursery but have the run of the house was unusual, although it was more or less the way she had grown up. But beyond that, their choices were purely personal, and often last-minute improvisations.

There was plenty to do, with four children and the renovations. But she was restless, beginning a lacy knitted jacket and cap for the baby and abandoning it, searching for curtain fabrics—perhaps she should embroider something on the uninspiring cottons and linens they sold in Falun—and then losing interest. Nils's friend Lars Vogt had given him an eighteenth-century pattern book, and she stared at its festoons, garlands and cartouches, looking without much success for inspiration for the cottage.

They bought an old ceramic stove at the auction rooms in Falun, covered with tiles in the yellow of rich new cream. The tiles were decorated with the folk painter's alphabet—crowns, flowers, hearts and pairs of birds in red, blue and a brighter yellow. Once the stove was installed in a corner of the parlour, Nils wanted to paint an echo of the tiles, a fan-shape of birds and flowers, on the ceiling above the stove. He is gilding the lily, she thought, initially amused—something he never does in his paintings.

"Let well enough alone," she told him. He paid no attention.

Now he stood on the ladder, palette in hand, literally overshadowing the lovely, self-sufficient stove. She busied herself at the other end of the room, her back to the stove, playing with some silhouettes and engravings she wanted to arrange on the wall.

"You don't like it," he complained when she made no comment on his work, inflating his hurt feelings to camouflage them.

"The stove is beautiful, all to itself. Let it do its work."

"Wait until I am finished," he insisted, and went on painting.

Annoyed, she talked reason to herself. This degree of good fortune would have been unimaginable to him as a poor, overlooked child. It was only natural that he wanted to put his mark everywhere on the cottage. She trained her eye to look at the midpoint of the stove, and not the pointless fanfare painted above it.

Up until now, in France, Stockholm and Gothenburg, she and Nils had shared a bedroom. Many bourgeois couples did not sleep in the same room, and Sofie had assumed that, in the larger space of Askebo, Nils would have his own room. Rather than build another single bedroom, it would be simpler if she slept for a while with the three little girls.

They were talking over their plans one night, at the dining room table. They wanted to extend the long window in the parlour almost to the full width of the room. But first the National Museum needed to send Nils his prize money for the fresco competition. While they talked he kept drawing versions of the window, varying the panes, the hardware, the number of casements. Nothing satisfied him. He scowled, erasing design after design.

Finally he said, "I don't understand why you think it is necessary to sleep in the nursery."

So *that* was the trouble with the window. "Well, since I have to get up in the night with the baby, why not avoid waking you by sleeping closer to our little broken alarm clock?"

That was what they called Birgitta.

"Of course," she continued, playing her trump card, "my parents always had different rooms, so that seems normal to me."

"Of course. Yes, I see that would help with the baby. We can try it for a while."

They never talked about their different origins. Nils liked to think of himself as a socialist and sometimes, when he became aware of the way the middle classes did something, he objected as a matter of principle. But usually he complied, as unobtrusively as possible.

Things would be different in Askebo. She watched him thinking about that while she darned Markus's sock and he sketched a set of windows with casements at either end. For one thing, she would no longer wake in the night and find him nuzzling at and then sucking at her breast, especially when she was nursing a baby. Its hardness would soften with his suckling, something that at first slightly disgusted and then aroused her. And the way he curled around her was sweet, until she needed more air. But she assumed their bed-life would go on, regardless of where he slept.

That night in her bed in the corner of the nursery, Sofie could not sleep. Her mind filled with cranky children, cheap curtain materials and a man who had to paint his signature on every surface. Even at past ten o'clock, the Swedish midsummer light was so strong that, if she had had a window by her bed, she could have moved aside the curtain and written a letter. But she had no window, so she lit a candle and began to write.

> *Dear Professor Malmstrom,*
>
> *I know I thanked you at the time of my marriage for the sketching umbrella you sent me. It still works perfectly and is a very clever invention. While cleaning out my husband's studio recently, I came across it. Of course, I had given it to him. Perhaps you do not know that I gave up painting when I married.*
>
> *I would just like to ask you one question, if I might. Why, since you troubled to give me a sketching umbrella, did you not encourage me more when I was your student?*
>
> *Yours sincerely,*
> *Sofie Falkner Olsson*

She had no idea why she wrote this aggressive letter, since it could never be posted. Still, she supposed it did no harm.

Chapter Five

FEBRUARY 1899

In the brilliant midwinter cold, Nils took her to Bingsjo, to see the work of an eighteenth-century folk painter, Winter Carl Hansson. The way to Bingsjo, almost directly north of Askebo and near Lake Amungen, sparkled with ice, coating the branches of trees, fringing roofs with icicles, glinting up treacherously from the ground. The house they wanted to see, square and dark red, was hardly warmer inside than outside once you were a few metres from the porcelain stove. Many of the family, who had crowded into the main room, wore their jackets and coats. Sofie huddled in her furs. In spite of the cold, the room was full of the flowers Hansson had painted on the stove, the walls, the doors and the big blue chest that stood in the corner. Flat blossoms rose symmetrically from low bowls on the panels of the chest. A long garland heavy with buds and leaves bloomed all around the wall close to the ceiling. It was like being inside a pleasure garden or a conservatory in an ice palace.

A loom dominated the room, the way a piano would in a middle-class drawing room. Against the wall a woman sat spinning wool, her foot, hands and wheel moving in a rhythm as intimate as breathing. Another woman, old and smoking a pipe, stood and worked at a piece of two-end knitting between puffs, and a young girl, also standing, whittled something. The woman at the spinning wheel did not speak Swedish and Sofie did not understand her dialect, but the spinner needed no words to see that the woman in furs was interested. Without taking her hands off the wool she was feeding onto the bobbin, she inclined her head toward the wheel to beckon Sofie over. *Look*, her fingers said, *it's easy. You just take the tufts of wool, spread them out to loosen the fibres and let them catch on to the end of what has been spun.* Pumping the treadle steadily, she pinched the wool with one hand while pulling down on the twisting fibre. With her other hand, she thinned out the tuft. It looked impossible, like twisting a cloud and expecting it to become a strong piece of thread or yarn. And yet it worked. The accommodating fluff stretched and did not break; a simple twist transformed it into wool.

Come, the woman smiled, sliding off her stool and patting it. Nils had gone off to see the painted walls in the bedrooms and probably expected her to follow, but this interested her more. Sofie folded her coat onto the floor and sat down on the stool. Pressing Sofie's thumb and forefinger against the wool, the woman demonstrated without words: pinch firmly, pull down and then slide your fingers back up. Later, Sofie would learn the words—whirl, bobbin, flyer, roving, slubs. She learned to like sheep's wool because even when cleaned and carded, it had a certain stickiness that meant the tufts adhered easily to the end of the spun wool. Except on the coldest winter days, she would spin barefoot or wearing only a stocking because it helped the connection between foot, treadle, wheel, hands and wool. But now, she let the woman guide her hands and felt more at home than she ever had at the piano.

After a few months, once she was comfortable with spinning, Nils bought her a loom and set it up in the workshop. The loom was so large and its bump-bump-shudder so loud that she felt as if she entered a small, impregnable house each time she stood before it. Although this house only had one wall, the noise shut out the children, the maid, decisions about dinner, everything but the demands of warp and weft. It gave her more privacy than she felt at her desk in the upstairs hall.

But it was trying work, frustrating her impetuousness. Unlike the oil painting she had been taught at school, where you could follow your instincts and redo what you had done before, weaving demanded a finished design and the warp strung perfectly before you began. The discipline irked her. At the beginning, she often walked away from the loom in irritated impatience. You are impossible! she told it. But she hired a woman from Bingsjo to come and teach her, and gradually made her peace with its demands.

Chapter Six

CECILIA VOGT HAD not been exaggerating when she said that the Olssons' house was famous throughout Sweden. Sofie and Nils never considered it completely finished and tinkered with it for years, but word of mouth began to spread almost before they gave up the Gothenburg flat and moved to Askebo permanently, in 1898. After 1899, when Nils published *How We Live*—twenty-four water-colours of the house with short essays inspired by the pictures—it seemed that most Swedes wanted to see the house, or at least pictures of the house. The Crown Princess, who had married the heir to the Danish throne, was one of those people.

In June of 1901, shortly after Sofie had first met Cecilia, a letter arrived.

Siljevik, 25 June 1901
Dear Mrs. Olsson,
    I did not intend to write again so soon after your visit, but curiosity—one of my besetting sins—compels me. When you were here, you mentioned that the Crown Princess would be making a visit to Askebo. No doubt,

she will find your house fascinating—I doubt there is
anything like it in Copenhagen. If it is not too pre-
sumptuous,
I would enjoy hearing how it all went.
> With my best wishes,
> Cecilia Vogt
> P.S. I wonder if you have had the time to begin
> reading Mrs. Gaskell.

Sofie was relieved. This was significantly warmer than
Mrs. Vogt's last letter, when she had skirted Sofie's question about
marriage. Well, she reminded herself, if you will ask questions
that are baffling if not rude, you must be prepared for a cold
answer.

> Askebo, 28 June 1901
> Dear Mrs. Vogt,
> How nice to hear from you. Please don't make
> apologies for your curiosity—many people would say that
> a seemly interest in the royal family is one of our Swedish
> duties! But seriously, the Princess arrives on July 1, and I
> will be sure and report afterwards.
> Alas, I haven't yet found the time for Mrs. Gaskell.
> We have had an early crop of strawberries and the usual
> rhubarb, so preserving them occupied me for some days.
> Also, Nils is painting the children and me having a picnic
> under a tree in the garden, and the posing eats into my
> reading time. He will be done with us soon, I hope, as the
> children are impatient to go fishing and swimming and I
> to read Mrs. Gaskell.
> I will write soon with details of the royal visit.
> Cordially,
> Sofie Olsson

The Swedish Homecraft Association was more than happy
to help with arrangements for the Crown Princess's visit. Miss
Zickerman, the Homecraft official who had already guided scores
of dignitaries through the house, made her usual conscientious
("stuffy," thought Sofie) plans. Usually she came round to a grudg-
ing appreciation of Miss Zickerman's carefulness, but this time
Sofie was out of sorts.

Dear Miss Zickerman,

*I am looking forward to welcoming the Crown Princess
next Monday. I hope you will not take it amiss, but I would
like to do something different for her visit. I would like to give
the tour myself, rather than rely on you as usual. It will begin at
the lintel over the door on which my husband painted, "Welcome
to the house of Nils Olsson and his wife," and it will give a
picture of our home and family rather different from the one
familiar throughout Sweden. I fancy that Her Highness, and
perhaps ultimately others, may find this of interest.*

Until Monday, dear Miss Zickerman, I remain,

Yours truly,

Sofie Olsson

Of course, she did not send that letter. Instead, she wrote,

Askebo, 28 June 1901
Dear Miss Zickerman,

   Thank you for your note about the Crown Princess's
visit on Monday. I have read of her interest in Japanese
prints, and I will put out some examples of my husband's
collection on the picture rail in the workroom for Her
Highness to examine after your tour. If her schedule
permits, I hope that she will be able to stop for some
coffee and apple cake afterwards. The peonies should

be fully out by then, and it is one of the best times to sit by the river.

Looking forward, as always, to your tour, and until Monday, dear Miss Zickerman,

Yours truly,

Sofie Olsson

Askebo, 2 July 1901

Dear Mrs. Vogt,

Well, normal life resumes again. The early fruits are bottled and waiting for winter in the storeroom, Nils has finished his picture of our picnic (where we all look better behaved than we usually are), and the Crown Princess has returned to Denmark. So I have the leisure to write to you about her visit.

The Princess seemed pleased, and Miss Zickerman, her escort from the Swedish Homecraft people, also thought it went well. Between us, the Princess has a slightly weak chin and an expression in her pale blue eyes of being ready to be pleased. That might be part of the training of a Swedish princess, but it looked deeper than that. Perhaps because she lives in Copenhagen with her Danish prince, she seemed particularly touched by unpretentious but plainly Swedish pieces—a painted wooden box, for example, or an embroidered wall hanging from Bohuslan.

The Princess wears a bracelet made of cameos linked with golden chains. It is old-fashioned but, she explained, it had belonged to her mother-in-law. Each cameo pictures a different member of the Danish royal family. Whenever Miss Zickerman described something as "typically Swedish," the Princess half-cleared her throat and rotated her bracelet. I wondered, was it aggressive

("Take that!" to the crowned heads in Copenhagen), nervous, or just something she does? I don't know, but Nils laughed when I told him about it. He avoids these visits, and had gone to Falun for the day.

I could see that Her Highness, like most visitors to the house, was taken aback by its smallness. After years of looking at Nils's paintings of the rooms, which he always paints from the wider side, people credit our simple cottage with a spaciousness that does not exist in reality. Visitors do not expect the dense warren that we live in, where one room opens unceremoniously into another without the dignity of a corridor. But the Princess adjusted, exclaiming with pleasure when she saw the location of a favourite picture, nodding happily when Miss Zickerman pointed out some of the landmarks—the row of hooks for the children's coats that climb the side of the staircase, the folkloric dining room, the blue-and-white parlour, filled with light and inspired by the eighteenth century.

In the dining room, Miss Zickerman talked about our casual family life, where even the youngest children take all their meals with their parents. That was a new idea for the Princess.

She turned to the little drinks cabinet on the wall and said, "Mrs. Olsson, would you be very kind? I love the picture your husband painted from here, the one where you open the cabinet to take out some aquavit. Would you mind standing just there for a minute?"

I did as I was asked, turning from the little wall cabinet with the bottle in my hand, exactly as I had posed for the picture. The Princess was charmed that I was wearing the tortoiseshell comb that stands up in front of my topknot, just as in the picture. She thanked me, and promised she would remember that moment.

So, I think we acquitted ourselves well, and the
Princess returned to Copenhagen with a good supply of
stories about Nils Olsson's famous house. And now, you
and your husband must come and see it for yourselves!
With all best wishes,
Sofie Olsson

Of course, she could not describe the whole visit to Cecilia Vogt.
One of the things Miss Zickerman had pointed out to the princess
was the weaving by Sofie that hung between Nils's bedroom and
the dormitory where Sofie slept with the girls. While Miss
Zickerman talked about the way they had opened up the dormitory,
Sofie stared, not listening, at her weaving and the flowery border
Nils had painted on the wall above it, for her birthday. Her laboured
attempt to make something in the fashionable Glasgow style, cen-
tred on that stiff rose, suffered from its closeness to his effortlessly
flexible, unspooling line.

As always, when she really looked at his blossoms, her body
yearned. When she was younger, it had concentrated itself in her belly.
Now it located itself further up, in her chest and head. The suppleness
and strength of that line. The tenderness. Sometimes she wished that
Nils would move with the times a little. But she could imagine what
it would cost him to suppress that easy flow for something more nervous, more modern. Something more like her unsatisfactory rose.

In the dining room, Miss Zickerman pointed out the tapestry
Sofie had designed for Nils's bench at the head of the table, and the
princess admired it. Saying obliging things was no doubt also part
of a princess's training, but what truly seemed to spark her enthusiasm was the room's red-and-green colour scheme.

"So bold," she said, sighing sympathetically. "And so reminiscent
of Nils Olsson's paintings." Miss Zickerman was skilled at following
a distinguished visitor's interests. She seconded the princess's appreciation for the red and green with remarks about Nils Olsson's colour

sense and flair for decoration. Sofie kept her face neutral, like a modest wife whose husband is being praised.

In the Long Hall, the princess asked about a painting Miss Zickerman had passed over.

"This oil of an artist in his studio. Is it an early work?"

Miss Zickerman looked at Sofie, almost apologetically. Sofie understood why. It was muddy and pedestrian, a portrait of her teacher, Professor Malmstrom. She had painted better pieces, and she had never understood why Nils chose this one, and only this one, to hang.

The princess was surprised at the answer.

"I did not realize that Mrs. Olsson had ever painted."

Your gracious Highness,

Forgive me. I should have corrected Miss Zickerman at the time of your visit when you praised the dining room colours. My husband wanted something that continued the Gustavian look of the parlour, perhaps pale yellow and blue to go with the parlour's blue and white. But the furniture in the dining room is stronger and more peasant-like, and I convinced him, finally, that those favourites of the Swedish countryside, red and forest green, were right for that room. It was my doing. Now he often writes about the need for strong, bright colour in this land of dark green forests and white snow.

With many thanks for your visit, and especially for your advice about the peonies. I will do as you suggest and be sure and let you know, through Miss Zickerman, if the bloom improves next season.

Yours respectfully,
Sofie Olsson

She did not send that letter, either.

Chapter Seven

OCTOBER 1901

THE AUTUMN AFTER the princess's visit, Sofie read in the *Dagens Nyheter* that Dorotea Jonasen, her Danish colleague from her days in Grez, had three paintings in the Stockholm Salon. Nils was painting a triptych and was too busy to go. Although she loved looking at pictures with him—they stood close together, talking in lifted eyebrows, puffed cheeks, pursed mouths and half sentences that the other understood perfectly—Sofie was relieved. He would not have been the ideal companion for this excursion. After arranging to meet Hanna Hirsch—now Hanna Pauli since her marriage to Georg Pauli—she took the train from Falun.

As she made her way from Stockholm's Central Station down to Stromgatan, she ran into Lars Vogt coming out of a cafe with a well-rouged woman. It was not yet noon, but they breathed brandy. Sofie was taken off guard, but Lars greeted her with his usual enthusiasm. He introduced them airily, "Mrs. Olsson, Mrs. Holmgren," and he and his companion went south toward the Old Town.

Sofie headed east, to meet Hanna at the National Museum. Marriage and children had not noticeably relaxed Hanna. She opined her way through the permanent collection ("Never understood his reputation," "Now that one *is* good") as they walked toward the second-floor rooms reserved for the Salon. Searching for Dorotea's work on walls crowded with paintings of peasants, flowers, sheep huddling in fields and rain pooling on lamplit streets, Sofie felt the gallery-goers behind her making room for a determined stride. Unconsciously and efficiently, Cecilia Vogt had a way of parting a crowd.

"Cecilia! What are you doing here?" Hanna said. They had gone to school together as girls in Stockholm.

"Mrs. Vogt," said Sofie, flustered by the memory of her encounter with Lars. They shook hands.

"Please, it's time to be Cecilia and Sofie," Cecilia said. "Lars and I are in town because he is showing at a new gallery, on Sveavagan. He has a meeting with the owner this morning." Sofie nodded, and hid her confusion: Sveavagan was in the opposite direction from the Old Town where Lars and Mrs. Holmgren had been headed.

Cecilia seemed not to notice her silence. She chatted about the visit to Askebo she and Lars had promised, but not yet accomplished. Hanna and Sofie explained about their friend Dorotea, and with Cecilia's help they found her pictures. There was an unremarkable seascape, a fine portrait of a girl with a family resemblance to Dorotea, and a painting of a table set for breakfast in a summer garden that delighted Sofie. She put up her hands as if to touch the sun-dappled tablecloth. This one was worth the trip.

Cecilia smiled. "Yes, she has something, doesn't she?"

Sofie was scheduled to catch the afternoon train back to Falun, but had time for sausages and dill potatoes in a cafe around the corner from the museum. Once they had ordered, Hanna told Cecilia the story of Dorotea's painting teacher who had recommended dispatching her paintbox to a watery grave.

"How did she react?"

"Probably more politely than she should have," Hanna said. "We were brought up to turn the other cheek."

Cecilia looked at Sofie, wanting her response. Sofie lined up her knife and fork in parallel lines across the top of her plate. She was reluctant, but there was something imperative in Cecilia's gaze.

Slowly, because she had never thought about it so explicitly, she said, "It was such a new thing for all of us, a woman wanting to paint, that perhaps Dorotea didn't know then what she really wanted. Or how much she wanted it."

Hanna was busy cutting her potatoes, and Sofie stared into the middle distance, frowning a little.

"But after all," she continued, "she didn't take his advice. We've just been looking at the result of that. And the dishes the teacher sent for the wedding present are probably all broken by now."

Cecilia and Hanna smiled. Sofie thought of the cracked and chipped dishes at the back of her cupboard at home. No doubt Cecilia disposed of her broken dishes immediately.

"Yes, china breaks," Cecilia agreed. "Dreams should not."

Sofie considered the perfectly turned-out Cecilia, her fur thrown back on her chair while she ate her sausages with gusto. What are Cecilia's dreams, she wondered. And did they have anything to do with the woman who'd been in the cafe with Lars?

Still circling the question of Dorotea and her teacher, Hanna said, "Lots of people felt the way that teacher did, and many still do. Georg remembers the time when he praised one of Nils's paintings, and Nils answered that his greatest achievement was stopping Sofie from painting."

Hanna's tactlessness was famous. Sofie turned red, and said lightly, "That is Nils talking for effect. You know how he likes to stir things up."

Hanna shrugged and buttered her bread. Cecilia said nothing. Sofie thought, Why, when Nils and Hanna have behaved badly, am I the one who has to smooth things? And why does Nils say these stupid things, when he surely doesn't mean them? Something about Georg brought out a cruelty in Nils—Georg's sweetness, perhaps, or the way he indulged Hanna's painting life.

"Saying that to Georg was unkind," she said to Hanna, "when he has worked so hard to encourage your painting."

Now, she thought, I have been disloyal too. Before she left for Stockholm, she had said goodbye to Nils in his studio, where he was sculpting a frame for his painting. At the bottom of the frame, a nude was lying on her side, seen from the back. Her crooked elbow jutted out of the frame and broke into the real world. That little miracle was shocking and marvellous, and when she saw it, she had kissed him from sheer pleasure. Why would a man who could do that wonderful thing exult, even as a joke, at stopping her from pursuing a very small talent? That was a power any waiter or clerk had over his wife, if he wished to exercise it.

Her eyes on her plate, she made a minute adjustment to her fork and knife. Hanna was chewing her bread and butter, apparently still oblivious. Abruptly, Cecilia changed the subject. She had been rereading *David Copperfield*, she said, and still loved the idyllic scenes where the boy David visited his nurse's family on the Yarmouth coast. But this time, she was more impatient than she remembered being with David's first wife, Dora, who was such a dimwit. Could a reasonable man really love such an empty-headed baby, however pretty?

Cecilia pressed on, almost breathlessly. This is kind of her, Sofie thought. When Cecilia finally paused, Sofie had something to add.

"I agree with you about Dora, but at least David realizes he has made a mistake before she conveniently dies. It is Agnes, the choice of his maturity, who bothers me more. She is such a stained-glass saint, she endures, endures, endures—taking care of her alcoholic father and silly Dora, suffering her unrequited love for David in silence. Unlike Dora, she is going to be a helpmeet for David, but that is *all* she is. She seems to have no wishes at all for herself. I find her very tedious."

She could see that she had surprised Cecilia, although that was not her aim. Perhaps Cecilia thought Sofie was not in a good position to cast stones at Agnes. Certainly it was easier to be critical of a fictional character than of real people, or yourself.

When she got home, she went briskly up the stairs to her desk, saying "Later" to the clamouring children. She hoped that Nils had not heard the carriage from his studio.

Askebo, 15 October 1901
Dear Dorotea,

This comes to you with many congratulations! Your "so-called talent," as you used to call it, is alive and well. I admired all three pictures, beginning with the bold Persian carpet in *Portrait of a Girl*. It reminded me of Professor Lavartin's ideas about the buildup of colour, how well you learned that lesson. Hanna Pauli, who was with me—do you remember she married Georg?—was very impressed with that. Is the girl a daughter, or a niece? The set of her mouth looks like you. But my favourite is *Summer Breakfast*. It is idyllic, the mismatched chairs, all the roundnesses of teapot, goblets, cups and table, the sun glinting on the green-glass cracker box, all masterful. You have put your paintbox to very good use!

With fond memories of our time in Grez,
Sofie

After she addressed the envelope, she went downstairs to hear about the children's day and to see what progress Nils had made with his frame.

Chapter Eight

IT WAS A blustery Sunday when the Vogts finally came to Askebo for the day. After the Grand Tour, as the older children called it, and lunch, the men went sketching at a picturesque bend in the river. They pulled their broad-brimmed hats as low on their heads as they would go, so that the wind would not blow them off. Sofie and Cecilia sat down in the blue-and-white parlour with their knitting.

"Lars does not enjoy the sight of a woman knitting," Cecilia said. "We look so tense and hunched over. A woman can look graceful while embroidering, but I try to do my knitting when Lars is not with me."

The talk moved to books, and to Charlotte Brontë's novels. They had both read *Jane Eyre* over and over, beginning when they were girls.

"As I get older," Cecilia said, "I am more and more cross with Mr. Rochester for attempting a bigamous marriage with Jane, while his lawful wife raves in the attic."

Sofie defended Rochester. "He has been duped into marrying a lunatic, and divorce was out of the question. What is the poor man to do?"

"Well, he is not to take advantage of an innocent, respectable girl, and then coolly propose making her his mistress when she discovers the truth," Cecilia said crisply. "And"—another affront struck her as she grew more heated—"do you notice that we think nothing of the fact that Mr. Rochester has had an illegitimate child with a ballerina? Suppose that Jane had an illegitimate child, that would make an entirely different novel, wouldn't it? As a matter of fact, the English are too prudish even to write that novel. It would have to be a French novel."

This had not occurred to Sofie. Of course, there was a different measuring stick for men than for women, but she took it so much for granted that usually she didn't notice it. Now she would notice it in *Jane Eyre*, but she still forgave Mr. Rochester.

"He is a schoolgirl's dream," Cecilia insisted. Her irritation was still rising, but the sweater she was knitting needed her attention: she had reached the row where she had to twist the cables. "Passionate, unpredictable and needing 'a good woman' to reform him," she went on scornfully when she had finished the row. "Even the way he flirts with Jane by insulting her is the way you flirt with a girl, not a woman. But sadly, we feel his appeal long after we are schoolgirls."

Sofie thought, I do feel Mr. Rochester's appeal but I am not going to apologize for that. Cecilia was enjoying their argument as much as she was. They carried on talking about novels, companionably disagreeing and agreeing. The men returned and, after a last cup of tea, it was time for the Vogts to leave.

But first, Sofie had a gift for Cecilia. Using her new, small loom, she had woven her a handkerchief. Over its red, white and blue plaid, she embroidered a few lilies of the valley, Cecilia's favourite flower. Cecilia gave one of her croaks of laughter when she unfolded the tissue paper.

"'A handkerchief red, white and blue!'" she quoted the Irish song Markus had played in the Hall on their visit to Siljevik. "'But before I could wear it,'" she went on, "'he tore it in two.'"

"Not this one," Sofie said. "Keep it safe in your handkerchief box."

Chapter Nine

TWO MORE CHILDREN were born at Askebo, in 1902 a girl they called Tilda, and in 1905 the seventh and last child, Felix. When Felix was a baby, Ellen Key came to see the house. "Seeing" made it sound rather casual, Sofie thought: the truth was that Miss Key had come to inspect the house. She was a motherly, white-haired figure who favoured lace blouses, but underneath her mild surface she was one of the most powerful cultural forces in Sweden. She championed Ibsen's plays, women's suffrage and the Nordic Museum. Her lectures and essays could single-handedly exalt or sink a writer or a cause. *Beauty for Everyone*, her latest book, took William Morris's view that useful things should be beautiful and beautiful things should be useful. She believed that cultivating a simple beauty at home would make people happier and families stronger. So—Sofie thought stoically—a visit to Askebo was inevitable.

Miss Key, Sofie and Nils sat in Nils's new studio, on easy chairs set around a low table. The studio smelled hopefully of paint and varnish. It felt expansive and far from the family rooms, although that was an illusion. There was a fireplace, a grand piano and a player piano. On the wall at the working end of the room, hundreds of serious, uniformed boys and their teachers stood in prayer, in Nils's draft of a fresco for the staircase of the Norra Latin Grammar School in Stockholm.

"I got pushed out of the original studio," he complained half-seriously to Miss Key, while the baby played on the floor with a wooden train.

"All these children," he said, circling a bewildered hand, as if to ask how it happened that seven children lived here, "all these children wanted to play or work in the old studio. A workbench for Markus, plus Sofie's loom and two spindles and the sewing machine, gave me no space to paint. So I left it to them, and now I have a bit of elbow room."

"A bit of elbow room" was modest, considering he had already told Miss Key that this was the largest studio in Sweden. Sofie watched as their guest took in the pictures stacked against the wall, the easels holding paintings at various stages, the stepladder Nils used to reach the high corners of the monumental works he hoped would finally secure his reputation as a serious artist. A white stoneware jug stood on the table between them, its tin lid tipped back to accommodate coneflowers, sweet peas and trailing ivy. It looked as if a busy hand had dropped the flowers in the jug willy-nilly.

"That is Sofie," he said, following Miss Key's look. "In case I have no other inspiration, she makes sure there is always one here on the table."

Miss Key glanced at Sofie, who looked at the bouquet. The second-highest coneflower was a few millimetres too tall; she would cut it down before lunch. On the floor, Felix found that banging his train cars together made a very satisfying noise. When he found a bullying rhythm he saw no reason to stop. Sofie picked him up with a few cars and the engine and took him to Berta.

When she returned, Nils and Miss Key were braiding their similarities together—which in Nils's case meant retelling anecdotes he had already rehearsed to perfection. How he had wanted his watercolours of the rooms at Askebo to be exhibited in the industrial arts section at the Stockholm Exhibition, rather than the fine arts section, so that people could learn from his example when it came to setting up a home. How he began painting pictures of the house and the children after a dismal summer when it rained every day for six weeks, and even the sketching umbrella would not allow him to paint out of doors. Fed up with his sulks, Sofie had told him to paint what he saw indoors. As usual, he exaggerated Sofie's impatience and his own subservience. Sofie and Miss Key smiled at each other, two women indulging a man's dramatics.

Miss Key talked about how the way the Olssons lived had become an ideal, not just of a new way to furnish houses, but of family life. Nils's devotees were growing in Germany as well as Sweden, and the German translation of *How We Live* had added many more. She and Nils negotiated their differences, which mostly involved women's rights, as pleasantly as possible.

"Your lecture caused quite a storm in Stockholm," he said, sitting a little further back in his chair.

She moved a little forward in hers. "Do you mean the one I called *The Misused Forces of Womanhood*? Yes, they liked it better in Copenhagen."

"No doubt, we are more conservative here. We don't like hearing that marriage puts a woman into a kind of prison."

Miss Key repeated what she had said and written many times. "But I want equality for women only so that they can be better mothers."

Sofie was no stranger to Miss Key's views on motherhood. She was devoted to motherhood beyond anything. She supported equal property rights for women and female suffrage because, she said, women would never become perfect mothers until society allowed them their full development. Nils agreed with her that motherhood was a woman's highest calling, but he did not see why a mother would want to vote, or why it would be better for society if they did. Watching the two of them, their determined cordiality only occasionally fraying, Sofie's thoughts wandered to the unspun wool she had taken to the dyer in Falun. Half of it she wanted dyed the palest green possible, and the other half a dark grey. Then she would mix them in the spinning to make various shades for her tapestry, as you mixed colours on a palette.

The talk she heard at a remove, threading in and around her plans for the wool, was abstract. Miss Key, for all her good intentions, was neither a wife nor a mother. And Nils was probably more interested in a woman's wifely function than her motherly one. Or was there any difference? Sometimes it felt as if she had eight children, not seven.

Now they were talking of property law, which brought Sofie back to the threshold of the house and Nils's sign, "Welcome to the house of Nils Olsson and his wife." Although the house had been in Sofie's family for generations, according to Swedish law it now belonged to Nils, not her. If Miss Key knew more about the two of them, she might decide he had taken her house as well as her name. (She would not accuse Nils of taking Sofie's painting life, because Miss Key believed that mothers should devote themselves only to raising their children.) If she knew more, would she still agree with the Germans that they were a model family? As for the vote, if getting it would enable Sofie to find the perfect grey-green she wanted for her tapestry, with a hint of lustre like a piece of Chinese celadon, she would support it. Otherwise, it sounded like a distraction.

After dinner, the adults looked at Nils's watercolours of the house. In *At the Window*, Marianne watered the plants on the windowsill in the drawing room. The room's colours were pale blues and off-whites. The aunts' old rag rug lay muted on the floor, and the sofa was loosely covered in blue-and-white stripes. As happened often in Nils's pictures, Sofie had apparently left the scene just before the painter took up his brush. The creases on the chair cushion still

showed the weight of a body, and her knitting had been left behind
on the round table. In this pale, well-behaved room of rectangles
and circles, with Marianne in her faded grey dress and the terracotta
flowerpots dusted with powdery mould, the stocking Sofie was
knitting was an inky black blob. It was ungainly, ill-mannered, even
menacing. Its four needles stabbed into the ball of wool and
announced, "Don't touch me. I don't accord with this soft, relaxed
room, but I must not be disturbed."

They looked at another painting where Sofie had just left the
scene, a nighttime picture of the dining room. Nils's book was open
at the head of the table, and at her place on the side there was an
open newspaper, a bit of black ribbon, and a pair of scissors, opened
to an X, balancing on the edge of the table. These things looked like
the clues in a murder mystery. But who was killing whom? Was she
the murderer or the victim? It would have been pointless to claim—
to whom? to the judge?—that she would never go off to bed with
sharp scissors threatening to fall off the table.

Staring at that strange picture alongside Miss Key, Sofie
thought of Lars Vogt. She and Nils now travelled to Siljevik every
few months, and no visit was complete without a tour through the
Vogts' new acquisitions—blankets or clocks or furniture. On their
last trip, Lars had shown them a thick belt made of something dark
and ungiving, with a brass holder attached to it and a big loop.

"No one could call it pretty," Sofie said.

"No," Lars agreed. "It's the belt a bride wears in the villages
around this part of the lake. It must be made of moose skin, and
this brass contraption holds her needles, and she keeps her knife
in this loop."

Sofie thought, So much for our citified, modern idea of a bride's
beautiful dress. These are the important things a woman brings to
the house—the needles with which she will make the family's
clothes, and a sizable knife to prepare the food. Is that why Nils
so often painted her with scissors and knives? Because women,

apparently so soft and yielding, do their work with these dangerous tools? She wished she could believe that was the reason.

The motto for Ellen Key's lecture about women's rights was "Women's History Is Love." That was a motto with many meanings, deliberately hard to challenge. Did Nils paint her with sharp, dangerous tools because she was failing at love? Doubtless Nils took so much because he needed so much.

Once they had finished with Nils's paintings, they had a stroll through the village, up to the church and its full-skirted bell tower. Then Miss Key took a trap back to Falun and the train. Although Nils had seemed to enjoy her visit, once she left his mood darkened.

"Nils, come in to supper. The children are at the table."

He shook his head, and would not move from the big chair in the studio. But as she turned to leave, he caught her hand and kissed the inside of her wrist. An apology. His cockiness bored her, although she knew it was defensive. But his sadness never failed to move her. She knew what was wrong. He did not want to be known as the man who painted watercolours of his house and children. At the start of his career, he'd had difficulty being taken seriously because he had been an illustrator. Now, this unexpected fame. That people admired what he had done with the Askebo house was fine, but it was a sideline. His ambition was to paint monumental frescoes of great Swedish kings, blood sacrifices, the tragic doings of heroes. Those were the subjects a man painted. How curious that he said women lacked the virile spirit to be artists, and now he was beloved for his paintings of children at breakfast, of his wife mending, of toys and dishes and enamel coffeepots full of apple blossoms.

Chapter Ten

JUNE 1906

IN EARLY SUMMER, Cecilia sent a letter to Sofie. She was going to an estate sale at one of the old master miner's properties around the Falun mine. There might or might not be some interesting things in the sale, but she really wanted to look at the house's folk murals, which were rumoured to be good. Perhaps Sofie would be interested in seeing the murals? Afterwards, they could have lunch at the hotel in Falun.

As Sofie rode through the Kopparbergslagen, the copper mining countryside, she watched the incongruous melding of the rural and the industrial—the familiar look of farms with barns and animals interrupted by smelting houses and slag heaps. The master miners were farmers with the rights to take ore from the mine, and many had become rich from the copper they produced on their land. The farmhouse Cecilia wanted to see was a plain eighteenth-century house near Bergsgarden, at the northern end of Lake Varpan. The neglected farm included a smelting house, but from the looks of it, it had never been prosperous.

As Cecilia had anticipated, nothing in the sale interested the two women. Nils had a wooden box that Sofie kept filled with old dishes, so she sifted through the boxes of crockery as always. He sometimes hammered the dishes into shards and made a small mosaic he affixed in a likely spot inside or outside the house. But today no cup or tureen lid caught her fancy. There was a heap of old tools—planes, chisels, a drill and a rusty saw that Nils would have inspected and Lars would have bought instantly.

"Thank heavens Lars is not here," Cecilia said. "We have too many of these relics already."

The sale may have been disappointing, but the murals were wonderful, a glowing story of a pilgrim who travelled around the walls of the main room, doing good deeds and minor miracles, inspired by regular visits from a saint they could not identify. A dotted line connected the pilgrim on his deathbed to his patron saint waiting to welcome him in paradise.

"I like the way his landscape obeys no botanical or biological rules," Sofie said, "tropical plants and trees living side by side with northern species, leopards walking along with penguins."

Cecilia nodded. She had the look in her eye collectors get when they must have something.

"We cannot stand by and let this be destroyed. But how to save it? Removing the frescoes from the walls is possible, but expensive and time-consuming. We would probably have to import the craftsmen from Italy, and their work takes months, while the new owners want to raze the building and build another house. It would probably be cheaper and definitely faster if we bought the house and moved it to Siljevik. I know that is what Lars will want. Luckily, we have a little time . . . so we can talk about it."

At lunch in the hotel restaurant, where the French aspirations included Louis XVI chairs and an almost comically formal service, Sofie tried to divert a distracted Cecilia by telling her about Ellen Key's visit. As a young woman, long before she had become a national figure, Miss Key had been one of Cecilia's and Hanna Hirsch's first teachers. Jewish children were allowed to attend the public schools by then, but the Isakssons and Hirsches had sent their daughters to a small private school for both Jews and gentiles. Miss Key had taught them history and Swedish literature.

"She inspected everything in the house," Sofie said, "including the children's rooms."

"Yes, she would," said Cecilia, amused.

"And at least part of this was your fault. Miss Key said, 'Cecilia Vogt tells me your designs are very clever.' That meant I had to show her all the curtains, the tapestries and the bed coverings I had made. She admired them, more or less, but then she turned over the fabrics without any apology, just as if I were her pupil. You know how chaotic my work is on the wrong side."

"Our samplers and other embroidery had to be as neat on the wrong side as the right side."

"I got that impression," Sofie said. "My designs are one thing, but my messy execution is another. Something else that she probably didn't appreciate—Nils is very proud of a little eighteenth-century spice cabinet on which he has written in Gothic script, 'Nils Olsson bought this old cabinet to put junk and other things in.' Miss Key had nothing to say about that."

Cecilia sniggered.

"She takes old furniture, especially folk furniture, very seriously, so she certainly would not find that funny."

"I'm not sure she knew what to make of the children's free-and-easy ways, either. Only Felix still has his meals in the kitchen, so there were six children who sat in the dining room for dinner. Lately, Nils has instituted a new rule—they sit in alphabetical order, beginning at his right—the only way to stop their constant bickering about placement. Nils keeps several reference books beside him on the bench, so he can look up facts under discussion. He has painted a big 'Empty!' at the bottom of the soup tureen, so the children compete noisily to get the last spoonful of soup and expose the 'Empty!' Poor Miss Key watched all that without comment."

"Well," Cecilia said, "she has written that the twentieth century is going to be the century of the child."

"That is the theory," Sofie said. "She seemed a bit disconcerted by the reality. Miss Key told the children that until she was twelve, she and her brothers and sisters took their breakfast and supper standing at a table without chairs. At those meals they ate only bread and milk. It was a question of discipline, not economy. She never spoke at the table unless she was spoken to until she was sixteen."

"How did the children take these medieval reminiscences?"

"With a mixture of disbelief and sadness."

Cecilia laughed. Sofie, who could still find her slightly formidable, thought, We are getting on.

When they finished the main course, Cecilia signalled the waiter. In a voice so low and confidential that he sounded almost ashamed, he told them about the desserts.

"What do you recommend?" Cecilia asked him. He was young, and only partially successful with the dishes that had French names. Now he looked slightly alarmed, but Cecilia smiled at him encouragingly.

"I know you are well known for your cheesecake. Unless I am mistaken, it has a hint of almond flavour, doesn't it?"

He thought it did. He ventured to suggest that, if she had the time to wait until they were prepared, the crêpes Suzette or the soufflés au chocolat were very popular.

"No, thank you. I love those things in France, but we have so many delicious Swedish desserts, I will stay with them today. I think I would like the apple cake."

"Very good, madame."

"And please don't forget to bring me some of your lovely vanilla sauce," she said, as if he made it himself.

Sofie stared at her friend. Where did she find room in her small frame for all that food? And why was she being so friendly with the waiter?

"Nothing for me, thank you. I do not have what the English call a sweet tooth."

"And I do," Cecilia said happily. There were still important things like this that they did not know about each other. They agreed that "a sweet tooth" was a nicer expression than the blunt Swedish *sockergris*, "sugar pig."

When the waiter returned with the apple cake and a silver boat of sauce, Cecilia asked him if he would mind pouring it.

"I have a bad habit of drowning the cake, the sauce is so good," she said, smiling at him as if pouring the sauce herself was quite beyond her capabilities.

My heavens, Sofie realized. She is *flirting* with him.

The waiter retreated, after pouring a shallow pool of sauce around the cake, and Cecilia returned to her normal self.

"Speaking of your work," she said between bites, "the Swedish Homecraft Association sent Lilli Zickerman to see our collections and the Folk School, and she was full of praise for the aprons and bonnets and cloths we have been buying. It all seems so normal now, collecting these folk things, but I remember when my mother was astonished that anyone would want what she called 'the belongings of the poor.'"

She helped herself to more sauce.

"But about your own pieces—I must warn you that Miss Zickerman is very curious about your most recent weaving and designing, and you will hear from her."

"Well, that is fine," Sofie said. "She means well."

"A word to the wise if she comes to visit: she is dead set against aniline dyes, which she regards as a prime example of what she calls 'industrial degeneration.' You might want to put any guilty fabrics or threads out of sight if you aren't in the mood for a lecture."

"I will never please the purists," Sofie said. "What they see as gaudy and artificial, I see as vibrant. Now I hear they will not even admit rag rugs into their sacred canon because the rags come from cloth made in factories. The problem with the Folk people is that they want everything to stop, and stay as it was before factories came to Sweden. Much as we love the old things and admire people like Miss Zickerman—and Miss Key too—that's not the way the world works. Nor would I want it to. And I'm impulsive and not at all methodical: if I see a pink or green thread that pleases me in a shop or market, I take it without asking about the dye, rather than ordering a season's worth of vegetable-dyed threads. Miss Zickerman will not approve, but there it is."

Over coffee, they began talking about *Vanity Fair*.

"I stopped reading," Sofie said, "I got so annoyed with Becky Sharp. All those heartless flirtations with rich men."

This was another of the differences they were discovering about each other. Once Cecilia started a book, she had to read to the last page no matter what she thought of it, but Sofie walked away when she got bored or irritated.

"Becky is in a bad way," Cecilia objected. "She has no money or position, and she has to earn a living or find a man who will support her."

"I don't really blame her, I blame Thackeray," Sofie said. "Are there only two kinds of women in the world—either a selfless Angel in the House or a temptress who is willing to destroy everyone who gets in her way as she climbs her selfish way up the ladder? Thackeray's male characters come in many colours other than black and white. Why can't he tell the story of a normal woman, with strengths and weaknesses, who has to make her way in the world?"

"And why is it," Cecilia interrupted, coming round to Sofie's side of the argument, "that in so many novels—not just by Thackeray—the woman who has to leave home to go to work often comes to a bad end?"

"You mean, in so many novels written by men."

Sofie could not deny that Nils would sympathize with Thackeray's suspicions. He distrusted women who had ambitions outside the family, although he made exceptions—Miss Key, for example—for older, single women who admired his work.

Sofie thought for a few beats, and added, "Do you think women novelists do any better at imagining real women?"

"Sometimes," Cecilia said. "For example, Dorothea in *Middlemarch*."

Sofie nodded. "Yes. George Eliot teases her, if I can put it like that, about some of her blind spots, and takes her other shortcomings more seriously—but always with affection."

"So it is all the more disappointing," Cecilia said, "that Dorothea is quenched, if that is the right word, by marriage. Her first husband resents her intelligence and youth . . ."

"Fears it, really."

"Yes, he sees she could be a rival. Or expose his mediocrity. And then she marries Ladislaw, with whom she is happier, no doubt. But the young woman who had grand hopes of reforming society settles for life as a wife and mother. Ladislaw goes into politics, and she helps him behind the scenes."

"A bit of a comedown," Sofie said.

She felt Cecilia looking at her keenly.

"But Dorothea *is* happy," she added.

"Yes. But George Eliot says very plainly in the Finale that society turns idealistic and original girls into women whose work is to support their husbands' work. It reminds me of the end of . . ."

"*War and Peace*!" They said it together, triumphant at having recognized the same thing.

Cecilia leaned across the table, with her index finger raised for emphasis. "I'll tell you something about *War and Peace*. When I read the ending for the first time, when I was around seventeen, I was horrified at what had happened to Natasha. It seemed such a betrayal of all that vivacity and promise, the transformation of that quicksilver girl into that matron completely absorbed in her husband and children. I never got over the picture of her emerging from the nursery in her untidy dressing gown, happily brandishing a diaper stained with healthy yellow rather than worrying green—a sign that baby was better. That enchanting girl grown dull and dishevelled. But each time I reread it, every four or five years, I suppose, I grow more reconciled to the mature Natasha. Partly because I am more mature, no doubt. But also because she is doing something that is undeniably important, raising all those children . . ."

Sofie waited until Cecilia noticed her skeptical look and stopped. She said, "Now you sound like Tolstoy."

"But surely you can appreciate what Natasha is doing," Cecilia said.

"Not entirely. Her family is an extension of herself. Loving her children is a combination of instinct and selfishness. She is spoiled and demanding, she allows Pierre no life of his own . . ."

"Except his work," Cecilia interjected.

"All right, I agree, and that is important. But Natasha has no opinions or interests—she agrees with everything Pierre says, mindlessly, because Pierre says it. Her fate is a sadder decline than Dorothea's."

"George Eliot and Tolstoy seem to be in agreement about marriage and its effect on women."

"But there is a difference," Sofie insisted. "Tolstoy celebrates the narrowing of Natasha's horizons. But George Eliot regrets that something fine in Dorothea will never be used, never find the opportunity she craves."

How did I end up on that side of the argument? Sofie wondered. They sat silent for a few seconds. Then she asked, so that things did not become too dispiriting, "How did we get from *Vanity Fair* to marriage?"

"Is marriage the problem, then?" Cecilia responded, and they laughed, to show that it was not their problem. "And if it is, is there anything we can do about it?"

"Pay the bill," Sofie said, "and get home to our husbands, I think."

Chapter Eleven

JULY 1907

SOFIE WANTED TO do something with a sunflower: the tremulous yellow petals, each individual one weak but with a multitude of fellows, the rough black centres densely packed with seeds. Unfortunately, sunflowers were ubiquitous. Mr. Morris and his followers had strewn them all over their fabrics, wallpapers and carpets. But she could not stop sketching them, some in profile, with the thick, bristly stalk humped into an upside-down U, others full-face. How to make something fresh with a sunflower? Perhaps if she cut one in half. No, it was inert, unwieldy. It did not beg to be a part of a tapestry or a table runner or anything in particular. But—and here the patient hours of sketching suddenly took flight—what about cutting it in quadrants? Each quarter of the seed head became the corner of a cushion, and the golden petals fanned out from the seeds' nubbly darkness.

What stitch would best convey the texture of the seed heads, and how far should the petals encroach into the pillow? Sofie bent her head over her worktable. It was a moment she loved, when ideas came so fast that she could not decide whether to thread a needle and try out some stitches on a small piece of linen or carry on drawing the whole design.

She had been lost in her cushion for some time when she realized that Nils was standing on the other side of the worktable, holding a sketch and a large book.

"Sofie, I need you."

She wondered if French knots would work for the seed head. The difficulty would be crowding them in closely enough.

"Sofie."

Reluctantly, she looked up.

"What is it?"

"I need you to make some costumes for the mural. I can't get anywhere unless the models are properly dressed. Here, I have some pictures of Renaissance cloaks and these close-fitting men's hats that come to a sort of point on the cheek . . . and look at these high boots with red pom-poms at the top."

He was painting a mural he hoped would be hung in the main staircase of the National Museum, showing King Gustav Vasa's triumphant arrival in Stockholm in 1523. Riding a white horse decorated with cornflowers, the armour-clad king entered the city, which had just been liberated from the Danes. The subject had preoccupied Nils for more than a decade, and was another bid to be taken seriously as a painter of monumental, not domestic, subjects. Preparing for it, he had pored over Donatello's equestrian statues and Uccello's frescoes, he had studied the armour at the Royal Armoury and the anatomy of horses at the Veterinary College. He had hired a white horse and had himself photographed riding it. Marianne and Sonja were put to use as models, holding a thick rope made of more cornflowers, and he even persuaded his irritable father to pose, presenting the keys of the city to the king.

Such a large undertaking—an oil painting fourteen by seven metres—required money. Sofie had promised him ten thousand kronor from her inheritance. When he asked his patron, the Gothenburg collector Pontus Furstenberg, to lend him the same sum, Nils wrote him one of his mock-histrionic summaries: "Everything must be sacrificed to the painting! Sofie promises to give the maids notice. The children will be sent to the local elementary school. The farm, piano and books will be sold to the highest bidder, father and mother sent to the poorhouse—the main thing is that something is achieved in one's short allotted span." Sofie smiled obligingly when he showed her the letter. But she knew there was nothing jocular in the words "that something is achieved in one's short allotted span."

"Well, what do you say?" He was shifting from one foot to the other.

"But Nils, these boots . . . I'm not a cobbler. Nor a milliner."

"No, of course, forget the boots. But I'm sure you could make a hat like this one, that wraps the head closely. I'm thinking of that for my father. But the main thing is the cloaks. Do you see how this black one has slits for his arms and a stand-up collar?"

She ran her fingers over the picture, as if it would give her a clue.

"What about the fabrics?"

"You can send Berta in the carriage to Falun, or go yourself if you'd rather choose."

She took one last look at her sunflower. Then she turned to his book of Renaissance paintings and studied the pages he had marked.

"I'll go myself. You need something that drapes but has some body too."

Relieved, he kissed her.

"My darling muse. I can't do anything without you."

Muse, she thought. Rough seamstress, more likely.

"I'll leave you the book," he said. "And this sketch shows the figures who need clothes. I can work on the king's armour today, but could this fellow have a cloak and hat tomorrow?"

It would be a long evening and an early morning, she saw that. And she would need enough space on her worktable to cut out a cloak. She began clearing away her sketches, humming Markus's old tune.

He bought me a handkerchief red, white and blue
But before I could wear it he tore it in two.

Chapter Twelve

Siljevik, 12 July 1907

My dear Sofie,

I cannot argue that, literally, a cushion is a small thing compared to a mural that commemorates an important historical moment and is intended for the National Museum. But you know as well as I do, that is not how art is measured. The sunflower pillow sounds like a brilliant solution to an outworn motif, and I look forward to seeing it on my next visit.

Something occurred to me as I read your letter. When Lars and I were in America, I saw that they are making something they call handicraft kits, where, for example, the outline of the sunflower would be printed on a piece of fabric, and the kit would include the necessary thread as well as directions. It's a smart, very American idea, and I wonder if some of your designs wouldn't be good candidates for this kind of thing? It's something to consider, perhaps.

Nils is very lucky to have your support and the use of your skills. What wonderful news that the museum committee is pleased with his sketches. The mural too I look forward to seeing.

In friendship,
Cecilia

Askebo, 20 July 1907
Dear Cecilia,

How well you understand the way the anxious mind of an artist—or in my case, a craftsman—works. The handicraft kit is, as you say, a very American idea, and probably not for me. But thank you for mentioning it.

To change the subject, Nils had a letter from Glasgow recently. Before I began reading, I admired the writing paper, with a simple design of pink and green rectangles on top—just the kind of design that the Glasgow School of Art does so well. The writer is a teacher of engraving there, named MacDonald Lawrie. Mr. Lawrie has read the German editions of Nils's first two books about the house, and is taken with his ideas about decoration, as well as his paintings. He guesses correctly that Nils has studied the Japanese printmakers, as well as the English illustrators, especially Walter Crane and Randolph Caldecott. Mr. Lawrie is planning a walking trip in Dalarna, and wonders if he might visit Mr. Olsson at his famous house.

I convinced Nils that he should stay with us—it will only be for a night, and getting back and forth to a hotel in Falun is too much trouble.

I hope this heat wave is over by the time he arrives, next Wednesday. But I think an admiring Scotsman might be just the tonic Nils needs!

All the best to you,
from your friend Sofie

———

Mr. Lawrie had dark red hair, large red knuckles and an outrageously loud plaid suit that was far too warm for a Swedish midsummer. Sofie and Nils were baffled by his Scottish burr at first, but they caught his enthusiasm. Because Sweden was slow to industrialize, artists and writers from other countries found it a treasure trove of peasant arts, and nowhere more than in their own province of Dalarna. Mr. Lawrie had been walking around Lake Siljan, stopping off in the villages. He was charmed by the folk paintings, the weavings that hung from the rafters and the traditional dress women wore to church and in some villages every day.

When he arrived, Nils and Sofie took him out to the picnic table, hoping to catch a breeze from the river before they gave him a tour. Nils drank cider, Sofie and Mr. Lawrie elderflower juice. At the first sip, his flushed face puckered and she saw that he wondered why it wasn't more sugared, but he drank it down. Since they were strangers, they talked about mutual acquaintances. Nils asked about the Scottish artists he and Sofie had painted with in Grez. After leaving France, they had formed a group called the Glasgow Boys. Although they had since disbanded, several still lived in Glasgow. John Lavery had moved to London after his painting of Queen Victoria at the Glasgow International Exhibition impressed the English, but Mr. Lawrie knew him.

Nils remembered one of Lavery's paintings in particular.

"In the first summer we were in Grez, Lavery painted himself painting the main street, all done in greys, beiges, pale blue. We copied Bastien-Lepage and the other French painters in those days by limiting our palette. No trees, a few clouds in a pale sky, a poor street of plain, low, boxy houses."

"Those paintings of the artist painting himself painting out of doors were a feature of that time, weren't they?" Mr. Lawrie said.

Now that his glass was empty, he looked more comfortable in the dappled shade.

"As if they were announcing, 'No more studio, no more antique models,'" Mr. Lawrie continued. "'We will paint Nature as she is.'"

He probably meant to appear admiring but he sounded patronizing, as if he were describing a quaint but now unnecessary tactic. Sofie stared at the water, remembering another painting John Lavery had done, on another river, the Loing, the one of her in the hammock. The clink of the gold bracelet against the teacup, the sleepy river lapping half-heartedly at the bank.

Nils leaned across the table and tapped Mr. Lawrie's wrist.

"The Swedish painters had a saying when we returned from France. We said we had to take off our French gloves and get into our *peau-de-Suède*. We still wanted to paint Nature as she was, but now it was a Swedish nature. Brighter whites and darker greens, for example."

Mr. Lawrie stared.

"*Peau-de-Suède.* Oh, I see. Your Swedish skin, very good!"

He gave a tired laugh, as if his sense of humour was exhausted by the heat.

Nils showed him around the house. In the Old Room, he pointed out the seventeenth-century cupboard bed on whose doors he had painted the names of the famous people who had slept there. Mr. Lawrie did not recognize several of the best-known names, and Nils looked a bit crestfallen.

"You see here the name Prince Eugen," he said. "His father is the king, but he is a very fine painter who avoids court life as much as possible so that he can paint."

Mr. Lawrie nodded politely.

"And this is a mirror that belonged to King Oscar's mistress, Emilie Hogkuist. It was gold, but Sofie and I painted it this blue and white."

Now Mr. Lawrie looked embarrassed. Perhaps in Scotland one

did not discuss mistresses in front of one's wife, nor give their furnishings pride of place?

"But what is this?"

Mr. Lawrie had stopped in front of the table in the library, covered by a rough white cloth with a black-and-white checked tapestry border.

"Sofie made that. The peasant women at Bingsjo, a village a little to the east of your route, taught her to spin and weave."

"It's very fine. Very fine. But the designer knows something of the Wiener Werkstatte, and of the Japanese too. Perhaps Jessie Newbery in Glasgow. Who designed it?"

"Sofie," Nils repeated, as if he wondered why Mr. Lawrie was distinguishing between the maker and the designer.

Mr. Lawrie's cinnamon-coloured eyebrows rose.

"My congratulations, Mrs. Olsson. I wish my colleagues in Glasgow could see this."

She smiled and moved as if to go to the next room. But he was not done looking at the cloth.

"Your work reminds me of some pieces I recently saw in *The Studio*," he said.

"It's possible. We are subscribers."

"Really? I never thought of *Studio* subscribers living in Sweden."

"The mail comes to Askebo, Mr. Lawrie."

She gave him a teasing smile, but she wanted to end this exchange, which she knew was tedious for Nils. Mr. Lawrie's knuckles looked even redder, if possible, as if they were blushing.

"Of course. Very stupid of me. But where does this braided fringe come from?"

"It's a specialty of this region. Women unravel the warp in a weaving and do this intricate plaiting, in different patterns. Some wives do their own plaiting, but many rely on women who walk from farm to farm, plaiting the fringes of towels and table linen in exchange for a little money or food."

88

"And what about this decoration, with the dragonfly and the pear?"

"The dragonfly, I don't know how that came to me. But it is such a good shape, isn't it, that long body and those long wings at right angles to each other. As for the pear, while I was working on the design, Birgitta came into the room eating one. She said, 'Mamma, put my pear into your weaving.' Now, if you just come this way—watch your head—Nils wants to show you his bedroom."

When Nils showed him his room, with the bed tented in the middle, Mr. Lawrie's eye went to the curtain between it and the room where Sofie and the girls slept. He is quick, she thought, as his reactions moved across his face like clouds in a fickle sky. Now that he knows I make many of the house's table covers and curtains, he is not jumping in with influences. He knows we don't like them rubbed in our faces. And this hanging is the most indebted of all to the Glasgow School, with that rose blooming at the top of that ruler-straight stem.

She decided to help him.

"It was a present to Nils. I wanted to give him some privacy but as you see he has no window, so I needed to make it in as loose a weave as possible to let in light. You recognize the macrame, I'm sure, and the middle section is the plaited work the local women do. I called it 'The Rose of Love.'"

"And this little beast coiled around the stem?"

"It's the worm that destroys the rose. But he is so far away from the blossom that he will do no harm."

Nils took Mr. Lawrie to his new studio, pointing out, as usual, that it was the largest studio in Sweden. Sofie wondered why Swedes always had to tell you something was the biggest of its kind. The studio was filled with sketches and details of Nils's mural for the National Museum, as well as the mural itself, and Mr. Lawrie was suitably interested. But he also stopped at a square, low-slung rocker, painted red.

"This reminds me of the work of the American architect, Frank Lloyd Wright."

"Sofie's, again."

"You design furniture too?"

"Only in a small way. Our carpenter, here in the village, thought it so ugly that he delivered it under cover of darkness. He didn't want anyone to know he had made such a clumsy thing."

They had a second guest for dinner, a small bustler of a woman named Marta Jorgensen. Before she married, she had been a gardener for Crown Princess Victoria at Tullgarn Palace. The German-born princess, full of Swedish patriotism, had insisted that her servants wear the local folk dress and, to her surprise, Mrs. Jorgensen found that the full skirt, hemmed slightly above the ankles, was much easier to garden in than modern clothes, with their nagging corsets and longer, hobbled skirts. When she moved to Dalarna, she founded the Swedish Female Folk Dress Association, and she had come to Askebo to enlist Nils as a charter member.

For dinner they had boeuf bourguignon. The weather was far too hot for such a dish, and Mr. Lawrie seemed disappointed that they were not having a Swedish meal. Nils explained happily that Sofie had learned to cook in Grez. Now their cook, Anna, used the notebook of French recipes Sofie had compiled.

"When we set up housekeeping in Grez, Sofie's mother sent her a copy of the Swedish wife's bible, *Housewife in Town and Country*, by Mathilda Langlet."

As usual, the mere title was enough to make Nils and Sofie laugh—a little guiltily on her part. She tried to explain. Why would she want recipes for pea soup and meatballs, when she was learning how to make *soufflés au fromage* and *coq au vin*? Why live in the country dedicated to pleasure and grate potatoes for dumplings?

But Mr. Lawrie did not see what was so amusing, nor did Mrs. Jorgensen, although she knew who Mathilda Langlet was.

Nils steered the talk to Mrs. Jorgensen's Female Folk Dress Association.

"Sofie designed the Askebo costume just last year," he told her. "Run upstairs and put yours on," he ordered Marianne. She modelled the skirt lined with thin green, red and black stripes and the emerald-green bodice with silver clasps, worn over a white blouse. To demonstrate how a colour changed everything, she put on the red apron that was worn on happy occasions, and then the white one for funerals.

Mr. Lawrie was disappointed to discover that these charming dresses were modern inventions.

"Until recently, Askebo was too small to have its own dress," Sofie explained.

"Bigger villages do have traditional costumes," Nils said. "And because provinces like Dalarna stayed almost medieval in their customs, the dresses had just begun to die out when people first set out to collect them."

A few decades ago, he told Mr. Lawrie, collectors and their assistants had travelled through the countryside with their rucksacks and walking sticks, and found people who were happy to sell them the complete suits of folk costumes they had just abandoned, from the embroidered stockings to the starched caps decorated with drawn thread-work. These peasants were astonished that 'young gentlemen from the universities' would waste their time and money on old clothes.

Mrs. Jorgensen chimed in, wanting to describe all the strata of a folk costume to Mr. Lawrie. Methodically, she began with the first layer, the white linen shift. "When an engaged girl bundles with her fiance in the summer in the hired girls' shed," she told Mr. Lawrie, "she wears that shift."

"And bundling is?"

"Why, getting into bed and cuddling," Mrs. Jorgensen said, in the same businesslike way she had described the grafting of fruit trees.

Mr. Lawrie blushed again. Was bundling not a custom in Scotland, Sofie wondered. Or was it a custom that was not discussed in mixed company?

"But if the girl becomes pregnant, she is not allowed to wear the traditional Swedish crown at her wedding," Mrs. Jorgensen added, as if this would reassure him.

Seeing that they had a rapt audience, the Swedes talked on. For Mr. Lawrie's benefit, they explained why yellow was a mourning colour in many villages—because mourning clothes could not be luxurious and the yellow dye came from a common larch tree. They warned him not to put his nose in those lovely embroidered waist bags women wore to church. Their owners often stored an onion in them, chewing it in church to keep awake during the long sermon.

Since the conversation was taking care of itself, Sofie composed a letter in her mind.

> *Dear Mrs. Jorgensen,*
>
> *I congratulate you on the founding of the Swedish Female Folk Dress Association. Such an organization is so important, especially at this strange moment when we are losing so many traditional ways at the same time that a minority discovers them and tries to save them.*
>
> *I am curious why, when I designed the Askebo dress, you invited my husband and not me to join the association. Of course, he is known throughout the country, and his name will attract others to your cause. I understand that. But why not invite both of us? Surely an association devoted to female folk dress, founded by a woman, should welcome female members.*
>
> *With every wish for the success of your work,*
> *Sofie Olsson*

Later, in her corner of the bedroom, she would write out the letter, just for the pleasure of seeing it on a page. But she would not mail it.

As Mrs. Jorgensen was saying her good nights, she had a request for Sofie.

"I've seen some of the posters you designed for the Swedish Homecraft Association," she said. "I wonder if we could prevail upon you to design the letter paper for our association?"

Sofie smiled regretfully as she handed Mrs. Jorgensen her wrap.

"Now that is flattering," she said. "But I'm afraid I've already taken on too much work for the coming months. Some of the nearby villages have seen the Askebo dress and asked me to design one for them." She opened the door to the porch, and went outside with her guest. "Perhaps a student in graphic arts in one of the new vocational institutes might help you."

After Mrs. Jorgensen left, Nils wanted to spend a few minutes with his day's work. Sofie and Mr. Lawrie walked out to the water. Long streaks of pink lit up the sky, then disappeared, leaving it inky blue with a creamy edge in the west. They were both interested in the Wiener Werkstatte and their attempts to reform the applied arts. Sofie disagreed with their idea of throwing out every influence from the past, but she and Mr. Lawrie were taken with their designs, especially Josef Hoffmann's. They were still talking about Hoffmann's severe teapots and silverware when Nils came out to find them.

Once they had shown Mr. Lawrie to his room, Nils read the paper at the dining room table and Sofie let down the hems in Tilda's and Sonja's Sunday dresses.

"Mr. Lawrie was very impressed with your designs for the Comedy Theatre fresco."

Nils nodded, without looking up from his paper. His jaw seemed to lengthen, as it did when he was displeased. Apparently their moment of camaraderie over Mathilda Langlet's cookbook was over. The Glasgow School of Art specialized in applied art, so it was only natural that Mr. Lawrie would be interested in textiles and furniture. But she could not say that. They sat in silence until Nils rose to go to bed. He stood with his fists on the table, until she raised her eyes from her sewing. Then he winked and turned his head toward the stairs. Logically, the gesture meant nothing, since his bedroom and her bed in the nursery were both located at the top of the stairs, but it had always been their sign. And he had not used it for some time.

In his narrow bed, hung with Sofie's curtains and covered with the blanket she had designed (Mr. Lawrie had been garrulous in his admiration of its American Indian motifs), Nils took her with something that verged on a cold fury. He battered into her, digging his head into her collarbone as if he were marking out a territory, or re-staking some claim he had let lapse. She knew, without being able to see it, the set of his chin. There were no words, only the rasp of the bed on the bare floor. There was no thought of pleasing her, but she was pleased. And she knew better than to show it, because it would have diminished his sense of having evened some score.

In the morning, there was sour milk, Falun sausage, a ham, crispbread and lingonberry jam for breakfast. Mr. Lawrie was charmed, it was so Swedish. He said to Nils, "I cannot get your *Sunday Afternoon* out of my head; I thought of it for a long time after I went to bed. The way you have cut Mrs. Olsson up, if I may put it that way, and not put her back together—so that we see nothing of her, as she sits hidden behind the little room divider, except for her folded hands, her skirt, and her feet resting on the table leg. And then, the coup de grâce, the portrait of her head on the door, is a masterful stroke! Your fine black outline is so Japanese, and yet you make it so Nordic, and so your own."

Nils nodded briskly. The gangly Scotsman was sharper than he looked. He would take him back into the studio after breakfast and show him more of his sketches for the National Museum mural.

For lunch, in spite of the heat, Sofie had asked Anna to make pea soup followed by pancakes.

Nils came to the table all smiles.

"So it's pea soup, it must be Wednesday."

"Pappa!" the children howled, delighted at his ignorance, even though they knew it was a show. "Pea soup is for Thursdays!"

"And why would that be?" he asked, lifting up the big reference book of Swedish customs that sat beside him on the bench.

Markus raced to get the answer in before the book snapped open. "Because it's the maids' half-day holiday in Sweden, and you can make soup ahead of time."

"But why pea soup? Why not lamb-and-rice soup or beet soup?"

No one knew the answer to that one, so Nils read from the book that Thor, the god for whom Thursday was named, was associated with peas. That was all they wanted to know, but Nils read on, in his comic schoolmaster voice. Humans had offended Thor in some way, and he sent dragons to ruin the world's wells by filling them with peas. But the dragons dropped a few, by mistake, and they fell on fertile ground. Voila, a new vegetable grew, and Thor was more furious than ever. The humans tried to placate him by dedicating the vegetable to him and only eating it on his day, Thursday. The children were quickly bored by this, but Mr. Lawrie was enchanted at the spectacle of the artist in his uniquely decorated dining room, with his progressively raised children, who shouted out answers and behaved as if they belonged at the table as much as the grown-ups.

Sofie looked down the crowded table, thinking about dragons and pea vines. Bright green dragons, scaly and spiny, with transparent wings. As they flew on to destroy another well, a pea vine grew up behind them, tremulous but unstoppable. The vine, with its modestly drooping pods and thread-thin tendrils, was rooted to the earth, while the dragons mounted to the sky. An embroidered table-runner, perhaps? A tapestry cushion? The length of a runner would give her more scope to show the vines clinging to houses, fences and bridges. The brilliant but slightly disgusting crackle of the dragon skin would be the hard part—and also the most interesting.

Glasgow, 15 September 1907
Dear Mrs. Olsson,

I take the liberty of writing to you, and so soon after my bread-and-butter letter (another strange English expression), because I have been discussing your work with a few of my colleagues at the Glasgow School, textile designers named Ann Macbeth and Jessie Newbery. Of course, you know Mrs. Newbery's work from *The Studio*. I wish I had been able to take photographs while I was in Askebo but my camera is far too bulky to carry on a walking trip. Instead, I took the liberty of sketching the table covers in the library and the Old Room, and the cushions and tapestry in the dining room. Miss Macbeth and Mrs. Newbery were most impressed. They are interested in showing a few of your pieces in their forthcoming exhibition here in Glasgow next spring.

I will send more information when you assure me that you are interested.

Meanwhile, best wishes to your husband and all the children at Askebo,

MacDonald Lawrie

Glasgow, 7 October 1907
Dear Mrs. Olsson,

There is no need to apologize. Of course you must do as you see fit with your work. But please believe me, there is nothing amateurish about it. It holds its own with that of the best-known modern designers. It would have been a significant asset to the forthcoming exhibition.

I could not agree with you more about Mr. Olsson. He deserves a greater audience outside Sweden and Germany, and I too hope that he will find one in Britain.

I remember all the good times at Askebo, including
fishing with Oskar and playing hide-and-seek with
Markus and Sonja. Naturally, they had me at a
disadvantage, and showed no mercy.

The current *Studio* has a piece about the mingling of
folk traditions with modernist ideas, and I thought of your
work, especially the curtain near your desk. The author
claims that when the folk tradition relies on angular,
geometric forms, there is often little that needs translation
into a modern idiom. I wonder if you agree? If you have a
chance, I would be most interested in your response.

With greetings to your husband and the hope that
the National Museum appreciates his mural as it deserves.
I imagine him in his splendid studio, extending his neck
to see even better.

Yours very truly,
Mac Lawrie

Sofie put Mr. Lawrie's letter into her pocket. She suspected that
he was acting more naive than he really was, as British people sometimes did. Surely he realized it was the placement of the folk motifs,
the stags and bouquets that appeared in a slightly unexpected place
or relationship to each other, that added the element of the modern.

It was not difficult to keep Mr. Lawrie's letters from Nils. Often
she strolled to the mailbox at the end of the lane just before lunch.
And even when Berta collected the post, she brought it to Sofie, usually at a time when Nils was in his studio at the other end of the house.
Besides, there was nothing improper about their correspondence.

She wondered what Mr. Lawrie would think of Nils's mural, in
his heart, if he were to return to Sweden. Without a doubt, it had
all Nils's wonderful draftsmanship, his affinity with the Renaissance
masters, the fairy-tale charm of the victorious king entering the city.
Charm above all—Nils was always charming. But it was 1907.

Picasso and Matisse and Cézanne were no longer considered so very bizarre in many quarters. Would the Louvre or the National Gallery in London give its main staircase to such a picturesque, realistic painting? Probably Sweden was a little behind the times.

Chapter Thirteen

MARCH 1910

Nils's patron Pontus Furstenberg had redecorated his Gothenburg gallery and rehung the pictures and was having a party to celebrate. Sofie and Nils travelled there by train. It was March, and the world was mostly white, with heavy, colourless skies and thick snow, black trees and rivers, and the occasional beige stubble of last year's wheat in a field. Blond grasses stood up abruptly in the river, pressing their feathery tops against the train, as high as the windows, as if they were dusting them.

"I would like to embroider *that*," Sofie said, nodding at the matte grasses and the sulking, dimpling river.

"Yes," Nils said. "A good idea."

"But how would I stitch the contrast between the water and the grasses? The usual way would be green silk for the water, with black highlights, perhaps in wave stitch, and beige wool or cotton for the grasses, with the tops in Cretan stitch." Not that Nils knew a Cretan stitch from a wave stitch, but she was thinking out loud.

"And what's wrong with the usual way?"

"Nothing, I suppose. But it's so . . . predictable."

Nils went back to his newspaper, and she went back to frowning at the river. If she were painting rather than embroidering, there would be all kinds of ways to express the coexistence of the busy water and the calm, superior grasses.

The Furstenbergs lived on Brunnsparken, one of Gothenburg's most elegant streets, and their party was equally grand. Civic dignitaries, people from the National Museum and artists, many of whose works Nils had encouraged Furstenberg to buy, walked slowly up the broad staircase, past the Furstenbergs' two private floors, to the big gallery at the top of the house. The Furstenbergs received their guests at the entrance to the gallery, Gothilda in a cut-velvet dress the colour of garnets.

They went first to see the new home of the triptych that Furstenberg had commissioned from Nils around the turn of the century. Each panel was devoted to a different era of art: the Renaissance, the rococo and the modern. Sofie spent her time in front of the last panel, really to enjoy its frame, where Nils had sculpted "the nude with the elbow," as she thought of it.

The next room was dominated by a large oil portrait Hanna Pauli had painted of her friend, the Finnish sculptor Venny Soldan. The two women had studied in Paris together at the Colarossi studio and the picture dated from that time. Venny, a tall, solid blonde, sat on the floor near a few of her knives, holding a lump of clay in her hand. "Look, Nils, how good this is, the way her black dress is so undetailed, and Hanna saves up all the realism for Venny's head and hands."

He looked at it, but not very closely.

"Yes, it's all right."

"It's still very bold, isn't it—her sitting on the floor, that foot in its slipper sticking out. It was unusual when it was painted and portraits were more formal, and even now . . ."

Her sentence trailed off as she felt his stubborn lack of interest.

Changing direction, she said, "Hanna and Georg's children must be very grown up now."

Nils looked at the picture more seriously.

"She is so homely, no wonder she paints. Did you see Georg's portrait of her in the other room, wearing spectacles?"

She nodded. So, now only ugly women who wore glasses were allowed to paint. Just as only lame ones, like Selma Lagerlof, were allowed to write. And only unmarried women, for whatever reason, like Ellen Key, could go into public life.

"Apparently, not everyone thinks Hanna is as homely as you do. I heard last week that she and a Sicilian man have fallen in love. They met when she was in Italy last summer, trying to recover her health."

Nils stared at her as if she had lost her senses.

"Whatever do you mean? She is over forty. She has grey hair. Even when she was young, she was no beauty. Who told you that?"

"Cecilia."

She could see he was struggling to think of Hanna—intense, driven but self-doubting—as a femme fatale, and failing. "But how does Georg react?"

"They say he is very unhappy, and wants her to come with him to Paris, where he is studying the new painters."

Nils looked as if he did not know which was more incomprehensible, wanting to keep an unfaithful wife or throwing over a mature style to learn how to paint like those ludicrous French daubers. He turned back to the portrait of Venny Soldan.

"That's very clumsy, painting her with her mouth open."

"Maybe she thinks better that way. She is looking at her work, it seems."

She had heard something recently about Venny Soldan, that she lived in a ménage à trois in Helsinki with her husband and her sister. The husband had sons with both sisters. She was not going to tell Nils, it would only make him more vehement about women artists.

The Vogts approached, Cecilia looking soignée in black and pewter–grey. She wore a long chain Sofie had not seen before, that looped several times around the neck, with oval stones in blue, green and pink topaz at long, irregular intervals.

Lars had designed it, Cecilia said, when Sofie admired it. Not the easiest thing to wear, but she hoped that, since this dress was so simple on top . . .

A thought like a little worm intruded on Sofie. Lars must have someone new. Or he'd had a particularly fine time with someone who was not new. Were men not embarrassed by their own transparency? When she and Nils had been in Stockholm a few weeks ago, they had bumped into Lars in an out-of-the-way cafe. Pink with champagne and high spirits, he'd been sitting with a few male friends and two women whom Sofie could see were from the demimonde. Now she wondered, as she had before, whether this broke Cecilia's heart. You're just a naive girl from Hallsberg, she scolded herself, and turned her attention back to Hanna's painting. Some of Nils's former students from the Gothenburg art school had joined them. Lars, who as usual had effortlessly become the centre of the circle, was appraising the picture.

"Look at the way the woman's weight rests on the knuckles of her right hand, that is well done. And the way she is half alert, half relaxed, with that big foot in its flat shoe sticking out . . . Very fine."

Nils was not interested in hearing Hanna praised, but before things became awkward, his students took him off to explain his triptych to them.

"Walk with me to the buffet," Cecilia said to Sofie, taking her arm, "before it gets too crowded."

There was already a tail of hungry and thirsty art-lovers extending beyond the long table at the end of the hallway, and they took glasses of champagne while they eyed platters and chafing dishes full of delicacies. No caviar, thank you, they told the server. It would be too difficult not to spill it on their dresses or on the beautiful new floor.

While they made their way down the buffet, they began talking about Jane Austen. Sofie was reading her way through the novels in chronological order. Cecilia could talk about books at the same time as she scrutinized the provenance and quality of each dish. Sofie could not divide her attention in that way, but she cared less about the food.

"Did you enjoy *Emma*? I suspect those shrimp may be a little tired."

"It was very clever," Sofie said, nonetheless helping herself to the shrimp, "all the farcical twists and turns of the plot, like a long country dance of a novel, with several possible couples—at least in Emma's imagination!—taking their turns dancing down the middle. And the end could not be more perfect. I don't know that I have ever been happier at the prospect of a wedding, real or literary. But Emma's meddling irritated me so much, at points it interfered with my pleasure."

Cecilia said, "Surely Emma's meddling is Jane Austen's point."

"I realize that." Sofie allowed herself the faintest hint of frost. Sometimes Cecilia seemed to think she was not terribly bright. "But she causes so much pain with her interference in that poor simple girl's life—Harriet Smith, I mean. I hope Emma's marriage with Mr. Knightley will put an end to this tendency."

"There is nothing wrong with trying to help people," Cecilia said, filling her tiny plate with the smoked salmon the Furstenbergs imported from Norway. "Emma's flaw is not that she is a busybody, but that she is not an intelligent busybody. She's so infatuated with Harriet that she doesn't see that her friend is too limited to attract even so silly a man as the pastor, Mr. Elton, much less someone as sophisticated as Frank Churchill. Emma is a romantic, when she needs to be a realist. You have to be sensible and clear-eyed about people you want to help—you have to think about what is possible for *them*."

Indeed, thought Sofie. She allowed herself to say, "I think trying to manage other people's lives is a tricky business."

Cecilia looked up from her smoked salmon. "But when you succeed in helping them, such a satisfying one."

Sofie wandered through the rooms alone. She never knew when what she thought of as "the bad feeling" would descend. Usually it was not inspired by the expected things, like the work of people she had known at school. It was never attached to Nils's work. Typically it would be sparked by a painter who was more distant, more neutral. His work would exasperate her, sometimes because she could see the joy in the making of it, or sometimes because the opposite was true and she saw that it was mechanically done, the artist going through worn-out motions or following a new fashion by rote. At the Furstenberg gallery, people were enthusiastic about the work of a young artist who painted barren northern landscapes, mostly around Vasterbotten. Nils found her in front of one of these paintings and they stood looking at it together.

After a moment, he shot her a look. "Sofie?"

She covered her vexation with an expressionless face. But he understood the face and spoke into her ear. "But what is it?"

"His skies do not interest me."

In bed that night in the hotel, Nils repeated his question.

"Sofie, what is it?"

"Nothing." She was trying to escape the featherbed, which was too hot, without bothering him. He liked a warmer bed than she did. "I'm probably just a little excited from the party."

He fell asleep, clinging to her. She managed to extricate one arm and both feet from the featherbed, while she went on thinking.

My dear friend Cecilia,

I keep returning in my mind to your remarks about Emma. And how the helpful person has to pay attention to who the beneficiary really is. I am touched that you want to help me, although I don't think of myself as needing assistance.

But I urge you to apply your wise assessment of Emma to yourself. How many times must I tell you that I do not want to start a business making embroidery kits? You would do an excellent job of starting and running such a business. I would not, nor do I wish to.

Friends wish the best for their friends, of course. But, as you suggest, the important thing is to understand what is best for them, not you.

Yours very sincerely,

Sofie

She knew the letter was unfair, in that she made it sound as if she knew what was best for herself, when she didn't. But Cecilia would never see the letter, and perhaps now she could sleep.

Chapter Fourteen

APRIL–MAY 1910

Glasgow, 3 April 1910
Dear Mrs. Olsson,

I wonder if you have any plans to visit your sister in Hampstead this spring? I am often in London on business for the School, and it would be a pleasure to see some of the exhibits at the Victoria and Albert Museum, in South Kensington, with you.

Yours truly,
MacDonald Lawrie

Sofie had not seen Martina for more than a year, since her sister's last visit to Sweden. She told Nils she would like a trip to London for her birthday, which was in May.

"You want to go alone?"

"Yes, why not? You are so busy, and I don't want to take the children out of school. Besides, I'll only be alone on the train and the ferry. Martina and Francis will take care of me once I reach London."

"It's just that I had another idea for your birthday . . . I was planning to paint some nosegays of local flowers on the walls in your bedroom."

You mean, she thought, in the nursery where I sleep in the corner.

"Nils, what a lovely idea."

"Now you will have both. When will you go?"

Siljevik, 10 May 1910

Dear Sofie,

This is written on the fly, as I have a mountain of small *crises*, delays and artistic egos to tunnel through on the way to Lars's upcoming exhibition. I envy you your visit to London, and I insist on hearing all the latest news about Martina's family as well as any galleries, concerts, etc., you think worthy of mentioning.

I have a commission for you, if it is not too much trouble. My Boston friend, the collector Isabella Stewart Gardner, writes that I must read an American novel called *The Awakening*. The author is Kate Chopin, and it aroused quite a controversy when it first appeared, just at the turn of the century. Set in New Orleans. Bonniers does not carry it in their lending library, nor does Hemlins sell it. Could you inquire about it when you are in the London bookshops?

Many thanks, and I will write more civilly next time, when I hope I will have a bit more leisure.

Your harried friend,

Cecilia

P.S. I wonder how your Scottish friend will strike you when he is closer to home. I will need a full report on your excursion with him.

London, 18 May 1910
My dear Cecilia,

First, my commission. Unfortunately, Foyle's knows nothing about *The Awakening* either, and the clerk managed to convey a subtle doubt that a novel by an unknown American author could be worth pursuing. However, his good manners and business sense reasserted themselves, and he is undertaking to order it and send it to you in Sweden.

It was no trouble getting to Foyle's, as Charing Cross Road is not far from Regent Street, where Martina and I had been looking at upholstery fabrics in Liberty's. The treasure trove that is Foyle's drove all ideas of tassels and cording and jacquards from my mind immediately. I exclaimed and pored and piled up my choices, and then chose again and piled up different choices. I was giddy, until even the long-suffering Martina was chafing to leave. In the end I settled for four books by a writer who is new to me, E. M. Forster. The superior clerk seemed to approve of this choice, and I am anxious to begin reading.

But it will probably have to wait until I return home. This is a busy house. Martina's husband, Francis, still works at the Natural History Museum, but he is almost equally occupied with his work for women's rights. At dinner on my first night here, he talked about an address given to the Rational Dress Society by a suffragist named Louisa Becker. Although the Society is ardently opposed to corsets and lacing, Miss Becker supports moderately tight lacing because she claims that it releases the blood from what she called "an inactive locality" and leaves it available to be used in the brain. Heresy! The members of the society were so upset that their patron, Lady Harberton, convened a meeting in her drawing room, so that all could express their objections.

"Look at Aunt Sofie!" one nephew said to the other, during this edifying dinner table conversation. "She doesn't wear any corsets at all." All the family talk of undergarments leads to comments that would be impossibly rude in other houses.

"Lucky you," I said to my moderately tightly-laced sister, "you have so much more blood available for your brain." Francis did not find that funny, as he takes these questions very seriously.

Martina is redecorating her drawing room in the Arts and Crafts style, in rose and a soft green. She took me to Morris and Co., on Oxford Street, to look at fabrics and wallpapers. The customers sit on high stools, paging through sample books of wallpapers, or stand, fingering the textiles ranged along the walls. In spite of the fog outside and the amber light that falls from hanging lamps, we had stepped into a world of English meadows, orchards and thickets. Sometimes all the vegetation rambles uncontrolled over bolts of cloth or wallpapers, at other times it is held in check by trellises and fences. Martina reacted at Morris and Co. the way I had at Foyle's—first drawn to a wallpaper with old-fashioned roses, then to one with clumps of primroses and bluebells, then to another with interlacing lilies.

Like many Morris designs, they all struck me as too dark and congested. But this is a heresy almost as grave as Miss Becker's support of moderate lacing!

I steered my distracted sister to "Willow," a simpler, lighter green paper under-printed with white hawthorn blossoms.

"More versatile," I told her. "And it will work with your Japanese things."

Then we found our favourite, an airy pattern called "Arbutus." The tree's diamond-shaped leaves and strawberry-like fruits hang from slanting, knobbly branches.

"See how clever, the way Mr. Morris added depth with this under-pattern of pale grey leaves on white," I said to Martina. "Very *japoniste*."

"Beg pardon, ma'am," the attendant said. "Of course, the designer understands Mr. Morris's principles. But her name is Kathleen Kersey."

No doubt, London is so large and the British so enlightened there are more opportunities here for women. We took a sample of Miss Kersey's pattern, and I expect that Martina will order it.

My visit to the Victoria and Albert Museum with Mr. Lawrie is scheduled for tomorrow, and I will send you all the details. And I expect a letter from you about what I am sure will be a triumphant show for Lars.

With friendliest wishes to the two of you,
from Sofie

The day appointed for Sofie's visit to the museum with Mr. Lawrie was silvery grey, with rain that sounded like well-disposed but not overly enthusiastic applause. Still known to most people as the South Kensington Museum, it had been renamed the Victoria and Albert at the turn of the century. Its confident red-brick sprawl went on for blocks. She watched from the main entrance as Mr. Lawrie followed his umbrella down Cromwell Road. It bobbed, feinted, rose and fell in its owner's attempts not to collide with other umbrellas on the crowded street. Mr. Lawrie bounded up the steps when he spotted her and dropped the umbrella, which immediately began collecting rain. Retrieving it in such a way that it dribbled water over her skirt, he shook hands happily.

"Mrs. Olsson, how delightful to see you. Would you like to leave your overcoat?"

He smiled down at her from his plaid height. Cecilia's instinct had been prescient. Seen in something closer to his natural habitat, Mr. Lawrie looked less red and raw-boned. Even the checks on his suit seemed more muted. He manoeuvred her through the door to the coat check, fussing with her things and eventually handing over her coat, scarf and umbrella to the attendant.

"I wonder if you would like a cup of coffee in the restaurant before we go to the Textile Rooms."

He led her down what was called the Ceramic Staircase, lined with gleaming yellow and white tiles painted with flowers. It was like being inside a gigantic centrepiece for a table. As they descended, he mentioned that the Victoria and Albert was the first museum in the world to have a restaurant. Sofie was amused: unlike the Swedes' pride in having something that was the biggest in the country or the world, the British preferred having something that was the first or the oldest. She and Mr. Lawrie kept bumping into each other, because she did not know where she was going, and he kept stopping abruptly to tell her something else about the museum.

The dining room had been designed by William Morris more than forty years earlier, although in many quarters Morris was still considered "modern." Below the green plaster, midway up the walls, were small panels painted with lemons, oranges, cherries, leaves and the occasional medieval damsel. Their gold background lit up the green gloom.

"Nils would love the berries and fruit on the panels," Sofie said. "But I cannot get him to England very often. He says it is because the English did not choose to publish his books. That is partly a joke, I suppose."

Mr. Lawrie was usually interested in anything to do with Nils. But now he smiled absently and drew her attention to the stained-glass windows by Edward Burne-Jones and Philip Webb. And to the waiter who was ready to take their order.

"Will you not have something to eat with your coffee? Their scones are very good. Or a Chelsea bun, perhaps, they have candied fruit in them but are not too heavy."

She knew what a Chelsea bun was, but she was not hungry. A little more of the museum's weak coffee, and she would be ready to see the exhibits.

On the top floor of the museum, the Textile Rooms were high-ceilinged and so cold she was glad she had kept her merino shawl. When she turned without warning and made contact with Mr. Lawrie's tweed jacket, it gave out its own welcome warmth for a few seconds. Fabrics from faraway times and places were pressed between thin sheets of glass in wooden frames, and stored in oak cabinets. You pulled out a frame by means of a brass handle, then stared through the glass at a worn or fragmentary cloth, trying to penetrate to the soul of a Hungarian apron or an Irish shirt. Dutifully, she stared at the examples of what the curators called "peasant art"—the bouquets, the pairs of birds and stags, the double-headed eagles that decorated fabrics all over Europe. Was she only echoing the same meagre, repetitive vocabulary? Was it all as boring as it looked in these low-lit rooms?

And then, in a glass case against a wall, something spoke to her. It was a full skirt from Crete, in a warm, off-white mixture of linen and cotton. Like her own clothes, it had no waist. It began high, at the breasts, and was held up by two broad shoulder straps. A jacket or shirt would be worn on top of it, but there was a deep opening down the middle, for breast-feeding, perhaps, or ease of putting it on and taking it off. From the hem up to the knee, the skirt was covered with black embroidery, an intense garden of stylized flowers and plants. This maker, she thought, marvelling at the wildness and control of the design, did not judge herself against the work of others, did not fret about unimportant things, simply ornamented a useful garment with disciplined abandon. She was being silly, she knew nothing about this embroiderer. But there was something so assured about the black-and-white skirt.

"Look . . . the maker has signed it."

Mr. Lawrie nodded. The signature was neither little nor large, but perfectly legible across the top of the embroidery band.

"Maria Pappadopoula, 1757," he read. "Does the fact that it is signed surprise you?"

"Of course. Does it not surprise you?"

"Phoebe Traquair signs all her work, whether it is metalwork or embroidery or bookbinding."

"Miss Traquair works in Scotland at the beginning of the twentieth century, which from your account sounds like a paradise for craftswomen. Maria Pappadopoula, whoever she was, worked in the middle of the eighteenth century in Crete, which I doubt was as enlightened."

"I was teasing you. Do you not sign your works?"

"I put 'S.O.' in an out-of-the-way spot on most of the tapestries and hangings, sometimes on a tablecloth but never on clothes or curtains. I know, there is no rhyme or reason to it."

On the way down from the Textile Rooms, they stopped on the second floor to look at the miniatures. She put her face as close as she dared to the cases, staring at portraits on vellum or ivory, almost small enough for a dollhouse.

"Here are a few by someone named Annie Dixon," she pointed, "and this one is signed Christina Robertson."

"Yes, it was a form in which a woman could make a living without much fuss, because it was considered a craft and not so demanding as a full-size portrait."

She looked at him to make sure he found that as ludicrous as she did and, reassured, she moved on to the next case. Anna Mee, born Foldsone, had painted a self-portrait on ivory at the end of the eighteenth century. Her eyes were almost violet and her runaway curls held strategically in check by a white kerchief. Mr. Lawrie said that she had supported her widowed mother and eight siblings with her miniatures.

"When she married Mee, he allowed her to continue painting as long as she confined her work to female sitters."

She laughed, but she understood Mr. Mee. The relationship between the artist and the sitter was charged—although in her experience, the artist was almost always male and the subject female. She thought about Nils's models. The children had grown up thinking it was quite natural for their father to spend the day closeted with a woman who was wearing no clothes. Sometimes they were assigned to guard him and the model when he posed her outdoors, leaning over the little bridge in the woods or lying under a tree. If anyone approached, they sounded the alarm. She thought back to the pictures—clothed ones—he had made of her when they were courting and newly married. Yes, there had been something. But not now. Now when she sat for him, she felt something almost like resentment coming from him. Or a hope that if he painted her from the back, as she tinkered with a shrub or set out linens to bleach, he could in some way contain her. Reduce her.

As they left the museum, Mr. Lawrie said, "I have a surprise for you."

The surprise lived in a white-plastered house with heavy Doric columns at 5 Cromwell Place, just south of the Natural History Museum. It was John Lavery, their old colleague from Grez, and he was expecting their visit. As Mr. Lawrie had told Sofie and Nils in Askebo, Mr. Lavery concentrated on society portraits these days, inching closer and closer to the royal family. He was a widower, with a daughter away at school. In his second-floor studio, lit by a triple window, he was painting a portrait of a woman in a velvet evening dress, with a necklace of starry diamonds. Just before they arrived, he had been working on the irregular, softly gleaming folds in the midnight blue velvet. They admired the studio and the portrait, and then he took them downstairs, to a parlour lined with Japanese prints.

Nils would have exclaimed at Hiroshige's actor in his mixture of plaids and patterns, his legs akimbo and his baggy pants pushed up high, or Kunisada's picture of a mother bending to slide the heavy baby on her back to a better position. Just for a second, Sofie missed him.

Although John Lavery was only a few years older than she was, his dark, attentive face was lined and his under-eyes pouchy. They scrutinized each other, and she remembered hot summer nights and parties that went on until dawn.

"Your clouds," he said in a soft Irish whisper untouched by his years in Glasgow and London. "That is what I remember. And the striped stockings you wore at one of our fancy dress balls, when you were meant to be a Moroccan girl. They were a mistake. The clouds were not."

Mr. Lawrie looked at them quizzically.

"I think perhaps Mr. Lavery means the clouds in my paintings," she explained.

"Of course I do. Your skies were remarkable."

A maid in a smart black uniform brought the tea tray, and Lavery asked Sofie to pour. The blue-and-white china was paper thin, and she had a sudden, vivid memory of the much thicker blue-and-white cup she had twisted her body to reach, when she posed for him in the hammock in Grez. As she passed the cups, she put her pleasure at his remark about her clouds off to the side so she could enjoy it alone, later.

He asked about her work, and Mr. Lawrie leaped in with an enthusiastic description of her tapestries and weaving. Lavery listened politely, and when Mr. Lawrie had finished, he turned to her. "And your painting?"

She explained: the children, Nils, the more manageable demands of the textiles.

He nodded, his face neutral. Lawrie and his colleagues in Glasgow, he said agreeably, were doing interesting work in the applied arts. The two men talked of their Scottish connections, the annual Academy Exhibition, John Singer Sargent's newest portraits of Americans in their novel sports clothes. Mr. Lavery knew vaguely about Nils's work, but more of Lars Vogt's, since Lars was a fellow portrait painter. The two men did their best to include her in the conversation, but she let them go on without her.

At the door, John Lavery took her hands in his. He had a powdery, pleasant touch.

"Come back when you visit your sister next time. I would like to introduce you to my daughter."

"Of course," she said. "I would enjoy that."

"And think about those skies."

She smiled, noncommittal.

On their way back to Martina's, she and Mr. Lawrie walked through Hyde Park, past the Albert Memorial. It looked like a piece of a great cathedral that had broken off and stood by itself. Perhaps that gave it its forlorn air. More than the crockets and arches and finials, it was the depth of Queen Victoria's devotion to Prince Albert that impressed her.

"She really loved him," she said with surprise.

"Something of an understatement, Mrs. Olsson. But you strike me as a devoted wife yourself."

There was no way to answer that seriously. She said something facetious about not having the funds, when the time came, to erect a Nils Memorial.

That evening, Martina's children seemed unusually noisy. Francis read aloud at length from the report in the *Times* about the Sixth Conference of the International Women's Suffrage Alliance, to be held in Stockholm next year. We can all read here, Sofie thought, why does he insist on reading to us?

"You haven't had a fine day," Martina said, with the acute eye of a younger sister. It was a family half-joke, since their father had always taken his seat at the dinner table while saying, "And did everyone have a fine day?" On the rare occasions when someone told him they hadn't, he was surprised and disappointed.

"No, I did. It was most interesting."

Maria Pappadopoula, Anna Foldsone Mee, Queen Victoria and Prince Albert, Francis and the Suffrage Alliance. John Lavery. It was in no way Mr. Lavery's fault, but she had hoped that her happiness could have lasted longer. Almost before she had absorbed his praise, his memory of her skies had turned from a pleasure into something else. She must be missing the children.

That night in her room, with her trunk open, she wrote two letters.

> Hampstead, London
> 19 May 1910
> My dear Cecilia,
>   This may reach you before the *vernissage*, and soon
> you may be able to tell me about Lars's show in person. I
> have had a fine time here, but am cutting my trip short by
> a few days. Perhaps I have become such a country mouse
> that life in the city is almost too much for me. You were
> right about Mr. Lawrie, he seemed more relaxed and,
> sometimes, even rather graceful here. Our day at the
> museum was very rich. I fell in love with a skirt
> embroidered in Crete in the eighteenth century, I learned
> that women were skilled painters of miniatures, and that
> Queen Victoria was extremely devoted to Prince Albert.
> Of course, I knew the last! But seeing the Albert
> Memorial touched me more than I would have imagined,
> and made me almost sad. Mr. Lawrie took me to have tea
> with John Lavery, the portrait painter—we painted
> together in Grez all those years ago. He admires Lars's
> work. This letter is an impossible jumble, I'm sorry. But I

must start to pack and I promised Martina a few sketches
of possibilities for her refurbished drawing room.

This time I am the harried friend!

And one with fondest hopes of seeing you soon,

Sofie

That letter required a desk, pen and paper. The other did not.

Dear John Lavery,

*You remembered my skies. And that is what I have never
told anyone. When I awake from a dream of painting, it is
always of a sky, on its own in a thin Swedish blue or overtaken
by clouds or sliding brazenly into darkness. If I could paint, it
would be skies. And you remembered mine.*

Thank you.

Sofie Falkner Olsson

Chapter Fifteen

OCTOBER 1910

SHE WANTED TO weave a storm, a fury of destruction. She wanted to weave the sound of paper ripping, of feet kicking at a door, of a voice shrieking until it ran out of sound. A tapestry of anger and fear. But why was she paying any attention to servants' whispers? Anna should not have left the kitchen door open while she gossiped with the new maid. Sofie had been passing through the dining room, looking for her needlepoint, when she heard Anna talking about how much Markus and Oskar resembled their father.

The new girl replied, "And they say there are more little Olssons, with the same sharp features and coppery colouring, running around Stockholm's back streets."

Her heart had begun pounding before her ears fully heard or her brain comprehended. At first she thought confusedly, But Nils has no nephews or nieces, what can the girl mean? Then she felt a thirst beyond any she'd ever known. Perhaps she heard Anna murmuring that she didn't know anything about that. Perhaps she'd only imagined that. The thirst stayed with her. She was parched, parched, parched. No matter how much water she drank, her throat was unspeakably dry.

It was obviously untrue. But where had the girl heard that?

That day the children were quarrelsome and Nils spoke sharply to them and then retreated to his studio. The sky was bright blue, with smoky clouds inside a thin outline of metallic white, but it was too cold for them to play outside for long and too crowded inside. When Tilda would not stop pushing her doll carriage into a town Felix was building with his bricks, he tripped her. Tilda fell onto Felix's favourite toy omnibus, which Nils had made from wire and thin sheets of wood, and it broke.

She left the crying children, one with a skinned knee, the other with a ruined omnibus, and shut herself in the workshop, hoping to weave herself into some calm. She was working on a wall hanging meant for the library, an abstract design of the four seasons. When all seemed to be going well, the maroon thread snapped.

Anna cooked Falun sausage with fried potatoes for supper. Nils began telling the children about the oxen who powered the Falun mine before they had steam power. When the oxen got too old to work any more, their hides were used for rope and their meat was smoked and became Falun sausage. Birgitta put her hands over her mouth and looked at the fat sausage on her plate.

"Oh, the poor ox!"

Markus was less tender-hearted. "Think how tough the meat would have been."

Birgitta was not to be distracted. "Is this ox?" she quavered, torn between pity and disgust.

"Of course not, darling. The mine doesn't use oxen any more," Nils said.

"What's the difference?" Sofie said sharply from her place at the foot of the table, by the door to the kitchen. They all started: her voice was so different.

"The sausage is from a pig, or a cow or a baby cow," she said. "Animals we eat every day."

No one said anything. Birgitta flicked nervously at her braids.

Nils hated it when she withdrew behind a closed face, sitting at her mending after supper without registering his presence. Once the house was quiet, he tried to woo her back with perceptive remarks about the children, with jokes, with questions about his sketches for the theatre murals in Uppsala. She was civilly, sullenly unresponsive. Finally, when they went upstairs, he took her hand and pulled her, indifferent, onto his bed. He used every trick at his disposal, slowing down until she sucked her lips inward to keep from moaning, moving his hands from breast to thigh, prolonging things until the inevitable. And then, when she could bear it no longer, and pleasure triumphed in long waves, she burst into thudding sobs. All the water with which she had tried to quench her thirst left her body in tears and cries.

"My little bird, what is it?"

She would only say, "Everything is broken. Everything is broken."

"But darling, it's only a toy. I'm sorry, but they were misbehaving. And the thread in your weaving just needs to be plucked out back to the edge, and you can attach a sound one. You know that."

"Everything is ruined."

It was all she could say.

"Sofie, I don't understand why you are sending the new girl away."

"You needn't put it like that, I am sending her to work for your parents. The housework is getting to be too much for your mother."

"But why? I thought Anna was pleased with her."

"That's not the point. Your parents need help, and we'll find someone else." Not that she believed a word the girl had said. Not for a minute, now that she had come to her senses. It was only a vicious little rumour, like the worm making its deliberate way up the stem of the rose, but she did not want it under her roof.

Chapter Sixteen

Falun, 20 January 1911
Dear Mrs. Olsson,

As you no doubt are aware, the International Woman Suffrage Alliance meeting will be held in Stockholm this summer. It is a great honour for Sweden, and we of the Falun Suffrage Society look forward to marching in the opening day parade with women from all over Europe and the Americas. We would like to distinguish our band of some thirty women by commissioning something special for the parade—a banner designed by you.

We all know your Askebo dress, and the blankets being woven to your design. We feel sure that a banner by Sofie Olsson would not be like that of any other society, and that it would be as progressive as our cause. Some of our members are excellent needlewomen, and they would do the embroidery. I would be most happy to discuss the details with you at your convenience. We all hope that we can interest you in this project.

I remain, with best wishes,
Otillia Lundeborg,
President, Falun Suffrage Society

Askebo, January 23, 1911
Dear Mrs. Lundeborg,

Thank you very much for your letter and your kind invitation. This is an honour I did not expect. Unfortunately, this year is a very busy one for me, mostly with my family and commitments at home. So I must decline your invitation, with regret.

Wishing you good luck in finding another designer, and all the best from
Sofie Olsson

Sofie put down her pen, and took an envelope from the drawer in her desk. She heard shouts from below and looked out the window to see the children at war in the snow. Felix, as usual, had lost a mitten and was playing on, his bare red hand inviting frostbite. She ran her hand over the curtain she had woven, with its austere, modern decoration. Most of the banners she had seen in parades and demonstrations were florid, nineteenth-century things. It would have been interesting to design one that suited the new century. She reread her note, and picked up her pen again:

P.S. But, dear Mrs. Lundeborg, I would like you to know that I think it is a very clever idea, and very disarming to some who are wary of female suffrage (as I was for some years myself). A beautiful banner, made by women, shows that we would not give up our home-loving hands and hearts if we became full citizens. I agree with you that a clean, simple design would suit your forward-looking cause. I am sorry I am unable to help, and again, my most sincere good wishes.

She wondered why the letter had come from Mrs. Lundeborg and not from Selma Lagerlof, who had been active in the Falun Suffrage Society for years. She was their neighbour, now that the older children needed a better school than Askebo could provide and the Olssons lived for much of the school year in a yellow house on Blindgatan in Falun. Nils had painted Miss Lagerlof's portrait when she won the Nobel Prize. Perhaps she knew something of Nils's opinion of female suffrage and wished to spare Sofie any embarrassment.

That night, Sofie lay in the bathtub and tried to rest her head on the leather strap suspended at one end. She was not completely comfortable, as the strap was either too thin or too low-slung. But she marvelled at the bathtub—the pipes that travelled importantly down the wall, the faucets that produced hot and cold water, the perfect whiteness of the baked enamel finish. No more heating water on the kitchen stove, no more balancing on your haunches in a tub the size of a large mixing bowl, no more piecemeal washing in the bedroom with a basin and ewer. Nils was fiercely proud of the house's first bathroom, recently converted from the smallest bedroom. He had painted its portrait, posing Marianne next to the tub, in a Japanese-style robe, with her sandals discarded on the slatted wooden floor. The thrillingly ugly plumbing was front and centre, along with a menacing brush and scraper in a holder on the wall. As part of the picture's mock-Japanese look, a potted lily stood on an overturned milk pail.

The lily was long gone, but a gardenia had taken its place. Sadly, the blossoms had died almost overnight. The leaves were brittle and the defeated flowers were brown at the edges and hung head down, yet their perfume remained. Strange that its rich-smell-ing heart still beat. The maid had wanted to remove it, but Sofie hesitated. Which was more important, the looks or the perfume?

The evening sky had arranged itself in irregular stripes of pink, turquoise, blue. Show-off, she thought. I could weave you.

She gave up on the strap, unhooked it and accepted that her hair would get wet. It was probably time to wash it anyway. It had been a few months since her last shampoo and people were beginning to advise washing the hair more than three or four times a year. She bent her knees, two bare mountains in the soap-slick water, think-ing back to a dream she'd had recently. In it, she and Nils lived at the top of a hill. Climbing up to their house involved sinking her feet into mud, then laboriously freeing each foot with a revolting sucking sound. She wanted to leave Nils and their remote house, and the dream-Nils offered to show her what he called "our trea-sure." If she left him, he said generously, as if speaking of a distant possibility, she could use it to support herself. He produced a leather box with hinges, filled with rubbishy paste jewellery, gaudy and obviously fake. She stared at the jewellery, thinking, could he really believe this was valuable? And yet, peeking in and out of the paste jewels, she could see some real ones. Separating the real from the counterfeit would take forever. Thinking of it made her tired.

When she awoke, she smiled at the idea of Nils encouraging her hope of leaving. And why in the world would she want to leave him?

In June, at breakfast one morning, she and Nils read in the paper about Selma Lagerlof's address to the suffrage convention in Stockholm. Backed by tiers of women students dressed in white, she read her speech, which was called "Home and State." Home, created by women, was a gentle, loving place that tried to make use of every talent, and State, the creation of men, was "great and strong but not happy." The State's problems would not be solved, Miss Lagerlof claimed, until men accepted the help of women in the public sphere.

Nils rattled the paper. "She is a curious choice for their main speaker."

Here we go, she thought. "Why do you say that?"

"There is so much gossip and innuendo about her relationship with that writer Miss Elkan and now Valborg Olander. I doubt she will help the suffragists' cause."

Miss Lagerlof shared her Falun house with a woman named Sophie Elkan, and also had a great friendship with Miss Olander, a teacher of Swedish. People said the two women competed to be Miss Lagerlof's favourite.

Sofie finished buttering her bread, and applied a thin varnish of lingonberry jam.

"Surely people talk much more about the fact that Selma Lagerlof is the first woman to win the Nobel Prize for Literature. And that she bought a sizable estate with the profits from her books, one that employs many people, yet she cannot vote."

In one fluid, irritated movement, Nils put down his cup and the paper, and scraped the chair away from the table. Once he was standing, he pulled off his glasses.

"I must get to work."

He would sulk now, at least for a little while.

"Will you be wanting Felix and me, or are you working on something else today?"

The rhubarb was ripe and she and Felix had prepared most of the crop for bottling while posing for Nils. In his painting, the stalks were piled on one side of the low table in the kitchen garden, with bowls of trimmed and sliced rhubarb on the other side. Felix's tongue distorted his cheek in concentration as he pulled off the peel in the broadest ribbons possible. Wearing her French bonnet, she leaned forward, pulling the last strings from a stalk. At their feet, a carpet of fan-shaped leaves, peel and strings deepened.

"In the afternoon, if it's still fine. I want to spend the morning on sketches for the Gustafsson portrait."

He was painting a portrait of the writer Richard Gustafsson. She nodded, without meeting his eyes. He left for the studio, and she returned to the paper.

Miss Lagerlof, like Ellen Key, couched the struggle for suffrage in terms of women being able to be more, not less, womanly when they had achieved their rightful place in society. Sofie reread the passage from her speech about the home being a loving realm where every talent is respected, then put down the paper. Miss Lagerlof, for perfectly good strategic reasons, idealized home life. On the other hand, as she had never married, perhaps she believed what she wrote.

Chapter Seventeen

THE DERRYS, AN English couple whom Sofie and Nils had met through Martina and Francis, were staying with them in Askebo, and the Vogts had invited the four of them to dinner and to spend the night. On the lonely road, as they neared Siljevik, they passed a cart and horse going in the opposite direction. A young woman was seated next to the driver, with a trunk in the back.

Cecilia was dressed in a forest-green watered silk that Sofie had admired before. But tonight it did not suit her. Her face looked drawn and distended at the same time. Lars seemed more or less his usual self, happy to show the Derrys around his collections, but he watched Cecilia out of the corner of his eye.

Apparently something had gone wrong with the servants. The maid who waited at table was too small for her lovely broderie anglaise apron and didn't seem to know the proper side from which to serve.

"Forgive us," Cecilia said to the Derrys, "Agnes is new to serving at table."

In between the soup and the fish, Cecilia excused herself for a minute and Sofie went to the washroom on the second floor to sponge off some soup she had spilled on her dress. Coming out of

the washroom, she found a strange, contorted shape in the hall, in
the niche where the Vogts displayed a very large Chinese bowl on
a stand. The shape was crouched over the broad bowl, almost as if
it wanted to get into it. Its arms extended around the lip, but not
protectively. It looked as if she—for now Sofie saw that the shape
was Cecilia—was furious with the bowl and wanted to squeeze it
almost to the point of shattering it.

"Cecilia, are you ill? Shall I call someone?"

She had no idea whom she would call, but Cecilia's abandon
and near-retching posture confounded her. Cecilia uncoiled herself
from the bowl but lost nothing of her tenseness.

"No, don't call anyone. I am a little under the weather, that's all."

"Just let me get Lars," Sofie began, but Cecilia transferred her
rage from the bowl to Sofie.

"Don't get anyone!" she whispered so ferociously that Sofie
instinctively stepped back. "Did you hear what I said? I just need
some cold water on my face."

Sofie gave an unconvinced half nod, and stood where she was,
bewildered.

"Stop fussing!" Cecilia hissed, as if Sofie were making an
unconscionable scene. "This has nothing to do with you!"

And with that, she vanished into the washroom. The rest of the
evening was unremarkable. Agnes seemed finally to grasp that food
was served from the left and drinks from the right. Cecilia reappeared
with her livid face somewhat restored and chatted about her collection
of English first editions with Charles Derry. And Sofie noticed only
one other small, untoward thing, as they said good night to the Vogts
before going to their rooms. Lars would often put his arm around
Cecilia at this point in the evening, as they accepted their guests'
thanks. This evening, he moved to do that, when an almost imper-
ceptible stiffening on Cecilia's part stopped his arm in mid-air.

"What was it, do you think?" Sofie whispered to Nils, as they
settled into bed in the smaller guest room.

"Cherchez la femme."

He began to unbutton her nightdress.

"What do you mean?"

"Something to do, perhaps, with the woman and the trunk in the cart we passed on our way here."

"Oooh." He *was* clever. Another troublesome maid. Although she suspected this was a different kind of trouble. She shifted a little, releasing more of the nightdress to her front, so that he did not tear it with his unbuttoning. Poor Cecilia.

Chapter Eighteen

FEBRUARY 1912

ABOUT SIX MONTHS later, the Olssons were invited to dinner at Wilhelmina and Walther von Hallwyl's new mansion in Stockholm. Walther von Hallwyl was on the board of the Comedy Theatre and the Lyric Theatre, both of which had commissioned works from Nils. The Hallwyls gave three formal dinner parties each February, one for the diplomatic corps and Stockholm society, one for family and the last for friends. Neither Stockholm society nor family, the Olssons were not really friends either, although that was the dinner to which they were invited.

Sofie admired the house's dignified, closed street face on Hamngatan, but inside, things were not to her taste. The architect paid homage to a different, but equally sombre, historical style in each of the public rooms. Although the decor harked back to the seventeenth or eighteenth century, the house had every modern invention—elevators, indoor plumbing, a long-distance telephone. It was all hidden. Even the piano was smothered under a baroque cage of ormolu mounts and marquetry.

It was a relief to spot the Vogts in the baroque drawing room, standing in front of a marble fireplace so massive it might have been the entrance to a small house. Lars needed to consult with his engraver, and he and Cecilia both wanted to look at the seventeenth-century Dutch silver at Gustav Mollenborg's shop, so they too had accepted the invitation and come to Stockholm.

"I wonder why there is no fire," Lars said, looking into the great black hole of the hearth, the only empty space in the tapestried, coffered, chandeliered room. Waiters with trays of champagne flutes, each in his own obsequious dance, glided and bowed from one group of guests to another.

"Because Wilhelmina Hallwyl finds fires dirty," Sofie said. "These public rooms have a kind of air heating, and the less important rooms, where pipes and radiators would not be so objectionable, are heated by steam."

The drawing room's pièce de résistance was a monstrous gilt cabinet, filled with equally ornate gold-painted teacups and teapots. Looking into its gleaming depths, Nils whispered, "You see, they like simple things too." Sofie had to turn away before she laughed too loudly.

Dinner was a procession of thirteen courses, beginning with *Hors d'oeuvres* and *Potage á la Victoria* and going on to *Filet de Turbot á la Normandie*, *Filet de Boeuf á la Parisienne*, *Vol-au-Vent* and *Perdreaux rôtis*. Following a short intermission of greens, *Salade* and *Asperges nouvelles*, the guests staggered through no fewer than five sweet courses.

After dinner they were invited to tour the Hallwyls' collections on the top floor of the house. Armour, porcelain, silver and paintings were displayed in separate galleries. Sofie and Cecilia strolled arm in arm and Cecilia, who knew a great deal about silver, pointed out the finest pieces to Sofie. The paintings looked as if they had been bought by the metre—one each of every Old Master still on the market, please—but even as she thought this, Sofie shrank a little from its snobbish sound.

Lars scorned the Rembrandt, although his own was equally dubious. He and Nils were no more enamoured of this conservative collection than Sofie was, but as they walked up and down the gallery, the men began to disparage artists the Hallwyls certainly would not have bought, the painters still called new. Picasso and Matisse took the lion's share of their criticism, although Cézanne, Kokoschka and Kandinsky also came in for abuse. Lars, in some ways more modern than Nils, was scathing but calm. The fame or notoriety, as he saw it, of the new painters wounded Nils more closely. "They are malignant," he said darkly, his forehead lowering at the thought of their baffling, deliberate clumsiness.

"Congratulations," Sofie said. "You and the pope are in agreement. Pius X has just called for Catholics to take an oath against modernism."

Nils looked disconcerted. He insisted, "They will not last. It is a fad. In fifty years, no one will remember their names."

"It is hardly a fad," Sofie said. "Cézanne has had a retrospective at the Salon d'Automne. Matisse is represented by Bernheim-Jeune in Paris, and Picasso by Kahnweiler. He has powerful patrons in the American brother and sister, Leo and Gertrude Stein. Matisse interests me especially, he is so sketchy and bold, with great blank spaces in his canvases. His flowers are wonderful, I think."

It was not a long speech, but she meant it to have a bite. Cecilia gave her a look. The conversation stopped abruptly and the men drifted away to look at the Murillo. She and Cecilia sat down on a bench in front of a rather sweet Van Ruysdael.

Cecilia wore an expression that meant she had something to say, and would not be stopped. Sofie resigned herself.

"Sofie, everyone who sees them thinks your fabrics are superb. Ellen Key was telling me about the tablecloth and napkins on heavy linen you designed, each napkin embroidered with a different Swedish berry. Have you thought of having some of your designs reproduced, or even manufactured?"

"Not manufactured," Sofie said sharply. "No. Some women in Askebo are weaving copies of the Navajo blanket I made for Nils's bed. It's a good way for them to make a little extra money. But other than that, no."

Cecilia swept past the "no." "I asked my brother about what would be involved in manufacturing some of your designs. Of course, he doesn't work with fine fabrics, but talking with him would be a start. Look at the success William Morris's fabrics and wallpapers have had."

Sofie smoothed an invisible lock of hair.

"I have never understood the appeal of Morris's claustrophobic vines and predatory flowers. Most of his designs are just a continuation of the gloomy rooms we grew up in."

This gave Cecilia pause, but only for a moment. "Of course, your work is much airier and lighter than Morris," she agreed cheerfully. "And more modern. I quite see that. I only meant that there is a market for good-quality textiles, and not only in Britain. And Fredrik would be happy to meet us—I thought I would go with you, for the first meeting anyway. Are you free next week?"

Sofie's smile said, I am making an effort to be pleasant, but you are on thin ice.

"It's kind of you to think about it, Cecilia. But there's no point in wasting your brother's time. Or yours, or mine. I don't want my designs manufactured."

Dear Cecilia,

Please don't make appointments with your brother to discuss arrangements that do not interest me. I am quite capable of . . .

No. No, no.

Dear Cecilia,

I was too abrupt at the Hallwyls'. I do appreciate your generous interest in my work. My reason for saying no is not

what everyone imagines, that Nils would not like it. I know
people think that, but I refuse for another reason. I don't
know how to put it. I can only say I am not a designer of
textiles except in the small way you know. I want something
else, maybe I am something else. Forgive me, this sounds so
silly, I don't even know why I'm writing it. Really, I only
wanted to apologize and thank you.
     Your stubborn friend,
     Sofie

Cecilia would have found both those letters incomprehensible,
and the second even more than the first. As she did herself. Besides,
she did not discuss Nils in that way with anyone.

Chapter Nineteen

APRIL 1914

Siljevik, 13 April 1914

Dear Sofie,

We had a rather interesting visit yesterday. Lars and I have been talking of hiring someone to do some curatorial and administrative work. The management of his work, the school and my other commitments keeps me more than busy. We would like to do something permanent, perhaps establish a public gallery of Lars's work and our collections, in the way our friend Mrs. Gardner has done in her house in Boston. The old buildings Lars is buying need to be restored and displayed properly. And we talk of willing our house to the country, with its furnishings intact. All quite a lot of work, for which we need help. A young woman, a university graduate, came to be interviewed for this rather nebulous position. She has written a dissertation on Sweden's traditional wooden buildings and apprenticed as a curator at the Kaiser-Friedrich Museum in Berlin.

Her name is Lisbeth Gregorius. She is neither pretty nor plain, exactly, although she has a lovely carriage and does nice things with her hands when she talks. She is tall and still, but her questions were apt, and she had already done some thinking about our "foundation," as she called it. I expect that Lars will choose one of the two young men who have also come to be interviewed, although their credentials are in no way better than hers. A pity, because I would have enjoyed getting to know Miss Gregorius.

I look forward to welcoming you and Marianne to my lacemaking school next week! It must be very satisfying to have a daughter who shares your interests— or at least some of them.

Your friend,
Cecilia

Marianne did want to learn how to make lace. But, she hastened to tell Sofie, not the quaint figures and even stories sometimes found in peasant lace. Instead, she wanted to learn some geometric, abstract patterns she could use to make bookmarks for her friends. Cecilia was happy to teach her, so Sofie and Marianne had arranged to spend a few days at Siljevik. In a corner of her study, Cecilia had equipped a small table with bobbins, the lacemaking pillow, pins, perforated pattern sheets and pictures of various patterns.

"Not Bockarna, certainly, not Krakspark, and not Halrad," she said to Marianne, pointing out some of the most difficult. "Those are for later."

"Those are not what I had in mind," Marianne said, casually dismissing the Alpine peaks of the lacemaker's art. "I like this one," she said, of a simple-looking pattern with a diamond shape.

"That one needs a bit of experience too. Beginners start with a kind of lace called 'Torchon.'"

"As in the French for tea towel?"

"Yes, exactly, because women edged their tea towels and even their underwear with it. Some lacemakers call it Beggar's Lace because it uses a thick thread and not many bobbins." She began pinning a pattern to the pillow and set Marianne to winding thread around the bobbins.

"You're going to start with this bookmark."

It was a loose honeycomb pattern with a tighter, diamond-shaped bit in the middle. So that Marianne could see the emerging pattern, Cecilia did the first few rows, twisting and crossing her bobbins and moving her pins with a dexterity that looked misleadingly easy. The bobbins made a gentle clacking sound. Then she slowed down so that Marianne could learn: "Cross over your threads, twist from right to left, and then place your pin under the stitch."

"Did Mr. Vogt's mother teach you?" Marianne asked, struggling to remember the order of the bobbins.

"She was my best teacher, and she taught me the patterns used around here in the Dalarna villages. But bourgeois girls in Stockholm in my day went to lacemaking classes, so I was not quite a beginner when I began to study with her."

Sofie had planned to knit during the lesson. Now she uncoiled her skein of wool, which looked like a braided loaf of bread, and looped it around the back of Cecilia's desk chair. She began winding it into a ball while Marianne whispered, "Twist, cross, twist, cross."

Eventually, as Marianne got more comfortable with her bobbins, she began talking about *The Ordeal of Richard Feverel*. Before she had had children, Sofie assumed they would all be eager readers. This was not the case—Tilda, for example, found in music the solace and the challenge Sofie found in books, and neither Sonja nor Felix enjoyed reading. Marianne was the keenest reader, and she had just finished George Meredith's novel. She found the heroine, Lucy, supremely aggravating.

"She is such a perfect Patient Griselda—her bridegroom abandons her, she has no idea where he is and she is left to give birth and care for their baby alone. And when Richard reappears and confesses that he has been unfaithful to her, all she cares about is whether he still loves her. You can't even speak about forgiveness, really, because she doesn't seem to realize that he has done anything wrong. I wanted to shake her."

Sofie kept on winding her yarn.

"You're doing well," Cecilia said to Marianne, "just remember to place your pins at an angle so the thread doesn't slide off."

"Don't you find that pathetic?" Marianne asked her mother.

Sofie gave a noncommittal shrug.

Cecilia said, "Marianne, make sure that your pairs of bobbins stay separate from each other and from the other pairs. You mustn't let them tangle."

"But don't you find that pathetic?" Marianne repeated, while she tidied her pillow.

"I don't remember that part terribly well," Sofie said.

"Perhaps the book is rather out of date," Cecilia said. "It's about fifty years old, I think."

"Are you saying that you don't think there are women who would respond the same way today?"

"I have no doubt there are," Cecilia said, "but perhaps your generation feels differently."

"Twist, cross, twist, cross," Marianne whispered until she came to the end of the row. "Richard is allowed to do whatever pleases him, and Lucy doesn't think she has any rights at all. And then—of course!—she dies of brain fever because she is so worried about a duel Richard is fighting. It's ridiculous."

Sofie decided she had had enough of this talk about Lucy. "Clearly, she was too good to live," she said with a smile she hoped was conclusive.

"I would never forgive a husband who treated me like that," Marianne said. "Never."

She was so occupied managing her bobbins, pins and opinions that she didn't seem to notice that her mother and Mrs. Vogt were not very talkative.

"But seriously," she persisted, "is Lucy the kind of woman men think is ideal?"

"Men have all kinds of silly dreams about women," Cecilia said slowly. "And we probably have silly dreams about men, but not so many, I think. Or perhaps we let go of them sooner. And the novel is far from sensible, I agree."

Blessed Cecilia, Sofie thought.

By the time Lars looked in, around lunchtime, Marianne's work was starting to look like a bookmark.

"Quite a little hive of homecrafts here," he said, bending over Marianne's work. "Cecilia told me you want to learn to make lace. Is that Torchon?"

He tightened her last twist, then placed her pin at a sharper angle.

Sofie gave a sigh of mock exasperation. "Please don't tell me you can make lace too."

"Why not? It was an army doctor named Mats Pettersson who is responsible for Pettersson lace."

"Not entirely," Cecilia said. "Pettersson came back from service in Pomerania with his Bohemian wife, their two daughters and his stepson. They were all lacemakers, and they introduced novelties like pricked paper patterns and pins into Sweden."

"In what ancient century did all this take place?" Marianne asked, amused.

"Just the last ancient century," Lars said. "Around 1800. Pettersson's stepson, Jacob Ernst, was a teacher as well as a lace-maker, and the 'Schoolmaster Edging' pattern is named for him. Cecilia has used it for the kitchen curtains, isn't that right, Cecilia?"

But Cecilia was having none of his bids for attention. "That's enough now, Lars, we have work to do. I want Marianne to settle into the proper rhythm of crossing and twisting. I'm sure you can find something to do," nodding her head in the direction of his studio.

He wants to be part of things, Sofie mused. But then, he always does. And Marianne finds him charming, like most women. But Cecilia does not—or at least not this morning.

By the end of the second day, Marianne had made several bookmarks and was flirting with the idea of edging some guest towels. Cecilia made her a present of the pillow, a few patterns and a dozen bobbins. "Give our love to Nils," she said, tucking carriage blankets around them before they set off for the train, "and tell him he owes us a visit. If he doesn't bring you all back within a month, I will insist on teaching him lacemaking too."

In the carriage, Sofie thought about Cecilia's kindness to her children. Everything about Cecilia seemed so complete that she rarely wondered if she minded not having children. She should give that some more thought. She laid her hand on Marianne's knee.

"What is it, Mamma?"

"Nothing. Just that you are a nice girl."

Siljevik, 20 April 1914
Dear Sofie,

   The geranium cuttings you gave me are flourishing, all over the dining room window. I wonder how many bookmarks Marianne has finished, and if she is still contemplating guest towels. She learns quickly, and it was a delight to have the two of you.

   I am giving some talks on traditional embroidery at the Folk School. Lars is in Germany, where he writes that war looks inevitable. At the same time, "everyone" assures him that it will be a very short war. I don't take much comfort from that, as even a very short war is horrible.

   I take advantage of my free time in the evenings to work on some napkins with a plaited fringe. The pattern came from Mrs. Mansson in the village, and I've adapted it slightly. If they succeed, I will send you the pattern.

Your tapestry sounds daunting—I will look forward to seeing it on my next visit.

One more piece of news. To my surprise, Lars has decided to hire Miss Gregorius, the young woman I wrote you about. She will start almost immediately. It will be strange, but I am looking forward to having a female colleague.

Your friend,
Cecilia

Chapter Twenty

JUNE 1914

MARTINA AND FRANCIS were celebrating their twenty-fifth wedding anniversary in the summer of 1914, and Sofie decided she would take Marianne and Markus with her to London for the party. Her oldest children, like Martina's, were in their early twenties, and the cousins got along well—the days when the English young people had snickered at their cousins' Swedish accents were long past.

The party itself was a rather stiff affair, filled with Francis's suffragist connections and his colleagues from the Natural History Museum. One group did not mingle much with the other, and the guests seemed to expect very little of Martina's sister, whose English they assumed was inadequate.

Trying to make conversation, one of Francis's colleagues asked Sofie about Falun's copper mine and the worry that the ore was running out. She confessed that she knew very little about that. He assured her that the bigger the crater—and the Falun crater was now very large—the less they were able to extract from it. She nodded, trying to look intelligent. It was rather a relief when the guests left, and she and Martina could gossip about them on her bed in the guest room.

Happily, Lars and Cecilia were also in London with their new assistant, Miss Gregorius. They were looking at private collections of art that had become museums, with a view to setting up their own, and suggested meeting Sofie at Lord and Lady Wallace's museum. Now open to the public on a quiet square in Marylebone, it was a cache of treasures collected by the third and fourth marquesses of Hertford and Richard Wallace, the illegitimate son of the fourth marquess. When Sofie mentioned that Mr. Lawrie too had business in London—he was always happy to schedule a visit when Sofie was visiting her sister—Cecilia insisted that she bring him along.

Sofie agreed to meet the Vogts in the afternoon, but she and Mr. Lawrie arrived at the museum earlier, to see more of the collection. She wore a new dress from Liberty's that Martina had convinced her to buy, a soft green-and-yellow print, with Grecian ribbons crisscrossed closely over the breast. It was different from her usual embroidered yokes, where the fullness began above the breast, and she felt almost shy when she took off her light wrap.

The museum's first floor bristled with weapons and armour. It reminded her of the newspapers, filled with angry threats of war.

"Why do men love these instruments of violence so much?" she asked, sighing at yet another room lined with dully gleaming breastplates, helmets and swords.

"No doubt the sight of all this weaponry rouses something in us," Mr. Lawrie agreed, peaceably. "But look at how beautiful the acid-etching of pomegranates is on this visor, or the inlay on this breastplate."

He showed her how the rings in a piece of mail were so tightly interlaced that not even the smallest, sharpest knife could penetrate them.

"You work with fabrics," he said, taking her elbow for the briefest of moments and turning her in the direction of a dowdy piece of mail that went over the shoulders. "This is a cloth. You can imagine how supple it is." His warm hand cupping her elbow confused her, and she retreated into flippancy.

"It looks like a bed-jacket," she said and immediately regretted it. Men did not like it when you belittled their enthusiasms. But he laughed.

"Yes, it does. But far more useful."

A suit of armour, he told her, was an extra skin, thin but impenetrable and as flexible as the body underneath it. He pointed out *couters*, elbow plates, *cuisses*, thigh plates, and *pauldrons*, shoulder protectors. The armour for shoulders, hands, knees and feet was made in thin plates called *lames*, which slid over each other as the body moved. This simple, flawless suit, he said, pointing to a glass case, was made for the Holy Roman Emperor Maximilian I by his court armourer, Konrad Seusenhofer.

"However did you learn all this?"

"My grandfather had a forge in Ayr, and he loved metalwork of all kinds. I spent hundreds of hours with him in the forge, and when he died I inherited his armoury books."

She looked at the visors, shaped variously like dogs, birds and gravy boats, the puffed-out breastplates, the braggingly narrow waists and the calf-guards as tight as hose. There was, as Mr. Lawrie said, something rousing about armour. She did not want to be roused. But when she took a deep breath, she was conscious of the ribbons that emphasized her breasts and she wondered fleetingly if he would find it necessary to guide her again by the elbow.

At the appointed hour, they met the Vogts and Miss Gregorius in front of the main staircase. Introductions were made: not only was it Sofie's first encounter with Miss Gregorius, but Mr. Lawrie was new to the Vogts as well as Miss Gregorius. Cecilia took in Sofie's dress and gave her a half nod, half smile that meant she approved. Miss Gregorius, who was blonde and more attractive than Cecilia's description had suggested, was agreeable but quiet. At first Sofie thought she might be subdued by the company of four older people. Then she realized that Miss Gregorius was here on business. The museum had been the Wallaces' London house before the widowed Lady Wallace willed it to the nation, and Miss Gregorius was intent on the way everything, down to the stables and the coach houses, had been converted into galleries.

Someone from the museum, a Mr. Holcross, had been assigned to tour Mr. Vogt and his party through the museum and answer any of their questions. He pointed out the changes made in the private rooms to accommodate the art. The billiard room, now devoted to furniture by Boulle in turtleshell and brass marquetry, had been dominated in Lord Wallace's day by a vast billiard table. No admirer of Boulle's obsessively elaborate armoires and desks, Lars sighed over the removal of the table: "What a shame!"

Sofie wandered through the galleries with Miss Gregorius and Mr. Lawrie, listening as he asked Miss Gregorius about her time in Berlin, and what it had been like working with Max Friedlander at the Kaiser-Friedrich Museum. Sofie noticed that she answered his questions amiably enough, but her real attention remained fixed on the galleries and their adjustments. Mr. Lawrie changed the subject, asking Miss Gregorius about the dissertation she had written at Uppsala on the ancient log buildings of Sweden. Sofie's dress with the Grecian ribbons no longer seemed so remarkable to her, which at least allowed her to stand and walk more naturally. After a while, she found their conversation a little tedious, so she joined Cecilia and Mr. Holcross.

Mr. Holcross was pointing out the adaptations made to the smoking room, which now held medieval and Renaissance pieces. When Lord Wallace's male guests had repaired there after dinner to smoke cigars and pipes, the walls and floor had been covered with Minton tiles. They had not survived the house's refashioning, Mr. Holcross explained, except in an alcove lined with Turkish-inspired tiles.

The alcove was small, so it was not surprising that Cecilia was standing quite close to Mr. Holcross. What *did* surprise Sofie was Cecilia's bright, unwavering smile.

"I'm so glad you preserved this," Cecilia said. "Such a perfect example of the period when exotic decoration was all the rage. Very glamorous."

"The tiles were practical in a room for smoking," Mr. Holcross said, "because they could be washed with soap and water."

"And they are so decorative that I suppose no one missed the curtains and rugs that would have harboured the smell of smoke," Cecilia added, like a student who wanted to please her teacher.

"That's right," Mr. Holcross said, and smiled back at her. Cecilia gave a small laugh of pleasure.

Really, Sofie thought. Why is everyone flirting today? What is Cecilia thinking? Mr. Holcross is probably twenty years younger than she is.

Mr. Lawrie and Miss Gregorius joined them, as did Lars, who had wandered off to see the Fragonards. Mr. Holcross must not have heard all their names properly. Encouraging them into the Boudoir Cabinet, he suggested to Mr. Lawrie, "Your wife may enjoy the miniatures and snuffboxes." He aimed a slight bow in Miss Gregorius's direction. Mr. Lawrie blushed his most violent red, but Miss Gregorius only smiled slightly and did not seem at all bothered. The others laughed, and Lars explained that Miss Gregorius was the Vogts' assistant.

"You should have realized they aren't married," he teased an embarrassed Mr. Holcross. "Mr. Lawrie is clearly enjoying Miss Gregorius's company too much for them to be man and wife."

Mr. Lawrie's scarlet face, which had begun to fade, blazed up again.

"Lars, you are quite horrible," Cecilia said. "Stop it, please."

On the second floor, Sofie and Cecilia stopped in front of a portrait of a Dutch family. Lars and Miss Gregorius had gone ahead, and Mr. Lawrie was nowhere to be seen.

"Isn't Miss Gregorius a find?" Cecilia asked happily.

Sofie nodded, although she was not sure how she felt about

Miss Gregorius, at least not yet. The young woman was no doubt very competent and organized, two things that Cecilia would appreciate. She was self-contained but not at all timid, and there was nothing wrong with that. Sofie was not suspicious of anything in particular, but she would wait and see. Perhaps Cecilia felt motherly toward her. And no doubt Lars enjoyed having a young woman around the house. Sofie trusted there would be no problems in that direction.

"Mmmm," she said, hoping this would pass for assent.

Mr. Lawrie joined them, and all three turned their attention to the painting of the Dutch family, who were seated at the edge of a forest. The father wore a red velvet coat and was hemmed in by two greyhounds. His small daughter held a platter of green peaches just touched with pink. Seated between her husband and child, the wife wore feathers and pearls, and a white satin dress. The odd thing was what she held at the centre of the painting, over her immaculate satin lap—an upside-down dead hare, with a wound in his lower belly. She grasped his two hind feet with one hand, letting his head and front legs fall free. The woman looked straight ahead, apparently unworried about getting blood on her beautifully painted skirt.

"She's not sure what expression to wear," Mr. Lawrie said. "There's something half-proud and half-ashamed in that plain Dutch face."

"But what does it mean," Sofie asked, "this woman in evening dress holding a dead animal?"

"Hunting was fashionable, something you had to be rich to do," Mr. Lawrie said. "So this shows their wealth and their power."

Sofie was not convinced. The woman's face had resignation mixed in with the pride and awkwardness. Did domestic tranquility always come with a price?

"At least this time it is the hare that has been sacrificed," she said dryly.

"You mean, instead of the woman," Cecilia said.

Mr. Lawrie looked bewildered. Sofie smiled. Sometimes the way she and Cecilia could read each other's thoughts was uncanny.

"Well, their holdings are astonishing," Miss Gregorius said to Lars and Cecilia in the cloakroom, after Mr. Holcross had said his farewells, "but so was the marquesses' wealth. In any case, it's not what you have in mind, I think—a private house turned into a gallery, with all the personal elements erased."

"No, I suppose we are thinking of two buildings," Lars agreed. "A new one for the art, on the opposite side of the house from the churchyard, and then leaving the house as it is, as its own museum."

The Vogts and Miss Gregorius were going back to Durrant's Hotel, just across from the Wallace Collection. Mr. Lawrie offered to accompany Sofie back to Martina's house. As they said their good-byes, Mr. Lawrie suggested some galleries in Glasgow and Edinburgh that might furnish Miss Gregorius with other models. He wrote down the Vogts' address and promised to send her the names. Sofie doubted that the Vogts would find it necessary to extend their research to Scotland, but Mr. Lawrie was always so helpful.

In the second week of her visit, a letter came from Nils. It was a catalogue of his problems. He needed her advice about the fresco for the Opera House, there was something wrong with it that only she would spot, he couldn't bear to show it to the artistic director until she had seen it. The children missed her, and quarrelled all the time, which meant he could get no work done. Since the party was over, when was she coming home?

Sofie thought back to the Falun mine, which was running out of ore. In a marriage too, you could mine and mine until the ore ran out. And then what? It was tiring, humouring his pretense that she was his idol while really being his mother. She had too many children as it was. At the same time, she missed him.

Later that morning, Mr. Lawrie visited her in Martina's rose-and-green parlour. He chose an armchair upholstered in a tired-looking rose linen; she sat on the chaise longue. Big cloisonné urns held grasses, and Japanese fans stood open along the mantel. The Morris paper was a success, but Sofie still thought the room had too many bits and pieces. She showed Mr. Lawrie sketches of her latest work: curtains for Marianne's room and a tapestry for the village church. Markus had taken some photographs, which were not very clear, but gave an idea of the scale. Every once in a while, Mr. Lawrie would temper his admiration with some small suggestion and she would smile at him and say, "That is a fine Glasgow idea, Mr. Lawrie, but not very Askebo." He would laugh, and agree.

When he had seen everything, he turned serious and said, "Mrs. Olsson, there you are, in a village deep in the Swedish countryside, and your work is as new as anything in Vienna or Paris."

There was nothing unexpected in this. He often said such things. But there was something discouraging about this particular damp morning and the dim room overrun with painted and dried vegetation. About Nils's letter. When she thanked him, her voice thickened and she cleared her throat. Just for a second, but he heard it.

Suddenly, he was sitting next to her on the chaise longue, holding her arms above the elbows, as if she needed steadying to stay upright. A small Moroccan table had shuddered as he collided with it on his way to her, and at first he looked as confused about being so close to her as she was to find him there. But now he had gone too far to stop.

"Mrs. Olsson, Sofie, I mean. I cannot do this with your last name. I meant never to tell you, but I see you are unhappy. So perhaps there is some point. I care for you, you know that. I would do anything to . . . help you, to make you happy."

There was nothing more to say, so he stopped.

She was stone, ice, covered in impenetrable armour. A dense hedge full of thorns. But sad for him, and sad for something else, too. Of course, she had known it. But, like him, she never expected to hear it.

"Mr. Lawrie, I am so sorry. But you must know it is impossible."

"Of course. It is I who must apologize. I forgot myself." Forgetting yourself, another odd English expression. But an acute one, too. Somehow they righted themselves and the ornaments on the Moroccan table. Sofie began flipping distractedly through the pages of *The Studio* Mr. Lawrie had brought with him. The maid came in with coffee, which had no flavour whatsoever.

She ached with disappointment. He had capitulated too quickly. Why had he not pressed his suit? She must be suffering some kind of aftershock. What are you thinking, her sensible side said. Would you leave the children, Askebo, Nils, Sweden?

But he knows me, she thought, her fingers trembling ever so slightly around her coffee cup. And he loves me.

The sensible Sofie qualified that: he knows and loves *your work*.

And is that so unimportant, she thought, while Mr. Lawrie chattered on nervously about the Austro-Hungarian folk furniture in the *Studio*. He looks long and intently at my work, then at me. I fell in love with Nils through his work, and perhaps it is similar with Mr. Lawrie's feeling for me. Nils never looked at my work for long, but he looked at me. Now he rarely does. But such a dense web of strings binds us together. I do not see how I could cut it.

Chapter Twenty-one

FEBRUARY—MARCH 1915

NILS SAID, "SOFIE, there is no need for you to go. Or I will come with you."

"No, I want to go. To go alone. I'll take the trap and be back within the hour." And she left.

The photographer's premises were at the end of Kristinegatan, a long cobbled street under the spreading left wing of Falun's Kristine Church. The door had a plaque that said "D. Helmersen, Artistic Photography Studio." The "D" turned out to stand for Dora, a fair, youngish woman who somehow expressed her condolences with almost nothing in the way of words. If she started giving full condolences to all the customers who wanted their dead photographed, Sofie thought, she would never finish. But there was sympathy in this woman's frank grey eyes.

"If you can have your son brought here . . ."

"No. I want you to come to our house, on Blindgatan."

"I can do that, Mrs. Olsson, but it would be simpler here."

"No. He has been moved about too much already."

She did not need to count the moves: they were too recent and each one fixed in terrifying high colours. From Askebo, where the pains in his stomach began, to the doctor's here in Falun, then to the hospital, where it seemed all would be well now that his appendix was removed, then the infection, cutting through the giddy relief, and the sudden, terrible end.

"He will stay at home now until the funeral."

"Yes, of course, then. Morning light is best, so if you can have your boy dressed in his suit, I suppose, at nine in the morning . . ."

"Not his suit. He never liked it and almost never wore it. He will wear one of his ordinary blue-and-white striped shirts."

She could see that Dora Helmersen had not photographed a dead person in a blue-and-white shirt before.

"Whatever you wish, Mrs. Olsson."

Miss Helmersen entered Markus's name and the other details in a dark green ledger on a neat desk. Behind her, hung on long wooden rods, were the various painted backdrops against which people posed—a summer garden, the cathedral in Stockholm, a skating pond. There were chairs and chaises longues arranged against the walls, and tables with albums of photographs to inspire her customers.

Sofie was so unaccustomed to her bereavement that she could not keep her attention on it. As yet, it had no content. She did not know what to do with it, so her mind went elsewhere.

"Tell me," she asked abruptly, "how you come to have your own business."

Miss Helmersen showed no surprise at the turn in the conversation.

"My uncle had the first photography studio in Borlange, and he showed me how the camera worked when I was a girl. I liked it. And because photography is a new thing, it is not controlled by the guilds. A woman can start her own studio."

Sofie nodded. A dull silence fell, as her wretchedness returned.

"And you will make your own arrangements for flowers?"

"No flowers. Just my son."

Carl and his trap and horse were waiting outside Miss Helmersen's studio. Sofie wanted to walk home, but within half a block, she saw some people she knew crossing the street to speak with her. Carl had been following her at a snail's pace, and she climbed quickly into the trap.

Falun, 25 March 1915
Dear Mr. Lawrie,

   Thank you for your kind words. I will always remember Markus luring you into that very unfair game of hide-and-seek the first time you visited Askebo. We have had greater luck with our children's health than many families. But now that misfortune has found us, it is as sad as any parent fears. Worse, really. And it seems cruel to lose him just as he was emerging into manhood. But I know it would be cruel to lose a three-year-old, or a baby, or a child of any age.

   My husband has been hit very hard.

   Perhaps when the war is over, we will meet again in England or here at Askebo. When I read the terrible numbers of young men Britain has lost, Sweden's neutrality makes me very uncomfortable.

   And thank you for your ever-ready hospitality and friendship.

   With good wishes,
   Sofie Olsson

In Falun she often walked down to the Miners' Church, not far from their house. It stood tall and stoic on its lawn, where the fine old trees kept a respectful distance. The graves scattered in the church-yard were hemmed in by wrought-iron fences. Like her heart, she thought, which felt surrounded by iron. If she breathed too deeply, or let herself remember Markus in a certain way, the iron would crack, and they would be in even greater trouble. Nils had found her sobbing over an old photograph of the children grouped around the Christmas tree, and she did not want that to happen again. The ancient Greeks in mourning threw cloths over their faces. It seemed too dramatic a gesture for Sweden, but she saw the point of it.

She went to collect Miss Helmersen's photographs, which were not consoling. The photographer had done her best, but Sofie did not want to remember Markus dead, or sleeping, as people liked to say. She thought back to the sketches and watercolours she had done of him as a baby, and burned when they left Gothenburg. Trying to love him, the one who had turned out to be the most steadily lovable of her children. She had photographs of him, posed in calm groups with the other children, or alone for his graduation. And she had Nils's paintings, mostly from his childhood—Markus blowing a toy trumpet on Christmas morning, or in a noisy procession to her bedroom on her name day.

But she had nothing that she had painted of him. And there was nowhere she could close a door in this house and paint him. The workshop was lined with windows, her desk was still in the upstairs hall, she did not even have her own bedroom. And Nils came looking for her often, in the workshop, the kitchen, the garden. Usually he had nothing to say. He would sit for a while with her, holding her hand while his tears flowed silently. He did not sob, and his blank expression never changed as the tears welled up and washed his face, over and over. In bed at night, she listened to his breathing next door, waiting for the point when it changed from the light sound of alertness to the longer sound of withdrawal and return, like waves on a shore, that meant he slept. She never heard that now.

While she listened, she painted Markus in her mind—launching his paper boats on the river, hurling himself joyously out of the carriage in Askebo on Friday evening after a week's school in Falun, pulling his cowlick as he trudged through his English grammar.

Finally, after several months, when Nils was in Gothenburg painting a fresco in the public library, she helped herself to brushes,

paints and paper from his studio. At first she worked numbly, painting the subjects she had pictured during those long nights. Then
sullenness succeeded numbness, and she kept on painting—Markus
in the confirmation suit he never wore again, Markus hiding behind
the big cupboard in the workroom while Oskar searched for him,
Markus suddenly more a man than a boy. Finally, she became angry,
painting her sweet boy with bitter speed, and those were the best
pictures. She could not turn off a rhythm in her head that repeated
over and over, "What a waste. What a waste. What a waste." After
a while, she stopped trying.

Chapter Twenty-two

JULY 1915

Askebo, 1 July 1915

Dear Cecilia,

Do not reproach yourself for your absence. We both know you would come at a moment's notice if Nils and I had the spirits for a visit. It's just that we don't, as yet. I say "as yet" because everyone puts it like that. I have to trust that they are right, and that we will not always feel this enormous inertia, this numbness that can shift unpredictably into something much worse. For now, it seems all I can do is sit with the family. We don't have to look animated or cheerful or sad, although we can be all those things, at moments. And we don't have to apologize for any of those moments. Every once in a while, one of us murmurs a memory of Markus.

And yet I miss you. Nils is decorating the village church, hoping to find some peace in that. Between us, he is painting some stylized angels who do not look at home in the ground-hugging little church. They are almost fussy, and Nils is never fussy. Here and there on the white walls he has painted some fine wildflowers, primroses and violets. But on the whole the work is weak and unsteady, an echo of the painter's state of mind.

I too find myself stepping into churches and sitting for a time. I can't say I feel comforted there, but maybe I feel more resigned. Grief has put me in a category too large to be resisted, as if I have joined hands with strangers down through the centuries who have lost someone. I seem to accept that while sitting in a pew.

Forgive me if I touch on a tender spot. I think so constantly now of children and losing children, and I know we have never talked about you and Lars not having them. I am sorry about that, that is all I want to say.

One thing I cannot do is read. Immersing myself in other people's lives or characters seems an impossible task. I will say "as yet."

Your friend,
Sofie

Siljevik, 17 July 1915
Dear Sofie,

Sad as it is, I was relieved to receive your letter. Lars and I both fret even more than usual when we don't hear from you, although we understand why letters come infrequently. We think of you every day, and of Markus, too. We talked this morning at breakfast of his first visit here, when he was eight, and his curiosity about what were considered "modern improvements" in 1901.

Thank you for thinking of our childlessness in the midst of your great loss. Your customary generosity. We longed for children, but the sorrow of not having them is surely small compared to loving a child for more than twenty years and then having him snatched away.

And this is the fate of so many parents and sons in this ghastly war. Just as we think the news from the front cannot be worse, it gets worse.

In infinitely more trivial news, we are awash in decisions here, close to choosing the architect for the Vogt Museum. Miss Gregorius and I lean toward Ragnar Ostberg, Lars still sitting on the fence. I will write when we have a final decision.

And meanwhile, may your sorrows ease, which does not mean that you or we will ever forget Markus. Lars joins me in this.

Your friend,
Cecilia

Six months after Markus's death, Sofie sat in the Kristine Church in Falun, looking at the baroque statues of the saints that lined the nave. Although she had known these statues for years, she was struck for the first time by how loose-bellied they were, as if they had given birth recently. They reminded her of the flabby middle and round breasts, stretched like drums, that came with a baby, the helplessness she had felt when she could not summon up feelings for Markus, and the surge of relief when she succeeded in loving him.

When she left the church, she walked up the street to D. Helmersen's Artistic Photography Studio. Miss Helmersen was dusting her painted backgrounds, moving her feather duster over a winding path in an autumnal forest.

"Mrs. Olsson," she said uncertainly when she turned and saw Sofie standing there. "Good day. I hope that everything was satisfactory with the pictures . . ."

"Yes. As much as they could be, perhaps."

They shrugged in unison, acknowledging that nothing about a twenty-two-year-old's death could be satisfactory.

Then Sofie had to think why she had come here. She shook her head lightly, hoping that would clear it. "My son was the photographer in the family."

"Really," Miss Helmersen said politely. "What kind of photographs did he take?"

"Oh, just informal pictures of the family."

Miss Helmersen nodded.

"I wondered—some time when you are not busy, of course—I would like to see something of how you develop your pictures. And, perhaps, how you organize your business."

She was not aware until she spoke that that was what she wanted, and even after she heard herself she wasn't sure if that was really the point of her visit. But Miss Helmersen took her request at face value. She showed Sofie the darkroom, a small, windowless room where she moved briskly through the mysteries of developing fluids, stop baths and fixers. She demonstrated how she used filters to increase or decrease the contrast between dark and light, and how to "dodge," reducing the light to one part of the picture, and "burn," giving more exposure to a particular part. They talked about subjects who fidgeted, grimaced or were otherwise difficult. Miss Helmersen mentioned, neutrally, that in one way photographing the dead was easier than working with the living, who had to hold a pose for long seconds.

As the afternoon lengthened, Sofie watched the green trees and blue sky and brick buildings outside the studio windows turn black and white, like a photograph. Was that why people accepted the black-and-white world captured in photography so easily? Because as day turned to evening, the coloured daytime world turned briefly into a photograph? Then black-and-blue, and finally black.

On another afternoon, the two women drank tea and Sofie looked through some of Miss Helmersen's albums. Worn Falun miners conscious of their Sunday suits, flanked by their families. Serious boys and girls in white arm bands, bearing a white candle, at their confirmation. Brides and grooms, the bride standing behind her seated husband, her hand solicitous on his shoulder. One photograph, as carefully composed as a painting, showed a boy in his confirmation suit standing by the open coffin of his twin, looking down at his mirror image.

Then Sofie came to a loose picture of a mother and a little girl. Or was it four little girls? The mother sat in a chair and the girl stood by her knee, and played with blocks in a corner, and strolled her doll in a wicker pushcart, and teased her cat with a bell on a ribbon.

"What is it?" she asked, baffled.

A look of annoyance flickered over Miss Helmersen's face. "It's nothing, just a little experiment. It shouldn't be here, with the albums. I was playing with multiple exposures."

"Is it a mourning picture?"

"It's just a little girl who lives in the neighbourhood and her mother. I was working with masking and something called lens capping, trying to see how many versions of her I could get in the picture. Why did you think it was a mourning picture?"

"Because this is what mourning is like, that you see the child everywhere and remember him in all his little pastimes."

Looking at Sofie staring at the images of the girl, Miss Helmersen seemed to make a decision. She moved to a chest of narrow drawers in the alcove, and from the keys at her waist, chose one and unlocked the top drawer. Riffling through the pictures inside, she found the one she wanted and took it to Sofie.

"This is a mourning picture."

A vase decorated with a painted cherub held about a dozen daisies. In the centre of each of the flowers, there was a child's head, a different one for each flower.

"It's . . . it's a bouquet of children," Sofie said, trying to puzzle it out. "Why do some of them have their eyes open and some closed?"

"It's something I do every year, just for myself. They are all children I've photographed in the last year, and they have all died. The ones whose eyes are open died after I took their photograph. The ones whose eyes are closed were photographed after death."

Sofie stared at the vase full of dead children.

"It's a simple technique, really," Miss Helmersen continued. "I cut out the heads, re-photograph them to the same size, paste them on the photograph of the vase and daisies, and then photograph that."

Reluctantly, Sofie looked up from the photograph.

"Could you show me more of your experiments?"

From the top drawer came pictures that were bizarre and oddly prosaic, even banal. Miss Helmersen was seen talking with herself, pouring coffee into a cup held by another Miss Helmersen, while yet another Miss Helmersen consulted a ledger. In another picture, four Miss Helmersens held a garland. The simplest way to accomplish this, she explained to Sofie, was by making a separate negative for each pose. Then she printed the negatives together in such a way that it seemed the figures were in the same room at the same time. She would have said more about these techniques, but Sofie was not so much interested in her trade secrets as in the strange power of the pictures.

"But what does it mean? What were you intending?"

Miss Helmersen rarely had an answer for that kind of question. Sofie had seen a few photographs that commemorated her sister, who had died. In them, pictures of her sister framed on the wall, painted on a vase and on a pillow coexisted with four images of Miss Helmersen. But usually there was no rhyme or reason to her creations.

Miss Helmersen was awkward. She was not shy, exactly, but she gave no sign as to whether she enjoyed Sofie's visits or did not enjoy them. One day, in her brusque way, she asked, "Would you like to pose for me?"

"Do you mean, for a regular portrait?"

"No, for one of these." She indicated the top drawer of the chest in the alcove, where she kept her experiments.

"Why me?"

"I think you would suit the form."

The picture she made showed four Sofies, one at a spindle where the thread she was spinning reached across the whole photograph and circled the other three Sofies, who were embroidering, holding a bundled doll meant to stand in for a baby, and staring off into the distance. Miss Helmersen had wanted her drawing or painting, but Sofie refused. She found the finished picture dismaying.

"There are so many of me."

"Yes, of course," Miss Helmersen said impatiently. As if to say, *like everyone.*

On another visit, Miss Helmersen said, "If you like, we could compose a picture about you and your son."

"Do you mean, like the one you did about your sister?"

"Rather like that, yes. We could plan it together."

Sofie brought photographs of Markus from home, and Miss Helmersen re-photographed them and put them in the room she was preparing, in frames and on a jardinière. The wonderful part came at the right edge of the picture. Using a full-length photograph of Markus, originally taken with Tilda in front of the Askebo house, Miss Helmersen placed him next to a full-length photograph of Sofie, overlapping his arm slightly against hers. It looked as if they were about to take a walk. Sofie pored over it, sometimes laughing at the legerdemain, sometimes weeping. Occasionally, when she had wept a long time, Miss Helmersen would bring her a fresh handkerchief. Tears did not bother her, and at those times Sofie was grateful for her remoteness.

She never talked to Cecilia or Nils about her visits to the photography studio. She knew what Nils would think of Miss Helmersen's work—childish, self-indulgent, probably demented. It was strange, no question, and Sofie didn't always like it. But she felt sure Miss Helmersen was an artist.

Chapter Twenty-three

NOVEMBER 1916

Askebo, 20 November 1916

Dear Cecilia,

Nils's painting of our Christmas dinner, which he painted just after Christmas last year, is a great success at the Stockholm Exhibition. The critics say it pictures the Swedish Christmas at its most idyllic, and a nodding ring of visitors gathers in front of it as soon as the doors open each day.

I cannot look at it without a sinking heart.

Anna stands at the centre, holding a punch bowl and wearing the Askebo folk dress, her waist bag thickly embroidered, the silver buckles on her bodice gleaming. She looks rested, happy, hospitable, a far cry from a real cook at a real holiday dinner! All around her, other people in snow-white blouses and bright-coloured skirts and vests are helping guests at the buffet. Sometimes I think I would be happy never to see another striped skirt and tightly laced bodice.

A creche with Mary and Joseph stands on the main table, along with the platters of ham and gravlax and the tureen of meatballs. But all I can do is look at myself, dressed in plain dark blue, not at all a holiday dress, one hand at my waist and the other under my chin. I am bending over my father-in-law, who sits brooding and alone at the head of the table, and I look as if I have no idea what to do with him.

At the opposite end of the studio, Nils turns away from the party and stands, looking glumly out the window. Father and son, both retreating from the festivities. Is Nils looking for Markus, at what was our first Christmas without him? But there is nothing to see, as the window is covered with ice. Even the painting's title, *Here Is Yuletide Again*, which Nils took from the Swedes' favourite holiday song, seems to stress the weariness in the "again."

But the Olssons are not weary at the prospect of seeing you and Lars over the holidays. Please consult your book and let us know a time when you can join us. At least for that day, we will try and forget the war, and rejoice in the company of friends.

Yours always,
Sofie

Sofie had decided to make something about the war. It was odd to try to communicate its merciless impersonality with something as domestic as a cushion, but that would be part of the point. The background would be black, with embroidery in innocent pinks and white. There would be shells, fire and tears, no comfort in the images.

She gave the cushion to Nils for his birthday. He looked at the shells exploding like holiday firecrackers and the flames like big tears. He took off his glasses and wiped them. Then he looked again. "Sofie," he said, "this is very good. Very, very good."

The work was clumsy, not from her usual impatience when it came to technique, but consciously, pointedly clumsy. If it had been painted by a French man instead of embroidered by a Swedish woman, Nils would have railed against it as a piece of modern art. Strange that he, who retreated more and more into the past in his own art, praised her modern efforts. This one especially, which was jarring in its juxtapositions of the cozy and the terrible. Perhaps he thought it was part of their bargain, that if she could not paint, he would at least admire her work on cloth. But, thinking about it later—after he had ceremoniously given the cushion pride of place on the sofa in the workroom—she doubted Nils had any sense that a bargain might have been called for.

Chapter Twenty-four

BIRGITTA WAS TO be a bridesmaid when her friend Hedy got married and Sofie was making her dress, a filmy white cotton batiste with a tucked bodice. Nils wanted to paint Sofie hemming the dress while Birgitta stood wearing it. The women protested that no one would hem a dress while the owner was in it, but Nils did not care, he liked the composition. He positioned them at one side of the picture, while the boxy Biedermeier sofa and table from their Falun parlour held the centre. On the table was a tray with cups nestled on their side, waiting to be filled from the copper chocolate pot.

"Nils, why would I be wearing a hat in my own parlour?" Sofie put up her hands, as if to unpin it. The hat was a wide-brimmed white straw, with a gauze scarf wrapped around the crown. In a long-sleeved dress and with her head down to attend to the hem, all that showed of Sofie were the sewing hands.

"That doesn't matter, it's good the way the white hat echoes the white dress."

"You mean, it's good the way the hat hides my face," she said.

Birgitta shot her father a glance, and Sofie and Nils laughed, to show her it was a comfortable old joke. Birgitta was in profile, her lovely bare arm and neck only slightly less white than her dress.

While they posed, Sofie holding up her needle and Birgitta look-ing down at her hem spread on her mother's lap, they talked about Sonja, who was coming home from art school for the midterm holiday. Curiously, Nils had raised very few objections to Sonja studying art, only insisting that she do it in Gothenburg and not in Stockholm. His resentment against the Academy still burned, but other than that, he seemed content with her choice—perhaps even half-proud. Did that mean that a daughter's talent for painting was different from a wife's?

Sofie's mind leaped from Sonja's arrival to Cecilia's latest letter. Forbidden to move, she addressed Birgitta without looking up. "I wonder if you girls would like to go to Stockholm when Sonja is here and see the new production of *A Doll's House* at the Svenska Teatern. Mrs. Vogt and Miss Gregorius saw it last week, and they thought it was very fine."

Nils and Birgitta spoke at the same time.

He said scornfully, "I'm quite sure they did," as if enjoying a production of *A Doll's House* confirmed his blackest thoughts about Cecilia and Miss Gregorius as well as Ibsen.

Birgitta said, "Oh, Mamma, *A Doll's House* is so old-fashioned!"

Sofie raised her eyebrows, invisible under her hat. She attended to Birgitta first.

"Miss Gregorius does not agree with you. She commented to Mrs. Vogt that the play is more than thirty-five years old, but the relationship between Nora and her husband is still being played out in houses all over Scandinavia every night."

Nils said, with even heavier emphasis, "Yes, she would say that."

"Whatever do you mean?"

"I only mean that it doesn't surprise me that Miss Gregorius, being a university graduate and apparently some kind of art his-torian, would sympathize with a story where a mother leaves her husband and young children. Keep your head down, please, Sofie. It was perfect before, when only the tip of your chin showed."

She left that one to Birgitta, who said, "Oh, Pappa!" with a fond, dismissive roll of her eyes. Sofie could see her thinking, *My father is a darling reactionary, and my mother speaks up for progressive ideas she doesn't practice in her own life.* Nils, like so many men, disliked Ibsen's heroine, and for him the play pressed on a particularly tender spot. She remembered him telling her in the early days of their marriage that when he came home at the end of the school day, his mother was always out, doing other people's laundry. He was so grateful, he said, that when he and their children came home, Sofie would always be there.

Without changing her position—she had been posing for her father since she was a toddler—Birgitta asked, "Pappa, do you think that Miss Gregorius and Mrs. Vogt have what the Americans call a Boston marriage?"

"A Boston marriage" was ambiguous, since it described two women who were closely bound and set up housekeeping together, with or without an erotic entanglement. Nils laughed, agreeably shocked at his daughter's quickness. Sofie was also shocked, and not agreeably. Where did Birgitta get these ridiculous ideas?

Nils said, "Well, if it's more than thirty-five years since Ibsen's Nora slammed the door, who knows what can happen these days? But Mrs. Vogt already has a Siljevik marriage."

Sofie said nothing. Birgitta's suspicions sprang from a young woman's overheated imagination, but she was encouraging her father in his wish to think the worst of educated women with careers.

The painting of Sofie and Birgitta was a diversion, but Nils was most occupied these days by a work that was as violent in its way as Sofie's war cushion. It was a monumental painting, destined in his mind for the upper landing of the National Museum, portraying a tragic event he had half-imagined from the Nordic past. The twelfth-century *Edda* had told the story of the Swedes sacrificing their king, Domald, in the hope of ending a famine. In Nils's version, the king was not captured but offered his life for the sake of his people. Having just thrown off his bearskin robe, he stood, nude, while his executioner, in a red cloak, held his knife behind his back. Noble and vulnerable, the king waited for death, his hand just touching his throat.

At one side, a writhing band of women were dressed like Samis, their patterned mittens, braided hair and anguished dance a strange melange of the folkloric and the horrific. One of them, a brown-haired woman who turned her distressed face to the viewer, looked like Sofie. At least she was not wielding a knife, Sofie thought, although other women in the painting wore knives, scissors and dangerous-looking tools at their waists that reminded her of the bride belt Lars Vogt had shown her years ago.

The museum committee wanted Nils to omit or soften the central motif, of the king sacrificing himself. Wounded to the quick, Nils threatened to stop work on the painting but, privately, Sofie thought the museum was being quite forbearing. After all, they had not commissioned this vast canvas—it was all Nils's idea. And they had not yet officially accepted it.

Askebo, 13 October 1918

My dear Cecilia,

I confess, and only to you, I am weary of riding the ups and downs as Nils torments himself over his painting of King Domald. The painting itself is beautiful and entirely painful. Of course, you have only to think of Kandinsky and Kokoschka, of cubism and futurism or, closer to home, the work of Isaac Grunewald and Sigrid Hjerten, to see that its combination of realism and romanticism is not the way to win over today's art world. As for the subject matter, I would not be surprised if the museum people find the ideas of ritual suicide and our stark Nordic past a little naive in 1918, if not sinister.

He takes it all so personally. I suppose that is because it *is* so personal. It is embarrassingly clear that he identifies with the king and his fate. By painting an unpalatable subject, he almost guarantees that his own career will have an end he sees as tragic. In one minute he crows that the Germans have bought 200,000 copies of his latest book, *When the Sun Shines*, and that so many soldiers carry it to the front, along with the New Testament, that it is almost standard equipment. (How indescribably sad to think of the Germans, or soldiers from any country, in their trenches poring over those serene pictures of home and family.) Then, in the next minute he is convinced that everyone is against him and his career is in ruins. I cannot imagine where this will end. I try to comfort without encouraging any more of these dead ends, but he is quick to spot that distinction.

Your friend always,
Sofie

Siljevik, 30 October 1918
Dear Sofie,

I am sorry about all this. If only it were possible for Nils to accept that he had his day—a beautiful, bright, shining day—and now we are living in a different one. I appreciate how hard it must be to stop expecting that each new work will capture the attention of the world, or at least the Swedish world. That is an ugly bridge almost every successful artist has to cross, when he is no longer the dernier cri. But, even if Nils's work is not going to be received with the rapture he has grown used to, some of it will live forever. And the same for Lars. People will not tire of Nils's watercolours of the

Askebo house and his portraits of Strindberg and
Selma Lagerlof, any more than they will of Lars's
engravings and the Siljevik paintings. Their pictures
will always be part of us.

Actually, Lars does not fret about his place now or
in the future. He is doggedly confident about his art. If
people prefer the work of the new artists, he is sure that
they are making a mistake, but he does not brood about
it. It is his ebbing strength that infuriates him.

About Nils, though. This is no help to you, it is only
telling you things you know already. And I am not an
artist, so I had better stop writing about matters I do not
understand. Just know that I am always ready to listen.
And to see you, either here or in Askebo.

Miss Gregorius is keeping us on our toes. She wants
so much information for the forthcoming museum that I
realize we need a catalogue. Rather to my surprise, I am
thinking of writing it.

Ever your friend,
Cecilia

Dear Cecilia,

*Forgive all that soul-baring. I feel quite guilty writing
about Nils in that way, but you will understand. I cannot
talk with any of the children about it, and obviously with
Nils least of all.*

*Our mothers would not approve. I can hear mine saying
that it is a wife's job to guard her husband's good name above
everything. But I am quite worried about Nils's state of mind,
and worry is a lonely business.*

*If my mother were here, I would assure her that Nils's
good name is safe with you!*

*You are quite right, there is not much help for it if Nils
cannot understand the part he has assigned himself in this sad
drama.*

But thank you.

She would not send that letter. There was nothing especially
wrong with it, but she had already said more than enough. And
Cecilia knew these things without being told. She imagined her
friend sitting very upright in her Louis XVI study and breaking the
seal on one of her letters. It took Sofie back to the first time she had
seen that study, on her first visit to Siljevik. The children had been
so young: Marianne barely ten, and Tilda and Felix not yet born.
More to the point, she, Sofie, had been young—even if people considered a woman in her thirties to be fully mature. Now, midway
through her fifties, she saw that wife who had visited Siljevik with
her husband and four children as green and ingenuous. If anyone
had told her then that the daunting Cecilia Vogt would become her
confidante, she would have laughed. It was an intimacy with strictly
defined limits, of course—whole areas of life were out of bounds—
but even so, the fact of it could still take her by surprise.

PART TWO

Prelude

JUNE 1901

LARS'S FRIEND NILS Olsson was bringing his family to Siljevik for the day. It was not terribly convenient, because Cecilia was busy ordering books for the village library and supervising the installation of more cupboards in the studio, but Lars had insisted on having the Olssons before he and Cecilia left for summer in the archipelago.

The visitors were all seated at the table on the porch by the time Cecilia joined them. She noticed, first, the bashful, curious boy, and his poised older sister, who looked around ten or eleven. Where did girls of that age get this precocious social awareness, while the boys stayed absorbed in their own obsessions? And there were two smaller girls, one only interested in the cinnamon rolls and the other only in her doll. Nils Olsson looked cheerful and a little jittery, an apparently indulgent paterfamilias on the watch for any lapses in politeness.

And Sofie: knitting a stocking without taking her eyes off the youngest girl, who was drinking from a glass her mother clearly regarded as too fragile. Sofie—Cecilia thought of her as "Sofie" although they were still at the Mrs.-Olsson-Mrs.-Vogt stage—dressed like a New Woman, in loose dresses, but she did not act like one. People said Nils Olsson did not want another artist in the house, so his wife had given up painting when they married. Perhaps that was all right, Cecilia thought. After all, she has five children. But perhaps it was not.

Lars was winning over Sonja, the older of the two smaller girls, by covering a sheet of paper with drawings of her doll driving the carriage, drinking coffee and reading to the children. Captivated, Sonja demanded more drawings and Lars, not for the first time, fell victim to his own charm. Cecilia found it hard to take her eyes off the smallest girl, Birgitta, who was trying to get the Vogts' dog Mouche to shake hands, but her duty lay with Sofie. After a few false starts, including the usual disparaging remarks about the Swedish climate and the late spring, the two women settled on gardens. Cecilia knew Sofie's natural, almost wild plantings from Nils's paintings. But Lars did not paint gardens, so Cecilia's rectangular beds, lined up with military precision on the broad front lawn, were new to Sofie. Looking at their formality through her guest's eyes, as they sat together on the porch, Cecilia said, "It is a French garden, I suppose. And yours reminds me of the English herbaceous borders, that look so relaxed and no doubt need a great deal of work."

"Which I never have the time to give them," Sofie said, "so the weeds outnumber the flowers. Whereas I cannot see a single weed in your perfect beds."

Cecilia thought, I hope she is not always so self-deprecating. She said, "You must come back later in the season, or in September, when the rose garden at the back of the house is at its best. I make a bit of a specialty of old-fashioned roses, and they give that garden a more informal look."

Their talk wandered to an early portrait of Sofie with Marianne, her first baby. Nils, who had been chatting with Lars at the other end of the table, turned to them at the mention of his portrait. He joked that, these days, Sofie accused him of painting her sun bonnets instead of her face. Cecilia suspected that this was a regular part of his repertoire, including a wife who laughed on cue. Making a show of extravagant devotion to his "darling muse," he fussed over cushions and drinks for her and fretted about her comfort.

Sofie seemed entertained by this, but when Nils was not drawing attention to her, she looked abstracted, the way she did in his paintings. Sofie's looks and the clothes she designed appealed to Cecilia—the advantage of beauty was unfair, but it was undeniable that it gave pleasure. And it was not only Sofie's beauty that drew Cecilia: there was her good-humoured calm and, perhaps most attractive of all, something enigmatic at the heart of her.

Lars led the tour of the house, he liked doing that. The two couples had a shared taste for Swedish antiquities and peasant handcrafts, but Cecilia could see that some of their collections, the silver and pewter, for instance, interested the Olssons less. Perhaps they found the house dark. Judging from Nils's paintings of their own house, it was filled with light as well as eccentric touches. She was curious to see it.

In the Great Hall, the children began playing Vikings under the high-pitched roof. That left Sofie free to walk the length of the room, admiring the weavings hung along the walls. But it was Cecilia's books that loosened her tongue. Lars occasionally mentioned Cecilia's first editions in his tour, but never the rows of English novels that had Sofie exclaiming and questioning. Both women loved Dickens, with all his faults, but that was only a start. They began trading likes and dislikes, opinions and recommendations. Sofie thought Charlotte Brontë was a far better novelist than her sister Emily, and Cecilia held strongly to the opposite opinion. But both agreed that the third sister, Anne Brontë, was undervalued, especially her novel *The Tenant of Wildfell Hall*.

Bored by this talk of novels, Lars and Nils had moved on to the bedrooms. By the time their wives joined them in Lars's bedroom, the men were standing in front of Nils's portrait of himself and his nude model, Margit.

"Lovely thing," Lars said, nodding at the painted Margit as if she could hear.

Cecilia thought, A painter and his nude model was a typical subject for Lars, not Nils Olsson. But one of Nils's more characteristic paintings, of his house and children, would not look so at home in the manly retreat that was Lars's bedroom.

After lunch, Cecilia walked Sofie across the graveyard that bordered the garden, into the village church. As always, the church's bright whiteness and severity daunted Cecilia. The synagogue in Stockholm had a brown coziness, like a parlour, but there was no comfort here.

Sofie murmured something about how exposed she felt in the space and light. Surprised, Cecilia thought: She senses it too. This constant burden of looking into one's heart. The wish to forget, if only temporarily—which the austerity of the place made impossible. What did Sofie want to forget? Cecilia did not know, but clearly there was more to this woman than embroidered cuffs and hand-knitted stockings for her husband. She turned to smile in fellow-feeling, and saw that her guest's eyes were filled with tears.

"Mrs. Olsson, can I help you? What is it?" She unlatched one of the pews, which opened with a small, complaining wheeze, in case Sofie wanted to sit down.

But no, Sofie said it was nothing, she was sorry that she was being so silly. She did not need to sit. Cecilia did not know what to say, so there was silence. Finally, Sofie said that she was weaning her baby, and it made her tearful. She apologized again.

Cecilia thought, Well, perhaps that is it. Neither she nor Sofie had anything more to say on the subject, so she retreated to the architecture, pointing to the preacher's golden pulpit, high up on a column.

"It is the only colour in the church. No wonder my husband prefers the churches in Spain and Italy."

In the early evening, in the hall, the Olssons' son, Markus, played an Irish song on his fiddle, while the two older girls sang the words.

When I was single I wore a plaid shawl
Now that I'm married I've nothing at all.
He came up our alley and he whistled me out
But the tail of his shirt from the trousers hung out.
Ah but still I love him I'll forgive him
I'll go with him wherever he goes.

Another unruly husband, another forgiving wife, Cecilia thought. She tried without success to think of a song or a poem in which a husband forgives a demanding, irresponsible wife. After the Olssons extracted a promise that the Vogts would return the visit, and the Vogts insisted that the Olssons must visit again when the roses were in bloom, the guests left in a blur of sweaters, shawls and tired children.

Once they were alone, Cecilia and Lars sat for a while in the Hall. They had left Sofie's birthday present for Lars, a cushion, on an easy chair. Cecilia straightened it and said, "She studied with Malmstrom at the Academy of Fine Arts, and now she embroiders cushions."

Lars didn't agree with her dismissal. "No, I meant what I said to her. She has talent as a designer."

Cecilia looked again at the cushion. Its balance of the usual motifs with the unexpected, its slightly off-centre sensibility. Perhaps he was right. He usually was about things like that. It could be interesting to see more of Sofie Olsson.

A few days later, a thank-you note arrived from Sofie. After the usual compliments, she asked an abrupt question.

"Do you ever look back on your wedding day and feel surprised at how your life turned out? I was so young, and so sure that Nils and I were making a new kind of marriage, something that my parents, for all their care for each other, hadn't known. But perhaps they too thought they were at the start of a new thing. Maybe everyone who gets married thinks that."

Quickly, Cecilia put the note face down on her desk, as if that would erase it. Surely she does not think that I would discuss whatever people may whisper about Lars and me. Then she told herself, Your imagination is running ahead of your common sense. You are too thin-skinned, at least on this subject. She read the letter again. Poor woman, she thought, this is something to do with her. I wonder whether it is related to those overflowing eyes in the church.

Surprised at how your life turned out? She was not sure that was a useful question even to ask yourself, let alone another person. Probably Mrs. Olsson meant it innocently enough, but this was a bud that needed nipping.

CECILIA

Chapter Twenty-five

1888

ALTHOUGH CECILIA HAD spent her life with paintings, beginning at her parents' house in Stockholm and after that with Lars, as a child she loved lists more than paintings. Her parents said that when she was about six, she began classifying their art, sorting it into oils, watercolours, drawings, etchings and engravings, with separate pieces of paper for each type, before giving up. There was simply too much of it. Just as she would think she had finished a room, she would find another stack of engravings in a drawer.

Her grandfather Isaksson collected the Swedish painters and made a specialty of pictures with Viking themes. Even the smallest ladies' sitting room in her parents' house had paintings that climbed the walls from the wainscoting to the ceiling. When her widowed mother moved from the house on Drottninggatan to a big flat on the Stureplan, Bukowskis auctioned off more than two hundred pictures.

It was the Isakssons' fondness for paintings that first brought Lars to their house. Cecilia's sister Natalie's house, more exactly, which was a flat on Master Samuelsgatan. In the winter of 1888, Natalie commissioned a rising star from Dalarna named Lars Vogt to paint her son Erik. The young painter had recently made a sensational debut in the Student Exhibition at the Academy of Fine Arts with a watercolour of a pensive woman in a mourning veil. Not only had the reigning art critic, Carl Rupert Nyblom, praised it in the *Dagens Nyheter*, he'd engaged the student to paint his son. Stockholm society took up the young man and, flush with commissions, he left the Academy without a diploma. At the time, it looked like hubris. In retrospect, there was nothing more the Academy could teach him.

"Cecilia, could you possibly help me out?" Natalie had asked her when the family gathered for Friday night dinner at the Stureplan flat. "Erik needs some entertainment while Mr. Vogt paints him, and I have meetings for the Orphanage Benefit almost every afternoon now."

Cecilia agreed that she would go to Natalie's two afternoons a week after Erik's nap. On her first visit, when he woke and discovered Aunt Cecilia, the two-year-old was more than happy to build bridges and towers on the parlour floor with her. His face clouded over only when Mr. Vogt entered the room: he already knew what that meant. Cecilia got to her feet and wiped her hands on the sides of her skirt, although Natalie's floors were impeccable. She and the artist shook hands.

"Mr. Vogt. How nice to meet you."

"Miss Isaksson. Your sister told me you would be here to amuse Erik. I'm afraid Erik finds me very boring, so we both thank you."

He was tall and serious, not from shyness but because he had work to do.

"Well, better save your gratitude until we see if I can make things any easier for you. Erik, would you like me to read you a story while Mr. Vogt paints your picture?" Not a flicker of enthusiasm. "Should I bring out your puppet theatre and put on a little play for you?"

What Erik wanted was to slam his toy coaches and streetcars into his mother's gilt-edged commodes, or to move the Turkish runners aside and slide on the glassy floors, not to sit perfectly still while a man painted him. No wonder he trembled on the edge of a pout in the finished picture.

Gradually, Cecilia found a rhythm that worked—short sittings interspersed with frequent treats and breaks. Later, when she told the story of meeting Lars, she always said, "Lars painted, and I made a fool of myself to distract Erik, with mimes and silly games and outrageous stories." And Lars always said, "I was more diverted than Erik was by this uninhibited girl who worked so hard to keep him still."

People often remarked that Lars was a cross between a yokel and a gentleman. He could have enormous savoir faire and courtliness and then erupt without warning into a joke fit for a barnyard. But in those days, when he was still making his way in the world, the gentleman prevailed. He called Cecilia "the charming aunt" and told Erik, "If your lovely caretaker permits, we will stop soon for a cup of chocolate." Cecilia wasn't fooled. She saw, at the edges of his politesse, something brusque and coarsely woven. Something unpredictable.

They were both twenty-one.

After they married, the only painting by Lars that she kept in her bedroom was that watercolour of Erik, with his dark blond curls and weary, long-suffering gaze.

When the picture was finished, Cecilia and Lars began meeting in town in the daytime. The evening would have required some kind of chaperone, and besides, Cecilia was busy in the evenings, with family gatherings and the opera and theatre. She had mentioned to Mr. Vogt that she frequently went to the National Museum on Wednesday afternoon with her cousin Eva Bonnier. The cousins were there on a miserable February day, with the sky and the Norrstrom channel both a sullen grey. Eva was poring over some Watteau drawings. Cecilia was looking out the window at the windy channel, where the boats were knocking against each other in the harbour and people hurried by, their faces huddled into their chests.

A voice behind Eva said, "It's a very good example, but I think you'll find an even better one over here in the corner."

Eva was not pleased. She had graduated from the Academy of Fine Arts and she did not need the guidance of a boy from Dalarna with a German name. Much less one who was having a fly-by-night success because he had dropped out of the Academy. But Mr. Vogt strolled with them through the eighteenth-century galleries, as if they had invited him, and gradually he mollified Eva by taking her opinion seriously. Or at least seeming to. They reached a truce, finally, because they both loved the domestic details in Chardin's paintings. Afterwards, the three of them walked up the street to the Grand Hotel and drank coffee.

It seemed that Wednesday afternoons were also a convenient time for Mr. Vogt to visit the museum, and the cousins met him there more than a few times. While Cecilia listened to Eva praising or disparaging the paintings on the walls, she eyed the doors, wondering if Mr. Vogt would make one of his sudden, almost silent appearances.

As spring approached, Cecilia and Lars walked in the Djurgarden. She would spend the morning working at Aunt Rosa's clothing depot near Strandvagen, and afterwards it was a simple thing to meet him on the other side of the bridge for a stroll along the canal or on a wooded path. One day they went to Rosendals cafe, and ate thin cardamom cookies while they traded biographies.

Rumour had already told her the outlines of his. Lars's mother was a country girl who had gone to work in a brewery in Uppsala and had a child after a liaison with a Bavarian brewer. His father, whom he never met, sent money for Lars's school fees and died when his son was twelve. Now Mr. Vogt filled in some of the details, with a detachment that was almost amused, as if he knew a mythology was building and he did not want to disturb it.

"I was born in a stable," he said, straight-faced.

Cecilia nodded, as if most people she knew were born in a stable.

"My grandparents' farmhouse was full," he continued, "because the fur skins we needed for warmth in the winter had just arrived. My mother knew her time had come, so she went where there was quiet and space."

His birth certificate described him with the harsh word *oakta*, meaning not only illegitimate but shoddy and false. This indictment coloured much of his childhood, but he only talked about that to Cecilia long afterwards. In the early days, he stayed close to the facts.

"My father's employers punished his indiscretion by sending him to a brewery in Finland," he said, tracing the rim of his saucer with his fingers and sometimes pinching it, as if he were modelling it from clay. "My mother's parents brought me up."

"Where was your mother?"

"Farming is never easy in Siljevik, my village, because the soil is rocky. That, and a series of failed harvests when I was a boy, made us desperately poor. The first thing I remember is bursting into tears when my mother walked into the main room of the farmhouse carrying her suitcase. Like many of the villagers, she had to leave for work—in her case, back to the brewery in Uppsala. She stayed there until I was in my teens."

Cecilia pictured a little boy begging his mother not to leave. She asked about his grandparents.

"They were strict. They were touched by the religious revival that swept through Sweden in those years, and games and dancing were forbidden. The only music they permitted was hymn singing. They took me to Bible meetings, where it seemed that the shame of my birth meant that I was damned forever."

Now he was moving the plate with cookie crumbs around on the wooden table. From what she could see of his face, she suspected he had strayed into territory he meant to avoid.

"And yet," he said, righting himself, "my grandparents loved me. At one point, my grandfather was ready to sell his summer pasture to pay my school fees. I wanted to help as much as I could, and I learned to sew and knit as well as doing the usual farm chores."

As a boy, he loved three things above all—whittling animals and people from small pieces of wood, the high summer pasture where he lived in a cabin near the cattle, and his mother, whom he called Mona, the word for mother in the Siljevik dialect.

"Everyone assumed I would be a carver," he said, "because I sculpted birds and rabbits with a big, clumsy knife. But when I saw a friend's set of watercolours, I changed my course."

He was fifteen when he entered the Academy.

"Although we were not supposed to work while studying, I did odd bits of carpentry and painting portraits of the dead to support myself. My speed at portraits started there, when I raced the clock to capture the dead person's likeness before they nailed the coffin shut."

It sounded to Cecilia like the hero's lonely determination in one of Hans Christian Andersen's mawkish stories. But something about Lars Vogt—his confidence, perhaps—made her sure that, unlike Andersen's heroes, he would have a happy ending.

Cecilia had learned her family history in the way most children did, through a combination of stories intended for her and other, more interesting ones that she overheard. She added to that an interest in the family wills—they were, after all, lists—that were kept in the easily opened secret drawer in her father's desk. At the end of the eighteenth century, her great-grandfather, David Isaksson, had perfected a way to print patterns on cotton so that their colours did not fade. That transformed him from a small businessman into a manufacturer. When he died, in 1811, he left sixty pounds of coffee beans, ten pairs of linen sheets, twenty-two shirts, ten pewter plates, a pair of silver shoe buckles and a walking stick with an embossed silver knob. To the end, his favourite foods were salted peas and gefilte fish made from Pomeranian pike.

Her grandfather, Joakim Isaksson, died in the 1840s, leaving four cut-glass mustard containers, eleven dozen plates, three punch bowls, six carafes for vodka and three cummerbunds. (He was a dapper man.) Her father carried on the family business, now called Ideal Textiles, and his Stockholm factory printed calico as cheaply and quickly as possible. He died when Cecilia was fifteen, leaving three houses, eighteen million kronor and uncounted art.

Cecilia's grandparents were Rakel and Joakim Isaksson, Sara and Moses Magnus. Like many of Stockholm's Jews, they descended from Germans who had arrived in the eighteenth century. Wanting to be as Swedish as possible, they gave Cecilia's parents Swedish names, Carl-David and Fanny. Her own generation kept their Jewishness for their middle names—Cecilia Rebecka, Natalie Leah, Fredrik Nathan.

Facts like those were the logical starting point of her story, Cecilia thought, as she accepted a second cup of coffee from the waiter. But those were not the kind of things she wanted to tell Mr. Vogt, or not just yet. Like most Swedes, and especially those from the country, he knew almost nothing about Jews, so she started with trifles. As her parents did, she minimized the differences between gentiles and Jews.

"Of course, we didn't have Easter eggs or Christmas trees or Christmas hams at home," she told him, "but we are quite used to them in the houses of our friends."

"Are you telling me that Tomten never left you any Christmas gifts for being a good child?" Mr. Vogt asked. He shook his head, in mock pity.

"He never did," she smiled, to show it was nothing. "But when my nephews complained that he never visited their house on Klarabergsgatan, he left them a few token presents."

We shrugged at things like that, Cecilia thought. If we did not practice a certain nonchalance in the gentile world, we would never thrive. On the surface, there was not all that much difference between them and other prosperous Stockholmers. She and her friends lived in roomy, high-ceilinged apartments or houses on

Drottninggatan and its cross-streets, borrowed the latest books from Bonniers' lending library, read the *Dagens Nyheter* and ate saffron buns with their coffee on the feast of Lucia. In the summer, they rented big wooden houses on the archipelago outside Stockholm. Taking the ferry from Stockholm to the archipelago, Grandfather Isaksson had worn a navy cap and the naval insignia on his jacket— not that the Royal Swedish Navy accepted Jews, but he had the typical Stockholmer's love affair with water and boats.

Just below the surface, of course, Cecilia understood that her family was different from their gentile neighbours. Until 1859, Jews had not been allowed to attend the public schools. Until 1863, they could not marry gentiles. They were only allowed to become full Swedish citizens in 1870. The Isakssons preferred not to make too much of those milestones, but Cecilia learned about them by osmosis.

"By the time I was twelve or so," she said to Mr. Vogt, changing the subject, "I wanted to understand my father's business. How many bolts of cloth was he manufacturing? What markets did they go to? Would some of these new looms and presses increase the output? My brother looked at me oddly when I pressed these questions on Pappa. Fredrik wanted to talk about pretty girls, the boat they used in the archipelago in the summer, and the change in the menu at Hasselbacken. But it was Fredrik who would take over the business."

"What about your parents? Did they look at you oddly?"

"Pappa was only too happy to talk with me about his plans. And Mamma looked proud, thinking, no doubt, what a good wife I would make some ambitious businessman someday."

She smiled, almost apologetically, and after a second he did too.

Cecilia noticed that charm has different faces. When people describe someone as charming they usually mean the person who tells amusing stories and takes centre stage easily, as if it were his natural place.

You leave an evening with this type and think how delightful he is. With another sort of person, you leave thinking, I must be more interesting than I thought I was. The charm of this second person is that they draw you out and make *you* feel charming. There is a third type of charmer, more difficult to describe. This kind neither dominates nor draws out the other person. Something about their physical presence, the way they incline their body toward you or look at you, the way they simply *are*, is beguiling. That was Lars Vogt. It was not what the English call animal magnetism (although he had that too), or simply a question of living easily in his body (although he did). It was more that he had a particular quality of relaxed attention. Without seeming to exert himself, he convinced Cecilia that her annual birthday excursion as a child to the marionette theatre or the family Sunday dinners at Hasselbacken were singularly interesting. She preferred hearing how he rolled out big wheels of *tunnbrod* with his grandmother, baked them on the farmhouse fire and then dipped the thin, crisp bread in pans of cream. They each found the other exotic.

She told herself she wasn't deceiving Mamma by not mentioning her meetings with Mr. Vogt. She was simply not worrying her mother with trifles. As long as it was in the open air or a relatively public place in the daytime, a young lady was free to meet friends. And when Mamma asked her about her day, Cecilia had plenty to say about the clothing depot and Aunt Rosa's flyaway mind.

"It's infuriating. She needs to make an inventory of every donation that comes in, separated out into skirts, shirts, jackets, trousers and so forth, with a rough guess about the sizes. Then when a man or a family comes in, we could make up a box for them, and cross the items off the inventory. It's very simple. But everything is harumscarum, nothing is sorted, and Aunt Rosa rushes around, exclaiming at the sad state of every single person who has been forced off the farm and come to town looking for work. It takes ages to find a girl's skirt or a pair of warm socks."

"But darling," Mamma would say, "what a good idea. Why don't you tell your aunt you'll set up an inventory for her?"

Cecilia expected that eventually someone would see her strolling in the Djurgarden with Mr. Vogt and remark on it to Mamma. And then she would figure out what to say. But before that happened, Mr. Vogt suggested that they visit Professor Hazelius's collection of peasant objects, and she had to tell Mamma. The new museum was at 72 Drottninggatan, a few blocks from their house and right in the middle of the shops where Mamma did her afternoon errands.

She did look a little taken aback, but not for the reason Cecilia expected.

"Really? Hazelius? Isn't he the man who has collected milking stools from all over Sweden?"

"I don't know. But Mr. Vogt says his collection is extraordinary."

"What can be extraordinary about a milking stool from every province? I don't know why I think he has only one from each province. Perhaps he has even more than one."

That possibility seemed to move Professor Hazelius in her mind from a harmless eccentric to something more pathological. She widened her eyes and set down her embroidery.

"Why don't you bring Mr. Vogt here afterwards? All those things will probably be very dusty, and you'll want some refreshment."

Sofie said something about Mr. Vogt being busy with his commissions. She knew he would be happy to have coffee and cake with Mamma, but she wanted to keep him to herself a while longer.

A few days later, on a day in early summer when the Norrstrom glinted in the sun, she and Mr. Vogt made their way down the commercial blocks of Drottninggatan. At the end of the street they could see the palace, but the buildings on their side of the river were sober storefronts with just enough cut-stone trimmings to show that the businesses they housed were successful.

"Hazelius is a professor of Nordic languages," Mr. Vogt told her. "He travels in Dalarna during the summers, and he likes watching the people around Lake Siljan setting off on Sundays in their church-boats."

In those days she knew very little about the provinces, nor did they interest her much.

"What is a church-boat?"

"It is how people in the remote coves travel to a bigger place that has a church, for Sunday service. Each settlement has its own rowboat, big enough to accommodate the whole village. One day, Hazelius watched people boarding their boat to go to Leksand and he noticed a woman carrying an ordinary purse instead of the traditional embroidered waist bag. Another wore a modern jacket, without the folded blanket in which women hid their hymn books. Hazelius thought, This is all going to die. All these ancient ways and things. He decided that he must preserve them while he could. He began by buying the folk costumes that were just on the point of being abandoned and moved on to the contents of farmhouses when a family died out or, more often, when poverty drove them to the cities or to America."

Professor Hazelius's collection was kept in a stone building that looked like all the others on the block. Even though Mr. Vogt had prepared her, she never could have imagined what waited behind the plain door with the small, hand-lettered sign that said "Nordic Museum." Professor Hazelius had not only acquired things that most people, like her mother, did not consider beautiful or interesting, but his way of displaying them was something new under the sun. Cecilia was used to the paintings hung from floor to ceiling in the National Museum. When the Isakssons visited a collector, they would be shown his Wunderkammer, a room whose glass cases were crammed with everything from ostrich eggs encrusted with silver to intricate carvings on walnut shells. But the professor had taken his spinning wheels and bed-hangings and tables and furnished whole rooms as realistically as he could, so that it was as if she and Mr. Vogt had walked into a farmhouse in Skane or a carpenter's house in Ystad. It was like catching a grown man methodically building a life-size dollhouse. And he'd even added the dolls, wax figures who wore the leather apron of Gagnef or the short jacket of Floda, embroidered with woollen blossoms.

Cecilia had never met a woman who cared about waist bags or earthenware jugs, much less a man. But Hazelius's things reminded Mr. Vogt of his mother and grandparents.

"Hello," he greeted a rough blanket woven in browns and reds. "My grandmother had one something like this."

She stared at its straightforward design of diamonds alternating with stripes and chevrons. She was willing to find this, and Professor Hazelius's other things, appealing or impressive or splendid, but mostly she didn't. For her, the Nordic Museum was another chance to stand next to Mr. Vogt, to listen to his voice, which sounded like a confidential whisper no matter how loudly he spoke, and to earn his approving look when she could summon up some honest praise. The more refined a piece was, the easier it was for her to admire it. When they looked at some of the fringes the Dalarna women made for their hand towels and curtains, she murmured something about the delicacy of cobwebs. She knew it was a cliche, but Mr. Vogt was pleased.

As for him, the less delicate the better. Once nostalgia brought him to a piece, he would begin appraising its line or the unknown maker's canny ways with a limited palette.

"Look at the way this one has used the swell of the pitcher for the face he's painted on it," he would say, rounding his hands in the air. "He knew what he was doing."

The Nordic Museum became one of their regular haunts. One day they stopped in front of an infant's shirt, which Professor Hazelius had put on a most unconvincing doll lying in a carved cradle. The loose shirt, simply embroidered with rosebuds at the neck and wrists, was eloquent. Had a girl embroidered it for her first child, dreading the peril of childbirth but hoping that she and her child might be two of the lucky ones? Had more than one baby slept in its fine white wool?

She pored over it, wanting to touch it but knowing that was not allowed. Mr. Vogt must have seen something in her eyes. Just for a second, he covered her gloved hand with his bare one. He almost never wore gloves in Stockholm, which he said was like a hothouse compared to Siljevik. Then he spoke quickly, a rare sign of shyness.

"Shouldn't we be Cecilia and Lars? Miss Isaksson and Mr. Vogt sound so unfriendly."

She found his face, with his wide-set eyes and short, straight nose, very German. Very beautiful. His square hands and tapering fingers. The way his shoulders filled up his coat. If they moved to first names, it would end the pretense that they were merely friends. She nodded. Whenever she thought back to that moment, she saw the two of them on either side of the cradle. An embroidered baby shirt from Visby had sealed their fate.

Chapter Twenty-six

1889–1893

SOMETIMES LARS SAID it was her blue eyes that had drawn him. More often, he claimed it was her laugh. People said her laugh was bigger than she was. Her brother and her aunt Rosa, and no doubt others, thought it was horrid. Lars liked it. He said it was like being in a perfectly calm, tidy room that was suddenly overtaken by a racket.

The Isakssons' Swedishness and gentile first names did not mean that they celebrated the feast day of the saint for whom they were named. But name days were important in Lars's village and on November 22, the feast of Saint Cecilia, he gave her a letter opener he had carved, with her profile in bas-relief and her initials looping underneath it. The profile, almost impossibly detailed, showed her heavy-lidded eye and the tendril of hair that swung loose at the back of her neck. She ran her finger over and over its tiny perfection, but only in her bedroom. She did not show it to Mamma, or anyone else.

Perhaps because the Isakssons rarely went, perhaps because their going was usually timed to a holiday and a family party, Cecilia liked going to services at the Stora Synagogue on Wahrendorffsgatan. The building was like a big square cake with white frosting, banded with gold-and-white stripes. Whenever members of the congregation got together, someone was bound to complain that it looked too much like a church. Then someone else would say that, on the contrary, the architect, Mr. Scholander, had modelled it on the "Assyrian style." Cecilia had never met anyone who knew what that meant, but it sounded better to the congregation than Gothic or Romanesque. She knew the synagogue didn't look like a church because churches had spires.

Inside, it was painted gold and soft brown, with brocade hangings in the same colours, pattern on intricate pattern, rich but homey—as if God had the taste of an indulgent grandmother whose candy dish was always full. Cecilia loved the solemn moment when they pulled back the curtain on the altar to reveal the Torah scrolls with their silver crowns. The dark blue background on which the scrolls were propped was painted with golden stars and, although it was morning, it looked as if someone had opened a window on a starry night sky.

The Stora Synagogue had an organ, something the members' forefathers had never known. And now some of the hymns they sang had melodies that sounded more like those of the Swedish Church than the sinuous Eastern tunes that undulated like the stems of Pappa's nasturtiums. Old Mr. Eliason shook his head about the organ, but Aunt Rosa said, "An organ is nothing. The Jews in Gothenburg have a Catholic choirmaster!" The Gothenburg Jews were always ahead of the Stockholm Jews.

Pappa and Fredrik sat on the main floor where a little sloping compartment in front of them was labelled "Carl-David Isaksson." Inside the compartment was Pappa's black velvet skullcap and his tallis. With ease, although he only did it a few times a year, Pappa swung the black-and-white tallis over his jacket and the shawl seemed to know what to do. It crumpled, swooped and clung, transforming a Swedish businessman who was praying a stone's throw from Stockholm's music theatre into a desert tribesman.

Seated between her mother and Natalie, Cecilia looked down from the women's balcony, where a rounded iron railing wrapped around three sides of the synagogue. Its design was like the lace mantillas Spanish women wore. She and Natalie boasted to Fredrik, We are above you, that means we're better. Fredrik claimed that he was better, because he was closer to the ark. No one told her until later that women sat in that filigree cage because they were too tempting, too distracting, for men to see while they were supposed to be praying. Lars would have found that very sensible.

When Cecilia began learning English in school, she and her classmates had struggled with *Our Village* by Miss Mitford. But once English became easier they read more entertaining books, and now she was a habitué of her Bonnier cousins' lending library, which stocked the latest titles from England, France, Germany and Sweden. If someone had blindfolded her, she would have known she was in Bonniers' from the sound of the bell attached to the door, with its slight shudder at the end of the clang, and the shuffle of the clerk, Mr. Eklof. He made his way slowly from the back room through the mingled smell of glue, paper, leather and toilet water to the oak counter where she rested her gloves.

"Good morning, Mr. Eklof. I'd like to borrow *Wuthering Heights*, please."

"I believe it is out, Miss Isaksson," he said, looking doleful. "But I'll just look."

He consulted his ledger.

"Why, no, we have it, returned the day before yesterday. But . . . but it was you who returned it."

"Yes."

There was no point explaining her need to read and reread.

Although he seemed to regret the necessity, Mr. Eklof was running his finger deliberately down the B's, where the Brontës' titles were listed with their borrowers. Speaking of her in the third person, he said, "Miss Isaksson likes the Brontë sisters' work."

"Yes. I like all that emotion and property."

He nodded, wrote down her name and went off to fetch the book and some brown paper and string.

Thinking of Lars, she began a mental list of fictional couples with disparate fortunes.

1. The maidservant in Richardson's novel *Pamela*, who marries her wealthy employer, Mr. B.
2. Jane and Elizabeth Bennet in *Pride and Prejudice*, who move up the social scale by allying themselves with Mr. Bingley and Mr. Darcy.
3. Fanny Price, from Jane Austen's *Mansfield Park*, who marries her cousin Edmund, from the rich side of the family.
4. Another master–servant couple, Jane Eyre and Mr. Rochester. Although, with Charlotte Brontë's usual originality, Jane comes into an inheritance before she accepts Mr. Rochester, now blind and missing a hand. In other words, she makes them more equal.
5. Amy March in *Little Women*, who marries her rich neighbour Laurie.

But it was easy to find wealthy men marrying poorer women. Wealthy women marrying poor men were hard to come by, and that inequality was often a sign of corruption. Dickens, for example, seemed to favour couples whose fortunes were roughly equal, and fallen. Little Dorrit gives up her inheritance rather than hurt Arthur Clenham, and Dickens rewarded the couple by making Clenham rich by the end of the book. Less romantic, George Eliot solved the problem—but why was she thinking of it as a problem?—in *Middlemarch* by having Dorothea Brooke renounce her fortune to marry Will Ladislaw, and no rescue was forthcoming. And, of course, there was *Wuthering Heights*. Cecilia found the passion and social inequality between Catherine and Heathcliff exciting, but finally there was too much madness in the book for her.

Her family's money and Lars's poverty worried her, but she had to trust that Lars's talent would narrow that gulf.

Now that the family had judged Erik's portrait a success, Mamma had mentioned a few times that perhaps Mr. Vogt should paint Cecilia. Mamma was capable of a momentary enthusiasm that she later forgot, but when she said something two or three times, she generally acted on it.

When it became clear that she was persisting with the idea of the portrait, Cecilia knew it would be wrong to take more advantage of her innocence. She and Lars had to tell her how things were. In fact, it was not a question of telling, it was a question of Lars asking her brother for her hand. When he went into the parlour with Fredrik, Mamma assumed they were settling the price of the portrait. Cecilia took her mother into the little family sitting room and explained. Her mother's face went blank with pure astonishment, followed rapidly by a combination of fascination and something softer. Guileless, she loved a shocking story, preferably also a romantic one. Like almost every woman, she felt Lars's appeal. Then reality set in. She had been a widow for six years, determined to honour what she knew would have been her husband's wishes. The Isakssons' liking for art did not mean they imagined their daughter marrying a painter.

Lars was having a harder time in the parlour, Cecilia was sure. After that first discussion, she insisted that the four of them meet together. It was silly to imagine that the men could decide this. Fredrik tried to impersonate Pappa during their meetings, but without his warmth. Later it seemed strange to Cecilia that Mamma and

Fredrik made nothing of the fact that Lars was a Christian. She cared more than they did that she would be leaving the family's comfortable Jewishness—comfortable, no doubt, because it was so loose and undemanding. It was not Lars's religion that concerned her mother and brother, it was his poverty. Fredrik mentioned his illegitimacy, of course, but even he seemed to realize that this was not an insurmountable obstacle for a painter.

Privately, she insisted to Fredrik that it wasn't her money that interested Lars. Fredrik probably disagreed, at least in the beginning. But Lars never asked anything from her family, and as it turned out, he never needed their money.

The four of them had a few long meetings in which Mamma alternated between looking troubled and fond, and occasionally teared up. Fredrik remained stern. The secret engagement, just within the immediate family, was Lars's idea. There would be no public engagement until he had proven that he could support Cecilia in a fashion that Mamma and Fredrik considered proper. If he had not accomplished this within a certain time, the engagement would be broken. Then they bickered about how long that would be.

"One year," said Fredrik.

No, that was impossibly short.

"Two, then," said Mamma, relenting.

"Lars is not just trying to establish his reputation in Stockholm," Cecilia argued. "He will have an international career, and that will take time." She continued, talking about the gradual growth of an artist's career as if she understood those things. Five years, she bargained.

"Five years, darling," Mamma said, patting the circles under her eyes with her handkerchief. "You will be twenty-six in five years."

"You mean I will be too old then to make a more advantageous marriage," Cecilia said shortly. "That does not worry me at all. Lars and I will marry then, if not before."

Lars stuck to one point, that he would work immensely hard to win her hand. He and Cecilia prevailed, because Mamma yielded. On July 2, 1889, they were secretly engaged.

Although most Swedish painters began their careers with a sojourn in France, Lars chose to try his luck in England and Spain. Once he had left Stockholm, Mamma suggested, brightly, that Cecilia needed a diversion. Wouldn't she like to spend a month or two in Baden-Baden? How hopeful she is, Cecilia thought. As if the tedious one-two-three, one-two-three waltz of life there—sipping the disgusting sulphurous waters, stepping gingerly into the mosaic-lined baths, drinking coffee and eating cake in the Kurhaus while admiring the fancywork of other ladies and insisting that one's own was very simple in comparison, making polite conversation with boring young officers—would not make her long all the more ardently for Lars. To please Mamma, she agreed, that would be nice. She and Mamma went to Baden-Baden, and she longed for Lars more keenly than ever.

For the first year or so of Lars's absence, Mamma and Fredrik clung to the strong possibility that he would not earn enough money to support Cecilia. But Cecilia knew better. He was soon busy in London with commissions from Swedish expatriates and wealthy Londoners. In Spain, his ambition was to paint the king, and he got as far as the Duchess of Alba. His engagement to Cecilia was announced publicly on July 2, 1893, four years to the day after their secret agreement.

Once it was official, Lars took Cecilia to Siljevik to meet his mother. It was like travelling to another century, and almost another country. The village was not particularly charming, being just as flat as Lake Siljan, which it bordered. There was a fine, austere church and not much else of interest.

Mona, Lars's mother, showed Cecilia the parts of the local dress—a black skirt, always, with different-coloured aprons depending on the occasion or the time of the church year. Red for weddings and christenings, blue for funerals and Lent, green for spring and summer. The bonnet strings were important: unmarried women wore red-and-white ones, married women blue-and-white. To Cecilia, all this was like penetrating a secret room hidden behind a mirror or painting. Smiling inquiringly at Cecilia to see if she understood, Mona used the dialect words for the colours. She had not spoken Swedish until she went to work in Uppsala, and her Swedish vocabulary was still best when it came to brewing terms. She and Lars always spoke dialect with each other.

Finally, Lars painted the portrait Mamma had wanted. It was a watercolour of Cecilia in her bride's dress, an ivory figured silk, with an overlay of glass beads. It was rather sentimental, she supposed, the bride in profile, her eyes cast down as she contemplated her new station. The dress was made by Stockholm's best dressmaker, Mme Akkerman. Mamma had some extravagant thoughts of Worth or another Paris couturier, but Cecilia and Fredrik agreed that Mme Akkerman was quite good enough. As for Lars's wedding suit, Mamma and Fredrik assumed that he would buy it at Uncle Goran's shop, the Englishman's Tailor. They were perhaps a little hurt when Lars told them he had already had his suit made by a real English tailor, in London. And perhaps a little impressed.

They married in September, in a civil ceremony at the Stockholm Town Hall. The synagogue would not have accepted Lars, of course, nor would a church have married Cecilia. So there was no chuppah to stand under, and no crown, which the Swedish Church lent to its brides. Pretty customs both, but they did not miss them. Mamma gave a dinner the night before at Hasselbacken, and a reception after the ceremony in her flat. Next day, she made good use of her handkerchief at the train station, alternating between waving with it and wiping her tears. When Cecilia and Lars settled into their seats, as the train slid off to Paris, they reached for each other's hand. They had done it.

We have come to the end of the novel, Cecilia thought. Now what?

Chapter Twenty-seven

1893–1895

SHE KEPT A picture from their honeymoon, taken in a photography studio in Constantinople. What a shame that the backdrop was a conventional scene of trees, not the Hagia Sophia or some other extraordinary sight from that mirage of a city. Wearing a bowler hat and carrying a cane, hooking his hand in her arm, Lars looked serious. She looked happy. Her suit, a navy serge, was in the latest fashion, the skirt a complication of drapes, the fitted jacket made so that it buttoned only once, at the breastbone, then fell open down to her waist and hips, as if to suggest that she was too well endowed to be able to button more of it. That was not the case. All that showed of her hat was a fall of dark feathers atop her head, like a bird's tall crest. She and Lars looked surprisingly well matched in size. Of course he was taller than she was, but not by so much.

She saw herself as meagre, with hooded eyes and a mouth that turned ever so slightly down. Lars said she was not meagre, she had a beautiful delicacy. But he preferred to paint women who bloomed like apples, round and firm, creamy and rosy. Or like peaches. He liked them out of doors, without clothes. When he painted her, it was indoors, dressed a la mode—as in her portrait in red silk with pale yellow polka dots, sleeves like pillows to the elbow and then tight to the wrist. That one was painted at their apartment in Montmartre, as she posed looking through a portfolio of his work. His paintings of models were timeless because they were nude. She could date his portraits of her by an out-of-style collar, an exaggerated shoulder, a hat that shouted its year.

Once, soon after they were married, Lars did paint her out of doors. Seen in profile from the back, in a forest, she wore a tailored lavender walking dress. Her hat was small and feathered, very smart at the time. She might have been a skittish, easily frightened bird turning into a woman, or a woman, timid but resolute, becoming a bird. A thornbush caught her skirt, lifting it slightly to show her high-heeled boot, and she turned to see what was impeding her. Later, what struck her about that picture was the love with which it was painted.

In Paris, they rented an apartment in Montmartre, on the Boulevard de Clichy. They lived, and Lars worked, in a space smaller than Mamma's drawing room. He was careful about money and his books were in order, but why should he keep accounts when she could do that? Within a month, she had taken over the business side of his work. She learned how to shop for his paints and materials, and she cleaned his brushes. Such an easy job when he used watercolours, and such loathsome work when he painted in oil. But Lars's customers wanted oil for their portraits, and she could not deny that it was his metier.

She introduced him to the Wallersteins, who were a distant family connection, and the Levertovs, who in turn introduced Cecilia and Lars to the Hallers and the Salmons. They had large families and cousins everywhere, so the commissions multiplied. Not that it always went smoothly, because a proud father would insist that his boy's mouth did not really purse in that sour way or that he himself was by no means so heavy, and Lars would only compromise so far. Sometimes he did not compromise at all. Cecilia was the one who had to satisfy both parties.

They had a very small maid, Françoise. She had to be thin, they said, because there was so little room in their flat. Most artists' wives in Montmartre cooked the meals. Cecilia considered it, and Mamma's cook had shown her how to make a few things, but there didn't seem to be much point to it. She was busy enough managing Lars's affairs. So Françoise arrived each morning with a baguette, and Cecilia made the coffee. They kept a little cheese and meat in the cold box for Lars, who did not think much of the French breakfast. Or, as he put it, "The French breakfast does not think much of *me*, or any man with a normal appetite." At midday, Françoise would collect a hot meal for them from one of the nearby restaurants, and they would go out for dinner, to a restaurant or to the apartments of friends or clients. Cecilia saw that she was better dressed than most of the wives, partly because she had brought her trousseau from Stockholm, and partly because every once in a while Mamma would send her the money to buy something new.

She did not miss Sweden in those Paris years, at least consciously. But occasionally she could not sleep, and as she lay there, she took to reciting the names of lace patterns. Some were designs she had learned as a girl, and some Lars's mother had taught her. Jerusalem's Gate would run through her head, a densely crowded pattern. Buske, Krakspark, Halrad, Gunsud, Gullviva, Buskra. Buske, Krakspark, Halrad, Gunsud, Gullviva, Buskra. And Bockarna, of course, the most difficult of all. Some designs were purely abstract, others tiny pictures as detailed as Lars's carvings. Over and over she repeated those names and summoned up those designs, until she woke to the slate roofs outside the window and the pewter light of a Parisian morning.

Wearing her red suit and a new hat, Cecilia was trying to look nonchalant. The occasion was Lars's first Stockholm show of work done in Paris, and he had made a beautiful little bronze that could be held in the hand, of a faun and a nymph embracing. Standing behind her, the faun planted one leg between the nymph's two, grasped her breast, and she cupped his hand with hers. Her head was thrown back in joy, his was bent forward on her collarbone in concentration. Cecilia found it very strange to have her husband sculpting intimacies that only their bedroom had seen. Even more strange to watch clients and friends and family walking around the bronze, appraising it.

Aunt Bette and Aunt Rosa arrived together and Cecilia thought, Oh dear. She began walking away from the statue, which by now was the piece that had attracted the largest crowd, but the aunts were too quick for her.

She need not have worried: they ignored the statue and assessed her outfit.

"Cecilia, you look so well. Is your hat from Paris?"

"Come closer, so I can see how they attached the veil. Is this single feather the latest thing?"

"And is this suit new too?"

No, she said, it was from her trousseau.

"Very bright," Aunt Rosa said. Not a compliment.

The aunts turned her around so that they could see her bustle, but Cecilia knew they were really looking her over for signs of pregnancy. Once they were satisfied that nothing showed, they moved away to talk with Uncle Goran.

As they left, Aunt Bette said over her shoulder, "You must be taking good care of your husband—look at all the work he's done."

Mamma arrived, and was enchanted by the faun and the nymph. "Lovely, just lovely," she said, shaking her head in appreciation and congratulating a quietly triumphant Lars. The confetti of red dots on the price list, indicating the pieces that had been sold, pleased Mamma too. Lars's prices were always high, and that seemed to encourage, rather than discourage, sales.

Mamma's friends rushed over to greet her and to tell Cecilia what a brilliant artist she had married. As soon as Cecilia saw that she was not expected to say anything but the vaguest pleasantries—or even to look closely at the pieces—the evening became much easier.

Chapter Twenty-eight

APRIL 1896

A FEW MONTHS after their return to Paris, Cecilia received a letter from her sister. Mamma was not to know about the misconduct of her darling son, Natalie warned her, but she had to tell someone. Fredrik's family was in a terrible state. The children's nursemaid, Inga, was going to have a child, which was upsetting enough. But it was worse than that. It seemed the father—Cecilia stared at the letter, at first unable to take it in—was Fredrik. Poor Inga would never have told her mistress the identity of her seducer, but the man-servant had gotten drunk and out tumbled something about "the master's by-blow" in little Jorgen's hearing. Jorgen didn't understand what a by-blow was, but he repeated it to his mother. Cecilia was shocked and very sorry for her sister-in-law. But what disturbed her most, although it was far from the most important part of this calamity, was Lars's reaction. "What's all the bother?" he said. "These things happen."

Apparently they did. But his coolness took her aback.

Their joy in the night was still there but it happened less frequently. That was probably normal, she thought. Lars was often out late in the evenings with his men friends. When he came home, she would turn to him in bed, but he usually slept almost immediately, worn out with food and drink.

For the first few years of their marriage Cecilia had been so happy she did not miss having a child. None came, and after a while she wondered why. After another while, she wanted one, and then she wanted one very much.

In the third spring of their time in Paris, she and Françoise were putting away the winter clothes and sorting through the lighter ones. Françoise must have made a small noise, a humph or a surprised start of some sort, that made Cecilia turn to her.

"What is it?"

"Nothing, madame, nothing at all. I caught my fingernail on a stray thread."

But Cecilia was looking at her, and she could hardly hide whatever she had found in the inner pocket of Lars's heavy brown suit. Although Cecilia hadn't the faintest idea what the object was, she knew at once that it was not good. She kept her eye on Françoise while she considered out loud whether the weather would turn cold enough for her to wear her grey worsted walking costume again, and whether it should go to the cleaners before being put into the trunk. Finally, when she thought that enough time had elapsed, she sent Françoise out of the room for more sheets of tissue to lay between the clothes.

At first, the small thing mystified her. A round, hard rim and a rubbery centre. She put it in her pocket and before Françoise returned, she laid Lars's brown suit in the trunk. By the time they had finished for the day, she was frantic. Not with an idea, more a shapeless suspicion that was just beginning to take on contours. Her mother had never discussed with her what went on between a husband and wife. Nor had anything like this object ever appeared in her English novels. She was reading French novels by now, although she did not care for them greatly. Compared to the Brontës and Dickens, the French ones were cynical and heartless. But some of them alluded to ways and means—not that she understood these veiled references, but this object reminded her of those passages.

She thought of consulting Otto Jespersen's wife, a forthright woman from Lund. But she decided someone French would be better, partly because all the Scandinavian artists' wives in Paris gossiped about each other, but more because somehow this seemed a French subject. Camille Desjardins was a better choice: her husband painted landscapes, and they lived in an apartment in the Marais with their three little girls. Cecilia arranged to visit her, and Mme Desjardins gave her jasmine tea. They talked about the Salon for a while, the work their husbands were exhibiting and the cheap place in Normandy the Desjardins had rented for the summer, close to the sea.

Then Cecilia said she had a question. Mme Desjardins nodded, testing her cup for heat with her chubby fingers.

"When a husband and wife do not want children, or perhaps do not want children at that time, is there anything . . ."

She stopped. The Frenchwoman looked surprised. And uncertain. "My dear Mme Vogt. I had a different impression . . ."

"No, no," Cecilia said, "it's not to do with my husband and me. It's that I have been reading Zola, and he makes references to such possibilities. I'm afraid mothers in Sweden do not explain these things to their daughters."

She hoped her hostess would not ask which Zola novel she had been reading.

"Ah, well then." Mme Desjardins smiled ruefully, thinking where to begin. "None of them, I'm afraid, are very nice."

She could never remember getting home from the Desjardins' flat. She must have walked, because she had a memory of Françoise clucking at her wet feet and sodden beaver cape, unpeeling her kid leather boots and taking them with the cape to the kitchen, after installing Cecilia in front of the fire with tea. Everyone was giving her tea today, she thought, as, like Camille Desjardins, she wrapped her hands around the cup's fierce heat. She did not drink it. She was sure she would never be warm again. She felt hollowed out, as if her heart, lungs, belly had been suddenly emptied. And yet something deep inside was pumping hard.

It was undeniable now, and yet she was counting on Lars to deny it. Only he could make it all disappear. What if he did not? While she decided how to proceed, she wondered what she had done wrong. She was too thin, her breasts were wrong, her breath smelled or her feet. That was it, her feet smelled. She took to washing them several times a day, as well as her teeth. The coated sensation of the tooth powder disgusted her. Lars could see something was wrong; she was no actress. She either clung to him in bed or turned away, saying she was exhausted.

"What is it?" he asked.

She shook her head. Nothing.

"Is it that there is no child yet? Because, you know, we will have one."

She shook her head.

He got up, and soon she heard him whistling in the little room he used for a studio.

Finally she grew tired of all the feeling. She wanted it to go away and, reckless, she did not much care how it ended. The next time he asked what was wrong, she went to her jewel case, took out the thing at the back of the bottom drawer and opened her hand to show it to him.

At first, either he genuinely did not understand or he was a better liar than she realized.

"My sweet girl, that is the last thing we need."

"I found it in your suit."

Even now they had not reached the point of no return. He could still tell her he was holding it for a friend, or it was part of a prank. Instead, he turned rather formal.

"My dear, I beg your pardon. It was a momentary lapse."

She said nothing, not out of strategy but simple shock.

"I was feeling discouraged," he said, as if that explained it.

Then, a little shamefaced, he extended his hands, with his elbows close to his sides, and took a step as if to embrace her. For an instant, she thought of the letter opener he had carved with her profile, but there was no time to reach it on her desk. She pushed him hard instead, and watched herself fly into a rage. Except that there was shrieking and not singing, it was like a scene from an opera that she had rehearsed again and again.

"How dare you! How dare you? I am cleaning your dirty brushes and introducing you to my parents' friends, and you betray me with a prostitute, or a model. What kind of stupid cliche are you living in? You promised to love me!"

There was more, equally pointless, and finally she stopped because she was out of breath. He assured her that he did love her, that there was no intention to betray her, he begged her pardon again. But a look had passed across his face, just for a second, while she was screaming, a look that she did not understand for a long time. Much later, when she knew more, it came to her: a prostitute would have provided this object herself. Cecilia wasn't sure about a model, but the fact that Lars had to provide the protection suggested that the woman was a lady, perhaps. Or a servant.

A painting flashed through her mind. Years before, she had seen an early Renaissance Annunciation at some collector's house, she had forgotten whose. Instead of the usual calm conversation between the angel Gabriel and a humble but willing girl, this painting was a scene of horrific ruckus and disarray. Gabriel, wearing bright blue and much larger than Mary, almost burst out of the frame. His ostentatious headdress and barely controllable wings, a frightening combination of muscle and feathers, were an affront to the girl's quiet bedroom. In her shock, Mary had spilled her work—thread, needles and scissors—all over the floor, and her speech ribbon unfurled in a frightened stammer. She half-turned from Gabriel as if to say, "No. Please. This is a mistake. I was sitting here peacefully sewing and you want to turn my life upside down." In some ways, not everything had ended badly for that timid Jewish girl, who enjoyed centuries of honour and devotion. But Cecilia could see no good whatever in this news for her. Something beyond her control had invaded her well-ordered room. Even if she thought she could restore its order, something more fundamental was broken.

Lars looked sorry for her, told her that she was his beloved, his darling. And she told herself it would not happen again. But he never promised that.

Next year, at Lars's Stockholm exhibition, there was another small statue of a faun and nymph. This nymph was somewhat taller, closer in size to the faun, who resembled the earlier faun. But their bedroom had not seen the posture that was transporting them. Cecilia told herself, Stop looking at the statue. And she did. Her naivete was laughable: last year she had been dismayed that she recognized the doings of the faun and nymph, and now she was concerned that she did not. Well, she told herself. Surely an artist, of all people, uses his imagination.

Chapter Twenty-nine

1899–1901

As THE CENTURY waned, the Vogts began building a house next to the churchyard in Siljevik. Once it was ready, they would move back to Sweden after almost six years in France. In 1899, Lars returned to Paris after their summer in the archipelago, but Cecilia stayed in Sweden for a few weeks to consult with the builders.

When she returned to Paris, she found Lars working on dozens of oil studies and pencil sketches of a woman on the Place Pigalle. What preoccupied him was the contrast between the yellow-white electric light from a nearby cafe, and the gaslight on the street. The woman, who stood between the two kinds of illumination, wore brilliant crimson—either velvet or the softest merino wool—with a waist-length fur cape that tied at her neck with a big brown satin bow, and a muff. She had a way of holding her head, with a look of triumph and wounded pride, that told Cecilia the woman and Lars had been lovers. And that the affair was over. But perhaps she was wrong, because Lars said the model was a streetwalker. Not one of his usual types.

Absorbed by the technical problems of the different lights—one relentless, flooding every corner, the other muted, soft and focused—Lars wanted to work around the clock. In the evening, when he had an idea, he pressed Cecilia into service as a model. She stood for hours, resting her arm with the muff against a pillar (standing in for a tree), and lifting her skirt with the other hand. Her head had to be inclined to the right, just so. She remembered the expression on the woman's face, assured and resigned, a touch of bravado that signalled defeat, and imagined it on her own. Although Lars was not interested in her face. Finally, she said no.

"I don't want to pose any more."

"But why?"

"I'm not a streetwalker."

"What are you saying? No one is going to recognize you. I'm keeping the model's face; I just need you for the twist of the body and the way her skirt folds into two panels when she lifts it out of the mud."

"I don't care. I'm not a prostitute."

"My dear woman, I don't understand you. Are you becoming such a prude that you can't help your husband?"

"I would rather help you in other ways," she said shortly, and walked away.

The house in Siljevik was finished only a little behind schedule, thanks to Cecilia's management, and they moved to Dalarna in 1900. Siljevik was Lars's village, but he and Cecilia had never lived together in Sweden, except for summers in the archipelago. Absorbing as their years in Paris had been, it was time to return home. Lars's career was at a stage where it could flourish in Sweden, and Cecilia looked forward to helping that happen. The ground was prepared: now their real life could begin. She concentrated on adjusting to life in a village, mastering the local dialect and, without trampling on too many sensitive feelings, trying to organize a library and a folk school. An orphanage would come next. She still half-hoped all this effort would make a difference in her marriage.

In her first autumn in Siljevik, feeling sentimental and at loose ends, she went back to Stockholm for the Jewish New Year. Mamma was happy to see her, although she thought travelling so far to go to a service at the synagogue was a curious idea. Afterwards, the family convened for tea at Aunt Bette's. Cecilia listened as her cousin Lena lamented over a burglary at her house when the family had been away for the summer. There was much shaking of heads and clucking while Lena, the expert on break-ins, chattered on.

The first time, she said, was terrible. You felt violated, and that nothing would ever be the same again. But that turned out not to be true. The second time and, if you were unlucky, the third time, it felt more like a nuisance. There was a sleepy watchman to be fired, and broken glass and lost valuables, but you didn't feel the wretched vulnerability that came with the first break-in.

Cecilia passed China tea and seed cake, concentrating on the pattern on Aunt Bette's cake plate, the Rorstrand one with innocent blue cornflowers scattered over a white surface. She wondered if having your marriage broken into was like a break-in at your house. The first time, or the first one she knew of, was an earthquake, a floor she had presumed was solid giving way without warning. She had thought it would never happen again, but even so, nothing would ever be the same. And she had been right that nothing would ever be the same—but right only about that. The second time, was it less or more painful? The second time meant that the first was not an aberration. And the third . . . What did the third time mean?

Better not to think these thoughts. Better to commiserate with Lena or ask Aunt Bette if she still bought her mille-feuille from the patisserie on Drottninggatan. Her store of hope was diminishing, but she still had flickers that Lars's escapades might end, or become very rare. She might never again be the centre and the whole of his desire—probably would not be—but in time he would see that no one would ever love him as she did. As she still did, and the panic and anger she felt at each unwelcome revelation only increased that love.

In the second autumn they lived in Siljevik, Lars acquired a new dealer, and he and Cecilia went to Stockholm so that Lars could talk with him. By now Cecilia sat in on many of his business meetings, but Lars liked to have his first one with a dealer alone. That left her free for a few hours, so she headed for the National Museum. There was usually something interesting at the Salon. Making her way through the crowded galleries, she ran into Hanna Pauli and Sofie Olsson, who had come to see the work of a Danish woman they had studied with in Grez.

"Mrs. Vogt," Sofie said, looking awkward for just a minute. Cecilia felt a twinge. The Olssons had visited Siljevik in the spring, but she and Lars had not yet managed a return excursion to Askebo. She really must organize that.

"Please," Cecilia said, "it's time we went to first names."

Sofie smiled and agreed.

After they had toured the Salon, Cecilia sat in a cafe between Hanna, whom she had known since they were schoolgirls, and Sofie, whom she was just beginning to know. She liked looking at Sofie's rounded features and the yoke of her blue dress, embroidered with honeysuckle and ladybugs—no doubt her own design. Hanna and Sofie were telling her a story about Dorotea, their Danish friend, whose teacher had advised her to set her paintbox sailing on the river when she was about to marry.

"How did Dorotea react?"

"Probably more politely than she should have," Hanna answered. "We were brought up to turn the other cheek."

Hanna had jumped in, as usual, but it was Sofie's response that Cecilia wanted to hear. She looked at her inquiringly. Sofie's expression was wary.

"Until we went to art school," she said slowly, "most of us had never met another woman who wanted to paint. So we were easily discouraged."

But, she corrected herself, Dorotea had not been discouraged. "And the dishes the teacher sent for his wedding present are probably broken by now."

Cecilia thought of the Rorstrand china Mamma had given them for their wedding present, a pattern called Flow Blue that was a little old-fashioned even then. She remembered setting off on the train with Lars for married life in France, with a few place settings of the china carefully packed in a crate to use in their tiny Paris flat. She had been so blithe that day. The path to the wedding had been arduous, and it seemed as if they had reached the happy ending at last. She had looked forward to a union as devoted as her parents' but more passionate, to children, to growing old as Lars's one true love.

"Yes," Cecilia said. "China breaks, but dreams should not."

How sure the future had seemed as they travelled to Paris— really, not like a dream at all. She had never imagined its fragility. The china had fared better: few pieces had been broken, as she was strict with the maids about the proper way to wash it.

Now Hanna, typically blunt past the point of insensitivity, was telling a nasty story about how Nils Olsson had boasted to Georg that the greatest thing he had ever done was to end Sofie's painting career. Did Hanna just say the first thing that crossed her mind, without considering its effect on her listeners? It was more than embarrassing, it was painful. Blushing and obviously wounded, Sofie changed the subject to Georg—who worked hard to encourage Hanna's painting—rather than concentrate on her husband's disloyalty to her. Cecilia wondered, Is she really such a good wife? Or does she do that to save face?

When I was single I wore a plaid shawl
Now that I'm married I've nothing at all.

After a short, uncomfortable pause, Cecilia diverted the conversation to *David Copperfield*, which she was reading. Nervously, she fell into criticizing David's silly child-wife Dora before realizing this was a mistake. Wives of any kind were not an ideal topic after Hanna's story. But Sofie surprised her by mounting a robust criticism of David's second wife, the saintly Agnes. Sofie might have seen Agnes as a kindred spirit—except obviously she didn't. Well, Sofie Olsson is inscrutable, Cecilia thought. Then: And I wish I understood her better.

Hanna, who did not read novels, had nothing to contribute. The trio passed the rest of their time in half-hearted news of friends and acquaintances, until finally the cheque came and Sofie left for the train.

That night, in the Stockholm hotel, Lars said little about his meeting with his new dealer. Cecilia did not take much notice, still preoccupied with her lunch. Briefly, she considered which was worse: a wandering husband or one who forbade you to paint? She had no experience of the second, but it sounded important. When they got home, she would sit down with Lars and a calendar and fix a date to visit the Olssons at Askebo.

Chapter Thirty

TWO PREGNANT WOMEN were knitting in the parlour at Askebo. That is, Cecilia was almost sure they were both pregnant. Sofie was the more certain case, with a rounded belly that not even her loose dress could hide. Cecilia had not yet seen a doctor, but she was counting on her sore breasts and two months without her courses.

My goodness, she thought, looking at Sofie's fingers playing effortlessly over the four needles of her stocking. Another stocking. Another child, her sixth. Of course, neither woman mentioned her condition.

It was the Vogts' first visit to Askebo. As soon as they arrived, Nils had given them a tour, mimicking Miss Zickerman from the Homecraft Association until Sofie ordered him to stop. For Cecilia, the house was a mixture of the familiar and the unfamiliar. As Sofie said, visitors who knew Nils's paintings (and everyone knew Nils's paintings) were surprised at how small and unpretentious it was. Many of the house's improvisations were famous—the portraits of the children on door panels, Nils's self-portrait as a gargoyle under the roof, the caricature of himself painted on the soup tureen. Some of them were too clever by half, Cecilia thought, and many of them were about Nils. But the blue-and-white parlour, the dignified Old Room, the intimate library and even the big, barn-like nursery were as engaging as their painted likenesses.

It was Sofie's curtains, table coverings and other textiles that stirred Cecilia. These made their way into the paintings as details, but in person they were as original as anything in the house. Some of the designs, like the needlepoint bestiaries with which Sofie had upholstered the seats of antique chairs, were exuberant. Most were knowing and spare—Japanese seals embroidered on a hand towel, stylized animals parading gravely around the edges of a child's blanket, the diaphanous curtains for Nils's bed, embroidered in one of Sofie's signature motifs, a consummately simple alchemy of circles and straight lines.

Now the men had gone sketching, and the children had scattered. Sofie and Cecilia talked about books while they knitted. As before, Sofie's reactions took Cecilia by surprise: where did she get her soft spot for the grouchy, tyrannical and dishonest Mr. Rochester in *Jane Eyre*? Cecilia could find no excuse for Mr. Rochester.

Their talk moved seamlessly from characters in books to real people, from the Yorkshire moors to the afghan Sofie was making from the scraps in her wool bag. "Are you expecting a new niece or nephew?" she asked, nodding at the white baby cardigan Cecilia was knitting.

"Not that I know of," Cecilia said nonchalantly, stopping to count her rows. She sometimes knit past the row where the cables had to be twisted and then had to pull out the stitches. "But I like to have one or two things on hand for happy announcements."

Oskar made an appearance, with a partially undone diaper that trailed behind him like a short train. He was in the care of a maid, but he preferred his mother and had escaped. His nose ran and his hair stuck up on one side, a casualty of his nap.

"No, you do *not* want to kiss him, Cecilia. He has snot all over his cheeks."

Sofie kissed him instead, briskly, redid his diaper and passed him back to the maid. Oskar made a pro forma protest but accepted the inevitable. Cecilia watched hungrily, supposing that, as with other great joys, you gradually grew used to living with these small, miraculous beings.

As the Vogts were leaving, Sofie pressed a featherweight package into her hands. She had woven Cecilia a gift whose inspiration she recognized as soon as she unwrapped the tissue paper.

"'He gave me a handkerchief red, white and blue!'" she crowed, "'But before I could wear it he tore it in two.'" It was the Irish song Markus had played on his fiddle on the Olssons' visit to Siljevik.

"'He *bought* me a handkerchief,'" Sofie corrected her, laughing. "Keep this one safe in your handkerchief box, and no one will tear it."

"I will return the favour," Cecilia said, "and make you a lace handkerchief in Bockarna." It was a fiendishly difficult pattern, with a bearded ram seen in profile, his horn an upside-down comma. She had the patience for that, and Sofie did not.

The pains started in the carriage on the way home. She ignored them as long as she could, but by the time they got home, she knew it was no good. Telling Lars that she would explain later, she went immediately to the second floor. She had not told him about the baby, not wanting to rouse his hopes in case it turned out to be a false alarm. Sitting on the shiny new toilet, she rested her elbows on her knees and held her weeping face in her hands. The little cabled sweater would go to another baby.

Chapter Thirty-one

LYDIA BARNES LOOKED as if she were born to wear the Siljevik folk dress. Or no dress at all, one of Lars's full-figured, rosy-bodied nudes. But she was American to the core, a red-headed descendant of Congregationalist ministers and theologians. Lars and Cecilia had met her a few years ago in Paris, where she was married to Benjamin Barnes, a sculptor whose work with a bronze casting process called "cire perdue" interested Lars.

The Barneses were unhappily married, as it turned out, but the Vogts, or at least Cecilia, had not known that. They had visited the Barneses at their house in Passy and enjoyed themselves. Except for Lydia, who was about ten years younger, they were all in their early thirties. Benjamin Barnes had been helping Lars cast some of his bronzes, and Cecilia and Lydia walked in the woods while the men worked. The Barneses' little house was decorated with Japanese embroideries and prints, but Cecilia thought that Lydia Barnes was the most decorative thing in it.

Once Cecilia and Lars returned to Sweden, they learned that the Barneses were divorcing. That was a surprise, and so was Lydia's recent appearance in the Stockholm archipelago, staying with some friends. Lars ran into her there, while Cecilia had stayed in Siljevik, arranging the last details of the fall courses at the Folk School.

About a week after Lars had returned to Siljevik, he came to the threshold of her study, where she was writing to his dealer. He said casually, "I've had a letter from Lydia Barnes. She is coming tomorrow."

She lifted her head. She wasn't sure she had heard correctly.

"Lydia Barnes? Is that what you said?"

"Yes."

"But Lars, we've had too many guests. We agreed there would be no more until November."

"Well, she was so curious to see our place. And of course I owe Barnes a great deal for his help with the casting."

Since they had separated, this seemed an odd way of thanking Benjamin Barnes.

Cecilia never liked the centrepiece of the house, the Great Hall. Its bloated height and scale, its lumbering darkness, its Viking trappings struck her as foolish. And when Lars made an etching of Lydia at the billiard table there, looking like a blowsy, old-fashioned rose, bending over her cue so that they could all admire her figure, she liked it even less. For years afterwards, when Cecilia was in the Hall or even thought of it, the etching came to her mind.

Lydia and Lars played game after game of billiards during her visit. Cecilia gave up the pretense of waiting them out, and went to bed alone. In the early hours of the morning, she could hear the creak of the stairs as Lars tiptoed up to his bedroom. The Hall was on the second floor, along with their bedrooms, but the guest room was on the first floor.

If she had decorated the guest room with Lydia in mind, it could not have been more perfect. Lydia's red head like a flame in all the cool beige and ivory upholstery, the white and gold furniture. The broad planks of the floor with its few sheepskin rugs made Cecilia think of Lydia's forthright American personality, and something of Lars too. In addition to the canopied bed, there was a small sofa and even a chaise longue. Plenty of spots for dalliance.

Because the weather was fine, they ate their breakfast on the little second-floor porch. Lydia talked about Ibsen and his ideas about women. How marriage stifled a woman, turned her into a piece of property, and how in the new century these unjust arrangements would no longer be made. Lars looked bored. He liked it better when Lydia exclaimed about the beauties of Siljevik's church or the Viking look of their roofline. In his carelessly genial way he responded by talking about Strindberg's belief in the profound antagonism between men and women, how women tried to consume men and destroyed their art. In these circular arguments about the rights of women and men, women invariably quoted Ibsen and men Strindberg. Cecilia concentrated on trying not to think of how Lydia had looked playing billiards in her black lace evening blouse. How her breasts spilled like melons as she angled her arm and considered her shot.

A photograph remained from that visit, taken in the Hall. Cecilia could not remember who had taken it. Lars was in the foreground, bent over his cue at the billiard table, his back to the two women. As if he wanted nothing more to do with their tiresome rivalry. Lydia sat by the window in the morning light, reading her mail. Cecilia struck an oddly theatrical pose by the great fireplace, holding onto the mantel with one hand as if she needed its support, staring into the empty hearth. Had her heart been in her mouth? She supposed so. Both women wore full skirts, high-necked white shirtwaists and jackets with leg-of-mutton sleeves. Looking at the photograph, Cecilia could hear the clink of Lars's cue when it hit a ball, and the thunk when the ball went home to a pocket. She could see the set of his shoulders that said, leave me alone.

Lydia Barnes had been pursuing him, no doubt. And Lars did not like being pursued. After Lydia left for the station, Cecilia walked by the lake in the late afternoon. The waves hurried in to shore, and the sun on the water hurt her eyes. Apparently, Lydia had left in defeat. But this victory, if it was a victory, had a sour taste, or maybe no taste at all.

In the end, she and Lars did not have much of a scene. Perhaps it fell flat because it shamed her. Beyond the usual humiliation, it was mortifying to realize that she felt threatened by Lydia because of her class. She and Lydia were from roughly the same class, and that made her a rival in a way that a model or a maid could not be. And that was an unworthy idea. A Brontë heroine would not have made that distinction. Nor for that matter would Lars.

The next day Cecilia also left by train. She got off at Stockholm's Central Station, hot-eyed, pale, not having slept or eaten for two days, and took a carriage to her mother's flat on the Stureplan. Ignoring Mamma's questions, she went straight to bed. Next morning, after twelve hours' sleep, in which she dreamed she was a girl again and woke to find the wallpaper all wrong, and then fell back to sleep and dreamed that Lars and Lydia were playing billiards with her head, smaller and glossier than it really was, she sat in the familiar dining room. Everything was as usual, from the view out onto the square to the table laden with platters of cheese, meats and smoked fish that could feed eight, not just two small women. Two of Lars's Spanish paintings hung on the wall over the buffet, the shy senorita with her fan and long earrings, and the two black-haired girls gossiping by a well. A thick Iberian sun poured over the paintings, while the light on the Stureplan was thinner, a sun tinged with blue.

She drank some coffee and ate a roll. Mamma, who had worried that something was wrong with her health or Lars's, was relieved to hear the truth.

"Darling, that is very unpleasant but nothing to make yourself ill about. That is what men are."

They had never had this conversation before, but her mother's reaction did not surprise her. She felt obliged to protest.

"How can you say that? Pappa didn't have affairs, and certainly not with the wives of his business connections."

Neither of them remarked on the illogic in the last sentence. Mamma looked up from the slice of cheese she had chosen, as if she were considering that possibility for the first time.

"I have no idea whether he did or didn't. We certainly never discussed it."

Cecilia wanted to say, "But wouldn't your heart have been broken?" But that was not a question she could ask.

Instead she asked, "Wouldn't you have felt terribly humiliated?"

"I suppose. That's why we never discussed it. Besides, your father was a businessman. Lars is an artist, and it's only natural . . ."

Cecilia set her cup down on her saucer rather too smartly, and Mamma looked startled.

"Don't. You always take his part, and you make too much of artists. They're not exempt from the normal rules."

Suddenly, she missed Lars piercingly. He would be the first one to resist Mamma's glorification. Artists? he would say. We're just whittlers or daubers or makers of mud pies. Any fellow who can slap a fruit border on a jug gets to call himself an artist.

"Cecilia, men don't have the same rules as women."

"But we didn't start out like this. We started out as equals in love, not wanting anyone but each other. When did the rules change?"

"Darling, beginnings are always like that. That's why they're called beginnings. They don't last."

"Then why didn't someone tell me that?"

"Because you wouldn't have believed it."

Cecilia looked at her bone china coffee cup, ivory with a gold rim and her parents' interlaced initials, also in gold. Why were bones used in bone china? So much cruelty combined with fine feelings. So much fragility in things meant to endure. Hurling it on the floor would not be satisfying, because the thick Brussels carpet would muffle its fall. It would lie on its side, dribbling out the last vein of coffee. She concentrated on pressing it hard but not crushing it.

Mamma finished her bread and butter, extended her hand briefly to the meat plate and thought better of it. She had a last swallow of her coffee, and checked that her rings were in place.

"Why don't we call for a carriage and visit Natalie? She has a new étagère in the dining room she would love you to see."

Later, Lars would always deny that he and Lydia Barnes had had an affair. But while she fumed in Stockholm, he went to France and visited Lydia Barnes in Passy. He wrote coolly to Cecilia that she had converted her husband's studio into a library and a billiard room, "Siljevik style."

It was better to be away from him, because in these aftermaths Cecilia was usually torn between fury and the need to feel she could still attract him. It was an indigestible, slightly nauseating mixture. Back in Siljevik, he was in the last stages of packing for America, a trip that she had organized meticulously and that promised to be extremely profitable. She stayed with Mamma for a month and wrote him a letter full of a sense of injury and what she considered indisputable claims. He answered from the ship:

> You made me melancholy with what you wrote.
> You are of course correct when you say that you
> are what no other woman can be for me. I certainly
> miss you and care for you. But I'm feeling calm
> being away from you. It is as Strindberg says, that
> we come together in order to torment each other.
> Let's see if a winter's separation will make us
> both more reasonable.

Chapter Thirty-two

1903

No DOUBT LARS was telling the truth, and he was calm without her. Cecilia was not calm, at least not at first. Nor was she able to forget his doings in America, as she got frequent letters from him complaining about difficult clients and sometimes asking her to intercede. As his prices escalated, now to the giddy heights of four thousand American dollars for a full-length oil portrait, his clients became more vocal and he became more headstrong. His stay was limited, so there was rarely time for a long argument about the set of a head or the amount of grey in a moustache. Cecilia's transatlantic letters and telegrams to the painter, and occasionally his clients, calmed some of the storms.

As the winter progressed, she found she could attend to Lars's business problems without thinking about their own struggles. His painting was just that, a business, and her tormented feelings about their marriage had nothing to do with it. She craved order, and if she could not have it in her private life, she could produce it when it came to Lars's career. She had always been organized. Now people were telling her that she had a gift for persuasion and diplomacy. Not only was she rather skilled at all this, she was enjoying it.

Siljevik, 18 March 1903

Dear Sofie,

Forgive my silence. I have been having a particularly busy time with the Homecraft Association, the library and the school. On top of that, Lars's mother had a fever and cough that needed attention—and caring for such a self-sufficient woman demands large reserves of tact and patience. Which I do not always possess. At the same time, I succeeded in buying quite a large piece of land on the lake, to display the old log buildings Lars seems to be collecting. He bought the first few almost on a whim, but their timber construction absorbs him more and more. Now he has a dozen barns, storehouses and houses, some dating from the Middle Ages.

I'm writing today in the hopes that you and Nils will be coming to my exhibition and sale next Saturday. The roster of art and books could not be better, and I have high hopes of making enough money to buy new tables and chairs for the village library—so far we are using castoffs from deserted farms. My stroke of genius was to concentrate on artists from Dalarna, beginning with Lars and Nils. There are a few exceptions—although they are not from Dalarna, I couldn't resist asking my cousin Eva Bonnier (and she would never have forgiven me if I hadn't) and Prince Eugen for donations. They obliged, of course. Then, although she is a writer—but she does live in Dalarna—Selma Lagerlof donated a few of her first editions. After that, no one dared say no to a show with so much cachet, and the walls and tables are already gratifyingly full.

Looking forward to seeing you on Saturday in the village hall—

Yours in friendship,

Cecilia

———

There was a good crowd in the hall soon after the doors opened, and by the time Cecilia spotted Sofie and Nils, around noon, it was full. Farmers and the local shopkeepers, who had never attended an art exhibition in their lives, stood looking at the pictures and fingering the books and pottery. Teachers at the local school and the Folk School, the pastor, and more middle-class people from quite a few villages away, drawn by Lars's reputation, were also there, and willing to buy. If people could linger over coffee and sweets in the hall, Cecilia thought, sales would follow. So she arranged tables, chairs and trays of her cook's best pastries. A bashful maid went from table to table with a large jug of coffee, under strict orders not to spill on anyone's purchase.

Cecilia sat down briefly at one of the tables with Sofie and Nils. Sofie wore one of her big, stylish hats, a beautiful boat that sailed on top of her wavy brown hair. It balanced the bulk of her loose dress and toned down its eccentricity. Nils had a painting wrapped in brown paper under his arm.

"Well, what did you capture?"

Nils unwrapped it. Painted by Lars in France in the early years of their marriage, it was called *Cecilia Vogt Reading*. She was caught up in a book, holding it close to her face. Her dress was quiet, striped in darker and lighter greys, and her hair was held back by a ribbon, exposing the big ears she inherited from her father. It was one of Lars's most affectionate portraits.

Cecilia laughed and went quickly to the cashier, where he was holding something for her on the shelf behind his table.

Returning, she said, "We're on the same track. Look what I bought," before she pulled off the protective cloth. It was a painting by Nils of Sofie, wrapped tightly in a plaid shawl and reading under a shade shaped like a cactus flower.

"I know that pose of yours," Cecilia said, smiling at the woman in the picture, "thumb on your jaw and two fingers spread-eagled on your cheek."

Lars's portrait had been painted by the soft light of gas, but in Nils's portrait Sofie read in the all-over brightness of electricity.

"Is the cactus-flower shade one of your designs?" Cecilia asked.

"No, Nils made it."

The two women propped the pictures up side by side. Lars never cared for reading, but he was proud of his little bookworm. Nils, too, was not much of a reader. Two painter husbands, Cecilia thought, two bookworm wives.

"Speaking of books," Sofie said, "have you read *The Odd Women*? It made me think of you."

"No, I haven't. Is it by Arnold Bennett? Why did it make you think of me?"

"It's by George Gissing. Its heroine, who is called Rhoda Nunn, is a New Woman who runs a secretarial college to give women without means a way to earn their living. Like you, she is terribly organized and effective."

"That's promising," Cecilia said. "I would like to read a novel about a woman who runs a successful business."

"But don't hope for too much in that quarter," Sofie said. "I'm afraid Mr. Gissing is much more interested in the fate of three poor sisters and their many troubles. He is devoted to the French school of realism, which paints life in very drab, undramatic colours."

"Sounds like the French school of realistic paintings," Nils said, but the women ignored him.

Cecilia asked, "But you enjoyed it?"

"I did. It felt very true."

"I'll see if I can borrow it from Bonniers," Cecilia said.

"If you two are going to talk about books, I'll just have another walk around the exhibition," Nils said. He went off to have a closer look at Prince Eugen's landscape.

———

When Lars left for America, his hope that absence might make them more "reasonable" sounded too optimistic. But to Cecilia's surprise, once he returned it seemed too modest. He was glad to be home, glad to see her, grateful for her help in Siljevik. His drinking had slowed. He visited her room again in the night. They shared so much, after all. Many men, she told herself, lapse occasionally. They are contrite, and things return to what they were. But no, things did not return to what they were. And Lars could not really be described as contrite. The realist in her told her that the best she could hope for was that they would find an accommodation that suited them both. The dreamer in her hoped otherwise. She tried not to analyze it too much. If you kept taking a plant out of its pot to examine the roots, you would only harm it in the long run.

That summer they returned to the archipelago and the house Mamma rented. Lars went off in his sailboat every morning with one or two models, and a picnic lunch. He worked all day in the sheltered coves, the women turning their nakedness every which way, at his command. Perhaps they put their clothes on when they ate their lunch. Or perhaps they just draped some cloths around themselves. When Lars showed her his work, Mamma exclaimed with pleasure at the light, the shade, the rocks, the water, the models' hair or their arms. She did not remark on their private, female hair, although that too was in the pictures. Cecilia thought, If Lars spent his days looking at naked women but not putting them on canvas, Mamma would not have liked that.

In the evenings, before dinner, Lars joined the family on the verandah. The men drank arrack, and Cecilia sometimes had a glass of white wine. They looked out on the same placid world of water and rock that Lars painted, only now from a substantial wooden house. Everyone was fully dressed and if her own skirt had been more than six inches off the ground, Mamma would have found that in very bad taste.

It was a queer business, men making art.

With Lars's return came the return of their monthly disappointment. When would his optimism about a child end? When they still used privies, Cecilia would go out there to lament the coming of her courses. Now, with a toilet in the house, it was harder to get away but, she admitted, more comfortable. When she miscarried—once on the day of the visit to the Olssons' and once about a year later—she went to the toilet and the baby seeped out with the tears.

Now, once she had taken care of the monthly flow of blood, she often went next door to the church to sit for a while in its coolness. Its barrenness. One of the church's few paintings was a small medieval picture of a strangely bare-breasted Mary with Jesus in a stable. Mary had thrown her red cloak open, probably to nurse the baby. A farmer and his wife were hurrying to leave their stable, awkwardly carrying a lamb like an embarrassment, and Joseph rushed in with a blue blanket, all thumbs but trying to be helpful.

In his studio, Lars was also painting breasts, in a painting he called *Getting Ready for Church*. It was one of his favourite subjects, an older woman in folk dress, a younger one in the nude. The older woman adjusted her silver necklace, her big round calves in red stockings, her rump sticking out into the middle of the picture as she bent to see in the inadequate mirror. In the foreground, the younger one washed her gleaming shoulders and breasts in a small round bowl. Lars worshipped flesh, more and more these days. Sometimes Cecilia thought the big bums of the mature women moved him as much as the breasts of the young ones. What did it matter? She had neither.

Chapter Thirty-three

CECILIA PUT ON her jacket and then, because rain threatened, she took an umbrella from the "Viking" stand in the hall. She doubted that Vikings used umbrellas, in spite of the dragons who circled the stand's rim. The master miner's house that she and Lars had bought for its murals was due to arrive in Siljevik that day, and she needed to meet the movers at its destination near the lake. She also had business at the Folk School nearby. On her way out, she put her head into the studio, where Lars was stretching a canvas. He sometimes used prepared canvases but for this painting, a peasant wedding procession, he wanted something longer and thinner than any of the standard sizes available. Stretching canvases had been one of her jobs in Paris, but now she was too busy, and in any case Lars enjoyed every stage of making a painting. He made his own sizing, a starch paste, and after that dried he would apply one or more coats of white ground.

"Cecilia, what do you think? How many coats of the ground?"

"I like the smooth look you got with two coats for the bathhouse painting."

"I think this one calls for something a little rougher. Look at the difference here."

He held up two recent pictures for her to compare, one with a single coat of ground and one with two.

But she was anxious to be gone. "I can't stay. The house movers are due to arrive any minute. I prefer the more finished look—two coats."

Dubious, he looked at one painting, then the other. Without raising his eyes, he said, "I'll try and get down to the lake myself later, to see how the house survived the journey."

But Cecilia knew she would not see him at the lake. Once he started working, he behaved like someone in a folktale who was under a spell. His feet could not leave the studio until the charm was broken, hours and hours later. That was fine, she did not need him.

She walked through the street of shops on her way, and met Mr. Munten coming out of the baker's. He was on the orphanage board, and always greeted her with several problems that he insisted needed her immediate attention. Since he considered all of them urgent, she wondered why he never contacted her, just filled her ears when they met by chance. She found it difficult to have a short conversation with Mr. Munten, he fretted so. Should siblings be separated when it came to adoptions, he asked her now, shifting his bag of bread and rolls from one arm to the other, or should the orphanage governors try to keep them together, risking the possibility that they would never be adopted, either singly or as a family? They had a case at the moment where people wanted to adopt the older girl in a family—she was useful as well as pretty—but not her younger brother. As Cecilia considered this dilemma, he charged ahead with another before she could answer. In the case of a family farm that was sold, did the money from the sale belong to the orphans or could the orphanage take a percentage for their support? And if so, what should that percentage be? Both excellent questions, she told him, trying to be soothing and brisk at the same time, and he must be sure to bring them up at the next board meeting. And she made her escape.

Down by the water, the log buildings she and Lars had bought stood in dispirited clusters, and there was no sign of the house. The man in charge of the moving had sent a telegram yesterday saying he expected to arrive before noon, but a delay was always possible. Moving a house was easier in the winter, when ice smoothed the way, than in September, but the new owners of the property had been anxious to be rid of the house so they could start building its replacement. The moving was a complicated process that Cecilia understood imperfectly, involving screwjacks to raise the house above the foundation, rolling carriages on which it was secured with spikes, and a team of strong North Swedish workhorses to pull the carriages.

The villagers probably thought they were mad to waste money and time on a house no one wanted, but she and Lars could not have stood by while the frescoes in the parlour were destroyed. An eighteenth-century master miner's farmhouse was less local and traditional than the medieval log barns and store-houses they had collected, so perhaps they would place it slightly apart in the grouping. But she looked forward to seeing that room again, crowded with fantastical landscapes as a pilgrim walked steadfastly through the scene.

She walked away from the lake up to the Folk School, leaving word at reception that she should be called as soon as the house arrived. First, she drank coffee with Miss Hagans, the principal, in her office. The office did triple duty as a storeroom and archive, so the two women sat close together on a loveseat between filing cabinets and shelves filled with carved ladles, painted jugs, embroidered ribbons and lace pattern books.

They began talking about the divide in the Folk School between the adult literacy classes and those that concentrated on folk arts. The people who came to learn how to spin, weave, carve furniture and do folk painting were mostly middle-class women, while the adults learning to read and write were from the working class, from

Siljevik or the nearby countryside, and often only fluent in the local dialect. Cecilia had an idea for bridging that gap.

"Why don't we enlist some of the people in the literacy classes to help teach the traditional arts?"

Miss Hagans looked at her in confusion.

"But how could that work? Their Swedish is often not up to the mark."

Cecilia covered her irritation by accepting, with thanks, another cup of coffee.

"Surely that is no impediment," she said crisply. "I don't think there is anyone in the school who does not understand the Dalarna dialect."

"But the people in the literacy classes do not have the pedagogical skills or the organizational ability . . ."

"Of course, we would still have the main teachers but the literacy students could demonstrate, assist, criticize their fellow students' work, and so on."

She knew Miss Hagans did not like the idea, but would warm to it. It was a good idea, and when Cecilia was certain of that, objections did not touch her. After her coffee, she visited a few classrooms and looked in on the choir practice. The teacher was telling Cecilia about an upcoming concert when the groundskeeper came to the door. The house had arrived.

It looked like something in a dream, this farmhouse standing on rolling carriages. Cecilia could not wait until the house was taken off the flatbed to see the murals, so a tall chair was brought over and she climbed up and looked through the windows. There they were, the treasures hidden within the pedestrian house, their deep blues and garnets and creams just as she remembered them. And there was the pilgrim walking with his staff except when his guiding saint appeared in the clouds. Then he knelt, sending his thanks in a diagonal line of Old Swedish words up to the saint. She directed the movers to a likely spot, and watched them settle the house almost casually, as if it were an immensely large piece of furniture. She must write to Sofie and remind her of the day in June when they had seen the murals together.

It was late by the time she returned home but Lars, as expected, was still in the studio. The blank white canvas stood on the easel, waiting. While the sizing dried, he was making some rapid sketches. There would only be one coat of the ground, he told her.

She waited for him to detach himself enough from his painting to remember the rest of the world. He had always been like that. After thinking out loud for a few minutes about possibilities for his wedding procession, he asked, "Did the house arrive safely?"

She told him the full story of her day—her encounter with Mr. Munten, the visit to the Folk School and finally the wonderful arrival of the house.

"Is there a single pie in Siljevik in which you do not have a finger?" he asked while his eyes ricocheted back and forth between the white canvas and his sketches of a happy, untidy procession. Behind the self-conscious bridegroom and the triumphant bride, he began rubbing out a child so he could advance him into the road and make him more prominent.

"We will go tomorrow, first thing, to see the house," she said. "Before you go to the studio."

She left to see about dinner, unpinning her hat in the hall and returning the umbrella, which had not been necessary after all, to the Viking stand. The day had been so satisfactory that she looked at its silly dragons with more affection than usual. Lars and I have something in common, she thought. We both have a canvas, but mine is Siljevik. But she would only say that to herself: if she heard it out loud, it would sound pretentious.

Chapter Thirty-four

1907

WHEN LARS MADE his next trip to America, Cecilia went with him. On the ship going over she reread *Martin Chuzzlewit*, trying not to take it too seriously. After all, it was more than sixty years since Dickens had first visited America and no doubt the constant bragging and tobacco-spitting he described were things of the past. And, indeed, as she settled into their hotel rooms in New York and Boston, she found that many of Lars's American clients and patrons behaved like prosperous people the world over—she enjoyed her visits with the Boston collector Isabella Gardner, for example. New York and Boston had music, some of it very good, and she became a regular visitor to the Metropolitan Museum of Art, which was, astonishingly, more than thirty years old. And yet, she had to admit that she found America a bit rough-and-ready.

Men there were probably no more sensual than European ones, but Lars's American friends took less trouble to disguise it. One night she and Lars went to the opera in New York, sitting in a client's loge. Lars disappeared during the second act and reappeared to take her back to the hotel. Then he went out again, explaining offhandedly that Arthur Caton, a Chicago man whose portrait he had painted, had come to New York to give a party for men only, twelve of them, with Lars as the guest of honour.

At noon the next day, when he woke, she asked him, "Were there women at Mr. Caton's party?"

"Yes, twelve beautiful ones, one to go into dinner with each of us. We were introduced to them only by their Christian names."

"And were there animals?"

"Animals? Why do you ask that?"

"Because when I brushed your suit this morning, I found women's hair and animal hair."

For a second, he looked confused. Then he laughed.

"Of course. There were skins put out on the divans, for us to relax on with our champagne. Some of the women danced for us, in gauzy white gowns. And don't look like that, Cecilia. I took my beauty in to dinner and escorted her home, as politely as could be."

So, a dinner "for men only" really meant that wives were not invited. She did not want to know whether or not Lars was lying. Or perhaps she did not care. Of course he was lying. But she had work to do: she had to write to a client in Boston and explain that Lars's fee was not negotiable. If the man in Boston declined to commission a portrait, there was no lack of other people who would be happy to take his place. She was looking forward to the courteous thrust and parry of their correspondence. And she wanted to get a letter off to Lars's Stockholm dealer as well as to Sofie before she went to a lieder recital in the afternoon. Isabella Gardner was coming from Boston, and she and Cecilia were to meet at the recital. There was no time for a scene.

Waldorf-Astoria Hotel, New York City
5 March 1907
Dear Sofie,

How good it was to get your news from home. It sounds as if Nils is making great progress with his portrait of Gustav Vasa, and I'm confident all his years of preparation will pay off handsomely. But, as usual, you say nothing of your own work. What original and unexpected thing will excite my admiration on my next visit to Askebo? (And to the aforementioned admiration, you will say, "Oh, it's just a little experiment I've been toying with . . .")

Although we are having a most interesting trip, I confess I miss Sweden. Lars likes America more than I do, saying he is at home in a country where a man with no forebears can be an enormous success. Which is silly, since his success in Sweden is undeniable, but he says it feels different in America. For me, something raw seems always on the point of revealing itself here. I do remind myself that Europeans have had a longer time to work on the strength of our surface. Perhaps more important, we seem to want a surface, at least more than the Americans.

It's also a terribly busy trip for Lars. Although I am nowhere near as busy myself, I have had some work here, too. You are lucky that Nils does not paint portraits more often—those who do encounter rough waters with their subjects, and sometimes I am assigned to smooth them. Or to decide when it's time to sail away.

This is brief, as I have a few business matters that won't wait—just to let you know that we are well. We send our love to all at Askebo, and look forward to more news when you have the time. It's possible that I will leave before Lars, and I'll let you know if that happens.

Your friend,
Cecilia

The most recent "rough waters" had concerned the old New York banker Moses Loewe. Lars had etched his portrait a few years ago, and Mr. Loewe seemed content enough with the result. But his children had become increasingly dissatisfied, and now that Lars was in New York, their complaints intensified.

"Cecilia," Lars called to her from the sitting room of their hotel suite, "will you come here and tell me what you think of the etching?"

She left the bedroom, already too warm although it was a frosty morning. If she came again to America, she must remember to pack some very thin summer blouses, the rooms here were so overheated. She sat down next to Lars on a broad sofa, its brocade upholstery dimpled with buttons, and looked hard at the portrait. Two tufts of white hair hedged Mr. Loewe's round, balding brow. The eyes at first looked penetrating and worldly, and were finally sad.

She said, "He looks guarded, but noble."

"The family wants me to etch another portrait. I have refused, and I want to return my fee in exchange for the fifty prints I made. Do you agree?"

It could have been more than awkward, especially since Lars's relationship to the Loewes and their Cassel and Warburg connections had begun through Cecilia's family. But that was not his concern, and she realized that it was not hers either.

"I don't understand their objection."

"His son-in-law complains that I have distorted their elegant father into what he calls a 'hunch-backed Shylock.'"

Oh, the intricate web of Jews and our family feelings, Cecilia thought. We want to be seen and respected for what we are by gentiles, but our hackles rise quickly and God forbid that they should see us as stereotypically Jewish.

She looked again.

"Dearest," she said, "in the future I think you should take more careful notice of your male subjects' clothing. Women usually seem to know what clothes will paint well. Here, where the Loewes see a hunchback, I see a heavy fur-lined coat that rucks up in the back and seems too large for Mr. Loewe's small head. That is your only mistake."

She enjoyed it when Lars looked slightly worried and even bewildered, as he did now—it was rare. She kissed him.

"I congratulate you on a poignant character study."

Relieved, he kissed her back.

"My Cecilia. What would I do without you?"

He did not undertake another portrait of the old man. And the Loewes, who had promised that Lars's decision would make no difference to their friendship, behaved beautifully, unlike some of his more bumptious American clients.

The lieder recital was given by the Brookfields, both of whom had been painted by Lars, in their Fifth Avenue palazzo. The butler led Cecilia to the salon, where she found about two dozen people drinking champagne and waiting for the music. The salon was generously upholstered, as were most of the guests. Isabella Gardner and Cecilia, neither well padded, sat together. When the contralto began, the women guests looked soulful. Their husbands looked resigned to a late afternoon of culture and tiny sandwiches. The contralto sang of love, death, disappointment, morning light, waterfalls, and more love. Cecilia paid attention with half her mind, and admired the singer's phrasing. At the same time, she thought of Lars's forthcoming show in Stockholm, and of a new and troublesome client who had commissioned Lars to paint his wife and two young daughters. The plainer girl was the client's favourite and now he wanted Lars to prettify her, widening the space between her eyes, lengthening her forehead. How to convince him that truth was best . . . because Lars would never make those changes.

During the intermission, Cecilia looked longingly at the lobster tarts, the shrimp quenelles and the petits fours at the buffet, but Isabella ignored them. She had moved her gold-painted chair diagonally across from Cecilia's and cut off her exit. Sotto voce, she asked, "Have you heard the news about Gervase Williams?"

"What is it?" The artist Gervase Williams was a great friend of Lars's.

"Mrs. Williams has discovered that he is keeping a second family in New Hampshire, a mistress and a son who is not much younger than Mrs. Williams's boy."

Cecilia raised her eyebrows, as she knew was expected. Shadowy second families were not unknown in that set, and another friend of Lars's, the architect Stanford White, was rumoured to have had a similar arrangement. The marriage of Gervase and Margaret Williams had begun as a great love match not much more than a decade earlier, and he had painted many ardent portraits of her. Cecilia felt her left eyelid flickering, as it did when she was tired. Was everyone's story the same?

"Poor Mrs. Williams. How is she taking it?"

Isabella had slung her arm around the back of her dainty chair. Now she moved in closer and tightened her grip on the chair.

"She is distraught. But it is her husband's response to her that is so infuriating. Apparently he has written her with the greatest coolness, reminding her from a great moral height that sweetness and patient dignity become a woman most, and that his sins are mere peccadillos compared with Stanford White's or others of their circle. He writes that he has suffered greatly in this. And finally he begs her, more for her sake than for his, not to descend from the pedestal where she lives in his imagination."

Isabella was as worldly as they came, but clearly even she felt that Williams shifting the responsibility for good behaviour onto his wife was shameless. The two women ran through all the conventional expressions of wonder, scorn, disillusionment and cynicism. They flicked their fans shut and snapped them open for emphasis. Cecilia was not sure how outraged they really were. Superficially, she enjoyed the drama and the camaraderie with Isabella, but underneath she felt weary. Her eyelid quivered again. "Poor Mrs. Williams."

Isabella rested her hand just for a second on Cecilia's beaded bag. That was as close as she came to suggesting Cecilia might have more than the usual sympathy for Mrs. Williams. Then the contralto began again: Schubert's *Winterreise*, another unhappy love story.

On that American trip, Lars produced fifteen oil portraits, ten etchings and some watercolours of nudes. He was so fast that he could make up to $15,000 a week, so he took advantage of his popularity. As well as her own responsibilities piling up in Siljevik, Cecilia had to supervise the packing of Lars's canvases for the spring Salon in Stockholm, so she left New York in late March. Their leave-taking was tender. Lars wrote her that his eyes were red with tears when he returned from seeing her off, and he asked for a different suite in the hotel, one without memories. "My own loving woman," he wrote, "I shall never forget your searching eyes when I left the ship." Cecilia felt, not elation—by now she was too realistic for that—but satisfaction. They had narrowly escaped throwing out something they both valued.

Chapter Thirty-five

1909–10

Lars marked the feast of Saint Cecilia in November by giving her an eighteenth-century French portrait for her study. The picture, from the studio of François-Hubert Drouais if not from Drouais himself, was of an unknown woman whose neck and lightly powdered head rose from her blue gown like a flower just on the point of blooming. She had a French gloss and knowingness, a way of making the most of what nature had given her.

More interested in Saint Cecilia than this French woman, Cecilia took Lambert's dictionary of saints from the bookshelf. "Saint Cecilia, virgin and martyr, and patron of church music." The daughter of an aristocratic Roman family, she read, which had converted to Christianity, Saint Cecilia begged her father to let her remain a virgin, but he betrothed her to a pagan named Valerian. After a vision in which he saw Cecilia's true love, an angel with fiery wings, the compliant Valerian accepted his wife's wish to live as a virgin. The two did good works in the Christian community until Valerian was martyred. The Romans' attempt to behead Cecilia failed, but she died of her wounds three days later. She bequeathed their house to the bishop to be used for prayer.

As Aunt Bette used to say at weddings, every couple invents their own marriage. Cecilia imagined Cecilia and Valerian's union, a mixed marriage that never became carnal, dedicated to a higher cause. It almost made her smile, although poor Cecilia's martyrdom was gruesome.

It was Valerian who had done the accommodating in that marriage. But together he and Saint Cecilia had a divine purpose. And Lars and I, she thought, what is our purpose? Not Christianity, not children. Lars's work, certainly, and Swedish things and Siljevik. Was it enough? Viewed in one way—the way she would have viewed it as a bride—it definitely was not. Looked at in another way, it was not what she would have wished, but she had not known herself terribly well as a young woman. Now, at forty-two, she would say that her life was full, richer, more demanding and perhaps even more absorbing than she had imagined. What she had engaged her thoroughly. But was it enough? Silly question. Of course it was not enough.

In March, Cecilia went with Lars to Gothenburg for the reopening of the Furstenbergs' gallery. She chose a dress with the fashionable S-shape, thanks to the new corsets, and with it she wore the necklace Lars had designed for their wedding anniversary. It looked as if everyone who cared about art in Sweden was wandering through the Furstenbergs' big rooms, including, she was glad to see, the Olssons. But something was amiss between Nils and Sofie—he must have said or done something that annoyed her. Cecilia could see it in the way Sofie turned away from his usual jokes and did not even pretend to laugh. Hanna Pauli was there, and she often brought out the worst in Nils. So perhaps the unpleasantness had something to do with Hanna?

Hanna's portrait of the Finnish sculptor Venny Soldan hung in one of the main galleries, and Cecilia and Lars stood looking at it for a few minutes with Sofie and Nils. One of the things Cecilia found irresistible in Lars was the way he looked at other people's art. Now she listened to him appreciating the scope and the details of Hanna's portrait, and she loved him again. Generous but shrewd. Critical, but from the vantage point of what the artist had tried to do, not what Lars would have tried to do. He could always show her something she had missed.

Sofie, too, listened intently, angling herself between Lars and the painting. Cecilia wondered what it felt like for her to see this large work, prominently displayed, by a friend and fellow student. Was there no envy, no sense of failure? Pontus Furstenberg had never bought a painting by Sofie Falkner, much less Sofie Olsson. Except for the laboured oil of her teacher Malmstrom that hung in the corridor at Askebo, Cecilia had never seen a painting by Sofie.

By now Nils had gone off with some former students. Lars was still looking at Hanna's painting, which reminded him of something he couldn't quite remember. Inclining his head toward Venny, he asked, "Did I hear that she and Hanna were lovers?"

Cecilia let out a bark of laughter.

"So," he teased her, "nice girls from the Stora Synagogue don't take women lovers?"

"It's not that," Cecilia said quickly, although it was partly that. She reminded him what Ellen Key had told her, reluctantly, about the ménage à trois in which Venny lived with her husband and her sister.

He remembered, and was titillated.

"Pity I never fancied your sister," he began, but stopped when he saw Cecilia's face close down.

Sofie excused herself—she has had enough of misbehaving men, Cecilia thought crossly—saying she wanted to see the paintings of Vasterbotten by the young artist who had impressed all the critics. But Cecilia took her arm firmly, and led the way to the buffet.

While they chose from the Furstenbergs' bounty, they talked not about Lars or Nils, but about Jane Austen's *Emma*, which Sofie had been reading. Sofie complained heatedly of Emma's meddling, and Cecilia thought, She is the perfect reader—she relates so directly to the character she forgets that Emma is the carefully constructed creation of the writer. Then she repented: that was patronizing. She did not share Sofie's dislike of meddling, but perhaps that was because few people attempted it with her.

After she had eaten a few canapes, Sofie went in search of the works by the young landscape artist, and Cecilia found Lars in front of *On Place Pigalle*, his portrait of the woman in Paris caught between two kinds of light. He was staring hard at it, still trying to decide whether he had captured the difference between electric and gas illumination. Cecilia concentrated on the woman's face, with its look of swagger and disappointment. She didn't know if her suspicions of the model had been right, but now it hardly seemed important. Not because Lars's liaisons were over, but because these days the individual women rarely mattered.

Cecilia continued strolling through the galleries until two extraordinary paintings stopped her. One, called *Interior*, showed a room with two pieces of furniture and completely empty of people. The room was painted pink, a competitive, disturbing pink, with lighter trim. The mouldings and plasterwork were heavy and classical. The desolation of it. The elegance. The disappointment. The other painting had a single person in a room, a woman with her back to the viewer. The same Greek Revival moulding. The same frightening, truthful emptiness. She stayed in front of them for a long time and finally left. But she kept returning, unable to get enough of their beautiful sorrow.

Lars found her there, and said, "What do you see in those blank rooms? Come here and look at Liljefors's animals."

The pictures she loved were by a Danish painter called Vilhelm Hammershoi. As she and Lars were saying their good nights, Pontus Furstenberg said, "Mrs. Vogt has an eye. If Hammershoi comes again to Gothenburg, I will have a dinner and invite you."

But she did not want to meet the painter, only to look at his pictures. Gothilda Furstenberg smiled at her, as if she understood.

In the street, as they waited for a cab, Lars said, "The Furstenbergs seemed very happy."

"With their gallery, or in general?"

"Both," he said. "Don't you find them a devoted couple?"

She shrugged. A marriage was like a country. It might look thoroughly mapped, but there were always unknown and unstudied regions, even for those who lived in the country. It would not surprise her to hear Lars describe their own union as devoted.

Chapter Thirty-six

SEPTEMBER 1911

No OTHER WOMAN ever threatened Cecilia as Lydia Barnes had. What happened after Lydia was a slow wearing away rather than a dramatic rupture. In spite of the rapprochement with Lars, the old pattern resurfaced, and there were too many nights when he came in late smelling of other women. (Why did these women insist on wearing perfume that was so dense and clamorous?) There were a few models who startled more than necessary when Cecilia met them in the hallway—she never went to the studio when a model was there—while Lars brushed his hair down on his forehead into a reverse widow's peak and looked unconcerned.

Once she and her cousin Eva took shelter from the rain in a Stockholm restaurant and stumbled into a tryst between Lars and Klara Mertens, a client's wife. (Cecilia had to assume that this was rare, it was bad for business.) Lars and Mrs. Mertens were being shown into a private dining room off the main one. The woman, whose husband Lars had painted in his riding clothes, trailed a fur as if flaunting a guilty secret. Lars and Mrs. Mertens did not see Cecilia and Eva, and Eva pretended not to notice.

After a certain point she could almost turn a blind eye to Lars's dalliances with his models. For a painter, it was what the French call a *déformation professionelle.* When a man spent dozens of hours concentrating on the shadow on a throat, or the exact way light falls on a rosy haunch, perhaps only an angel could resist. Even Nils Olsson, the patron saint of family life, at least as far as the Germans were concerned, was rumoured to stray in that way.

Cecilia dared to hope that she had achieved a hard-won resignation, even an equanimity. She could expect that Lars's transgressions would be minor and would take place far from her sphere. It turned out she was wrong about that, at least about the latter part.

By 1911, the maid Hedvig had gotten too old for the house's heavy work and Cecilia sent her off to the Folk School, where they kept the textile collection. Hedvig could do some careful washing and stain removal and some basic mending. The girl who was to take her place stepped into Cecilia's study wearing the dress of her village—a white kerchief, a black skirt and a waist-length black jacket outlined with a thin red cord. Her yellow apron, banded in openwork stripes, announced she was in mourning. Although not particularly tall, she seemed in danger of bumping her head on the ceiling, as if a large but timid beast had been penned inside a Louis XVI cage.

"Sit down, Sigrid. Yes, right there. I see you are from Leksand."

"Yes, ma'am."

"And my condolences." Cecilia nodded at her apron.

"Thank you, ma'am. My father died just before Easter."

"Why is it you want to learn to be a maid?"

"To earn money for my passage to America, ma'am. All my brothers have left the farm and are in Minnesota. My sister works at a cloth factory in Stockholm to earn her passage, but the work is hard. The women have to do most of the hauling of the big bolts of cloth, and they work from seven in the morning until six in the evening. I'd rather stay in a small place like Siljevik than move to Stockholm."

"What factory does your sister work in?" Cecilia asked, dreading the answer.

SOFIE & CECILIA   255

"I think it's called . . . Ideal something."

Really, she thought, Fredrik should be ashamed. People were not going to tolerate these conditions for much longer.

"And how long do you imagine it will take you to earn your passage to America?"

"They say about two years, ma'am."

The girl seemed sensible enough. Mrs. Holm would show her over the house, explaining about the central heating and electricity, the room with a big bathtub fixed to the floor, and next door to that the room with a toilet whose bowl was always full of water. And the separate bathroom and toilet for the servants. Cecilia insisted that the maids who served dinner must bathe before putting on their blue dresses and white aprons trimmed with broderie anglaise. Lars laughed at her fussiness, but there was no point in using the good china or serving Chablis with the fish if the maids looked grimy or, even worse, smelled bad.

Sigrid settled in well, and the other servants had no complaints. One day, after she had been with them a few months, Cecilia was looking for the cook. Nils and Sofie were coming to dinner with some English visitors, and she wanted to serve rice pudding with saffron, Nils's favourite dessert. Normally they would serve something French, and Cecilia knew the cook would grumble at the idea of this ordinary pudding, but it would interest the English as typically Swedish. She put her head in the laundry room and found Sigrid mending the pocket on her apron—not the white one with the broderie anglaise, but her everyday red-and-white checked one.

There was nothing extraordinary about a maid bent over some sewing in the laundry room. But her face when she raised it and saw Cecilia said everything: fear, guilt, innocence, anger, disgust and, most of all, pity. She drew her arms together in a panic, like a bird pulling in its wings, trying to hide the telltale apron, which told nothing. In a second, Cecilia crossed the room, wrenched the apron away from her, needle and thread and all, and ran out with it across the lawn to the studio. On the way she thought, I should have told the girl she has nothing to fear. But first she had to go to the studio.

Lars was holding their dog, Mouche, standing back from a portrait of his mother to see what it needed, and he looked up with a smile. Until he saw her face, and the balled-up apron that she threw down on his worktable. A jar holding brushes tipped over when she banged the table, and an oily yellow-green stain began moving across the apron. The needle and thread swung from it like a pendulum.

"No. No! Not in my house, and not with one of my maids."

He nodded, and hesitated only briefly.

"No. Of course not. I beg your pardon."

Plainly, he hoped that it would end there, but she had more to say. How dare he interfere with the smooth running of the house, which he depended upon! These girls were given into their care, and now this one was no better off than if she had worked at Ideal Textiles— worse off, in some ways. She wanted to humiliate him, to make him contrite, to make him see it from her point of view, from Sigrid's point of view. That had always been fruitless and was still fruitless, and she knew it but could not stop. Lars paid extravagant attention to Mouche, stroking her, checking her mouth. Cecilia took no notice.

"Not in my house, not in the Folk School, where I see you have your eye on the weaving instructor, not at the orphanage, no one from the Homecraft Association, nothing in which I am involved. In your studio, I know nothing of your models, nor do I wish to. But not there"—pointing across the way to the house. "Not ever."

"Of course, my dear. I knew better."

What struck her most was the expression on his face. He did not look sorry, nor ashamed that he had humiliated her, nor angry that she was trying to curb his masculine liberty. He looked bored. Bored that they were wasting their time talking about something that was not going to change. Something that was going to happen again and again, and pretending otherwise was silly. Fine, she could draw a boundary beyond which he could not go, but that was all. It was nothing to make a scene about. Now he wanted to get back to his painting.

That moment when she saw his boredom was the moment when the whole thing tore—not on a seam as with Sigrid's apron, where it could be mended unobtrusively, but right in the centre of the garment. It could be repaired, if the wearer needed shelter from rain and cold and public shame, but the mend would be ugly and crooked, an unwholesome scar. The piece might still be serviceable but would never again be beautiful.

She had one more thing to say.

"Nor will I socialize any more with Klara Mertens. I will not invite her or her husband here, nor dine with them in Stockholm."

If he was surprised that she knew, he gave no sign.

After Sigrid, they retreated into an old-fashioned marriage. No, that was wrong. Lars had gone there ahead of her, and now she joined him. They had his work and their family. Although there were no children, there was Lars's mother and her mother as well as the nieces and nephews. He depended on her and cared for her. But their original promise of being "all in all to each other," as silly Flora Finching says in *Little Dorrit*—of being a new kind of couple—had come to nothing. Perhaps Lars never made that promise, in spite of the years he worked to win her hand. Perhaps she had just assumed it. Mamma, if she were here, would say that was a childish idea. "New kind of couple, old kind of couple," she imagined Mamma saying, "they all come to the same thing in the end." Looked at from Mamma's point of view, she could understand the bored look that had crossed Lars's face. Men were going to have affairs, and their wives were going to be more or less unhappy about it. And that was going to continue. Probably their parents had got that right. Somehow her generation, or at least the women, had come to expect more of men than human nature could bear.

Mamma would also have said that she had great freedom in her own separate realm: that that was something new, since she was so bent on newness. But freedom was not what she'd had in mind when she pleaded with Mamma and Fredrik to let them marry.

Sigrid took the money for her passage without comment. Looked at cynically, she had earned it more quickly than she had planned, but neither she nor Cecilia were cynical. After the Olssons and their English friends left the next morning, Cecilia spent the day in the storeroom of the Folk School, where they kept the textile collections. So many baby shirts with big upstanding collars, white bonnets with a woven blue-and-white ribbon covering the back seam, blankets for the carved cradles. There was an infant's shirt very like the one they had seen in Professor Hazelius's museum years before, with a simple ring of rosebuds around the neck. Lars came up to see what she was doing. They were still wary and sensitive with each other, but on the surface they behaved normally. Usually he left the textile collections to her, but now he looked at the pile of baby shirts and said, "My dear old woman, don't you have enough of these?"

She made it known to him that he would be welcome in her bedroom when it was the time of the month when a woman might conceive. Only then. She still had her courses at forty-four, although many women her age did not.

This arrangement lasted until the courses stopped, and after that there was no point.

Chapter Thirty-seven

To Cecilia's disappointment, Sofie was too far from her at Walther and Wilhelmina von Hallwyl's gleaming dinner table for conversation. She sent Sofie a look, and they retreated to the powder room, although neither wore powder.

Replacing her comb in her bag, Cecilia said, "These Frenchified dinners are when I think your refusal to wear corsets is most brilliant. Even with my notoriously hollow leg, I could only eat a few bites of each course once we got to the *vol-au-vent*."

"I suppose we should go back," Sofie said. They had installed themselves on two brocaded chaises longues, resting their evening-slippered feet.

"No, let's stay here a little longer. It's cooler."

Cecilia wanted to ask Sofie if she had thought again about the American embroidery kits, but something held her back. To bide her time, she asked about the children. Was Markus still saving money for a camera? And were Sonja's plans settled yet? Sonja, who hoped to study art, was a favourite of Cecilia's.

"I finished *The Awakening*," Sofie said abruptly, breaking into Cecilia's questions about the family. Foyles Bookshop had sent Cecilia the American novel that Isabella Gardner had recommended so highly, and she had passed it on to Sofie after reading it herself.

"I loved the portrait of the summer colony outside New Orleans," Sofie went on, "the sense of the heat and the sea, and all the details of life in New Orleans—the women's at-homes, those strange American drinks they call cocktails (I wonder why?), the way the heroine gets around the city, walking or on the streetcars, other small things."

"But what about the centre of the book," Cecilia asked, settling in for the conversation, "the stirring of the heroine's sensuous life, and her love for the young man?"

"I suppose that was very well done, too," Sofie said less enthusiastically, "but I felt sorry for the woman's husband. He wasn't really so awful."

"Are you serious? He was selfish, inconsiderate, concerned only with his business and how his wife's behaviour would affect it. Honestly, Sofie."

"Well, I did feel sorry for him," Sofie said. "I can't help it. And even leaving the husband aside, how could she take her own life when she had two little children? I know the writer tells us she was not a 'mother-woman,' but that is unforgivable—even incredible. I cannot believe a disappointment in love would lead a mother to do such a thing."

"You make 'a disappointment in love' sound very small," Cecilia said. "But the young man, Robert, was her great love, and he had renounced her. She had nothing to live for."

"Oh please, Cecilia. You seem so hard-headed, but you are such a romantic! You would never do anything like that."

"No, probably not," Cecilia agreed. "But while I am reading, I understand her despair. And you always take the husband's side."

Sofie laughed. "That is so outrageous, I'm not even going to argue it." Cecilia made an effort not to roll her eyes. How could Sofie be so blind to her own bias?

Sofie continued, "And I suppose you think it is all right, then, the affair she has—what is her name? Edna? yes, Edna—the affair Edna has with the playboy when her husband is out of town?"

That was rather a bold question. They didn't usually ask each other so bluntly about things of this sort, but *The Awakening* was a bold novel.

"Well, I'm not sure," Cecilia said slowly. "Her husband has not brought her that kind of joy . . . perhaps she is susceptible to the playboy because she is really falling in love with Robert . . . I'm not sure."

Sofie looked skeptical.

"But there's something else," Cecilia said. "When she starts changing her life, Edna begins to draw, and even to sell her drawings. It's a sign of her growing independence, and she works at it. Didn't that intrigue you?"

"Not very much. The author is so much more interested in Edna's romances than in her drawings. And the real artist in the story, the pianist—Mademoiselle Reisz—is the old stereotype, a homely, bitter spinster who lives alone and only for her music. It's not a happy picture of the artistic life for a woman."

"Yes, I suppose," Cecilia said, reluctantly.

"It's the small touches, almost like genre paintings, that I will remember about that book," Sofie said. "The women and their children on the beach like great white seabirds, the mothers' white robes and veiled hats blowing in the wind. The glamorous, dimly lit dinner party Edna gives in her new little house, with the oddly matched guests and a feeling—almost—of imminent danger."

They sat silent for a minute, each remembering that scene. Then, sighing a little, Cecilia swung her legs over the chaise longue, and Sofie took one last look in the mirror.

An hour later, Cecilia was sitting with Sofie on a bench in front of a too-pretty Van Ruysdael, while they waited for their husbands to return from a stroll through the Hallwyls' private gallery. Their silence was more strained than companionable. After dinner, Sofie had uncharacteristically lost patience with Nils's usual anti-modernist tirade. Her response—brief, irritated and powerful—had taken all three of them aback. Then, when the men retreated to look at the pictures, Sofie had rapped Cecilia's knuckles when she had proposed a perfectly sensible idea about Sofie manufacturing her fabrics.

"Well?" Cecilia greeted the men when they returned. "Have you finished enumerating all the heinous crimes of the new French painters?"

"We do not have enough years left to finish that list," Lars said, straight-faced. He could joke about it, but not Nils.

"The Hallwyls do have a Poussin worth seeing," Nils said, looking almost reluctant to admit it. "If you go down this side . . ."

But Sofie interrupted him.

"Not tonight, Nils. It's late."

She said this impatiently, a small coda that echoed her earlier testiness. This time Cecilia covered any awkwardness by agreeing that it was time to thank the Hallwyls, get their coats and set out into the night.

The Hallwyls really had been very hospitable. While they accepted their guests' thanks in the front hall and asked about Lars's and Nils's latest projects, Cecilia felt slightly guilty that the Vogts' and Olssons' attitude to their hosts, if not their behaviour, had been rather cavalier. But probably the Hallwyls had noticed nothing.

A servant laden with furs emerged and lined them up carefully on a large table. After he helped her on with hers, another servant motioned her to a chair, where he fastened her boots. The hall was full of people being shouldered with dark, heavy coats by straining servants, or buttoned into boots, while the Hallwyls made sure the leave-taking was as well organized as the rest of the evening. A Swedish winter scene.

Cecilia glanced over at Sofie, who was fastening the clasps on her fur. An ungenerous thought flashed through her mind. Sometimes there was something almost mulish about Sofie. Lars often said that

Cecilia was the driving force behind much of Siljevik. Why, then, was she powerless when it came to her dearest friend? Why did Sofie resist her plans—such modest, practical plans—for her textiles? Whether her balkiness was a sign of modesty or arrogance, or something else, Cecilia did not know. Sofie had so much that Cecilia did not—children, artistic talent, a husband who was not famous for philandering. And yet at times Cecilia wanted to protect her, and at other times to wake her up and stir her into activity. Her placidity was so irritating. But every once in a while there was a glimpse—or two or three, such as she had seen tonight—of a more tumultuous Sofie.

After the door closed behind them, the two couples stood for a minute on the sidewalk looking across the street at Berzelii Park. It had filled up with snow since they had gone in, and fat flakes were still falling at long intervals. The yellow light from the street lights illumined the blue-black sky and the snowy park.

Lars took a last look at the Hallwyls' house. Its sober front was dark, although the servants were still cleaning up in the public rooms that faced the courtyard.

"Well, it's more than a little old-fashioned."

"But they have an interesting plan," Cecilia said, "which is to leave the house and their collections just as they are, down to the dust cloths and brooms, as a museum. They want to preserve the daily life of prosperous art lovers of their time in amber, and to let the house speak for itself."

She turned toward Sofie as she spoke, trying to determine whether her friend was still annoyed with her. Sofie wore her usual peaceful face as she considered the Hallwyls' idea. "I suppose it comes from a certain self-importance, but it is original."

Lars said lightly, "Cecilia and I have been talking about doing something like that."

Nils was still cross. "It's a terrible, self-conscious idea and very morbid," he said. "I don't want any of you to think about it."

Sofie gave a small, dry laugh.

"Nils doesn't believe he is going to die."

Cecilia allowed herself a tentative smile. Well, at least I am not the only person here who is irritating Sofie.

With that, they said good night. The Olssons were walking across the park to the Berns Hotel and the Vogts, who were staying with Cecilia's sister Natalie, got into a cab.

In the cab, Cecilia stared out the window. When they passed a street light, Lars asked, "What are you counting on your fingers?"

"How few organized, effective women there are in novels."

"You mean bossy ones?"

She gave him the sniff he expected.

"That is how most people see them. I see them as strong and purposeful."

"I couldn't agree more. And I benefit every day from living with one of those women."

She gave him an absent smile, and went back to her list.

1. Mrs. Proudie, the domineering wife of the bishop in Trollope's Barchester novels.
2. Aunt Norris, the sycophantic, snobbish upholder of the status quo in Jane Austen's *Mansfield Park*.
3. Marian Halcombe, the mannish and courageous half-sister of the heroine in Wilkie Collins's *The Woman in White*.
4. Daniel Defoe's Moll Flanders, who supports herself as a servant, a thief and a farmer but mostly by marriages.
5. Sophia Baines in Bennett's *The Old Wives' Tale*, who runs a successful pension in Paris.

She was not very happy with this list, or sure these women had much in common. The only one with a good business sense was Sophia. Moll was indefatigable and ambitious, but there was not much more to say about her. Marian Halcombe was chiefly distinguished by her refusal to marry or otherwise bow to the wishes of men, but why did she have to have a moustache and a face too strong to be pretty? Aunt Norris was horrid, and especially unkind to the poor heroine, Fanny. And yet Jane Austen, scrupulously fair as usual, made a point of saying that the disciplined Aunt Norris would have done better with nine children and no money than her sister, Fanny's kind but feckless mother, did. The only one Cecilia liked was Mrs. Proudie in the early Barchester novels, decisive and resilient where her husband was weak and vacillating. But by the end of the series she had become a monster.

Chapter Thirty-eight

APRIL 1914

WHEN CECILIA FIRST picked up her pen to write to Sofie about the young woman who had applied to become the Vogts' assistant, she found herself at a loss. No matter how much detail she provided, she could not quite convey what was so extraordinary about Lisbeth Gregorius. Lars, as expected, had turned on the charm. First, because Miss Gregorius was a professional woman, he complimented her qualifications and experience in Berlin. What did she think of the idea of adding a museum of early German art on Berlin's Museum Island? Was it too ambitious? When he wanted to show how much he agreed with what she had just said, he would extend his arm almost to her arm or hand, as if to underscore his approval, although of course he did not actually touch her. Finally, his suit turned wordless: he turned his body completely in her direction, he held his teacup in the same way that she did, he nodded vehemently whenever she made a point.

And this was the extraordinary part. Miss Gregorius did not appear to see it. It wasn't as if she noted Lars's behaviour and decided to ignore it. She seemed simply unaware of it. She was focused on the work that needed to be done, the archiving, the conservation, the design of the museum she was envisioning, the presentation of the exhibits. Not on the man in front of her. Cecilia had never seen anything like it. Did they teach that at the university?

She felt sorry for Lars. She had never seen him at such a disadvantage. He kept trying to start again with Miss Gregorius, and Cecilia was reminded of how, in the early days of the automobile, people tried again and again to crank up the balky engines of those self-propelled wagons. But Miss Gregorius took no notice.

Siljevik, 30 April 1914
Dear Sofie,

Miss Gregorius has been with us a few weeks now, and I must admit, life is quite different. She slipped into the office we gave her, the room next to my study, as if she had always been there. Almost immediately she ordered, without apologies, a very large quantity of office supplies from Stromberg's Stationers in Stockholm. She likes the oak filing cabinet and desk we brought into the room, but asked if they could be moved to the opposite wall, so that she could overlook Lars's studio and the churchyard. I assumed that she would live with us, or perhaps with Lars's mother next door, but she said, with thanks, that she would prefer to live elsewhere in the village. That was a surprise, but I saw her logic. I made inquiries, and gave her a few likely addresses. She chose a room in the schoolmaster's house. I hope she will be warm enough: Mrs. Turesson is well known as a "careful" housekeeper.

She usually eats the midday meal with us, although she insists that it is not necessary, or not necessary every day. But I persist, because while Lars relaxes over a glass of wine, Miss Gregorius acquires useful information. With very little prompting, he reminisces about his work

with the animals as a boy in his grandparents' summer
pasture, or about his youthful belief that he would be a
sculptor of horses.

When Lars is away, I use the mealtime to ask Miss
Gregorius—her Christian name is Lisbeth—about
herself. She is the eldest child of a professor of philology
and his wife, and grew up in Uppsala, in an old house
near the cathedral. As a little girl, she loved pictures, and
when no one could find Lisbeth, someone would be sent
to the professor's library. There she would be, wedged
into the corner of the window seat, with a book of
reproductions bigger than she was. "The book is having a
look at Lisbeth," they would say, rather than the other
way around.

But enough of this. As you can see, I am enjoying
having her with us.

I wonder how things are at Askebo—what is your
latest project? How do you and Nils like Marianne's beau,
and has he banished all thoughts of Torchon lace from
her head (not to mention the more challenging patterns)?
But here is Miss Gregorius standing at my door with
what looks like an engraving she wants identified, so I
close hastily.

With love from
Cecilia

Chapter Thirty-nine

JUNE 1914

CECILIA LOOKED AT Sofie, who was watching Mr. Lawrie look at Miss Gregorius. Perhaps Sofie was sensing a spark between Mr. Lawrie and Miss Gregorius? The two had just met, here at the Wallace Collection in London. Cecilia's first thought was that a match between them made great sense, and might be delightful. Then she realized that Mr. Lawrie would have to wait a long time before Miss Gregorius would be free to move to Glasgow. She and Lars certainly could not do without her until the museum was open and all the other arrangements were in place. And even then, Miss Gregorius might have to stay in Siljevik for a year or so, perhaps more, for the sake of continuity. So no, it was not a good idea after all.

While their little party walked through the Wallace's galleries, Miss Gregorius making careful notes that related to the Vogts' future museum, Lars was talking salacious nonsense about the source of the museum's collections, the marquesses of Hertford and Richard Wallace. Cecilia could hear Lars assuring Mr. Lawrie that the marquesses were famous libertines, and that the fourth marquess's illegitimate son, Richard Wallace, had followed in his father's footsteps. He had met the future Lady Wallace when she was a saleswoman in a perfume shop in Paris. She bore him an illegitimate son when Lord Wallace was twenty-two, but his father refused his consent to their marriage. Lord Wallace waited thirty years, until his father died, and then they married.

"Well, that shows a degree of fidelity, at least." Mr. Lawrie was clearly less interested in this gossip than Lars, but seemed to feel he should make some response.

"Oh, there were many other women along the way," Lars assured him. He radiated the certainty that, given wealth and the tolerant atmosphere of France, where the marquesses mostly lived, any normal man would do as they did, following their sensual appetites wherever they might lead. Mr. Holcross, the pleasant, well-informed young man who had been assigned by the Wallace Collection to accompany the Vogts as they inspected the museum, affected not to hear these revelations. Cecilia walked by his side as he led the way.

At times like these, it felt particularly demoralizing being married to an old roue who tried to charm everyone except his wife, and whose magnetism still worked. When that happened, Cecilia would sometimes find herself trying to beguile someone—almost to see if it were possible, and usually unsuccessfully. Mr. Holcross's manners were irreproachable and, unsurprisingly, there was no answering flicker.

Just as Lars's pleasure in the marquesses' debaucheries was becoming intolerable, he stopped in the West Room, and looked around. "You can see how their sensuality informed their collection," he said, extending his arms to embrace the cherubs and beautiful women captured on canvas, tapestry, enamel and porcelain. "How their pictures and statues and even their small things, the snuffboxes, the porcelain, are perfectly finished, pretty, sensuous things. The taste of the eighteenth-century French court, in other words. There is not much work here that shows ugliness, violence or sadness. No unfinished work, no experiments. This collection is designed around pleasure."

There was the Lars she could never leave. Although it was infuriating wading through his dross—like an adolescent boy who had just discovered the pleasures of the flesh, he never tired of talking about it—there was always the promise of gold. She could see Miss Gregorius nodding.

In the Oval Drawing Room they found Boucher's portrait of Madame de Pompadour in her garden. She was relaxed, standing with one arm extending over the base of a statue, her hand holding a closed fan. The frills on her sleeves and skirt were furled like the leaves on the trees behind her. It was as if a particularly lovely shrub had taken human, female form. Miss Gregorius told them that Madame de Pompadour had commissioned the portrait to announce to the court that, although she was no longer Louis XV's mistress, she was something perhaps equally impressive—the king's confidante.

"How do we know that?" Sofie asked, sounding more skeptical than Cecilia thought was necessary.

"From the statue behind her, which is called *Friendship Consoling Love*," Miss Gregorius said, "and from her little dog perched on the garden seat, a symbol of fidelity."

Well, there was no denying that Miss Gregorius was very knowledgeable.

Cecilia turned back to the portrait. When passion ended or love changed in other ways, there was always a passage to be negotiated. If the Frenchwoman was feeling forlorn now that the king's passion had waned into friendship, her poise belied it. That, of course, was the point of the portrait, to demonstrate to the court that she was as powerful as ever. Besides, Madame de Pompadour had work to do—and work, Cecilia told herself, is a balm. Wilier than the king and more knowledgeable about politics, Madame de Pompadour was intent on shoring up his fading popularity. And yet . . . and yet. Some sadness would be natural.

Sofie did not look as if she were having a particularly good time. After a last glance at Madame de Pompadour, Cecilia followed her into the room with the Dutch pictures.

"Mr. Lawrie seems very nice," Cecilia said. "He and Miss Gregorius are getting on well."

"Yes, apparently," Sofie said.

Mr. Lawrie joined them in front of a strange Dutch picture. At the edge of a forest, a woman dressed for a ball in white satin held a dead hare over her lap while her husband and daughter ignored her. According to Mr. Lawrie, shooting game was prestigious, so the fact that the woman was chosen to flaunt the dead animal was a mark of favour. In theory. She didn't look as if she regarded it as any sort of privilege.

Married life, thought Cecilia. Someone always had to pay. Were the woman's white satin and the peaches the little girl carried on a platter worth the price?

"At least this time it is the hare that has been sacrificed," Sofie said.

Mr. Lawrie looked mystified, but Cecilia nodded.

"Instead of the woman, you mean."

Chapter Forty

1915

MISS GREGORIUS HAD already decided that her first task would be to catalogue all of Lars's works in Siljevik, from the house, the studio, the fishing lodge and even the Folk School, where his paintings were hung in rotation. After that, she would move on to the textile, pottery, silver and art collections, but first, Lars's works. He helped her with dates and provenance, if he remembered them. On occasion, he would lose interest in Miss Gregorius's precision and hazard a random guess or two. She paid no attention to these transparent inventions. Cecilia, who understood the need for accuracy, had kept records of sales. When Lars was away, Cecilia and Miss Gregorius worked together in his studio.

One day, they were sorting through some pictures, Miss Gregorius wearing the cotton gloves with which she rummaged through paintings or files of engravings. She extracted a painting called *Midnight* from a stack leaning against a wall. A woman, her dark blonde hair caught up in a knot, her heavy breasts straining at her blouse, rowed a small boat on a bright midsummer night. Her head turned toward the approaching shore, and her brawny arms wielded the oars as if the effort cost her nothing.

"She looks familiar."

"Yes," Cecilia said. "You may well have seen her in Siljevik. She is Clara Dahl, one of my husband's favourite models. She lives on Persvagen."

"Any idea of the date?"

"Yes, I have it here. 1891. We bought it back from a Gothenburg collector, Kasper Lennart, and he had taken it soon after the paint dried."

Miss Gregorius wrote the date in her notebook.

"And this?"

It was Clara again, braiding her hair in folk costume, with a red ribbon held in readiness between her teeth. In the background, a woman naked above the waist bent down with her back to the viewer, one breast swinging low.

"Pictures of Clara, with this pinky-orange colouring, are probably all from 1891. The Dahls needed money that summer, and she was happy to pose. My husband never sold this one. He was pleased with the way the light turned that long fall of her hair into copper."

Miss Gregorius peered at the half-nude woman in the background.

"Clara keeps her clothes on."

From someone else, Cecilia might have found that remark verging on impertinence, but she laughed.

"Yes. The Siljevik women who posed for Lars did not care very much if strangers in Stockholm, which is a world away to them, saw them in the nude. But once they realized that many of the pictures would stay here and be shown every once in a while in the village, it was a different matter. Clara's husband is a respectable working man, and their children went to the village school. The nude is not a local woman."

Miss Gregorius bent and detached another canvas from the pile.

"Nor are these two, I suppose."

It was a nude scene of a mother and daughter, titled *In the Bathhouse*. The daughter leaned down to dry her legs with a cotton towel, but the picture belonged to her mother. Slick with sweat, she planted herself in front of the fire, all glistening curves and globes, from her round head wrapped in a kerchief to her reddish buttocks to the calves that seemed almost too slender to support her stocky body.

Miss Gregorius tipped the painting into the light, as they studied its heat and lassitude in silence. A glowing line, the reflection from the great fire, traced the mother's breast, ribs, inner thigh. Finally, Cecilia said, "No, I don't know these women, or when this was painted. I must have been visiting in Stockholm."

Miss Gregorius put a question mark after the painting's title in her book.

Next they came to a portrait of Cecilia with her dog. Mouche brimmed with life, willing to sit on his mistress's lap but ready in an instant to spring up if activity, recreational or protective, were called for. Cecilia, on the other hand, looked careworn, all but swallowed up in her voluminous red coat and floppy red beret. The festive colour underlined her sallowness.

Sometimes when they had worked together for hours, lost in the look and smell of canvases and drawings, Cecilia heard herself say something that sounded more as if she were talking to herself than to another person. The contrast between the previous paintings and this one seemed to call for comment, and she said, "Here, Miss Gregorius, we have a change from his usual models."

She hoped her tone was dry, and far from self-pity.

"This is from 1902," she added.

Cecilia was looking at the portrait, so she did not see Miss Gregorius's expression, only heard the intake of breath. Then she felt a gloved hand placed briefly on her own.

"Please, call me Lisbeth."

Lars noticed the change.

"I see you call Miss Gregorius by her first name."

"Well, we work together so much. There doesn't seem to be any point in formality."

He nodded, but knew better than to attempt less formality himself. Cecilia wondered if part of Lisbeth's appeal was that she was oblivious to Lars's allure. She saw it and saluted it in his pictures, but not in his person. It was one more thing about her that was distinctive.

At first, Miss Gregorius doled out the stories she told Cecilia with care, but as the two women worked long days together, she told Cecilia more. The only girl, with two younger brothers, she had been the best scholar in the family. Unlike most fathers, hers was not inclined to ignore his daughter's promise.

"Lisbeth is meant for study," he declared, and he meant the university, which was still a fairly new possibility for women. Her mother fretted that if she went to the university fewer men would want to marry her. Her father said he hoped she would need only one. Lisbeth said that she did not intend to marry anyone, ever. Her father told the two of them to stop talking nonsense. Lisbeth put her arm around her gentle, stubborn mother and told her not to worry. "But I am stubborn too," she told Cecilia, "and I never took it back."

Cecilia was not sure what to make of that. It had never occurred to her for a single moment, as a girl or young woman, that she would not marry.

Meanwhile, Lisbeth was continuing her story. Armed with her degree in history and a few letters of recommendation, she convinced Max Friedlander at Berlin's Kaiser-Friedrich Museum to take her on as an apprentice curator. Berlin had a few women curators, while Sweden had none. In fact, her title was a glorification. She laboured away in the dusty storage rooms of the museum cataloguing, cataloguing, cataloguing.

Her three years in Berlin were a mixture of austerity and rapture. No doubt the austerity heightened the rapture, she admitted, as it had with the medieval saints who starved themselves and had mystical experiences as a result. Her meagre salary paid for an attic room and endless bowls of potato soup with rye bread that she ate on long benches in the artist cafes on Museum Island. The rapture came from the museums, from occasionally breathing in the pure air of Herr Friedlander's scholarship, and from her work, humble as it was. She had hoped to work with paintings from the nineteenth century, but the Kaiser-Friedrich collections were older. The Renaissance engravings she was assigned to catalogue did not particularly interest her at first, but gradually she came to love their earnest details. The care with which a messenger lifted his pointed shoe over a puddle, the guarded pride in Our Lady's look at the chubby Saviour lolling on her lap, the methodical way a mason built a wall, icing each brick with mortar like a *patissier*. She still hoped to move beyond the sixteenth century someday, but she was content.

Her colleague in the Prints Department and later her roommate in the attic room was a young woman named Marthe Schiller, who was also willing to wait. Marthe's passion was for the ornate wooden altarpieces of the South German carver Tilman Riemenschneider. She dreamed of a position in Wurzburg, where she could be close to the master's works, although a woman curator was unheard of in conservative Bavaria. Meanwhile, she catalogued alongside Lisbeth.

"It's nice you found a friend," Cecilia said into the silence that had fallen.

"Yes," Lisbeth said. "Marthe was like the people in the engravings we worked with—she did everything seriously. And her oval face with its high forehead reminded me of those medieval and Renaissance figures too."

Friday nights, Lisbeth and Marthe would go to the public bath in Oderberger Strasse and pay their ten pfennigs for thirty minutes of cleansing. Saturdays in fine weather, they took bread, cheese and apples and picnicked in the Tiergarten. In the evenings, after their frugal supper in the attic—more bread and cheese, some broth in which lentils floated like tiny coins—they read and wrote letters at the table, on either side of the lamp.

Lisbeth expected that she and Marthe would eventually move to more comfortable lodgings. As the years passed, Lisbeth imagined that she would be transferred to Paintings in the Neue Galerie. Marthe would find a sculptor in the Berlin collections she would love almost as much as Tilman Riemenschneider. They would spend their holidays walking in the Tyrol, and perhaps in England's Lake District.

But one winter Friday night, as they walked home from the public bath, Marthe had a surprise. She had accepted a proposal of marriage from a classmate at the university, a young man named Johannes who hoped to become a professor after he finished his military service. Lisbeth had noticed Marthe spending more time in the evenings writing letters, but that was all she noticed. Stupidly, she asked, "But what about Tilman?" as they called Riemenschneider. Oh, Marthe said, that had been a mad dream. The Bavarian museums would never hire a woman. Johannes had kindly offered to take a side trip to Wurzburg on their honeymoon so that she could see her favourite pieces once more.

"A farewell visit!" she said merrily.

With Marthe's departure for Hanover, where she and Johannes would live, Germany lost much of its lustre for Lisbeth. People were saying that a war was inevitable, but she was ready to leave in any case. First she went to Hanover for Marthe's wedding—a quiet ceremony in the family parlour and a breakfast in the garden, heavy with lilacs—and then she returned to Berlin to pack up.

Back in Sweden, prospects for work were not good. The National Museum in Stockholm was not about to hire a woman. When she heard through a friend of her father's that Lars Vogt was making discreet inquiries about a curator for his private collections, her first thought was, Water and skin. He does wonderful things with water and skin. Being around his pictures would be interesting.

———

Listening to Lisbeth recount the story of her journey to Siljevik, Cecilia thought: The timing is ironic. Lisbeth had come to them already intrigued by Lars's work, and now that she had been there some months, her enthusiasm had risen dramatically. At the same time, it was undeniable that Lars's star was falling in some important quarters. Criticism mounted when, with no experience in restoration, he persuaded the rector at Uppsala University to allow him to restore the university's sixteenth-century portrait of Gustav Vasa. Although his work was supervised by the conservator at the National Museum, in the end almost everyone considered it the ruin of a historic painting. Among the few who disputed the sorry outcome were Lars and Lisbeth. One newspaper cartoonist lampooned the scandal by drawing Vasa's head on the body of a voluptuous nude woman. Cecilia had to smile, ruefully, when she saw it, but Lisbeth was furious.

Lars had always been an eager customer for art, but his buying had recently taken on a new frenzy and credulity. Against expert opinion, he was convinced that he had bought a Raphael and then a Velázquez. Of the so-called Velázquez, he wrote to Cecilia from Munich that the modelling of the face in the portrait was one of Velázquez's strongest. "It is grand and I've never been so happy about a find." She wondered what had happened to his acuity. When they came to set up the gallery, she and Lisbeth would have heated arguments about that attribution, and others.

Most seriously, at least to Cecilia, critics were beginning to see Lars's work as passe. Lars and Nils Olsson still thought of themselves as modern painters who had freed the Swedish art establishment from its hidebound attitudes. Did they never notice, Cecilia wondered, that that had happened three decades ago? Compared with the younger generation of artists, who had turned painting inside out, Nils's and Lars's innovations had been subtle and small-scale. Lars, of course, saw no reason to change. Georg Pauli's interest in the new French painters he could regard affectionately, if a bit condescendingly. But when Prince Eugen, whose mind and work he respected more, spent some time in Paris investigating the Cubists, he was cross. The Swedes still loved Lars's scenes of peasant life and the Americans his society portraits. But the critics were losing interest.

Now he gave them another reason to dismiss him: a more and more unbridled sensuality in his nudes. Some of the latest ones looked more like the pictures men pass around in privacy than those that hang on gallery walls. The criticism that came his way because of this new ribaldry amused him more than it irritated him.

Which was why Cecilia knew she could bring it up at the midday meal, with no fear of distracting him from his afternoon work. As usual, he came into the dining room last. She and Lisbeth were at the table, and they could hear the cook pacing in the kitchen, trying to keep the dill sauce for the chicken from curdling. Cecilia thought Lisbeth looked particularly appealing that day, in a soft, rose-coloured woollen dress. Finally Lars slipped into his seat in his quiet way, and looked around expectantly for the tureen as if he had been there for some time, waiting.

After they finished the soup, Cecilia went over the morning's mail briefly. There was a request or two for Mr. Vogt to do a portrait etching, a rearrangement of a sitting for a painting, a note from his engraver in Stockholm about their next appointment, and several notices of auctions and irresistible finds from dealers. Then she came to something more notable, a letter from a Zurich dealer.

She put on her glasses and summarized. "Mr. Siebert says the police raided his premises and took some small reproductions of your nudes. The court fined him twenty francs for selling pornography."

Lars looked up from his plate with interest.

Lisbeth, Cecilia could see, was appalled.

"That is preposterous!" she said. "How dare they misinterpret your pictures . . . which ones have been reproduced?"

Cecilia didn't answer that, but added that Mr. Siebert interpreted the small fine as an admission that the police had been overzealous.

As for Lars, Cecilia knew he enjoyed being on the opposite side of "the half-educated middle class," as he called the Zurich police. If people could not see the poetry in his yawning nudes, their mouths gaping and their legs planted far apart, or barely awake in a dim, airless bedroom, splashing water on their warm bodies, their stretches so uninhibited that it seemed ludicrous to call them poses, so be it.

Lisbeth would not be appeased. She talked passionately about Lars's masterful way with shadows and skin tones in his nudes, about the way a secondary person could remain in the background but exert a powerful influence on the composition as a whole. And about the squalid minds of people who did not see what he was doing in those pictures, which was far from pandering to sordid imaginations. Cecilia wanted to put her hand on Lisbeth's fine cashmere sleeve, feel the tense forearm underneath and tell her not to upset herself.

Chapter Forty-one

FEBRUARY 1916

LARS WENT TO Stockholm, where he was beginning a few portraits, for a week. Cecilia had planned to go with him, because Bukowskis was auctioning a first edition of Mary Wollstonecraft's *Letters from Sweden, Norway and Denmark*, and she wanted to inspect it. But at the last minute, she decided to stay home. She and Lisbeth could work uninterrupted, and Lars would be happy to go to Bukowskis, look over the book and leave a bid.

Early in the week, Lisbeth stayed for dinner and the two began talking about a painting of Lars's from some twenty years ago, called *The Bath*. A woman, seen from the back, is reflected in the mirror as she stands in her shallow tub, squeezing a sponge against her breasts.

"That was how we bathed," Cecilia reminisced. "We had hip baths too, but no full bath with its own plumbing, until the beginning of the century."

"I remember those hip baths," Lisbeth said. "Very uncomfortable. You were always squatting in about six inches of water."

"But very good for painters. The body contorted in all kinds of interesting positions."

"I suppose so. Where is *The Tub* now?"

"We will look it up. I think probably Ernest Thiel has it, in Stockholm. But Lars took the pose, that of the woman with her arms level to her shoulders and squeezing the sponge onto her breast, and made the statue at the front of the garden in the same position."

Perhaps it was the talk of breasts and tubs. Perhaps it was the arrack punch they had had after dinner in front of the fire. Usually they drank no more than a glass of wine at the table, but it was such a cold night and Lisbeth had been talking about her university days in Uppsala. Arrack punch was the male students' favourite drink, and after a few stories of punch-inspired pranks, Cecilia sent her into the kitchen to tell the cook how it was made.

But the cook had already left and the maid was cleaning up, so Lisbeth made the punch herself and brought out the jug and glasses.

"*Punch* comes from the Hindi word for five," she said, looking through her glass as the drink heated their throats and reconciled them to the snowstorm outside.

"I know," Cecilia said, "because traditionally it contains five items."

They laughed. This had happened before: they often knew the same odd fact.

"Alcohol, water, sugar," Lisbeth counted, "lemon . . ."

"Or fruit."

"And spices."

"Or tea."

It was simpler for Lisbeth to spend the night rather than fight the wind and snow to return to Mrs. Turesson's. After they said good night, Cecilia heard her running water in the bathroom. More water than was necessary to wash her hands and face. The water kept running. It was so noisy that it cancelled out thought. Perhaps she needs fresh towels, Cecilia thought. The maids can be so careless about the bathroom. Then she thought, You fool. And before she could think any more, she went briskly to the linen closet, took out two large towels, rapped on the bathroom door and entered without waiting for a reply.

Lisbeth was in the tub, her back to the door.

"Oh, pardon me . . ." Cecilia began, but Lisbeth simply turned her head toward her and interrupted.

"Thank you," she said, referring to the towels. Then, as if it were the most natural thing, she asked, "Could you possibly wash my back? It's impossible for me to reach all the way . . ."

Cecilia knelt and washed her back. Conscientiously, as if much depended on how thoroughly she washed Lisbeth's back. It was long and slim, rounding out generously below the waist, but she washed only the back. She watched herself doing this. The clinical bathroom with its black-and-white tiles was silent, except for the peaceful lapping of the water, as she dipped her sponge in and out of the tub. Finally, when no one could have denied that Lisbeth's back was clean, she turned to Cecilia and kneeled. Cecilia washed her shoulders, her arms, her underarms, and her breasts. Carefully, she lifted the breasts to wash underneath them.

Lisbeth stood in the tub. Water streamed off her body. She held out her arms, and said, "But you'll get all wet."

"No matter," Cecilia said.

In the morning, she rang to have breakfast in her room, something she rarely did. Along with the tea and soft-boiled egg on the tray, the maid left a letter from Sofie. Cecilia stared at the familiar writing on the envelope. Sofie. She would read the letter later.

Although she was certain that Lisbeth was already in her office, she could not risk meeting her in the dining room. It was more than embarrassment that she felt. It was sorrow, and she wanted to be alone with it.

Sitting at the small table, ignoring her breakfast, she turned the sorrow over and over, like a paperweight she wanted to appreciate carefully. First she thought, Something clean and pure and innocent has died, and it is my fidelity as a wife. No matter how many times Lars had broken the promises he made on our wedding day, I had stayed true to them. It was like a shawl that gave no warmth and was not particularly handsome, yet I treasured the shawl.

Then she thought, You're being stupid and sentimental. What is the point of a fidelity that isn't returned? Your beloved English novels have let you down here. They are unable to imagine a moderately virtuous woman who no longer sees the point of one-sided marriage vows. French novels are more honest about these things.

But in all her novels, she had never read anything that approached what had happened the night before.

PART THREE

PART THREE

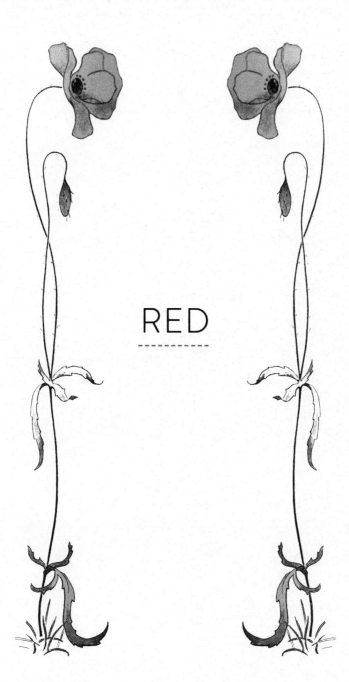

RED

Chapter Forty-two

JANUARY 1924

EVERYTHING WAS AS usual on the night that Nils died. Tilda was practicing a new song for her choir, accompanying herself on the piano. Sofie and Nils said good night to her, and went to their rooms. Sofie still slept in the nursery, although it had been many years since children slept there. She was in her nightdress but had not turned off the light when she heard something small break and something heavy fall, almost in the same instant. Odd, he was almost never clumsy.

By the time she had taken the ten steps into his room, Nils was on his side on the floor, with his mouth and one eye open. That eye was looking at the wall and not at her, even when she spoke to him. His hand clutched a little at the pocket of his worn red dressing gown, and then it stopped. In the parlour, Tilda was still singing. Sofie looked at the shards of the little Japanese vase that had broken in his fall, scattered around him like petals, and she thought, I must sweep those up before Nils walks on them in his bare feet.

In the days leading up to the funeral, she could not stay away from the loom. She stood very erect, looked straight ahead at the wool and concentrated on keeping the tension correct. She thought of Penelope keeping her suitors at bay by pretending to weave a shroud for Odysseus's father, and for a few mad moments, she considered weaving a shroud for Nils. Since that was impossible, she kept on with the wall hanging she had been making. It was nothing special, a wedding present for Erika next door. But the clunk of the shuttle and the treadle beneath her feet made her feel as if nothing had happened.

People said, "Sofie, come and sit down in the dining room, the Nordins have come to pay their respects," or "Mamma, come and play with the baby awhile." But the loom was the only place that felt right.

When Marianne stood at her shoulder and said softly, "Mamma, it is time to go to church," she pointed to the end of the weaving.

"Look," she said, "how much I've done."

She could hear family and friends worrying behind the closed door. Finally Cecilia, who had come with Lars, walked into the workshop. She tried to take Sofie's hands, but Sofie would not let go of the shuttle, so, awkwardly, Cecilia put her arm around her shoulder, something she had never done before, even when Markus died. But that, too, interfered with the weaving, so Cecilia rested her hand on Sofie's back.

"Sofie, I am so very sorry."

Startled at the interruption, Sofie's eyes left her loom for a second.

"Thank you. It's so kind of you to come all this way. But now I must just finish this blue section."

Sofie hoped she was not being rude. But the blue section was crucial.

Then Cecilia said something Sofie could not have predicted.

"Work is a balm, Sofie. Work is a balm."

Sofie cocked her head to one side. So, once again Cecilia understood. And she, Sofie, understood that this was not a comment on what she was doing now, but a promise for the future. Thinking about that, she moved the shuttle a few more times, slowly. Then

she put it down and said, "Yes. But now we must go to church."
They came out of the workshop together, Cecilia holding her hand.
Sofie thought wryly, Perhaps she thinks I will try to escape. But she
stood quietly as Cecilia and Marianne helped her on with the black
cape and the widow's cap.

When they returned from the burial, there was no more weaving. She put on Nils's red robe, and sat at her desk, or in the Old
Room, or in the library, doing nothing by the hour. Sometimes she
even came downstairs in the robe. About a week after the funeral,
no one could find her for a time. Then someone spotted a moving
clump of red in the big bulb garden that faced the river. It was Sofie,
still in the robe, uprooting lilies by the hundreds. As soon as she
exposed one mass of bulbs, their sickly-looking white roots upended
in the air, like a part of the body that should be decently covered,
she moved to the next, tripping over the robe and the shovel, wreak-
ing destruction on the carefully tended garden that had produced
flowers for Nils's pictures for decades.

"Because they're no good!" she panted, without pausing in her
work, when Marianne and Sonja begged her to tell them why she
was doing this. "No good at all!"

Only when she had taken out the entire bed and thrown the
bulbs on the lawn would she agree to go back in the house.

Chapter Forty-three

APRIL 1924

CECILIA AND LISBETH never discussed it. Lisbeth came to her in the night, or she did not. It surprised Cecilia at first that there was so much of her. Not, of course, that Lisbeth was as big as Lars, but a woman's body has so much more geography. Concave, convex, tapering calves, delicate wrists and meaty hands, full upper arms interrupted at the elbow and then meagre lower arms, breasts, cul-de-sacs, sudden broad expanses. Lars was a prairie, Lisbeth an intense place of mountains and valleys.

Even now, eight years after that first night together, she could still be surprised by Lisbeth's body. Still surprised to be in bed with Lisbeth's body. Partly, Cecilia knew, that was because it was secret, and illicit. And not as frequent as she wished. But partly, she thought—because she was in love—it was because of Lisbeth.

Lars was often away, in Stockholm, or at his fishing lodge, or travelling. Lisbeth slept in the guest room more often now; it was the press of their work, she told Mrs. Turesson.

In the beginning, the adultery seemed more important to Cecilia than the fact that Lisbeth was a woman—perhaps because it was easier to understand. She made a list of married women who had affairs in novels and poems.

1. Anna Karenina
2. Emma Bovary
3. The unnamed wife in Meredith's *Married Love*
4. Edna Pontellier in Kate Chopin's *The Awakening*

She stopped there, because she could not remember any others, and because the list did not raise her spirits. Anna Karenina threw herself under a train, Edna Pontellier walked into the sea, and the other two poisoned themselves. Perhaps one day a writer would imagine an adulterous woman who survived. As for Lisbeth being a woman, either thinking about it did not interest her much, or perhaps she simply did not know how to think about it. If she had written out, "I am in love with a woman" (which she did not), the words would have looked very strange. But, as she lived it, it seemed normal. The only thing she knew with certainty was that she loved Lisbeth in the way she had loved Lars at the start of their years together.

These days they were busy with the Old Farm, as they called the land near the Folk School where they had placed fourteen top-heavy log houses, storehouses and shops, some dating from the fourteenth century, and arranged them in a rectangle, mimicking a Dalarna village. Lisbeth and Cecilia had been working on the interiors, which they wanted to put in order before the weather warmed up and people began asking to see them.

One morning when Lars was at the fishing lodge, Cecilia stood in the clockmaker's shop at the Old Farm, looking at Lars's overflowing collections of tools and clocks.

"Three quarters of this stuff needs to go into storage," Lisbeth said in a tone that forbade argument. "I'll get Ingerson and his son to move it this afternoon." She began tying red strings around pieces that Ingerson could take away.

"But not those," Cecilia said of some tall clocks. "That group shows the evolution of the Dalarna clock. And not these," she said, less convincingly, of a heap of saws and clamps.

Lisbeth gave Cecilia a look.

"Then what will you choose?"

But Cecilia could not choose, so she said, "You can be infatuated with one of Lars's most unimpressive sketches, but I see you are more judicious when it comes to his collections."

Lisbeth ignored the sting in that. "Cecilia, fewer examples will allow people to see them better. Right now this is like a junk shop."

She knew Lisbeth was right, but paring down the collection was impossible for her. Lars loved these well-used tools and painted clocks so much that putting them in storage felt like banishing *him*. Tired of the argument, Cecilia left Lisbeth rearranging the stoneware jugs and made her way outside.

Winter hung on stubbornly, although there was no snow. The ground was hard, with a springy crunch to the grass. The lake sparkled near the leaf-drying barn, the malting house and the other buildings planted on the broad lawn. Many of their rooflines were decorated with the traditional row of Nordic pickets, which left scalloped shadows on the sides of adjoining buildings. The biggest building was the boathouse, probably from the seventeenth century. Lars had bought it long ago, one of his first buildings, and eventually filled it with a vast church-boat that held thirty or more villagers. Eventually Lisbeth found her there, a small, dark bundle in the dark boat.

"Where have you been? I've been looking for you all over. We need to decide about the milking stools so that the Ingersons can move them."

Cecilia remembered how bewildered Mamma had been by the idea that Professor Hazelius would collect milking stools. And yet by the time she died—five years ago now, and Cecilia still missed her— Lars had won her over to the belief that these things were important.

She said nothing.

"Cecilia, what is it?"

"Nothing. Nothing at all."

"But what are you doing here? Are you ill?"

"No. I'll meet you at the tithing house. Please."

Lisbeth left. Cecilia wrapped her hands around her knees as she huddled in the boat. When spots had first appeared on her hands, she liked them. She had always wanted freckles, and these were the closest she would come. But as they got bigger and more irregular, they looked less like freckles and she no longer enjoyed them. Now they were liver spots, an ugly name that belonged to an old woman. She was fifty-seven, and she needed reminding that she was an old woman. Lisbeth's hands were completely spotless. More and more, Cecilia noticed other differences between Lisbeth's body and her own. Compared with Lisbeth, she was thin but flabby. Lisbeth's skin fit her flesh perfectly, there were no dimples, no little lumps, no skin pocked like orange peel such as she was discovering on the inside of her upper arms. Lisbeth was a plum; she was drying into a prune. But Lisbeth did not seem to care.

While she sat in the boat, small, hard tears, like apple seeds, came out grudgingly. The boathouse, ancient, dark pine built with sober purpose and unfathomable strength, decorated only by the long logs that formed an X at its gable ends, summed up so much that Lars treasured. There was so much of him here. His years of self-indulgence were showing, but unaccountably, it was Nils who was dead—although older, he had moved as though he were younger than Lars.

And there was Sofie. What was life like for her in a house where many of the door panels, windows, walls and lintels were Nils Olsson paintings? Where Nils's inventiveness had touched everything from the weathervane to the doorknobs? Cecilia and Lars had visited her last month and Lars, the optimist, described her afterwards as composed. Cecilia said no, she was numb. Some things were moving too quickly, while others seemed cast in stone. She thought about Lisbeth, who loved her, and who also loved Lars's art but not his old tools and clocks. She thought about things and people and even marriages being put in storage. Finally, she went out to find Lisbeth in the tithing house.

Chapter Forty-four

NILS HAD FINISHED his autobiography, called *What I Am*, the day before his death. At first Sofie could not read it, but by June, six months after his death, she had. All the children had read it too, and there was to be a family meeting.

"Mamma, don't feel you have to come," Marianne said. "It may be too hard for you."

"Don't be silly, of course I am coming."

Marianne looked unhappy.

They had the meeting at the dining room table, under the picture Nils had painted of Sofie and himself as a young couple travelling in a romantic landscape of castles and hills. At the head of the table, where Nils had sat, her tapestry of the four elements was faded but still strong.

Oskar began.

"Of course, we will have to notify Bonniers that there will be no publication."

Sofie asked, "And why is that?"

Several of the children seemed to say at once, "Mamma, how can you ask that?"

"Well, I *am* asking that, so perhaps someone might tell me."

There were a few different answers. Marianne and Sonja objected to Nils's candour about the women in his life before Sofie, including the model with whom he had had two children who died as babies. Oskar did not want people to know about his father's melancholy, his lack of self-confidence, his grief for Markus that never seemed to lighten. Tilda and Felix thought that his long, humiliating struggle with *King Domald's Sacrifice* and the National Museum's final rejection should be kept private.

To Marianne's and Sonja's objection about the women, Sofie shrugged.

"That's what the life of a young artist was, in those days." She might have said, "And no doubt still is, today." She might have said, "That's what the life of a man is." But she decided not to. To the other stumbling blocks, she said, "That's what your father was. I see nothing to hide."

She stood up abruptly, startling them. No doubt they were expecting a long discussion.

"That's all I have to say. Good night. Oskar, will you make sure that all the lights are out when you go to bed."

Marianne came to her bedroom while Sofie was brushing her hair. It was thinner, although not much, and threaded with white, but she was still a dark-haired woman.

"Mamma, I'm sorry that you're upset."

"I'm not upset."

"Yes, you are. I know how you look when you are angry."

"All right. Your father had the right to write about himself in the way he found most true. You children don't have the right to interfere with that."

"Mamma."

Marianne took the hand that was not holding the brush, that was gripping the dressing table, and held it. This first-born knew her too well.

"That's not all you are angry about."

She continued brushing, counting on the long, deliberate strokes to temper her rage.

"Fine, then. You've read the book. He writes that I was his angel, his darling, his good Sofie, the person who believed in him when he despaired. He never once mentions that I was a painter. That I studied with Ernst Malmstrom at the Academy. That he and I painted together at Grez. That we decorated the house together, and that many of the ideas . . . Never mind. Never mind. Not one mention."

She wrenched her hand away from Marianne. Now she was past talk but not past putting down the brush, dividing her hair in two hanks with one violent motion, and beginning to braid the right side.

Marianne was aghast.

"But . . . I'm sorry. I had no idea you felt that way."

"Of course not, none of you did."

And none of them had noticed what was missing from the book. Now she had only a minute to get Marianne out of the room before she fell into a torrent of fury at all of them, at the children, at Mr. Lawrie for coming too late, at Nils for living the way he had and then for dying.

She swept Marianne into her arms, and said, "Now go, my darling. I'm very tired."

Chapter Forty-five

JUNE 1926

ON A BRIGHT spring day in 1926, Cecilia received a telegram from Hanna Pauli. Ellen Key had died at Strand, her country house. Incoherent and irascible, she had not been herself for a few years, probably since 1920. She had left instructions that there should be "no frivolity" around her death, and she wanted to lie in an oak coffin on top of bluebells and grasses from the beach, before she was cremated and buried in the family grave at Vastervik. That was fine for Miss Key, Hanna wrote with her usual asperity, but it left those who had been touched by her influence feeling the need of a gathering to mark her passing. Hanna and Georg would welcome those who wanted to remember Ellen Key on June 10, at their house in Storangen. Cecilia would go, of course, to honour her teacher, accompanied by Lars. Sofie wrote to say that she would see her there, for Nils's sake: she would not forget how Miss Key had celebrated his paintings of Askebo.

On the appointed day, eminent figures from Miss Key's various worlds—education, suffrage, aesthetics, literature, among others—gathered in Hanna and Georg's parlour. A few read appreciations of her contributions to Swedish life and thinking, interspersed with musical interludes on the piano. Hanna's oil sketch for her portrait of Miss Key stood on an easel by the piano. Then everyone drank coffee, ate spice cookies and chatted in small groups. That's where the real memories came out. Here was the whole Ellen Key with all her contradictions, Cecilia thought—the Christian turned radical socialist, the feminist who did not believe that mothers should have other work, the teacher who thought the state, rather than husbands, should support women and their children. Eva Bonnier, Cecilia and Hanna reminisced about their days in the schoolroom with Miss Key, and even Hanna was close to tears. Cecilia wondered, Would Miss Key consider all this "frivolity"?

"It was a fine way to remember Ellen Key," she said to Sofie on the train home.

Sofie agreed. "I suppose, if people do not want a funeral in a church, there will be more of this kind of thing," she said. "This was my first."

Lars had taken out his pencil and paper and was looking around their car for a subject. The trio would travel together as far as Rattvik, where they would change trains and head in different directions.

Sofie reached into her carpet bag for her knitting, and her fingers found a book first. She pulled it out to show Cecilia.

"It's called *Mrs. Dalloway*. One of Sonja's friends recommended it to me, so I ordered it from Hemlins. It's very modern, written in a style they call 'stream of consciousness.' Which sounds horrid, but it just shows one thought flowing into the next thought, which may not have a logical connection to the last thought but always feels right—like the way we think."

Listening to Sofie's enthusiasm, Cecilia thought, She looks well. And she sounds like the old Sofie. It had been two years since Nils died. "And Virginia Woolf is?" Cecilia asked, taking the book to have a better look at its black, yellow and white jacket. Even the abstract cover, she thought, announced its modernity.

"I have no idea. But her book is wonderful. It's about a day in the life of a London society woman who is giving a party. She's complicated and perceptive, but also conventional and sometimes a little snobbish. Some of the other characters think she chose a shallow husband. One of them . . . let me find that page, I marked it."

She riffled through the pages until she came to a turned-down corner.

"Here it is. An old admirer of Mrs. Dalloway is thinking about the differences between her and her husband: 'With twice his wits, she had to see things through his eyes—one of the tragedies of married life.'"

Both women liked that, and smiled at each other. They could say anything in front of Lars. He was sketching a little boy across the aisle who was sleeping against his mother's shoulder, and paid no attention to them. Every once in a while, Lars too dozed for a short time, which concerned Sofie. It wasn't the simple fact of dozing that worried her, but how unwell he looked when his usual alertness did not mask his heaviness and bad colour. After an event such as the one they had just attended, you noticed your friends' frailties.

But not, perhaps, your husband's. "Lars! Wake up!" Cecilia hissed into his ear, afraid he would start snoring or making other loud noises. Imperturbable, he opened his eyes and recovered the pencil that had dropped onto his lap.

Sofie went back to *Mrs. Dalloway.*

"And yet the husband," she began to say, but Cecilia interrupted.

"Let me guess. You're going to take his part, aren't you?"

Sofie gave a small laugh. "But so is Virginia Woolf taking his part! He doesn't sparkle, like the old admirer, but he loves Mrs. Dalloway, and she loves him . . . And yet!" Sofie said, excited, as she remembered the unexpected twist. "The thing Mrs. Dalloway calls 'the most exquisite moment of her whole life' is a kiss she gets as a young woman from her friend Sally Seton—a kiss on the lips. More exquisite than *any* moment she has had with Mr. Dalloway or any other man."

Cecilia struggled for the right balance of curiosity and calm on her face. She raised an eyebrow.

"Yes, exactly," Sofie said. "What do you make of that?"

"Well," said Cecilia, pretending to consider the question, while her heart beat fast, "I suppose it happens. I will have to read the book."

"I suppose it does happen," Sofie agreed. "But we don't often read about it in novels, and not about women who are fairly content with their husbands. Mrs. Dalloway's love for Sally Seton is the most romantic thing in the book."

Sofie noticed that Cecilia's neck looked blotchy. Well, it *was* warm in the train. There was one more thing she was curious about.

"Virginia Woolf writes about what she calls 'this falling in love with women'—that it is something quite superior to our love for men. More disinterested, more protective, a love with great integrity. What do you think, is there anything to that?"

But Cecilia only said again that she would have to read the book.

"Yes, I think you will enjoy it. I will send it to you as soon as I finish."

"Thank you," Cecilia said firmly, "but don't bother, I will order it."

Chapter Forty-six

CECILIA WAS ANXIOUS about Lars. He was having a hard time with his *The Red Suit*. He had painted himself standing braced, legs apart, against the timber walls of his studio, in a Falun-red three-piece suit. He was in defiant colour, while the studio looked almost monochrome. A cigarette drooped from his fingers. There were heavy bags under his eyes, and he looked resigned. Lars Vogt, the reluctantly civilized bon vivant. But he could not satisfy himself; he went over and over the same ground in different versions, working terrible hours.

Cecilia urged him to leave it for a while and do another self-portrait, this time wearing a coat made of wolf skins. But this became a relentless picture of an even more exhausted man, his head dwarfed by a body laden with furs. Another cigarette. Another flush under the cheekbone, which looked healthy at first and then sadly hectic. Here was the Lars who spent more and more of his time at Tallmon, his fishing lodge north of Siljevik on the Dalalven River. Half-savage in his animal skins, civilized only to the extent of his beaver hat and cigarette. Her dearest wild man.

There was one more picture from that time, a photograph

taken of the two of them by a visitor. Lars was at his easel, wearing his smock. Cecilia stood behind him. The large white pleated collar on her dark dress made her look like a nun who had taken off her coif. She stared at his work, on the easel, the way a mother watches over a sleeping child. He stared at the camera as if facing down his old enemy, time.

Siljevik, 6 March 1927
Dear Sofie,

Thank you for your kind note about Mona. Her death has hurt Lars very much, of course. In some ways she was more like his beloved older sister than his mother. He is designing a bas-relief of her head for her gravestone, which he will see from the window of his studio.

Miss Gregorius agrees with me that Lars is far from well. He is even heavier than when you saw him last, he moves slowly, breathes with difficulty and lights one cigarette from the last one. But he is determined to eat, drink and smoke more than ever, while he works as if possessed. He is deep in a portrait of Carl Eklund and another one of Lukas Wallenberg's younger daughter, and has gone to Stockholm to supervise the sales of his latest etchings. He has plenty of buyers, although the critics disparage him more and more. But he sloughs off the criticism like an old snake slipping out of a used-up skin.

Your friend,
Cecilia

Something had loosened Cecilia's pen. A few weeks later, she wrote,

Siljevik, 20 March 1927
Dear Sofie,

Once, when we were just getting to know each other,
you wrote asking me if married life had surprised me. I
did not really answer you, and I probably thought
differently about it then. These days I am impressed with
the permanence of temperament. You tried for so many
years, with so much patience and determination, to make
Nils happy. But he was not cut from that cloth. Whereas
my disappointment, which is mostly in the past now, was
that nothing I did could make Lars *unhappy*. I remember
Nils calling him "this magic animal"—and he was right.
If Lars has food, drink, De Reszke cigarettes, beautiful
women and work, he is happy. For him, work is as much
a physical pleasure as the others. And that is what he has
taught me. It is his work that binds us together, and
through that I have found my own work.

I am not sure if a man's character is more
unchangeable than a woman's. Perhaps men need to
change less than women do. Or perhaps we are naturally
more flexible. I have accommodated to Lars but, along
with difficulties, it has brought me good things I could
not have foreseen. I see that again I have not answered
your question, after all these years. Yes, married life has
surprised me! But not all in negative ways.

Your old friend,
Cecilia

As she put down her pen, she thought how strange it was that
she did not feel hypocritical writing about marriage as though she
were as virtuous a wife as Sofie had been. On the contrary, the
words felt natural. A man who has a mistress or consorts with pros-
titutes may still think of himself as a good provider, a good father,

a good husband. Now, with Lars, the shoe was on the other foot. Or rather, the shoes were on both feet. Still, it was curious that she was able to write about Lars more honestly now that she had her own secret. She wondered about including "beautiful women" in the list of Lars's necessities. Was she being disloyal to him, or humiliating herself, or just acknowledging what everyone knew? The last, she decided. So much went unspoken between women friends.

But that did not mean she would talk to Sofie about Lisbeth.

Lars now spent most days and nights at the fishing lodge in Tallmon, where he retreated into what he liked to think were the habits of his ancestors. He slept between furs, with no linen, and laughed at the occasional visitor from the city who brought a toothbrush. Instead, he ran naked from his bed to scoop up water from the river, which he gargled noisily and then spit out in a great arc. The only citified things he did not give up at Tallmon were his scotch and his fat cigarettes. He drew around him a circle of local people, carpenters, farmers, hunters, and spent his evenings with them. His favourite, Maria, played the guitar and the occasional visitor reported to Cecilia that sometimes they all sang desolate folk songs in a monotone. Cecilia did not go to the fishing lodge. Lars exaggerated his connection to that life, of course—his hard-working Lutheran grandparents would have been affronted by Tallmon and its goings-on.

Meanwhile he bought, bought, bought—peasant furniture and blankets and wooden bowls and buildings when he was in Sweden, more than they could ever display, and when he went abroad, more paintings and antique furniture and silver. He never enjoyed museums because, as he liked to say, "Why go there? There is nothing for sale." After his mother's death, his buying became a mania. He also endowed a professorship of Nordic Art History at Stockholm University, founded a poetry prize and set up a fiddling competition in Siljevik. It looked as if he gave away money as soon as he got it, but the careful old peasant survived. Half of every sale went in the bank, and he spent or donated the rest.

"There is so much defiance in this feverish activity," Cecilia said to Lars's Friend Archbishop Soderblom, as she walked with him one day in the garden.

Cecilia said this to Lars's friend Archbishop Soderblom, as she walked with him one day in the garden. Lars was at Tallmon, and had promised to come to Siljevik in time for dinner.

"He is not defying death," Soderblom half-corrected her, "but weakness and illness. He wants to go out quickly, the way a candle gutters."

Chapter Forty-seven

WHEN VIRGINIA WOOLF's next novel, *To the Lighthouse*, was published, Sofie and Cecilia both ordered a copy from Hemlins. Often they shared a book, but neither was prepared to wait for this one. Sofie put everything aside to read it, almost guiltily relishing the long evenings with no one to interrupt her or remind her that it was time for bed. While she read, she imagined Cecilia, sitting in her favourite reading chair, loving the portrait of Mrs. Ramsay, a woman in her fifties with eight children. It was not something Sofie could mention, but she felt Cecilia idealized women with children. Her own reaction was different: as she read about Mrs. Ramsay's tireless indulgence of her self-absorbed husband, Sofie found herself impatient.

> Askebo, 11 July 1927
> Dear Cecilia,
> 　　I think of you at Siljevik, with eyes only for *To the Lighthouse*, like me. And I know you will expect me to defend poor Mr. Ramsay. Perhaps this picture of masculine need and feminine solace, while undeniably brilliant, is losing its power for me, I am not sure. But I

will admit that Mr. Ramsay's combination of achievement and insecurity strikes a familiar note—not that I ever answered Nils's longing for encouragement with the angelic resourcefulness of Mrs. Ramsay! But he would have loved it if I had.

Thinking of Nils, I am reminded of your letter this spring when you considered my impertinent question of long ago: had marriage surprised you? You wrote about my "patience and determination" in trying to make Nils happy, and that filled my eyes with tears. Poor man, he had so much trouble with happiness, and I am painfully conscious that I should have done more for him. But thank you for seeing it so charitably.

But to return to *To the Lighthouse*. I appreciate the humour and the compassion with which Mrs. Woolf describes Mr. Ramsay's need—a man's need for a woman's admiration can be so intense that it is almost frightening. My heart does go out to Mr. Ramsay, of course, but now from a certain distance.

Does Mrs. Ramsay have you wrapped around her beautiful little finger?

Your friend,
Sofie

Siljevik, 19 July 1927
My dear Sofie,

Perhaps I have a surprise for you. Mrs. Ramsay is undeniably a figure with enormous allure. The beloved centre of her family and friends, the doer of good deeds, beautiful and instinctive, she is the perfect woman. Like everyone in the book and like many readers, I feel her attraction. Her siren song, really.

But I have to put that attraction a little to the side because it is pernicious. A strong word, I know. The appeal of Mrs. Ramsay and her ilk, the ideal with which we were raised, dooms us to frustration and disappointment. To think you can be all that, do all that—bolster an anxious husband, provide eight children with perceptive love, arrange *boeuf en daube* for houseguests and hand-knitted stockings for the poor, all without ever having a mean or even selfish thought—is impossible and even cruel as a goal. And, in spite of what dear Miss Key thought, how many women are actually satisfied with trying to achieve this kind of perfection? Mrs. Woolf is very clever, in that several characters, including his wife, see Mr. Ramsay clearly, as one who takes and does not give, as being venerable and laughable at the same time. Which might well call Mrs. Ramsay's constant solicitude into question. But in spite of that, I think that Mrs. Woolf, too, is infatuated with Mrs. Ramsay.

And I admit that I am too, at least when I am reading. Only later, when I gather my thoughts, do I see it in a different light. But the book is unforgettable, and like you I can hardly wait to return to it.

Your friend,
Cecilia

Well, this is a turnabout, Sofie thought as she put down the letter. She had always been the one with more doubts about these Eternal Feminine figures than Cecilia—knowing something about the laziness, insecurity and egotism that could hide behind the martyr's shield. But what was changing in Cecilia?

What Cecilia did not mention in her letter was that she, unlike Sofie, did not have the novel all to herself. Lisbeth snatched it up whenever she had a free minute. And Lisbeth had very decided opinions on Mrs. Ramsay and women's training in self-sacrifice.

Sofie, too, had not mentioned something: that the character who stirred her more than the Ramsays was the little, self-effacing, middle-aged painter Lily Briscoe. What moved Sofie about Lily was her relationship to her painting. She read over and over a passage in which Lily contemplates an unfinished canvas.

> Here she was again, she thought, stepping back to look at it, drawn out of gossip, out of living, out of community with people into the presence of this formidable ancient enemy of hers—this other thing, this truth, this reality, which suddenly laid hands on her, emerged stark at the back of appearances and commanded her attention . . . this form, were it only the shape of a white lamp-shade looming on a wicker table, roused one to perpetual combat, challenged one to a fight in which one was bound to be worsted.

This formidable ancient enemy of hers. This other thing, this truth, this reality. Sofie felt as if Mrs. Woolf had known her. She copied out the passage, and put it in the drawer of the table beside her bed.

Chapter Forty-eight

1931

In 1931, Lars insisted on going on his usual summer sailing and painting trip with Maria, his companion from Tallmon. Cecilia did not see where he could possibly find the strength for it, but he would not listen to her objections. With a feeling of dread, she went ahead with her visit to her sister's house in the archipelago. It was there that word reached her. The trip had proved too much for Lars and he was returning to Siljevik. While she made plans to catch the boat to Stockholm and then the train to Siljevik, another telegram was making its way to her.

Oddly enough, it was little Erik who had to break the news. Her nephew was little no more, a man in his forties with a wife and children, but in the family story he was eternally the frustrated toddler who did not want to sit still while Lars painted his portrait. Cecilia was packing when she heard someone climbing the stairs. Something in those reluctant steps told her what Erik had to say before he appeared at her door and took her hands in his.

In Siljevik, Lars lay in his red-tented bed, looking impossibly small. It made no sense, he'd had no time to lose any flesh, but he was diminished. His waxy colour accentuated the pouches under his eyes. His expression was concerned, as if he were missing something. He hated being without something to do with his hands, and Cecilia had the mad idea of weaving a twig and his little knife between those still fingers. They told her that just after he became ill, his hands had moved as if he were painting. He had talked about colours and his dog, Liten, while he wielded his imaginary brush. Then he had stopped talking, and his right side did not move again. Now there was nothing for anyone to do but wait for him to die. The doctors said they would not wait long.

> *He came up our alley and he whistled me out*
> *But the tail of his shirt from the trousers hung out.*

Until then, Lisbeth almost always came to her in the night. Lisbeth was the seeker. But that night and for a week of nights afterwards, Cecilia went to Lisbeth in the guest room and climbed into the narrow bed hung with ivory-and-gold draperies. On the first night, Lisbeth burst into a storm of tears after her satisfaction. Cecilia wondered, Who is comforting whom? Her eyelid had taken to flickering but she was dry-eyed, as she had been since the news of the stroke.

The next morning, Archbishop Soderblom and the mayor came to make arrangements for the wake. They assumed that it would take place in the Hall.

"No," Cecilia said. "He will stay in his bedroom."

"My dear Cecilia, his room is far too small," the archbishop said. "People will be lined up far down the road waiting to pay their respects. There is talk of putting on extra trains from Stockholm. And the circulation is all wrong, as people would have to leave through your dressing room."

"I don't care about that. I don't want him in the Hall."

"Cecilia." It was Lisbeth.

Both men stared. Lisbeth had called her by her first name.

"He would want to be there," Lisbeth said.

Cecilia was silent. This was no business of Lisbeth's. She also thought, more irritably than usual, how much she disliked the Hall. But Lisbeth was right. That was what Lars would want. The archbishop cleared his throat. Would Cecilia want Lars photographed after he died? She thought back to the post-mortem paintings Lars had done as a student, painting fast to get a likeness so that he could continue after they closed the coffin.

"No," she said. "He has painted his own post-mortems."

She meant the portraits in the red suit and the fur coat. But no one asked her what she meant, so perhaps she had not said it out loud. Usually Cecilia was the planner, but now she sat quiet while the archbishop and the mayor organized the details. Lisbeth sat on a chair against the wall. She was red-eyed, like a child whose father is dying or a girl whose lover is doomed.

In bed one night during that first week, there came a moment when both women were quiet but still awake. Then Lisbeth said, judiciously, "He will be the first Viking to be buried in a three-piece red suit."

After a startled second or two, Cecilia laughed. So did Lisbeth, and once they started they could not stop. The laughter would tail away and they would stay silent for a little while, but then the thought of the Hall with its Viking gear or Lars lying in state wearing a horned helmet and his red suit would set Cecilia off again, and Lisbeth would join her. Lisbeth made things worse by telling Cecilia what happened when a real Viking chieftain was buried. After days of being given strong drink and singing happily, the thrall girl who had volunteered to join her master gave away her bracelets and rings. She was given more bottles of drink, and six men went into the master's tent on his ship to have their way with her. Then they began beating their shields to muffle her screams. She was hanged and stabbed between the ribs at the same time, and after that the ship was burned. It was grisly and terrible, and Lisbeth and Cecilia laughed even more.

Cecilia imagined the candidates for Lars's thrall girl—Lydia
Barnes, various models, perhaps Maria? Or Françoise, their little
maid in Montmartre? There were others, so many women for whom
Lars's indolent charm had been not fatal but decisive. She thought
about her own forty years of devotion. But she was not ready to join
Lars in the afterlife, even without the stabbing and hanging. Finally,
she began to weep.

Askebo, 15 September 1931

Dear Cecilia,

I can't think which is worse, a sudden death like
Nils's or the cruel waiting you have now. Lars unable to
do things with his hands is unimaginable. I remember
the first visit we made to Siljevik, when he took up the
heel of the stocking I was knitting and turned it better
than I could have done.

Believe me, dear Cecilia, we are all thinking of you
and Lars, and hoping he will have a speedy release from
this purgatory. As for you, I feel far away and useless. But
if there is anything I can do to make this time even a little
easier, I hope you will tell me.

Here, the asters are blooming by the river. Marianne's
boys were rowing on it on the weekend and it seemed like
old times, to have noisy children running in and out of the
house. Nils loved the clatter and mess of the grandchildren's
visits, and it is sad to think he has missed the growing up of
the older ones and the arrival of the babies.

I wish I could settle into some work. Nothing satisfies
me, I don't know why. I seem to have stalled since Nils's
death. I remember what you told me on the day of his
funeral, about work being a balm. I believe that. But I
have not yet found what work that is.

And yet, I am no longer lonely, usually. For the first

few years after Nils died, I would find myself thinking, when something interesting or puzzling happened, I must tell Nils that or I must ask Nils about that. That is over now . . . and yet, having had a companion for all those decades leaves its mark. If I am honest, I probably still tell him things occasionally, or wonder what he would say.

But why am I rambling on about myself, when you have very serious things to think about? I should rewrite this letter, without the last few paragraphs, but I am rushing to catch the morning mail collection, and I flatter myself you would rather have an imperfect letter from me than none at all.

With much love to you, and of course to Lars too,
Sofie

But Lars did not die. The doctors shrugged. Well, even if it was not as soon as they had expected, it would not be long. He could not last in this state. For a week or so he lay, eyes closed and barely moving. Gradually his eyes opened more and he rocked his head back and forth on the pillow, as if he were tired of the position. Lisbeth insisted that they sit him up. Against the doctors' wishes and with the help of two men, Cecilia and Lisbeth propped him on pillows in an armchair. His right hand never moved, but curled in on itself in his lap like a small, hurt bird. The left one sometimes fluttered idly. Sometimes he seemed to have enough brain to be worried about that, to look at his hands as if to say, Well, what about you two?

He could not speak or walk and had to be fed soft things on small spoons. Here is the baby we never had, Cecilia thought, as the maids or Lisbeth fastened a big dinner napkin around his neck and began to feed him. Sometimes at that point he looked at Cecilia and she imagined that he was asking, Why do you not feed me? But she never did. For real babies, they had dozens of bibs in the textile collection that were hand-woven or crocheted, embroidered or otherwise trimmed with love and skill. For Lars, they had damask napkins at first, and later, when they saw how stained they became, they used plain muslin cloths.

After a month or so, Cecilia decided they would get a wheelchair. Even if Lars only used it for a short time, they could donate it later to the local hospital. Gradually, the doctors replaced their conviction that he would not survive with a conviction that he would never improve. Lisbeth and Cecilia wheeled him in the garden, and in the cemetery to visit his mother's grave. Between the garden and the cemetery, they passed his studio. He looked at it, unblinkingly, but gave no sign that it was of interest to him.

"Come and see my plans for some of the main galleries."

Lisbeth took Cecilia's hand, and drew her into her office, where she had made a little model of the art gallery they were planning.

"Wherever did you get these toy logs?"

"I brought them from home. I used to play with them as a child."

In the model Lisbeth had hung tiny versions of Lars's paintings along with some by Ernst Josephson, the Rembrandt etching, the Frans Hals portrait and others that were important to him. A few dollhouse pieces stood in for the Renaissance chest from his Montmartre studio and some rugs. The furniture was all right, Cecilia decided, although it did not seem essential.

She said, "I don't think we should combine his work with his influences."

"But it shows people whom he learned from, and to what he aspired."

"It's distracting. These galleries should be only Lars's work. Pieces by others from the collections will go in separate rooms."

"I don't agree. It puts him in a larger perspective."

Cecilia turned away, angry, not wanting Lisbeth to see her fluttering eyelid. She said what she expected would finish the argument. "It's not what I want."

"But this is the way it should be."

At lunch, they wheeled Lars in to the dining table, and Cecilia saw how grotesque their argument was. Here was the man who had taken what he needed from other painters and done his work. Nothing in their disagreement could diminish that or add to that. Cecilia had his chair placed close to hers, so that she could caress his shoulder, pat his knee, put her hand on his arm. He looked straight ahead while Gerda, the new maid, fed him soup and carefully blotted up the spillage.

"You've never touched him so much," Lisbeth said, that evening when she and Cecilia were alone, sitting on the porch where they faced Lars's statue of the bathing woman.

"That's because he was never still enough before," Cecilia said, but that wasn't true. He had never moved quickly, except for his hands. She had caressed him when they were engaged and newly married, but Lisbeth had not known them then. Now she touched him because there was a new element in her feeling for him: pity. It had nothing to do with Lisbeth, and everything to do with the fact that he could not draw or paint or carve.

Just after his stroke, when she had thought Lars's death was imminent, Cecilia asked Christian Eriksson to design their gravestone. After some time, Eriksson returned with his ideas, produced in miniature versions, much like Lisbeth with her little log museum. Cecilia thought, Lars has become a baby with bibs and diapers, and everyone is making toys. Eriksson's models were almost comical, as if a dollhouse had come with its own churchyard. There were the usual rectangular and spade shapes, but there was one that looked like a cradle—or was it a bedstead?—high and rounded at one end, and lower at the other end.

She touched that one, and looked up at him.

"Yes," he said. "It is based on the Romanesque coffin. There is a hint of Viking too. I would make it in something stark and heavy, like pock-marked iron."

Cecilia nodded. There would be nothing like it in the churchyard.

She showed the model to Lisbeth, because she had to. She found a good time, as they were celebrating buying back Lars's portrait of his mother and grandmother from a collector in Lund. The letter agreeing to their terms had arrived that morning.

Lisbeth stared at the model, bewildered.

"But it's a bed." It was an accusation.

"No, it isn't. It's Mr. Eriksson's interpretation of a Romanesque coffin."

And what if it were a bed? Cecilia thought. After all, we are husband and wife.

"And why Romanesque? It isn't a period Lars particularly liked."

"I think Mr. Eriksson wanted a strong shape more than a particular period."

Lisbeth did not say, "And where will I be buried?" But everything about her—the full eyes, the tense posture, the way she turned away—asked that question.

It is not that she wants to be buried next to me, Cecilia thought; she wants to lie next to him. No, that was unfair. She remembered how once, when she and Lars were visiting Boston, Isabella Gardner took them to see a famous cemetery. It was romantic, a park full of hills and dales and emotional statues and lachrymose inscriptions, far from the level Swedish churchyards they knew, full of blunt stones and iron crosses. On the crest of a little rise, underneath a willow, they stopped for a moment at a family plot. The parents' graves were two full-size stone bedsteads lying on the ground, complete with stone pillows. Between them lay a small bedstead, the grave of their child. The parents sheltering their child for eternity. That is what Lisbeth wanted, to lie forever between her and Lars.

Cecilia thought, I have had two partners in work, Lars and now Lisbeth. She had hoped for more from Lars, but that was not to be. She had hoped for something different from Lisbeth too, something less obstinate and headstrong, but perhaps what she had made a better balance. She had been so certain that Lars would not seduce Lisbeth, and she could not have been more wrong. But this was a different kind of seduction: Lisbeth loved his art. Now she and Lisbeth competed to be the one who understood his art and knew what he would have wanted. When he died, they would compete to be the perfect widow. But it was on the whole a bearable rivalry, a polygamy she could live with.

As for their partnership in the night, as hers with Lars, it happened less often now. But not because Lisbeth wandered. And when it happened, it was like throwing a stone in the lake. The circles spread for days.

Chapter Forty-nine

1931

THE WORKSHOP HAD become a whole world. Haltingly at first, Sofie had begun spending a few hours there, and then retreating for a few days, as if the work made her shy. But that period was brief, and now she spent every day there. Outside the workshop, there was another world—of economic failure, worries about Germany, grandchildren growing up and the house falling into disrepair. But more and more, that world ceased to exist when she opened the workshop door each morning. In there everything was possible, and there was no time she had to keep track of, no meals to plan or even attend if she was absorbed in work. Anna cooked what she wished, and if her mistress did not turn up in the dining room, she would knock and ask if Sofie wanted a tray brought in.

Except in the summer, when the light lasted until past bedtime, she stayed in the workshop to watch the sun set over the river. It stirred her so much she often did forget about dinner. The preamble was achingly slow, with the most delicate pinks, blues and mauves—colours you would paint on porcelain—politely changing places in the sky. But the great moment came when the mother-of-pearl sky turned fiery red, as if to say, Yes, all those pastels are lovely but now it's time for a surge of sheer power. A triumphant, shameless red. Marianne's older daughter, who was good at science, told her sunsets were red because the path from the sun to the earth at sunset was longer than at noon. Only oranges and reds, which had longer wavelengths than blues and greens, could stay the course.

She was astonished by the amount of time and solitude at her disposal. She tried to conceive of it only in small pieces, in case it became intimidating. The seasons in Sweden, she thought, were so extreme, with few hours of daylight in winter and almost no night in midsummer. Marriage—or did she mean the time you had to yourself in marriage?—was like winter, with short, ecstatic sightings of light and sun. Widowhood seemed more like summer, with a light that went on forever. In theory, she saw that that might become tedious but, so far, making up for lost time left her lightheaded with gratitude. She tacked up the quotation she had written out from *To the Lighthouse* on the wall, where she could see it from her work. This formidable ancient enemy. This truth, this reality.

One day, experimenting with colours, she found a new one. It reminded her of her early attempts at spinning varying shades of wool together into different colours, trying unsuccessfully to produce the calm sheen of celadon. This new colour she chanced upon was not red, although it had red in it. Nor was it blue, although at first it looked much like blue. She kept playing with it, thinking she would lose it, but she did not. She loved it. It was rich but bouyant, it had depth but movement. She could use it in all kinds of ways.

Still slightly dazed with her colour, as she thought of it, she left the studio for dinner. The dining room table was set for two, on a cloth she had embroidered years ago with Japanese chrysanthemum seals. She traced one with her finger, feeling for a connection with the woman who had stitched it. And there was Sonja, sitting opposite, waiting.

"Darling, what are you doing here? I had no idea you were coming. How lovely to see you."

"Mamma, you knew I was coming. I wrote to you about it last week. The term at Siljevik is over, and I'm on my way back to Gothenburg."

Of course. The little girl in Nils's picture, standing on a stool while she painted a flower border on her bedroom walls, was now this capable-looking woman who taught art at the Siljevik Folk School.

"Mrs. Vogt sends her greetings. She gave an end-of-term coffee party for the teachers. And Miss Gregorius also asked to be remembered to you."

Cecilia, yes. Sofie did not hear from her so often these days, she was so busy taking care of Lars along with her other projects. She missed Cecilia in occasional great gulps, but she, too, was busy. Sonja was looking at her oddly, and she found it difficult to focus on her daughter's presence, on Anna holding the tureen, on everything that was not her workshop.

Sonja asked, "What are you working on? Anna said I was not to disturb you."

"Well, something remarkable happened today," she said, side-stepping the question slightly. "I discovered a new colour, it fascinates me. I can't get it out of my mind, I have so many plans for it. There is some blue in it, but it's not blue, really. And some red too, but it's far from red. I can't think why we didn't know about it."

Sofie had more to say about the colour, until Sonja stopped her with a small smile.

"Mamma," she said, "for quite some time now we have been calling that colour purple."

Purple. Of course, purple. It was purple. How funny that it had looked like a completely new thing to her. But so much looked new to her these days.

Sonja had moved on to something more important. She took a sip of her soup and turned to Anna.

"Anna, your cream of mushroom soup, what a treat. No one

makes it as well as you do. Even with your recipe, it never tastes the same in Gothenburg."

Anna went back to the kitchen, looking happier than she had for months.

Sofie cocked her head toward the kitchen, turned to Sonja and waited.

"Anna told me all the village gossip," Sonja explained, "and all about the 'new regime,' as she calls it. She misses the morning menu planning with you, and she misses Pappa's exaggerated compliments about her cooking. She worries that you aren't eating enough, and she can't understand people—I wonder who?—who forget mealtimes. Her orders to the butcher and fishmonger are thin to the point of embarrassment. Nobody can turn back the clock, she says, but things were very different when Pappa was alive and the children were home. Poor Anna."

Yes, poor Anna, Sofie supposed, although she did not feel terribly sympathetic. Anna was right about one thing, though. Things had been very different when Nils was alive and the children were home.

Marianne and Birgitta came for Sunday lunch. Anna had outdone herself, making pork with onion sauce for Marianne and semolina with red currants, Birgitta's favourite childhood pudding. No doubt primed by Sonja, her sisters praised Anna's cooking to the skies. Sofie wondered when everyone had gotten so interested in food.

Finally, her daughters turned their attention to her. How was she?

"Fine, but I'm finding the workshop rather small. I'm thinking of moving my work into the studio."

They nodded quickly, without looking at each other. She could see they were surprised.

Birgitta said, without conviction, "Moving the loom could be difficult."

That was nonsense: the loom had been moved into the workshop, so it could be moved out into the larger studio. In fact, Sofie wasn't thinking of moving the loom, but she didn't mention that. Obviously, they had come to talk about something else.

"Mamma," Marianne said, "we want you to think about coming to live with us. Or to Oskar's farm. We both have plenty of room. It's too lonely for you to live all alone in this rabbit warren, in a village far from most of your children. If you came to us, we are close enough to Orebro that you would have all the things a town offers, shops, a doctor, even concerts. With Oskar, there's less of a town, but you would enjoy the farm and have his children for company."

Sofie pretended to consider this while she served the pork. She was mildly shocked, as always these days, to see that her beautiful girls were matrons, with a bas-relief of wrinkles around their eyes and their shining hair streaked with grey. She would never move in with the children—or only when she was too old to work. They were part of her, but she didn't want them underfoot. She needed to be able to visit her work in the middle of the night or early in the morning if the mood struck her, without having to explain herself or speak to anyone on the way.

Of course, she promised them, she would think about it. In late afternoon, after more compliments to Anna, the daughters left for the Falun station.

"The place comes to life when the girls are here," Anna sighed, watching the hired car until it was out of sight. "What a shame they can't come more often."

The weather had been uncertain, and now the clouds were bright orange with blue veins. She wondered how long the light would last in the workshop.

Sofie leaned in for a closer look: something was happening to Nils's screen, the one he had painted in France and used when his models

undressed and dressed. It pictured a jolly scene of Scandinavian painters in a French restaurant, laughing, making toasts, teasing each other.
In the background a waiter, wearing the long white apron of his trade,
held a tray of drinks. But at a corner of the table, where there was a
bit of space—the only emptiness in this happily crowded picture—
something was changing. A figure, seated at the corner, was emerging. There had been nothing there, and now it looked as if someone
was appearing out of a fog. As the pigments of the overpainting faded,
someone who had been skillfully painted out was making a come-
back. Sofie looked again at the returning figure. It must be Thérèse,
she realized, the model who had been Nils's mistress in Paris.

> *Dear Thérèse,*
>
> *Forgive me, I don't know your last name so I address you
> by your first although we never met. Nils never spoke of you
> to me, but I knew that he had lived with a woman in Paris,
> and once in conversation Georg Pauli mentioned your name
> by mistake. He was embarrassed, but I did not care.*
>
> *After decades of banishment, you are returning to Nils's
> studio, one you never saw. It seems only fair. I wonder, what
> was Nils like when he was with you? Could you make him
> happy? That was a hard time in his life, so I doubt it. I doubt
> anyone could have done that. He could be joyful—a sharper,
> shorter feeling—but even when things went well for him, he
> lived with a shadow. I think you took good care of him, and
> thank you for that.*
>
> *What has your life been since he left? I do not apologize
> for taking him away, because what would that mean? But I
> am sorry if it hurt you. We made a life that was not perfect,
> but I think it was a full one for Nils.*
>
> *I wish you well.*
>
> *Yours truly,*
>
> *Sofie Olsson*

Well, it was not difficult to be understanding to a woman she had never met, in a letter that could not be sent. But it was true, that what had come before her did not interest her.

Chapter Fifty

MAY 1933

AT FIRST CECILIA was not terribly concerned when she read about rallies in Stockholm for the Swedish National Socialist Party or demonstrations in Lund against "foreign influences." What she felt was bafflement: Why were the Swedes following the Germans in their dangerous delusions? Lisbeth was even less concerned, insisting that Cecilia was exaggerating the movement's importance.

"I do not exaggerate," Cecilia countered. "I notice." She would say to Lisbeth over the newspaper, "The Farmers' League is claiming that they will protect Swedes from 'inferior foreign racial elements' and 'degenerative influences.'"

And Lisbeth would respond, "Cecilia, what do you expect? You're talking about the Farmers' League."

On another day, Cecilia said, "I heard in Stockholm last week that the crown prince sympathizes with the Germans' plan for expansion."

"And that is only a silly rumour. And even if he did, it doesn't mean that anything would come of it, or that a sizable number of Swedes would ever agree with him."

But Cecilia knew—because by now she was following more closely, and was worried—that thirty thousand of her compatriots had voted for the Swedish National Socialist Party in the last election. The number sickened her. Thirty thousand was *not* insignificant.

Cecilia and the housekeeper, Mrs. Goransson, were making the final arrangements for the fiddling competition on the weekend. There was a boy from Jonkoping who was said to be wonderful, and Mikael Lennart from Falsterbo would defend his crown. In the final round, on Sunday, each of the three finalists would play his version of Bellman's complicated minuet, "Alas, thou my mother." In the past Lars would have loved seeing Lennart's stocky body in his vest and breeches and embroidered stockings, and the brave, plaintive sounds he would cajole from his fiddle. Even now, music seemed to animate him more than anything else, especially the old songs. He would strike his knee in time to Bellman's melodies, although there was no other sign that he recognized them.

As usual, there would be a lunch for the judges and the patrons before the final session. And afterwards, a reception that included the finalists and their families and more of the village dignitaries.

"I think we will be twenty for lunch," Cecilia said, looking up from her page of notes. "If Mr. Astrom has some very fresh haddock, then let's have haddock with mustard butter before the roast lamb, but only if Ingrid is absolutely certain of its freshness. And have her make sure to use only really ripe fruit in the tarts. Last Sunday the apricots were too hard. The blue-and-white dishes for lunch, and for the reception, use the 'Lilies' pattern."

"Yes, ma'am."

"And see if Peder can find enough hydrangeas to fill the big Chinese pots for the reception."

"Yes, ma'am."

But the housekeeper stood there, not leaving. Cecilia stopped ticking items off her list.

"Mrs. Goransson. Is there anything else?"

"Not really, only I just wondered . . . I wondered if Mr. Martensson or Mr. Lundholm would be coming to the lunch or the reception."

How strange. Mrs. Goransson had never asked about a guest list before.

"Mr. Martensson has been invited to both, as he is on the board of the Folk School, and Mr. Lundholm has been asked to the reception. Miss Gregorius would know if they have accepted."

Mrs. Goransson stared into her blouse, and felt for the watch that was pinned over her heart.

"It's only a silly piece of gossip, ma'am."

"Well, then, tell me what it is."

"I think it's foolish, really . . . but some people are saying that the only people who should wear the local dress are those who were born in the village. That's silly, of course, but they say that Mr. Martensson and Mr. Lundholm agree with . . ."

Why was the woman presuming to discuss what she would wear? That was her maid's province. She cut her off.

"Thank you, Mrs. Goransson, that will be all. I will plan my dress with Dorrit."

Even as she turned away, Cecilia felt as though some part of her had been anticipating this conversation.

Siljevik, 22 May 1933
Dear Sofie,

Each year the details for the fiddling competition seem to multiply. Although we are far from finished, I long for it to be Saturday, just so that the preparations will be over! And don't worry if it becomes too difficult for you to get here—I completely understand.

Annoyingly, in the midst of all the busyness, I find I can't shake off the conversation I wrote you about, the one with my housekeeper about the local dress. I wouldn't have worn the Siljevik dress in any case. I almost never do these days. My mother-in-law looked so beautiful, so ordered and placid in hers. As I age, I look haunted, almost disoriented in mine. A dark foreigner in spite of my blue eyes, a stranger who has mysteriously washed up on the shore of Lake Siljan without any clothes and been forced to put on the local dress.

This new "rule" is particularly twisted: would Askebo exclude you, the designer of the Askebo dress, from wearing it because you were born in Hallsberg? Of all innocent things to be touched by this madness, the Siljevik dress. But very little is innocent these days. Perhaps we succeeded too well when we set out to encourage the old customs. They were sick and dying when we started collecting bonnets and timber buildings and folk songs. And now they have become strangely powerful. Too powerful, because now they are being used to exclude people from the inner circle.

This reminds me of the story of Bernhard Zondek, which the newspaper placed low down, on a back page, where it would be easy to overlook. Miss Gregorius says I have eagle eyes for any stories about the Germans, so perhaps you missed it. Dr. Zondek is a German gynaecologist who invented a pregnancy test, something to do with mice. He was the head of his department at a Berlin hospital and a professor at the university, and dismissed from both posts as a Jew. A large number of British professors published a letter in the *Times* to protest the treatment of such a distinguished scientist. Then he was invited to join the staff of the Biochemical Institute at

the University of Stockholm. To our shame, one thousand
Swedish doctors objected to his admission. Fortunately for
him, Dr. Zondek has since moved to Palestine.

Miss Gregorius thinks I worry too much, but the idea
of a thousand Swedish doctors wanting to bar one
eminent scientist stuns me.

Your friend,
Cecilia

After she read Cecilia's letter, Sofie made a decision: she would go
to the fiddling contest and take Marianne's daughter, Ebba, with
her. She liked to say she had a grandchild for every occasion, and
Ebba was studying the violin. Of course, there would be no relaxed
chat with Cecilia, who would be busy, but it might be nice for her
just to see Sofie's face.

Rummaging for her letter paper in her untidy desk—she never
had a moment to straighten it any more—she thought ruefully of the
time when she believed that their shared widowhoods would bring
her closer to Cecilia. That had turned into a dark joke. Poor Cecilia
had the worst of two worlds, losing the bright spark of the old Lars
while inheriting the care of a baby who would never develop.

On the morning of the contest, Sofie decided against her folk
dress, although she knew many women would be wearing theirs.
She would have enjoyed responding to anyone who challenged her
right to wear the Askebo dress—one of the bonuses of being old was
that she had no trouble being sharp when the occasion warranted.
But Swedes were usually too polite for such confrontations, and it
was more important to give Cecilia some company. She chose a light
grey dress with red smocking at the yoke and cuffs. Ebba, on the
other hand, with the half-conscious arrogance of sixteen-year-old
beauty, wore the red skirt and jacket of her village, with the long
points of her white collar trimmed with lace.

The field where the competition was held was crowded, and tiny Cecilia in her dark dress with sheer voile sleeves was not easy to find. When they located her, she spread her arms wide to embrace them and was lavish in her praise of the embroidery on Ebba's jacket. But she and the master of ceremonies needed to consult about something, so Sofie and Ebba took the seats Miss Gregorius had saved for them. A wooden path had been built through the field so that Lars could be wheeled to the front row, dressed in his Siljevik folk suit with its white coat and knickers. Sofie remembered when he had been so handsome in that suit, and for a minute or two he could still look surprisingly good in his chair. But the long coat demanded a man who could stand. Sofie went over to him, to greet him and introduce Ebba. She took the hand that did not lie in his lap in both of hers and looked closely into his eyes, but Lars met her with a blank face.

They returned to their seats and while Sofie tried to read her programme, Ebba followed Miss Gregorius's movements.

"Just watch her, Grandmamma. She is everywhere, either showing people to their seats, or rearranging the contestants' chairs, or seeing that the ushers have enough programmes."

"Mmmm," Sofie said. Miss Gregorius was pretty, but otherwise she could not understand why Ebba was so impressed.

"And look at how well she and Mrs. Vogt manage things: Miss Gregorius will give Mrs. Vogt a look from halfway across the field, and it will remind her of something and she changes her direction."

"Yes, I suppose," Sofie said. Ebba could be over-imaginative.

Finally, after too many introductory speeches, the competition began. As always, the music opened Sofie's heart. While the fiddlers negotiated Bellman's difficulties she sat, filled with gratitude for Cecilia and Lars, whose love for Swedish things was astute as well as generous. Occasionally, when a fiddler played a daunting bridge with almost impossible ease, she even felt close to tears— this new and unpredictable tearfulness was a part of old age she did not enjoy. She looked at the audience, a sea of breeches and silver-clasped vests, and the threat of tears receded. It reminded her of a picture she had recently seen in *Das Bild*, of Nazi officials at a folk-dancing festival giving their smiling blessing to rows of blond men in lederhosen and women in dirndls. Except for the Nazi uniforms and the swastika floating over the podium, it looked like a vast version of the Siljevik fiddling contest. Perhaps Cecilia was right, and something wholesome they had nurtured was revealing an unexpectedly sinister side.

While the judges deliberated, Sofie looked around for a washroom. Miss Gregorius would know where it was, but she was nowhere to be seen. Sofie made her way across the field, toward a small tent some distance from the stage. There was often a place where the dignitaries could rest and take some refreshment, especially if it was a hot day, with a toilet at the back, and that was probably it.

She moved the canvas flap of the tent aside, and for one astonishing moment found Cecilia lifting up her hands to cup Miss Gregorius's face. With her arms around Cecilia, the younger, taller woman was bending down to . . . Sofie closed the flap instantly before she saw more. In the first distracted minute, she told herself that she and Cecilia, too, could have had such a tender embrace. For example, when Markus had died. Reticence had kept them from it, but it would have been possible. Although the idea of Cecilia taking her face in her hands . . . no, that was hard to imagine. And she would not think of the look on Miss Gregorius's face as she bent down. Sofie slipped away quickly, stepping carefully over the ropes that coiled like thick beige snakes in the grass. It would not do to trip, especially when her heart was beating so fast. They had not seen her, she was sure of that. Probably Cecilia had been having a moment of upset about the pro-German supporters in the village, and Miss Gregorius was comforting her. No doubt that was it.

The washroom would have to wait.

———

The crown went to the boy from Jonkoping, who was Ebba's favourite. As Sofie had predicted, Cecilia was surrounded by well-wishers
and no one, including Sofie, got more than a few hurried words with
her. Miss Gregorius insisted that they come back to the house for the
reception, at least for a little food before they took the train back to
Falun. Sofie agreed, if only because she still wanted a washroom.

Later, on the train, Ebba chattered happily about her resolve to
practice much more, so that she could become the first girl to compete in the fiddling contest. Then they were silent, while Sofie
watched the lake and the sky. Blue clouds in a pink sky moved
backward—she knew there was no backward or forward, but that
was the effect—in a stately way, as if to say, our direction does not
matter, we keep our dignity no matter what.

Ebba said, "Miss Gregorius is very nice, isn't she?"

"Yes. She is what the French call *serviable*, very willing to help."

Sofie still did not see what was so special about Miss Gregorius.

"Grandmamma, have you read *The Well of Loneliness*?"

Surprised, Sofie glanced at the book on Ebba's lap—but no, it
was a collection of Selma Lagerlof's short stories.

"Surely you are too young to read a book like that."

"I haven't exactly read it," Ebba admitted, "but I hear girls at
school talking about it."

"What put that into your head just now?"

Suddenly hesitant, Ebba said she wasn't sure.

Indeed. Carefully, she asked Ebba, "Do the women in *The Well
of Loneliness* have a Boston marriage?"

Ebba didn't know that old-fashioned term, so Sofie explained
that it could be two women who lived together as dear friends or
who were in love with each other.

"Yes," Ebba said, now looking as if she regretted bringing it up.
"They are in love."

The evening sky was the deep pink of a cyclamen, darkening
to red. Sofie was very tired and a bit uncomfortable, even slightly

cross. Not at Ebba, who was a dear, observant girl if only a little too talkative. The scene in the tent hovered at the edge of her mind, and she pushed it away. She would be glad to be home, in her own room. And there was one thing she felt sure of after today, at least. She did not need to feel guilty about neglecting Cecilia.

Chapter Fifty-one

CECILIA SPENT HOURS each day working on the catalogue of Lars's work that was going to be published when the art gallery opened. Her study's French formality was obscured, more and more, by paintings leaning against chairs, tables and walls, and by etchings and engravings piled on the slender-legged marquetry desk. It would have taken her quite a while to find the silver tray with her calling cards that had sat there for years in chilly splendour. Among the new office furniture that had been bought for Lisbeth was a heavy oak table, which she rarely used. Cecilia had it moved next to her own desk, where it looked like a doughty North Swedish work-horse standing next to a high-strung racehorse. The oak table was where she worked on the catalogue.

As she sifted through the pictures, memories slowed her writing. Early in their marriage Lars etched his own version of Rembrandt's *Self-Portrait with Saskia*. In both pictures, the wife was in the background while the man occupied the foreground, holding a tool of his trade, a brush in Rembrandt's case, an etching needle in Lars's. Saskia sat, moon-faced and serious, while Cecilia stood with her arm angled on her hip, young, round-cheeked and confident.

Confidence had never been her problem, but the round cheeks astounded her. In spite of the title, *Vogt and His Wife*, she saw herself as an equal, staring off into the distance, plotting the next move in Lars's career. Saskia was a muse, but Lars had painted a partner.

Next, she pored over an etching of a nude girl lolling on a bed. Lars had begun it in a hotel room in Boston. The atmosphere in the picture was close, almost claustrophobic. The unhealthy heat of so many rooms in America almost seemed to rise from the paper. Lars had an alarmingly high fever on that day but would not stop working because the girl was such a perfect subject. He lay propped up on pillows drawing at the other end of the bed, literally febrile, and it gave the etching its quality of erotic intoxication.

How many etchings Lars had made of other artists manipulating their nude models into exactly the right position, or sitting on the edge of the bed after intimacies. There was one of Gervase Williams with his mistress crouched behind him on the bed. Cecilia could see more in these pictures than she had when they were new. Now that she was old, and now that there was Lisbeth, she recognized how weary Williams looked, how worn compared to his glorious Minny.

She sighed over some of the American society portraits. The Americans loved them, but they showed Lars's weakest side, a superficiality that was almost flashy. Some were formidable, such as his picture of two thoroughbreds, Mrs. Thurston and her English setter, or his rhapsodic picture of Isabella Gardner on her balcony, flinging her long arms open to the Venetian night. With others he went through the motions, and most clients could not tell the difference. Lars had so much facility that he could be impressive even when it was not his metier. But you had only to look at Singer Sargent's portraits to see what a real master of that form did with his subjects.

She propped up yet another picture of a woman in a taffeta evening dress and her moustachioed husband against a stack on the floor. It must take extraordinary discipline to turn away from what you do very well, in order to concentrate on what you do superbly. Lars had that discipline before and after America, but in the years when he travelled there regularly, the fame and the money were irresistible. He thought she was too European to enjoy America, but it was its effect on his art that had worried her. And she was right: the American trips had weakened his work, and although he recovered himself when he returned to Sweden, in a small way the damage was permanent.

For one thing, the Americans were too prudish to appreciate his nudes, and few were sold there. Still, those who bought them were reluctant to sell them back to her. She did manage to buy an early one, a lyrical little oil of a mother introducing her boy to the water. The American owner had had the mother's private hair painted over, but Cecilia had a restorer return it to its original state. The thought of that did make her smile. What a craft, restoring private hair after it proved too embarrassing for previous owners.

Strange that Lisbeth, of all people, was blind to the crudeness of Lars's late nudes. It was vulgar to think of them as lip-smacking, but to Cecilia that was the inevitable word. Well, in spite of Lisbeth, they were not going to be shown in the gallery. Or anywhere else, at least the ones Cecilia owned or could buy back. The question was, how to dispose of them? Perhaps in a bonfire at Tallmon. That had a certain symbolic rightness. She would have to make a discreet arrangement with the caretaker.

Lisbeth was eager to read the catalogue and, even more, the essays Cecilia was writing to accompany it. She said, "I'd be glad to look over what you have finished, Cecilia. Or, if you'd like another pair of eyes on something you're writing, I'm happy to read it."

"Thank you," Cecilia said, "there's no need just yet."

She was determined to keep it from Lisbeth as long as she could. Lisbeth would not like her reserve about certain works, or her bluntness about others. She would say Cecilia was undermining their work by qualifying his achievement. But, as Cecilia told Lars's dissatisfied clients when they wanted shoulders painted broader or a neck made slimmer, there was no way around the truth. She would borrow the word Sofie often used to describe Lars's work—"robust." She would tell Lisbeth that his work was robust enough to bear it.

Thinking of Sofie put Cecilia in mind of the scene she had glimpsed in the tent at the fiddling competition. Out of the corner of her eye, as Lisbeth bent down to kiss her, Cecilia had seen a sleeve with telltale red smocking on the cuff open and then immediately close the tent flap. Lisbeth had not seen it, and Cecilia would not mention it to her. What did Sofie think? She could not imagine. Any more than she could imagine her life without Lisbeth.

Chapter Fifty-two

AUTUMN 1933

DORA HELMERSEN HAD come to Askebo to see Sofie's work. As usual, she spoke little. Watching the photographer walk around the workshop, Sofie realized she cared more about Miss Helmersen's opinion than she had imagined she would. Taciturn people had power, whether they knew it or not.

Miss Helmersen stopped at a winter scene where the snow bordering the river was mauve. She inspected smoky clouds inside a thin outline of pale gold, a mottled sky of red and purple, a blue sky almost covered by a white cloud cracked like plaster. Sofie stood by the window, remembering how she had waited for the verdicts of Mr. Lindstrom, her first art teacher, and Professor Malmstrom.

Finally, Miss Helmersen said, "Many sunsets."

Sofie nodded.

"And much red."

"I suppose so."

Miss Helmersen indicated a sunset seen through leafless branches, their black tangles like the struggles of a beginning lacemaker.

"You have been busy."

Sofie understood this was as much admiration as she was going to get from Miss Helmersen. It was far from the enthusiasm with which Nils had met her textiles, or the discernment of MacDonald Lawrie, but she was content.

Afterwards, they sat at the round table in the parlour, where long ago Nils had painted her ball of black wool and the unfinished stocking, and drank tea. Miss Helmersen said, abruptly, "And you are wearing red, too."

This was apparently a reference to all the red she had noted in Sofie's paintings.

"They say it's not a colour for older women, but since my hair is still dark, I still wear it."

She thought of Nils's red dressing gown. Marianne had had it cleaned and mended, but Sofie had never worn it after she had torn up the lily bed.

"In Asia long ago," Miss Helmersen said, "they covered sick people with a red quilt, in the hope that the strength of the colour would help the person recover."

"And brides in China and Japan wear red," Sofie added. "The custom began at a time when red dye faded quickly, which underlined its connection with young, passionate love." She hoped this was not too intimate a subject for Miss Helmersen.

But Miss Helmersen smiled drily and said, "We have longer-lasting dyes now."

A few weeks after Miss Helmersen's visit, Sofie entertained other visitors. But for these, she put away her paintings. Cecilia had written to Sofie that Miss Gregorius had business in Falun. If Sofie had time, Miss Gregorius would drop Cecilia off at the house. And if her appointment did not last too long, she might join them later. Miss Gregorius drove an automobile, a Volvo sedan with the latest accessory, a compartment under the dashboard in which to store your driving gloves when the car was not in use. While you drove, you stored your dress gloves in the compartment.

Of course Sofie had time for a visit from Cecilia. And Miss Gregorius too, if it was convenient.

On the surface, things went on as before for Sofie with Cecilia. They exchanged letters and occasionally met in Dalarna and Stockholm. At times Sofie forgot about the scene in the tent at the fiddling competition, and each time the memory returned the shock was less. But it left a small awkwardness in her behaviour. More important, when she allowed herself to think about it—and mostly she did not—Sofie wondered how well she really knew Cecilia.

Sofie and Cecilia walked along the river. Looking not at each other, but at the roots and changes in the ground along the riverbank, they talked about *Howards End*. They had both enjoyed the clash, comic but potentially tragic, between the bohemian, cultured Schlegel family and the conventional, business-minded Wilcoxes. And what a wonderful man E. M. Forster must be, Sofie said, to have created Margaret Schlegel, one of the most complex, intelligent heroines they knew.

The odd one out in the bourgeois Wilcox family was the mother, who was intuitive, with deep feelings. Cecilia was talking warmly about her when Sofie interrupted.

"Wait a minute. When we read *To the Lighthouse*, you told me you were through worshipping at the shrines of these Angels in the House. You said their influence was 'pernicious.'"

"But Mrs. Wilcox is different," Cecilia protested. "There is something almost mystical about her. She is unsophisticated, even naive. And she appears in the novel so briefly . . ." Her voice trailed off as she saw the skepticism in Sofie's face. "All right, perhaps I was extreme in my rejection of Mrs. Ramsay. All I meant was that we have to think hard about these models of apparent perfection. Their selflessness can be so seductive that we forget to question it."

Perhaps thinking it was better to distract Sofie with her own Achilles heel, Cecilia said, half-teasing, "I don't suppose that you will be defending Mr. Wilcox."

Sofie had finished the book, but Cecilia was just at the point when Mr. Wilcox, who had confessed to an adulterous affair, was proposing to shun Margaret Schlegel's unmarried sister, who was pregnant.

Sofie said, smiling, "I think, by the time you come to the end . . ."

"Don't!" Cecilia ordered, putting her hands up to her ears. "You know I hate to have the end ruined."

"Then my lips are sealed," Sofie said, and they both laughed. They were old hands at this conversation by now.

Cecilia changed the subject to the forthcoming Vogt gallery. She felt that she and Miss Gregorius had collected enough of Lars's American portraits, and in any case, not many owners were interested in selling them.

She added, "But Lisbeth does not agree, and she thinks we should cast our net wider in the hopes of buying more."

Sofie assumed calling her Lisbeth was a slip. Still, she kept her face expressionless, in case Cecilia looked up at her.

A few minutes later, Cecilia said, "Lisbeth and I have still not decided whether to hang all the etchings and engravings in their own rooms, or mix them chronologically with the paintings."

So, Sofie thought, this is deliberate. This is a step in a new direction.

They were heading back toward the house when they heard the sound of Miss Gregorius's car. They joined her at the little clearing where people parked.

"Well," she said, "what book have you two been talking over?"

The three women strolled toward the house, talking about Mr. Wilcox, when Sofie spotted Anna talking to a young man at the front door. Even at a distance, she could see that the housekeeper was upset.

Sofie said, "What is it, Anna?" and the man turned in her direction, holding his cap in his hands.

He was ginger-haired, with a strong jaw.

Sofie saw the resemblance instantly. She glanced at Cecilia. The look on her face told Sofie that Cecilia saw it too. To Sofie's surprise, she found she could act as if it were not a shock. The visitor resembled Markus most, with something in the set of the eyes that was like Tilda.

"What is it you want?" she asked him, while Anna wiped her hands, over and over, on her apron.

"I wanted a tour of the house, ma'am," he said, rotating his cap.

"A tour of the house?"

She was confused, on top of this strange calm. She pretended to herself that she was Miss Gregorius, who was regarding the scene with interest but nothing more.

Anna leaped in.

"I told him we don't do that. That is, if the Homecraft Association or something has a special visitor, or has organized a tour . . . but people don't just come . . . I don't know how he got this idea."

The young man said, "My mother said, since I was in the area, there was the house of a famous painter I mustn't miss. That people came from all over Sweden to see the house. I'm looking for work in Falun, so I came by, wanting to take the tour."

Where do you come from, she asked him quietly and was told, the Gamla Stan neighbourhood of Stockholm. Nils's old neighbourhood. But there was no work in Stockholm, so he was hoping to find a job in the mine.

"Well, as Anna has told you, we don't show the house in that way. But since you are here, I think Anna has the time to give you a short tour."

Anna looked astounded, but before she could protest, Sofie told Cecilia and Miss Gregorius that they must see the burning bush down by the river, which was having a particularly spectacular

autumn. She would take them to it. The young man thanked her.
She thought back to the long-ago day spoiled by the garrulous maid,
the broken toy omnibus and the snapped maroon thread. She had
known, or suspected, for quite some time now. There was no reason
to think Nils any different from other men. Or that it had made a
difference to their life together.

"And if there is no work at the mine," she said to the man's back
as he followed Anna into the house, "I may be able to suggest other
places to you."

The door closed, and the three women looked at each other.

"That was kind of you," Cecilia said.

"Well, he is hardly to blame."

Miss Gregorius looked attentive, but said nothing. Of course,
Cecilia would explain when they were alone.

"There are worse sins," Sofie added, "and I have forgiven them."

Cecilia looked into Sofie's eyes for a minute before she nodded.
She understands that too, Sofie thought. As the three women
walked back to the river, just for a moment Cecilia put her arm
around Sofie's shoulder.

Chapter Fifty-three

JUNE 1934

A FEW MONTHS later, Sofie asked Cecilia to visit Miss Helmersen's photography studio in Falun with her. Although Sofie had been friendly with Miss Helmersen for almost twenty years and had mentioned her photographic experiments, Cecilia had never met her. It was not a comfortable occasion, as Cecilia did not really want to go, and she doubted that Miss Helmersen wanted her to be there. Still, the photographer had an imperturbability that suggested nothing Cecilia did or said, positive or negative, could really affect her. Which was fortunate, because Cecilia doubted she was going to be able to join Sofie in her enthusiasm for Miss Helmersen's work.

They began by looking at the portraits, which were competent enough. Some of the landscapes were more than that, and Cecilia had a premonition that she had better stay with these views of snowy forests and lonely peaks as long as she could. To buy some time, she asked questions about simple technical details to do with the camera, and why Miss Helmersen had chosen to photograph such-and-such meadow or stream at this or that particular time of day. Then she asked about the finances involved in running a photography business. With her curious mixture of distance and candour, Miss Helmersen was more forthcoming than Cecilia had expected. Tersely, she explained how much she needed to bill each month to pay the rent as well as for the supplies and the occasional assistant.

Sofie was fidgeting with her reading glasses, which she wore pinned to the yoke of her dress. Cecilia could see that these delaying tactics were annoying her.

Miss Helmersen added, "The photographs of the dead carry the business. They account for more than half of my fees."

"That's interesting," Cecilia began, genuinely intrigued. But before she could continue, Sofie interrupted.

"Miss Helmersen, may I show Mrs. Vogt some of the pictures from the little chest?" She nodded toward the alcove.

Miss Helmersen indicated that Sofie could do whatever she chose, it was of no interest to her whatever. The pieces Sofie wanted Cecilia to see, the vases full of dead children's faces and the bizarre multiple portraits of the same person or persons, were even more baffling than Cecilia had feared. She could not fathom what Sofie liked about them. Luckily, a lifetime of going to vernissages had given her a stock of ambiguous adjectives, and she used them all when looking at Miss Helmersen's creations.

"My, this is most original. I have never seen anything like it."

"That is impressive, how you manage to picture a boy playing cards with three others, and they are all the same boy. The way this one leans over his neighbour to spy on his hand is very effective."

"The effect here is very intense."

"All most unusual. I congratulate you, this is all so new to me."

Miss Helmersen remained civilly aloof throughout. Finally, as gracefully as she could and with thanks to Miss Helmersen, Cecilia manoeuvred Sofie out the door.

"You did not like them." Sofie stated the obvious as they walked up Kristinegatan.

"No."

"I know they are strange, as is Miss Helmersen. She shows them to almost no one, and does not care about their reception. It was only because I asked as a special favour that she agreed to show them to you."

"Sofie, I could not recommend that a gallery represent her or that a museum exhibit her work. I am a bit of a businesswoman, but not a spiritualist."

Cecilia saw that she had made things worse, and tried to repair it.

"I'm not saying that Miss Helmersen intends to make that impression, but something about those multiple figures puts me in mind of table-tapping and people wanting to make contact with their dead."

As soon as she said that, Cecilia regretted what sounded like flippancy. It would be very natural for Sofie to long for contact with Markus and Nils, and that may have been part of Miss Helmersen's appeal for her.

But Sofie twitched her cape, although it sat perfectly straight on her shoulders, and said, with some heat, "It is not the spiritualism— if it even is that, Miss Helmersen denies it—that interests me. I think she is doing something akin to surrealism in her photographs."

"That may be, but it doesn't make me any more enthusiastic about what I see." Cecilia stopped in the street to face Sofie. "It's *your* work that I would like to help."

"Oh . . . me," Sofie said vaguely, as if she could barely summon up an idea of what that would mean. "Cecilia, you've been so patient with me. But I'm not sure what my work amounts to or if anything is to be done with it."

Cecilia sighed inwardly. It was more of the old, aggravating balancing act, keeping her protectiveness and her bossiness in check while she waited for Sofie to be ready.

Chapter Fifty-four

JULY 1934

JOHN LAVERY WROTE from London with the news that MacDonald Lawrie would soon be married, to an instructor of copper enamelling in the school.

In the spring, a letter came from Mr. Lawrie himself. He was leading a study tour to Sweden in the summer, taking perhaps eight students through the Dalarna villages famous for their crafts, and to the Vogts' old buildings and their collections of folk arts. He wondered if he might bring the students to Askebo? They would stay in the hotel in Falun, and it would mean so much to them to see her work. And, naturally, the famous house of Nils and Sofie Olsson.

Siljevik, July 1934
Dear Sofie,
      Mr. Lawrie and his students, all very keen and
enthusiastic, left this morning for Rattvik and Leksand.
I think they are planning to arrive in Askebo on Tuesday.
Lisbeth laughed at the extent of my preparations, and of
course the old buildings are nowhere near what we would
like them to be yet, but I felt we had Sweden's reputation

to uphold. At any rate, it went off well enough, and we even had some last-minute fiddling in the Hall for them.

I found Mr. Lawrie aging advantageously. Like so many men, and unlike us, crow's feet and grey hairs become him. When he was younger, he seemed an almost painful mixture of orange and pink, someone whose colouring Lars would have loved to paint but not otherwise to be recommended. But now that grey is calming his hair and he has added a bit of ballast to his slender frame, he looks much less raw.

And, I do not believe that he and the copper enamellist are engaged, or at least not yet. I asked him several questions about his plans, and heard nothing of a wedding.

He told me you have promised him and his students a crayfish party. You are a saint to go to that trouble.

Enjoy your time with them.

We are in the last throes of preparations for the ground-breaking of the gallery, so I will write more once that is over.

Your friend, in haste,
Cecilia

Mr. Lawrie and most of his students arrived in a cab from Falun. Two of the hardier ones had got up at dawn and walked the fifteen kilometres to the village. Sofie had wondered if she would feel uncomfortable when she saw him, but they shook hands like old friends. He introduced the students, six young women and two men. Although by now she followed the tangles and burrs of Mr. Lawrie's accent easily, it seemed that each new Glaswegian took a while to understand. It was like scraping barnacles off a boat, she thought. Unlike the English, who often seemed blind to the letter *r*, these Scots pronounced it—but only sometimes.

She took them to the church and showed them Nils's saints and angels, which she still found strained and unconvincing. On the other hand, she loved the portraits he had made of the villagers, which were hung in the village hall—the sad-eyed minister; the farmer whose hands, folded in his lap, were as big as his head; the cross-eyed carpenter who had delivered the furniture she designed under cover of darkness all those years ago. Prepared by Mr. Lawrie, the visitors were also keen to see her textiles and furniture. The closest questioning—about the big-boned rocker, the box-style plant stand and the cradle with the railing made of fence posts—came from the young women.

The crayfish party was a humid, tipsy success, made more wonderful for the guests because it was held under the birches at the little point that jutted into the river, the setting for Nils's painting *Preparing for the Feast*. They knew the painting by heart, and when she appeared with the glasses and the aquavit decanter with its tall stopper, one of them, a brunette named Margaret, cried, "It's the wee glasses and decanter from the picture!" By the time the mosquitoes came out, the aquavit and beer had done their work and they did not notice. The bibs, the obligatory juice-sucking before shelling and the messy shucking all loosened their inhibitions further. Sofie cast an eye over the mushroom pies, the salads, the Vasterbotten cheese. They would be ignored, as usual, until the crayfish were all eaten.

She had asked Birger and Evert from next door to come and sing the traditional drinking songs. Birger brought his accordion and an unsuspected knack for teaching, and soon the Scottish guests were singing in Swedish.

Helan går
Sjung hopp faderallan lallan lej

They sang lustily, with many swallows of aquavit in the appropriate places.

When they asked what it meant, Evert translated freely,

He who doesn't drink the first
Shall never, ever quench his thirst.

Sofie had no idea her bashful young neighbour was such a ready versifier. She smiled at Mr. Lawrie over a heap of crayfish topped with a spray of dill, its yellow-green blossom exploding like a firecracker. He had taken off his jacket and rolled his sleeves up to the elbow. With his bib, he looked like a brawny baby. Flushed with aquavit and the knowledge that the party had gone off well, she considered what it would be like to touch his forearm.

"It was as hot as this the first time you came here, do you remember?"

"Yes, but there were no crayfish then. Boeuf bourguignon and boiled potatoes, if I remember rightly."

They both knew that he remembered perfectly.

"Yes, it was a mistake. Nils liked to show off my French recipes."

He laughed. "That was a long time ago."

Some of the students were planning to walk to the mine next day, others to visit the churches in Falun or the old miners' neighbourhoods. If anyone wanted to see Nils's engraving shop in Falun, she had made arrangements for Mrs. Jansson next door to the Blindgatan house to let them in. Then they would spend a few days visiting the mine managers' estates that had especially fine folk murals. Before he left, Mr. Lawrie asked if he could visit in the morning.

After breakfast, in Nils's beloved bathroom, Sofie tried to pinch some colour into her cheeks. When she raised her arms, the flesh under her upper arms rippled like chiffon. She thought about Glasgow, which she had never seen. She had known as soon as Mr. Lawrie stepped down from the cab yesterday that the rumours of the enamelling teacher were not true. She thought about the bed-life she had had with Nils. It still seemed odd to her that she rarely missed it. Having it had been utterly natural, and often happy, for thirty-five years, and now not having it seemed equally natural. Perhaps it was a habit she could acquire again.

The house and garden looked particularly themselves that morning, with even the most attention-getting details absorbed into a harmonious whole. Anna brought the tray to the wooden table under the birch trees, overlooking the river.

"Wasn't there a flower bed here?" Mr. Lawrie asked.

"Yes, quite a while ago."

This time, it was obvious he knew what he was going to do. There would be no overturned furniture, no declaration that had nowhere to go, no uncertainty about what to call her. He made no pretense of drinking his coffee.

"Sofie."

She met his look.

"I am calling you Sofie because I cannot propose marriage to someone called Mrs. Olsson. I still love you. I have for twenty-five years, and now I hope that you will become my wife."

Perhaps his only mistake was asking her while they were sitting. Had they been standing, it would have been easier to take her in his arms—gently, confidently—and perhaps that would have done the trick. Or perhaps not.

They stayed sitting. She took his hand and held it.

"MacDonald," she said, "since you call me Sofie. Thank you. You are a very treasured friend. I need a little time. Could I think about it for a few days?"

Of course she could. As he was leaving, Marianne and her younger children arrived. The family was coming for their own crayfish party, and Marianne was the first. Her husband and the others would arrive that evening. MacDonald shook hands with Marianne and the children, sent his regards to the rest of the family, and left.

At lunch she said to Marianne, "I'm sorry, my love, you will be tired of mushroom pie. We are going to eat last night's leftovers, and then we will have more, fresh, this evening. But Anna can't eat all this, and I hate to waste food."

Marianne helped herself to a piece of pie. She didn't mind.

"Mr. Lawrie looked rather the worse for wear," she said, picking up her fork.

Sofie thought about that while she tried to interest the grandchildren in cucumber salad.

"Well, they all enjoyed the aquavit and beer, so maybe he was a little pale from that. I think he is looking quite distinguished."

Marianne made a face.

"Distinguished? Mr. Lawrie? I remember when we were children, whenever we encountered that peculiar word, *chilblains*, in our English lessons, we would shout, 'Mr. Lawrie!' Not that we ever saw any chilblains on him, but we were sure if anyone had them, it would be Mr. Lawrie."

Don't rise to this, Sofie told herself. But she couldn't help herself. The words leaped out, perhaps so that she could test whether it had really happened.

"He has asked me to marry him."

Marianne looked blank, then stunned. Then she laughed, the big cackle that comes when someone says something completely ridiculous.

"What do you find so funny about that?"

Marianne saw that she had miscalculated, but she was not about to back down.

"You mean, what *don't* I find funny about that. First of all, you aren't going to marry anyone. You are going to stay here, in the house you and Pappa made . . . I don't know quite how to say it, but maybe respecting his memory, keeping it going so that you can show it to people . . . so they can see how he wanted things, how you two wanted things . . ."

Sofie noted silently that although Marianne and Birgitta had recently wanted her to move, now apparently she was destined to tend the flame of their father's memory here in the house, forever.

"And if you ever did want to remarry," Marianne went on, "it certainly wouldn't be to MacDonald Lawrie."

"And why not, exactly?"

Marianne was treading a bit more carefully now.

"Well, for one thing, he lives in Scotland. No, if you were to marry, it would be someone like Axel Tallberg, or perhaps Ernest Thiel."

Touching. The engraver and writer who had championed Nils's work, and the banker who had collected it. What a loyal daughter to her father she was. What a darling, really. Sofie fought the impulse to stand, that would be unnecessarily dramatic.

"As a matter of fact, I am going to write Mr. Lawrie this afternoon and accept his proposal."

Which meant that Marianne left her mushroom pie untouched, after all.

Chapter Fifty-five

JULY 1934

THAT SAME MORNING in Siljevik, Lisbeth and Cecilia sat at breakfast. Dozens of their figures were reflected in the silver pieces on the plate racks and shelves. An old woman and one Cecilia still thought of as young, although she too had some grey in her hair.

"Listen."

Cecilia shook the newspaper and folded it in half, as if to stress what was coming.

"'The Ministry of Health asks that ten Jewish doctors be allowed to emigrate from Germany. A majority of students at Uppsala condemn the idea.'"

Lisbeth put a patient look on her face. They had travelled this way before, and she was going to point out the familiar landmarks once again.

"Cecilia, the students at Uppsala are some of the oldest fogies in the country. Everybody knows that. Don't upset yourself."

"'The students at Lund University oppose it also, in even greater numbers. The resolution from Lund says, "Immigration that leads to foreign elements being absorbed by our people seems to us damaging and indefensible."' Foreign elements."

"Cecilia, they are just students."

"They are the future elite of the country. The idea that ten doctors could damage anything . . ."

She left that unfinished and pushed her dishes away irritably, as if they too had voted against admitting the doctors. "I don't understand how you can be so blase about this."

"And I don't understand why you let yourself be so worried. It's natural that there would be a certain amount of sympathy with Germany. Our connections go back centuries. But the majority of Swedes will not stand by and watch the Germans make life seriously difficult for their Jews, if it ever comes to that."

If it ever came to that. It had already come to that. And it was not only the privileged Swedish students who didn't want Jewish immigrants. But yet again, Cecilia couldn't talk to Lisbeth about it; Lisbeth thought she was hysterical.

That afternoon, they broke ground for the art gallery, with all the requisite pomp and dignitaries. Lars, the raison d'être, sat in the front row, oblivious even when all the assembled stood to applaud him. For the next few years, Cecilia and Lars and Lisbeth would live between the perfect quiet of the cemetery on one side of the house and the noisy upheaval of construction on the other side, a drawback they had ignored until now. She and Lisbeth were still at odds on all kinds of details, but many of them were years down the road, and they were united, at least, on the design of the gallery. Odd to think how these sorts of decisions had been easier with Lars in a way, although they never planned anything so ambitious as a medium-size gallery. She supposed he had let her do things her way so that he was free to paint.

After the ground-breaking ceremony, Fredrik and his wife Regina and Natalie and her Paulus were to spend the night in Siljevik. Lisbeth joined them for dinner. Cecilia sometimes wondered how it struck her brother and sister and their spouses that the curator of the Vogt Foundation, a woman who was well-spoken and not shy, was almost always at family occasions when they visited Siljevik. Usually things went well, but sometimes when the talk became too intimate about the family or "the Jewish question," she could see that they were uncertain about Lisbeth's presence.

This time, it was Cecilia who started it. Over the fish, she mentioned that Ragnar Josephson, the director of the National Theatre and a Jew, had given a speech to the congregations in Stockholm and Gothenburg about the hard place in which Swedish Jews found themselves. He put the dilemma in blunt terms: Should we allow a small, select number of German Jews into Sweden on humanitarian grounds, and risk the precarious balance we have been building for a century and a half?

"What is the precarious balance, exactly?" Fredrik asked, moving a very small amount of the sauce off his cod. He loved caper sauce but had been ordered by his doctor and Regina to lose some weight.

"Convincing the Swedes that we are more Swedish than Jewish," Cecilia said rather sharply.

In the silence that followed, Natalie took Lars's left hand, and held it. He had been fed the soft things he ate earlier in the kitchen, and now he sat, looking more as if he were in a streetcar with strangers than in his own house with his family. Cecilia could still be saddened at how easily all of them ignored his presence. She pushed on, despite the fact that everyone except Lars and Lisbeth looked a little uneasy.

"The alternative, according to Josephson, is to support a larger number of German Jews and watch anti-Jewish feeling rise even higher."

Fredrik, who had bravado but not courage, agreed that the times were dangerous. With a partly furtive, partly apologetic glance at Lisbeth, he said, "We owe it to the community here to keep the number of immigrants down. That may be regrettable, but perhaps it is the only way to safeguard our fortunate Swedish lives."

"Nonsense," Natalie said.

Natalie thought she understood Germany because she took the waters every year at Wiesbaden. She believed the Germans were like the Swedes, only more numerous and suffering from wounded pride since the Paris treaty.

"There is not going to be any need to safeguard our fortunate lives, as you call them," she said. "Cooler heads will prevail in Germany before any serious harm is done."

The damask-covered table glittered with silver and cut glass, but Cecilia's mind went to homespun weaving, carved wooden spoons and rustic pottery. Until her housekeeper's revelation about the Siljevik dress, it had never occurred to her that there could be any disjunction between her Jewishness and the affection she and Lars felt for old Swedish songs and customes. Now, even as she watched their heritage being commandeered by German sympathizers, it still seemed incomprehensible. We worked for decades fanning those small, weak flames back into life, she thought. And now I stand by as they are added to a bonfire that threatens to consume us.

Chapter Fifty-six

JULY 1934

MACDONALD LAWRIE WAS over the moon. His letter in response to Sofie's was happily chaotic. He wrote, "Never feel you are saying goodbye to Askebo. We will return every summer." And, "Now you must call me Mac, as my friends do." And, "The biblical paintings at the Sweden estate are marvellous. But, compared with your note, everything is dust." He would rush over tomorrow, after escorting the students to a manager's house with particularly fine murals.

She told a sullen Marianne not to say anything about the engagement, she was not ready to talk about it yet. Marianne promised, and by the time the family party began, it was clear she had told Birgittta, Sonja and Tilda. Sofie did not have much appetite for more crayfish and aquavit. Probably one crayfish party a year was enough. The family crowded close together at the tables under the birches. The daughters-in-law and sons-in-law were always disconcerted by the way the Olssons squeezed ten people around a table that held six, but it was an old habit. As grandchildren hung across Sofie's lap, swinging from one uncle to another, or chased each other along the river, and their parents jostled her to get the cheese or the beer, she watched as if from a distance. They were so dear, and there were so many of them. They were so loud, and several of them clever. Of course she would return here in the summers, although she would be happy not to see a crayfish for a long time.

She went to bed, leaving the last of them still sitting at the point—the sons-in-law and Tilda, who loved a party. She dreamed that a Glasgow jewellery-maker was making her a pendant. It was in the Rennie Mackintosh style, with a few cabochons hung from a spiderweb of chains. There were two problems with it. The first was it was meant for a low-cut gown. She explained to the jeweller, a lovely young woman who looked like one of Mac's students, that she always wore high collars, but the jeweller answered that it would be impossible with this necklace. The more serious problem was that the jeweller was literally fashioning it on her body, hammering her collarbones and breastbone to get the brass backing into the proper shape and screwing the stones directly into her chest.

She woke and found the sheet draped tightly around her body, mimicking the kind of evening dress she never wore, the kind that would be perfect with the necklace. It reminded her of the pink dress she had worn at Helena Jolin's party, when she first met Nils. It is a dream, she told herself, unwinding herself from the sheet, and went back to sleep.

Then she dreamed that she was painting a mackerel sky. But no matter what she did, the painting kept turning into a dark carpet. One minute, she was holding a palette and painting the sky's cobbled surface; then, with no transition, she was standing at her loom, weaving pairs of birds into a carpet's black background.

At breakfast, the sons, who knew nothing, said, "Mamma, you look as if you didn't sleep a wink." The daughters were kinder and secretly hopeful. They asked solicitously, "Mamma, did you sleep well?"

She hoped that Mac would stop at the hotel in Falun on his way to see her, so that he could read the note she had sent in a car, early in the morning. He would want to come anyway, she knew that, but at least he would know before seeing her. But he had come straight from the house with the murals, and she had to cut through his joyful chatter at once.

"MacDonald, Mac, I am so sorry," she said, taking his hands and unable to face the hurt eyes and suddenly prominent freckles. She bent her head in shame, but he lifted her chin.

"No, tell me," he said, his voice dismayed and quiet.

"It won't work. I should have known that, but I hoped . . . And now I have hurt you, more than if I had known that immediately."

Was it the move to Glasgow? Because he would find a place with a fine studio for her. Was it leaving the children, or the house? But his questions were perfunctory and half-hearted, and this time she did not feel that he surrendered too soon. They sat together for a while, sadly, all awkwardness gone.

After Mac left, the daughters were excessively affectionate. Mamma, they said, show us what you are working on. Why is there nothing on the loom? The herb garden is flourishing, is that your work or Anna's? Sofie let their questions wash over her, feeling her bad conscience throbbing. She wanted to forget Mac's face, with the freckles like the bottoms of exclamation points standing out in the bewildered whiteness. She knew that, once the memory subsided, she would feel intense, guilty happiness. But now it was painful, and it should be. She looked around at the family, whom she loved greatly when she could think about them in peace, when they were not pressing on her with their talk and their wants. She could hardly wait for the house to be hers again.

Chapter Fifty-seven

EVEN WITH HELP, it had become too difficult to get Lars up and down the stairs. Cecilia and Lisbeth moved him to the first floor, where they improvised a bedroom in the room off the dining room with the built-in china cabinets. This move meant that he would not see his beloved Hall again, but it had to be. Cecilia had the Victrola brought down from the Hall and set up in the dining room, so she and Lars could listen to music in the evenings. They had a short ramp built at the kitchen door, and it was a simple matter to wheel him out for a walk.

But Lars's bedroom, now empty, continued to cause trouble. Soon after his move to the first floor, as Cecilia and Lisbeth were looking over blueprints for the gallery in her office, Lisbeth had asked, "What would you think of my moving into Lars's bedroom?"

She spoke casually, as if raising nothing terribly important. At first Cecilia was confused.

"Do you mean for your office? But you are so well set up here."

"I meant for my bedroom."

Sometimes Lisbeth's cheek stunned Cecilia. Yes, Lars had no need for that bedroom, but Cecilia was outraged. Disturbed was probably the better word, she told herself, she should learn to moderate these extreme reactions. But no, she was *outraged*. She thought of Lisbeth sleeping in Lars's bed, under Lars's red canopy, wrapping his green silk coverlet around her fist, as she did with Cecilia's white one, and it was all wrong.

"No, that's out of the question."

"Why are you so upset? It makes sense—I would be much closer to you there, instead of on the first floor in the guest room."

But Cecilia knew that was not the real motive. She wanted to sleep in Lars's bed. And that made Cecilia feel trespassed upon, even invaded. On her own behalf or his? Or on theirs, hers and Lars's? She did not know.

"I am not upset. But I don't want to hear any more about it."

Sofie came to Siljevik for the day, in time to see the roses' early September bloom. Cecilia met her on the porch, and they went looking for Lisbeth. They found her in the kitchen, where she was annoying the cook by arranging roses in the sink. She was trying to coax some white ones into a cut-glass vase.

"Why do people grow these cruel things?" she complained, carefully choosing a safe spot on a stem around which to place thumb and forefinger. But the thorns seemed to know she was afraid and no matter what she did, the branches whipped this way and that, hooking themselves into her blouse and skin.

"For their beauty," Cecilia said.

"And their scent," Sofie said. Neat-handed, she took up a few stems and dropped them in a tin beaker, where they looked better than in the glass vase. Stop showing off, she said to herself, although pleased with the effect. This is not a flower-arranging competition.

She atoned by passing likely-looking stems to Lisbeth, who persisted with her formal bouquet.

At lunch they talked about Selma Lagerlof, whom Sofie had visited in Falun. Her books had had great success in Germany, but now her outspoken opposition to the Nazis had affected her fortunes. "Germany has become vengeful," Sofie said, "making things difficult for her publishers. They will not forgive her for helping the Jews."

From there it was a short step to the Swedish Farmers' League, with their pro-German, xenophobic attitudes. As usual, Sofie and Lisbeth tried to temper Cecilia's darker view. Looking for a fresher subject, Sofie asked about some sketches propped up on the buffet. They were interiors of some of the buildings in the Old Farm where folk objects were displayed—blankets, wall hangings, wooden bowls.

Lisbeth, being of a different generation, was less partisan about folk art than Sofie and Cecilia. The older women remembered the early struggles to get people to see its value, while Lisbeth took that for granted.

"I suppose," she said, looking over a sketch showing shelves of jugs and bowls, "one of their attractions is that there are no surprises."

Sofie and Cecilia disagreed hotly. There were tremendous surprises! Just think of Carl Winter Hansson and his unexpectedly delicate flowers. Or the earthy humour in some of the biblical mural paintings. Or the anonymous potters and carvers who made deft and sometimes mischievous adjustments to everyday objects.

"All right," Lisbeth put up her hands in surrender. "There are surprises, but the vocabulary is very limited."

"Of course." Cecilia was impatient. "And that is probably what appeals to me, the order and the system, the doing much with little. The frugality."

Lars sat at the table, apparently paying no attention. Cecilia thought back to their visits to Professor Hazelius's first little museum on Drottninggatan. In those early days, Lars had been such a patient teacher. Yes, he had been courting her, but he genuinely loved those nameless craftsmen and the sturdy, homegrown things they made, and he had wanted her to know their worth. For a strong minute, she loved him more than anyone else in the room. How had this terrible thing happened to him, while the obstinate young woman across the table wanted to sleep in his bed?

"No doubt, the idea of a simpler life is part of the appeal of folk arts," Sofie said, conciliatory. "And that simple life wasn't all pretty."

She was thinking of Nils's painting of the king who sacrificed himself to end a famine while the dazed women danced.

Lisbeth turned toward her to show that she agreed and said, "Everyone knew his place. And there was no way out of your place."

Cecilia said crossly, "This is all too much theorizing for a simple piece of lace or a milking stool to bear."

But Sofie was thinking about what Lisbeth had just said. It was obvious once you heard it, but she had never heard it put so baldly. Everyone knew her place—that was reassuring, at least at first. But there was no way out. That was the important piece that was often overlooked.

Lisbeth was busy with the builders' contracts and sample materials for the gallery, and returned to her office after coffee. Clearly, things were not perfectly easy between Lisbeth and Cecilia, but Sofie was grateful for some time alone with Cecilia.

They sat in the garden, hemmed in by roses, all their colour and perfume. Cecilia had brought out the tin beaker with the white roses, and now she put it on a low table in front of them.

"The more complicated the architecture of the flower," Sofie allowed herself to say, "the better it looks in a simple container."

Cecilia looked her over as Sofie adjusted the beaker very slightly away from the centre of the table. Her hands were less veined and spotted than her own. Her neck was quite good, and those big French sun bonnets had left her skin unlined in most lights. No wonder MacDonald Lawrie still carries a torch for her, Cecilia thought. She considered asking Sofie about their meeting at Askebo, but decided not to.

"Do you notice," Sofie said, tipping a rose toward Cecilia that was mostly still a bud, with a double fringe of petals around it, "that the bud has more colour than the opened petals?"

Cecilia bent forward to look. The bud was a delicate pink, like a shell, but when the petals unfurled, they turned white. They opened recklessly, careless of their form. The fully opened flower was less beautiful and more vulnerable than the bud.

"As it opens, both the colour and the shape weaken," Cecilia agreed.

"So hard to keep the beauty of the new," Sofie said, as if to herself. "Things always lose their wonder."

"Except, perhaps, children," Cecilia said. "But I can only guess about that."

Sofie thought about it. "I suppose change is always possible with them, even with the grown-up ones you think are finished," she said. "But they all have patches when they are not wonderful."

The maid brought them elderflower juice to refresh them into wakefulness, but it was no match for the lulling heat. They inclined the backs of their slatted wooden chairs and closed their eyes. Wanting to keep the sleepy intimacy of the scene, with her eyes still closed, Cecilia said quietly, as if they had been discussing it, "I always thought that when I was old, I would have worked everything out, and I would have no worries."

"I thought the same thing," Sofie said in an equally low voice, amused. "Perhaps many people do. The problems change, that is all."

"What worries you?" Cecilia asked in the same offhand way. But she felt the boldness of the question.

"Oh, that Birgitta may have inherited Nils's melancholy. That Oskar's baby may be rather slow, although perhaps I imagine it. He seems to walk and talk later than the other children. That the sales of Nils's work have slowed, if not stopped, and the house needs a new roof."

"And . . . what about your work?" Cecilia had a sense that Sofie was working, but she did not know with certainty, nor on what.

"That does not worry me. It preoccupies me, almost constantly, but it does not worry me. I suppose I am still so happy that I am able to do it."

Cecilia nodded, afraid to press further. She waited, half-expecting some announcement about MacDonald Lawrie. Like her mother before her, Cecilia relished a love story, but her imagination resisted the idea of Sofie living in faraway Glasgow.

Instead, Sofie lifted her head, rested her elbow on the arm of the chair and looked at her, with two fingers open on her jaw, in the pose that Nils had painted so often. It was Cecilia's turn.

"Well, there is Lars, of course." She took a breath and added, "And the worry about Germany."

Sofie nodded quickly. Plainly, no one wanted to hear more from her on that subject.

"And, naturally, deciding on all the details of the gallery and the house museum, and then seeing that they become reality, is not easy."

That was as close as she would go toward Lisbeth.

When she was sure Cecilia had finished, Sofie said, "And yet some things are easier in old age. Small things trouble me less. What people think doesn't concern me much any more."

"Yes," Cecilia said, "although I never cared much what people thought of me." The only exception, which she thought but did not say, was her marriage: she could not bear the idea of people pitying her about the other women.

Sofie thought but did not say, Yes, you are fearless about others' opinions and that stands you in good stead now with Lisbeth. Although Cecilia and Lisbeth were discreet, there were several people working in and around the house. It would only take one with a suspicion and a weak allegiance to the mistress to set the whole village speculating about Mrs. Vogt and Miss Gregorius. Most likely it was already going on.

"Have you read any of Mr. Lawrence's novels?" Cecilia asked, breaking their brief silence.

"No, not yet. Do you enjoy them?"

"He can be clumsy and even indelicate, but I find the scenes where a man and woman rage at each other violently and then love each other just as violently are very powerful."

"I think I am happy to be done with that," Sofie said. "I am happy now to rage at my work, and enjoy the rapture that comes afterwards."

Aha, Cecilia thought. Poor Mr. Lawrie.

Chapter Fifty-eight

SOFIE INVITED THE family for Sunday lunch. Afterwards, while the mid-afternoon light was still strong, she ushered them into the workshop. She had placed her paintings all over the room, taking down Nils's pictures and using the same nails to hang hers on the walls, leaning them against the long window and the benches, even standing a few on her loom. She had not told any of the children that she was painting, and she had put away the paints and pictures whenever they visited. Now, she expected general astonishment.

Instead, they walked into the room lined with her work and although admiring were not surprised. They began appraising, and the grandchildren chose their favourites. Felix's little girl, Malin, asked her why she did not paint dogs, and she promised to paint her a dog. Birgitta's Filip said of a tree on a windy autumn day, "Look, it's snowing leaves." For that, she decided she would give him the painting for his name day.

Sonja, the only one with professional training, looked closely, and finally said collegially, "These are lovely, Mamma. You have a good eye. But then we knew that."

"But," Sofie said, not quite accepting defeat, "aren't you surprised that I have been painting?"

"We knew what you were doing," Oskar said.

"How did you know?"

"Well, there was nothing on the loom or the spindles."

"None of us have received tablecloths or blankets or wall hangings for Christmas or our name day for the longest time."

"As a matter of fact, you forgot a few red-letter days altogether."

"Anna dropped a few hints."

"You were so happy."

Sonja found some purple in a picture of a stormy day and told Felix, "Mamma invented this colour."

Sofie laughed at Felix's mystified face. "I never said that. I said that I discovered it."

That had been another clue, Sonja pointed out. It was easier to discover a new colour with paints than when spinning wool or buying embroidery thread.

Sofie felt cheated of the drama she had anticipated, but also relieved. Apparently no one was going to accuse her of disobeying their father's wishes. If that sounded like a scene from a nineteenth-century novel, it had not been out of the question. At a conscious level, her children probably knew nothing of Nils's feelings about her painting. She had never painted as long as they had known her, or almost never—a couple of them, perhaps, remembered her pictures of Markus after he died—and now she was painting. No doubt she had more time on her hands. In their minds, it could be as simple as that. At a deeper, unspoken level, they might well know how their father had felt about her painting. But their father, whom they loved, was dead, and their mother, whom they loved, was alive. Sofie had noted before that children were rarely as curious about their parents' private lives as the parents expected them to be.

That evening, after the family had left, Sofie looked again at her work. Something was missing. She'd had an inkling of it when she showed her paintings to Miss Helmersen, and now the feeling was stronger. Something was not quite as it should be. Something, now that she saw it all together, looked overworked or fussy. She hoped that was because she was still so new at it.

Chapter Fifty-nine

SEPTEMBER 1935

SOFIE HAD TO go to Stockholm for the name day of Mikael, Tilda's second son. He was a sweet boy, but all these family gatherings took time from her work. If Nils were alive, he would have said, "That's what happens when you have so many children," as if he'd had nothing to do with it. Cecilia was also in Stockholm, for a doctor's appointment and other business, so they arranged to meet at the National Museum, where there was an exhibition of Dutch painting.

In the entrance hall, under Nils's painting of Gustav Vasa, Sofie felt a throb of gratitude toward Lisbeth. She had become less like a lover and more like a spouse, in the important sense that her place in Cecilia's life left plenty of room for Cecilia's friendship with Sofie. While she waited for Cecilia, she watched as people met and parted, studied the map of the various galleries and looked up at the mural of the victorious king on his white horse. Women's hemlines now fell between the knee and the ankle, after the giddiness of the twenties' short skirts, and many of their suits and dresses were cut on the bias. From across the rotunda, she admired an old woman's finely tailored suit and veiled hat, until the woman was swallowed up in the swirl of people.

Suddenly the veiled hat and the suit, a periwinkle blue that matched the wearer's eyes, stood before her. My goodness, Sofie thought, how we are getting on. Cecilia had a fine beading of perspiration where her hair met her forehead, but it was a warm day. Sofie put a steadying hand on her arm, but she brushed it aside.

"Everything is fine," Cecilia said briskly. "It's just that, as usual, I tried to squeeze too many appointments and errands into one day. But now I'm here, and we can enjoy the pictures."

They walked to the rooms with the Dutch paintings. They both loved the orderly scenes of quiet courtyards, black-and-white tiled front halls, children being combed, linen being stored away.

"It's because we are Protestants," Sofie said, an old joke, and Cecilia smiled.

The religious paintings interested them less than the domestic ones, but they stopped at one from the seventeenth century with a strange title—*The Annunciation of the Virgin's Death.*

"I thought an annunciation always referred to the Christ Child's birth."

"So did I," Cecilia agreed. "But this is an end rather than a beginning. And this angel looks like a hearty Swedish husfru, the kind of sensible neighbour whose advice you would ask if your bread failed to rise."

The angel wore a red-and-gold priest's chasuble that left her goose-like white wings free, and she held one hand on her heart, the other on the wrist of the Virgin as if she were taking her pulse. The Virgin, also a square-faced Northern type with a well-developed chin, had been reading, her thick book propped on an overturned chair.

"And look how matronly the Virgin is." Sofie pointed to the upside-down chair. "Why in the world doesn't she turn the chair right side up?"

"Baroque painters loved untidiness, even mess. Upheaval outside mirrors upheaval inside."

Cecilia knew so much. It could be annoying or, as now, interesting. The Virgin looked distracted, as if she had not absorbed the angel's news enough to be worried. Of her approaching death, she seemed to be thinking, *Well, all right, if you must. But not before I finish my book.* Sofie sympathized. *Not yet. Not when she was just getting started.*

As they were leaving the museum, a round, excited man recognized Sofie, and shook hands with her. He was perspiring freely and reminded Sofie of her old drawing teacher in Hallsberg.

"Norberg," he introduced himself. "Ministry of Culture. How marvellous to meet you here, under your husband's magnificent..." He waved his arm upwards toward Nils's painting. He never quite finished a sentence, but it was easy enough to follow him as he ricocheted from one idea to the next. He flew from the picture to the Olssons' house, and "how much it means to people all over the... and the furnishings, how... and what a genius Olsson had been to mingle the old Swedish things with other, more..."

Sofie cut through his burbling to introduce Cecilia. His eyes widened and he began at once to talk reverently about Lars's *Dancing at Midnight* upstairs and about the work of the Folk School. "And it's so important, isn't it, just now, that we remember... as Swedes, we must stay true to the..."

Sofie felt a prick of apprehension. She had a wispy memory of reading in the newspaper that Mr. Norberg was a strong supporter of the Third Reich's cultural programme. He carried on. "And we must strengthen our national... you know, as your husbands did, rather than welcoming all these foreign... And it's not in the city... but in Askebo, and in Siljevik, that we find our real Swedish heart."

He stopped abruptly and looked at Cecilia, perhaps only now remembering her citified, even arguably foreign origins. She looked pale and small, unlike the beating heart of Sweden that was to be found in the countryside.

Cecilia stared back at him, impassive, while Sofie answered.

"But surely Stockholm, too, is part of Sweden, Mr. Norberg, and a rather important part. And our heritage includes a long history of accepting other people, and of tolerance."

"Silly man," Sofie said, after he said his effusive, unfinished farewells. Cecilia nodded dismissively.

"Let's go to the Grand Hotel for some coffee."

Leaving the museum, Cecilia thought, Sofie thinks I am taking that foolish man too seriously. But he speaks for many people in Sweden. Nothing would make me happier than to find myself wrong, and Sofie and Lisbeth right. But I do not think that will happen.

As they made their way to the Grand Hotel, Cecilia saw people staring surreptitiously at Sofie. In the country, she still looked charming in her usual clothes. But here, in a city crowd of people wearing modern clothes, her long, loose dress was odd. Sofie did not notice. Her cheekbones were sharp and her thick eyebrows a tweedy mixture of brown and white, but she moved easily and looked happy.

Sitting in the hotel's old leather chairs, they toasted their work with the Grand's good coffee.

"I will say this only to you," Cecilia said. "The thought of my name on the spine of Lars's catalogue thrills me. I have to think hard and write very well, to be worthy of that."

Sofie nodded. For a bookworm, there was nothing better than a book with your name on it.

She had told Cecilia about Mac Lawrie's proposal in the winter, but now she told her in more detail and was rewarded with Cecilia's distinctive, clattering laugh. Sofie joined her. The reason she too could laugh was that Mac had married the copper enamellist after all. An announcement had arrived, in the best Glasgow School typography, with a note from him. She sent him and his bride her warmest wishes and a tablecloth and napkins, woven and plaited in the Dalarna patterns he admired.

"I did feel sorry for him," Cecilia said, wiping away tears of laughter, "but I worried you would move away to Glasgow."

Putting her handkerchief back in her purse and treading cautiously, she asked, "Were you reluctant to start again? I mean, to live again with a man."

Sofie understood what she meant.

"I don't think that was the obstacle," she said, "but there are other things, now, that I want to do more."

She thought about the unstable red dye the Japanese and Chinese connected with young, passionate love. Since she and Cecilia were on forbidden ground already, she dared to ask the unaskable.

"Did you ever think of leaving Lars?"

"Yes. But probably not until it was too late. By then I was so tied to his work, or to my work, which was easing his work. It was what younger women call a career, and you don't walk away from a good career. And with Lars . . . there was always something that connected us, even when things were at their worst."

"I suppose we were too bourgeois to consider leaving a marriage," Sofie said. "Think of Strindberg's wives—Siri, Frida, and what was the name of the third one?"

"Harriet Bosse."

"Harriet, yes. Separation, divorce, remarriage, living together without marriage—they did it all without any qualms."

"But they were bourgeois too!"

"Not really. Siri was an aristocrat and Frida on the fringes of the aristocracy. Things were looser for them. Do you remember that Siri's first husband came to the wedding when she married Strindberg? They took it all in stride, in a way we couldn't have. And Harriet Bosse was an actress."

An actress, that was different. They fell silent.

"What about you? Were you ever tempted to leave Nils?"

"He needed me too much." That was true, but it sounded martyred. And not quite right. "And I loved him, sometimes as a husband, sometimes as a child, sometimes as a marvellous painter. I never could have abandoned any of those people."

"Sometimes I still wonder"—this was harder for Cecilia to say than anything so far—"if my family's money was not an attraction for Lars."

Sofie lowered her cup.

"Well, it certainly wasn't a drawback! For either of us. I can't imagine a painter who wouldn't prefer to have a wife with some money. Not that they ever needed our money, as it turned out."

Well then, that was all right. Cecilia had fretted about this for so long, and Sofie had erased it so simply. Why hadn't she mentioned it earlier?

Sofie added, "And it didn't mean they didn't love us."

"In their way."

After a pause, Sofie nodded.

"Yes, in their way."

So. If you lived long enough, Sofie thought, these astonishing conversations were possible. It was something she would never have dreamed of when they had begun to know each other.

Love, the bodily love they had each had for their husbands, and which Cecilia had for Lisbeth, felt like fate. It could distract you, or decide you on a course that might or might not be right. Sofie remembered hesitating in Grez, when she had first seen Nils's need. It was the body that had convinced her to accept him. That kind of love had an element of destiny. The love of friendship, on the other hand, felt more like a choice.

On the train to Siljevik, Cecilia thought back to the painting of the Virgin's death. It reminded her of the painting of another Annunciation, the one that had come into her head when she and Lars had had that scene in Paris about the contraceptive in his inner pocket. Those two serious Jewish girls—the Virgin, who spilled her sewing at the Angel Gabriel's news, and Cecilia, whose life had also turned upside down—had been so horrified. How hard it was now to summon all that racking feeling.

Unlike Gabriel with his terrifying wings, the motherly angel announcing the Virgin's death in this afternoon's painting had looked encouraging, as if she were saying, "Trust me. It won't be so bad." Still, the Virgin seemed reluctant, or maybe, as Sofie said, she hadn't taken it in yet.

Cecilia was like the Virgin. She wasn't ready, either.

Dr. Persson had tried to be reassuring, saying that, with a rest in the afternoon and perhaps less salt in her diet, she might be fine for some time. In her own mind, at the very least, she needed to finish the catalogue. But really, that was not enough. Although Lisbeth was devoted to Lars's work, Cecilia needed to be there to rein her in. No, she had that wrong: it was *because* Lisbeth was so devoted that Cecilia needed to rein her in.

The painting had put her in a retrospective mood.

Dear Sofie,

Once again I turn to the question you asked me in your thank-you note more than thirty years ago: Do I feel surprised at how my life has turned out? Some parts of my life seemed to have been there all along—from the small girl bent on classifying her parents' art to the woman in her sixties trying to do justice to Lars with the catalogue. But, of course, other things surprised me greatly. When Lars and I set out for Paris after our wedding, I thought I had come to the end of the novel. I never suspected that the hard part of the story was still to come. And not only the hard part, but the most surprising thing of all. Lisbeth. The friend and the beloved.

She broke off there, because the train was nearing the Siljevik station. And this was the merest outline of what she wanted to say. She needed to fill it in and she would, as soon as she finished the catalogue. It was time to answer Sofie's question properly.

Chapter Sixty

SOFIE HAD TAKEN a cab to Tilda's house from her coffee with Cecilia. Before the party—and now she was glad she had come, because Mikael really was a sweet boy, and it was an efficient way to see all the family at once—she wrote a note.

> Stockholm, 6 September 1935
> Dearest Cecilia,
> You have been very patient with your tortoise of a
> friend. I am finally ready. Please come and see my work.
> I will be very glad of your opinion.
> Always yours with love,
> Sofie

A week later, Cecilia came to Askebo. She had hired a man to drive her, rather than taking the train as usual, explaining to a surprised Sofie that it was easier than changing trains in Rattvik.

"I hired this fellow last week," she said, walking with Sofie from the automobile to the house, "when I went to see Miss Helmersen in

Falun, and it worked well." She knew that would shock Sofie, so she said it matter-of-factly.

"You went to see Miss Helmersen?"

"Yes. I'm quite impressed with her business sense. I've been encouraging her to look for larger premises and to hire a full-time assistant to do the hand-colouring in her pictures. She shouldn't be wasting her time with that. I plan to lend her some money for the higher rent she will incur—as an investment, of course."

Of course. So the visit to the studio in Falun had not been a failure, even if Cecilia was still blind to Miss Helmersen's artistry. It was more than a year since Sofie had introduced them, and how typical of Cecilia to keep her patronage a secret until now. Sofie beamed at her, but Cecilia was intent on getting to the house. She was in a terrible rush to finish the catalogue, she said, and she did seem very hurried, even flustered, until Sofie took her into the workshop.

Then she was all concentration, and much more excited than the children had been. When something moved her, she turned to Sofie and raised her eyebrows in conspiratorial joy, as if she had been let in on a great secret. She noticed the wilted piece of paper Sofie had pinned up by the easel, and read the quotation.

"'Here she was again, she thought, stepping back to look at it, drawn out of gossip, out of living, out of community with people into the presence of this formidable ancient enemy of hers . . .'"

Cecilia stopped. "Is that from . . . ?" She tried to remember.

"*To the Lighthouse*," Sofie said. "The painter."

"Yes, of course! Miss Briscoe."

When she had seen everything, Cecilia took both of Sofie's hands in hers and pumped them.

Then she said, "Could you get me a chair?"

"Yes, of course," Sofie said. "Are you tired?"

"No. But I'd like to sit here, in the centre, where I can see them all at once."

Once she was seated and had caught her breath and looked again, she said, "I think you want to paint in oils."

This had never occurred to Sofie, although painting in watercolours had never been a deliberate choice. It had begun as a question of thrift, since Nils had painted in watercolours and she used the paints he had left. Why would she want to paint in oils?

"Because they would suit you. Watercolours demand that you know from the start where you're going and work fast, with no regrets. Nils was made for the short dash of watercolours. You are different. You want to plunge in without planning—remember how weaving frustrated you when you began it?—but you doubt yourself, you change your mind, you want to double back, you want the possibility of reworking and thinking as you go along. That is what you can have with oils."

It was one of those ideas that made sense as soon as Sofie heard it. She had lived so many years with an artist who painted in watercolours that it was almost as if she had forgotten the alternatives. She still remembered when leaving oils for watercolours had been a new and progressive choice, but painting in oil did not mean that she would return to painting the trial of Socrates or any other of Professor Malmstrom's ideas. She would paint her skies and clouds, but in her own way.

"And now, my dear," said Cecilia, using the chair's arms to support herself as she stood, "I must go."

"But you came all the way from Siljevik, and we haven't had a proper visit! And Anna has made one of her special plum cakes in your honour."

"Tell Anna I am sorry to miss her famous plum cake. But I must get back to work."

"But we have set up a table by the river, where the mums are thriving. We could eat our cake there, and you would have a little rest before the journey home."

"And why would I need to rest before riding in a comfortable automobile?" Cecilia asked, almost sharply. At the same time, something about Sofie's entreaty took her back to the turn of the century and another pastry, another view. On Sofie's first visit to Siljevik, on the verandah facing the garden, they had made such stilted conversation over cinnamon buns.

Cecilia smiled at her and raised her eyebrows again in that conspiratorial way.

"But this has been a thrilling visit."

Chapter Sixty-one

SEPTEMBER 1935

At Mattsson and Berg's Fine Paints in Stockholm, Sofie found all the colour in the world neatly stacked on dark wooden shelves. It had been forty years since she had bought oil paints and now even the names thrilled her—Prussian Blue, Viridian Green, Yellow Ochre. As for the reds, she was incapable of choosing among Venetian Red, Alizarin Crimson, Winsor Red, Permanent Carmine and Quinocridone Red. She wanted them all, and she bought most of them.

A week later, still intoxicated by the riches at her disposal, she stood in front of a painting in the workshop. It needed more red— Permanent Carmine this time—but she was not sure where.

She was puzzling about that when Lisbeth called with the news that Cecilia had died.

That evening, a man driving Lisbeth's Volvo arrived at Sofie's house with a letter. He expressed his condolences, handed the letter to Sofie and left.

Siljevik, 20 September 1935
Dear Sofie,
    For some time we have avoided calling each other by

first names or last names, but now I think we must be Sofie and Lisbeth. At the very least, Cecilia would have wanted it.

News of a death is terrible however it comes, but I think it must be particularly dreadful by long-distance telephone. I promised you more details, and here they are. And forgive me if I go on too long or linger on things that are not completely relevant. I am not yet entirely myself, as you must understand.

I think again and again of our last days together, particularly one evening. We were sitting on the porch overlooking the garden, as we often did. The final weeks of writing and proofreading the catalogue had been intense and Cecilia still looked drawn. Knowing what I know now, I might write "pitiably drawn," but that word would have enraged her. I was still denying the obvious, still trusting that, after some days of rest, she would regain her strength.

I asked her what she would do next.

"What do you mean?" she asked. "I have finished."

I said that she had finished the catalogue. But clearly, she was a writer. Who or what would she write about next?

Cecilia gave me a look, in which skepticism mingled with affection and something else that I did not recognize.

Since she did not answer, I told her my idea, which I had had for a while. It was that she should write a monograph, or something longer, about Vilhelm Hammershoi.

Cecilia was so surprised that she laughed. Of course, you know the Danish painter—the master of beautiful, bleak rooms, as Cecilia called him—whom she had first

seen in Pontus Furstenberg's Gothenburg gallery
decades ago. But you probably do not know the number
of times Cecilia bundled me off to Copenhagen or
Stockholm or Oslo to see more of his paintings—more
of those women looking out from a window at a view
that is no more consoling than the room in which they
stand. Those paintings, unflinching in the face of
disappointment, which make something so fine out of
stoicism and longing.

Looking at Cecilia's doubtful face, I said, his
paintings speak to you, and I would like to read you
describing what it is they are saying.

Finally, she said, dryly and almost casually, "Lisbeth.
What an interesting idea."

The following morning she was very ill, and she
never again left her bed. When it was over, and I had
talked with Dr. Persson, I understood some of the things
that had bewildered me in the past months—small
moments of withdrawal or evasion, Cecilia's careful
husbanding of her energy, the look on her face when I
asked what she would do next. Her doctor was not
surprised. Nor was she, although she never told me.

Her brother Fredrik arrived on the first possible train
from Stockholm after her death. I told him that Cecilia
had suffered only a very short time and I took him to her
room, where she was laid out on the bed. The stillness of
the room seemed to emphasize her tinyness; she looked
like a white-haired child lying under the white blanket.
We had taken Lars in to see her, and his eyes filled with
tears. But when we took him a second time, he showed no
interest. Everything had been done properly, with juniper
twigs on the floor and sheets hung over the windows and
mirrors. My mother always put a sprig of ivy in a dead

person's hands, or on their chest, so I did that too. It did not occur to me until Fredrik arrived that we had arranged things properly in the Swedish style, but not necessarily in the Jewish way. Fredrik did give a half nod in the direction of the covered mirrors, so perhaps they were a familiar sight. I left him alone in the room, but he followed me downstairs almost immediately.

No, you have done nothing wrong, he said. It is just that Jews do not have the custom of spending time with the body. He said something about a special group that washes the body and watches over it. Then came the surprise. He had come, he said, to take Cecilia's body back to Stockholm on the train, as soon as the undertaker could deliver the coffin.

I was dumbfounded, I confess. I reminded him that she planned to be buried in the Siljevik churchyard, with Lars. That was fine, he said. But first she must have a Jewish funeral.

I still did not know what to say. I could only nod my head, but of course he was not asking for my agreement. He is her brother, after all, and Lars is past consulting. I wondered what Cecilia would think about it. Ten years ago, she might have called it a sentimental idea, and a great deal of expensive bother. Now, I think she might well have approved.

I decided not to go to the funeral. It is not my religion, not my family, not my place. But today, after Fredrik left with the coffin on the afternoon train, I held my own little observance. I sat in Cecilia's favourite reading chair, and drank a glass of the good white Burgundy she enjoyed. And I read the catalogue from beginning to end, for the first time. It has all the marks of Cecilia's discrimination and care. Her confident scholarship. Her elegant way with a sentence. Her refusal to make Lars more than he was, and her astute sense of where and how he was incomparable. Well done, Cecilia, I thought. I will miss all of you.

And you will miss her too, Sofie. Her dear friend of so many years. You know how much you meant to her. I cannot write any more now, but I will send you the particulars of the burial as soon as they are settled.

Your friend,
Lisbeth

Chapter Sixty-two

SEPTEMBER 1935

SONJA ACCOMPANIED HER mother to Siljevik for Cecilia's burial. All the children would be there, of course, but Sonja was the only painter. She still taught art at Cecilia's Folk School, and that was another point of contact. It was not strictly logical, Sofie knew, but somehow it was Sonja she wanted on the journey to Siljevik.

The trees that bordered the churchyard were red and golden, with a brilliant colour that meant the leaves were on the verge of drying and falling. Had Cecilia died a week later, there would have been no leaves.

Most of Siljevik had assembled in the churchyard, alongside friends and family. Lars's collectors and dealers past and present, all of whom had done business with Cecilia, were there. So were Hanna and Georg and the Bonnier cousins, who had also been to the funeral in the synagogue in Stockholm. Sofie's other children were scattered in the crowd, but the staff of the Folk School stood together, and Sofie joined Sonja with them. Nearby stood people from the orphanage, the library, the Homecraft Association and Cecilia's other projects. Sofie saw Miss Helmersen from afar, but the photographer hurried away after the burial and Sofie had no chance to speak with her.

Never before in the history of the village had someone come to rest in the Siljevik churchyard after a Jewish funeral. Tactfully, the minister chose to read a few extracts from the Old Testament, and left it at that. Lisbeth listened intently and, just for a second, caught Sofie's eye. In his chair, Lars looked handsome and unconcerned. Sofie had put the lace handkerchief Cecilia had made for her, in the Bockarna pattern, in her purse before leaving home. But it was too intricate and stiff to cry into. When the hot tears spilled down her face, Sonja passed her a plain cotton handkerchief.

Afterwards, at the house, Lisbeth gave Sofie a copy of Cecilia's catalogue and asked her to choose something of Cecilia's as a memento. Sofie was tempted by Lars's painting of a young Cecilia wearing a red silk dress with exaggerated sleeves, going through a file of Lars's engravings. But no, it was better there, in the gallery that was to be. She thought of Cecilia's copy of Mary Wollstonecraft's *Letters from Sweden, Norway and Denmark*. They had both enjoyed Miss Wollstonecraft's tart observations, and Sofie had always thought of Miss Wollstonecraft as a kind of accomplice on that warm Sunday afternoon in Grez when she and Nils had first made love. But that was all too fanciful. That also should stay there, in Cecilia's collection of first editions. In the end, she asked only for the handkerchief that she had woven for Cecilia, a cheeky reminder of the "handkerchief red, white and blue" in the song Markus had played in the Hall for the Vogts. Lisbeth looked bewildered, but Sofie insisted that was all she wanted.

When she returned home from the burial, she put the plaid and Bockarna handkerchiefs in a box on her bureau where she kept locks of Markus's and Nils's hair. She walked along the river for a while, but it was no good. The place where she could think most clearly about Cecilia was in the workshop.

Standing in front of her painting, she was full of wishes. She wished she had insisted more strenuously that Cecilia stay longer on her last visit, even though she knew that Cecilia was unpersuadable.

She wished she had told Cecilia more, and heard more from her. Still, they had made progress.

More than anything, she wished Cecilia could see her new work. Cecilia had been right. The buttery colour that emerged from those tubes of oil paint was the missing element. It was deep and forgiving, letting her return again and again to her sunsets and weathers, adding, subtracting, complicating, simplifying. There was no more overworked fussiness, but a full colour and a rich surface.

And now she really had to move to the studio. She could not imagine why she had stayed so long in the cramped workshop. But first, that red. She put on her smock over her black dress and stood again in front of the painting. This other thing, this truth, this reality. Almost at once she saw where the red should go—just at the edge, where the sky ran out of orange and pink. She narrowed her eyes, and picked up her brush.

Author's Note

Carl Larsson and Anders Zorn were two of Sweden's most famous painters in the last decades of the nineteenth century and the first decades of the twentieth century. Outside Sweden, Larsson is probably still his country's best-known artist; his watercolours of his house and family have appeared on innumerable posters, stationery and calendars around the world. Known for his engravings and his portraits, Zorn also enjoyed great success in the U.S., where he painted three presidents. Larsson's and Zorn's influence is central to *Sofie & Cecilia*, but it is their wives, Karin Bergoo Larsson and Emma Lamm Zorn, who inspired this novel.

As the Larssons were transformed into Sofie and Nils Olsson, and the Zorns into Cecilia and Lars Vogt, they acquired invented qualities, adventures and relationships large and small. Dates were shifted when it suited the story and the titles of their paintings and books changed. They became, in short, fictional characters.

Another fictional character, Lisbeth Gregorius, has a shadowy connection to Gerda Boethius, Sweden's first woman art historian and the first director of the Zorn Collections.

Most of the characters with whom Sofie and Cecilia interact are complete fictions, but I have preserved the real names of some historical figures who were important in Swedish society and in the international art world of the time. They include Eva Bonnier, Prince Eugen, Pontus Furstenberg, Isabella Stewart Gardner, Marta Jorgensen, Ellen Key, Selma Lagerlof, John Lavery, George Pauli, Hanna Hirsch-Pauli, Venny Soldan and Lilli Zickerman.

Zorn in America: A Swedish Impressionist of the Gilded Age, by William and Willow Hagans (Chicago: The Swedish-American Historical Society, 2009) was a rich source of information. Two of Zorn's letters, translated by the authors, appear in the book as letters from Lars Vogt.

From Per Wastberg's essay, "The Hirsch Family in Stockholm" in *Contemporary Jewish Writing in Sweden*, ed. and trans. Peter Stenberg (Lincoln: University of Nebraska Press, 2005), I borrowed many of the details in the Isaksson family wills, as well as the menu of the Hallwyls' dinner.

The photographic experiments of Dora Helmersen were suggested by those of Hannah Maynard, a nineteenth-century photographer in Victoria, British Columbia. *The Magic Box: The Eccentric Genius of Hannah Maynard*, by Claire Weissman Wilks (Toronto: Exile Editions, 1980) is a good introduction to her work.

Sofie Olsson's "discovery" of purple is a version of a story the artist Mary Pratt told Michael Enright when he interviewed her in 2013 on "The Sunday Edition" on CBC Radio.

The painting Cecilia Vogt thinks of in Chapter Twenty-nine, where the frightened Virgin spills her sewing, is "The Annunciation," by Jan de Beer in the Thyssen-Bornemisza Museum in Madrid. The painting with the woman holding a dead hare in the Wallace Collection in London is "Jochem van Aras with his Wife and Daughter," by Bartolomeus van der Helst. "The Annunciation of the Virgin's Death," by Paulus Bor, is in the National Gallery of Canada in Ottawa.

Acknowledgements

This book would never have happened had not my daughter, Sybil Carolan, taken me to Sweden. Thank you, Sybil, for indulging my wish to see the house of Karin and Carl Larsson, which is where *Sofie & Cecilia* began. Thanks are also due to my daughter, Hannah Carolan, and to Andrea Townson for answering my questions about strokes. Marta Braun explained the intricacies of experimental photography to me, and Tony Urquhart was enlightening on the differences between painting with watercolours and with oil.

In Sweden, thanks to Alberto Manguel, I benefitted from Anders Bjornsson's and Hans Henrik Brummer's wide and deep knowledge of Larsson, Zorn and their circle. My friend Margareta Eklof saved me from many mistakes about Swedish society. One of Sweden's premier translators, she also revealed a gift for creating place names: Askebo, Siljevik and Tallmon are her inventions.

At Knopf Canada, thank you to Deirdre Molina, Rick Meier, Anne Collins and Sharon Klein for their enthusiasm and intelligence, and to Kelly Hill for yet another brilliant cover and book design. Thanks, as well, to Angelika Glover, whose admirable notes and queries made this a better book.

My deepest gratitude goes to my agent, Samantha Haywood, and my publisher and editor, Lynn Henry. Samantha believed in this book as soon as she heard about it, years before she read it. She was its first, extremely astute editor and remains its tireless, canny champion. It's hard to pin down Lynn Henry's greatest gift as an editor—is it her keen eye for the smallest details as well as the big picture, or is it her insistence that all decisions are mine while she suggests changes that only a fool would resist, or is it her eloquent, encouraging emails? I don't know, but thank you, Lynn.

KATHERINE ASHENBURG is the author of four books and many magazine and newspaper articles. She has written for *The New York Times*, the *Times Literary Supplement, The Globe and Mail* and *Toronto Life*, among other publications. Her books include *The Mourner's Dance: What We Do When People Die*, and *The Dirt on Clean: An Unsanitized History*, which was published in 12 countries and six languages. In former incarnations, she was a producer at CBC Radio and was *The Globe and Mail*'s Arts and Books editor. In 2012, she won a Gold Medal at the National Magazine Awards for her article on old age.